The Cousins' War

THE RED QUEEN

PHILIPPA GREGORY

London · New York · Sydney · Toronto

A CBS COMPANY

First published in Great Britain by Simon & Schuster UK Ltd, 2010
This paperback edition published 2011
A CBS COMPANY

1 3 5 7 9 10 8 6 4 2

Simon & Schuster UK Ltd
1st Floor
222 Gray's Inn Road
London WC1X 8HB

www.simonandschuster.co.uk

Simon & Schuster Australia
Sydney

A CIP catalogue record for this book is available
from the British Library.

ISBN 978-1-84983-589-3

Typeset by M Rules
Printed in the UK by CPI Cox & Wyman, Reading, Berkshire RG1 8EX

For Anthony

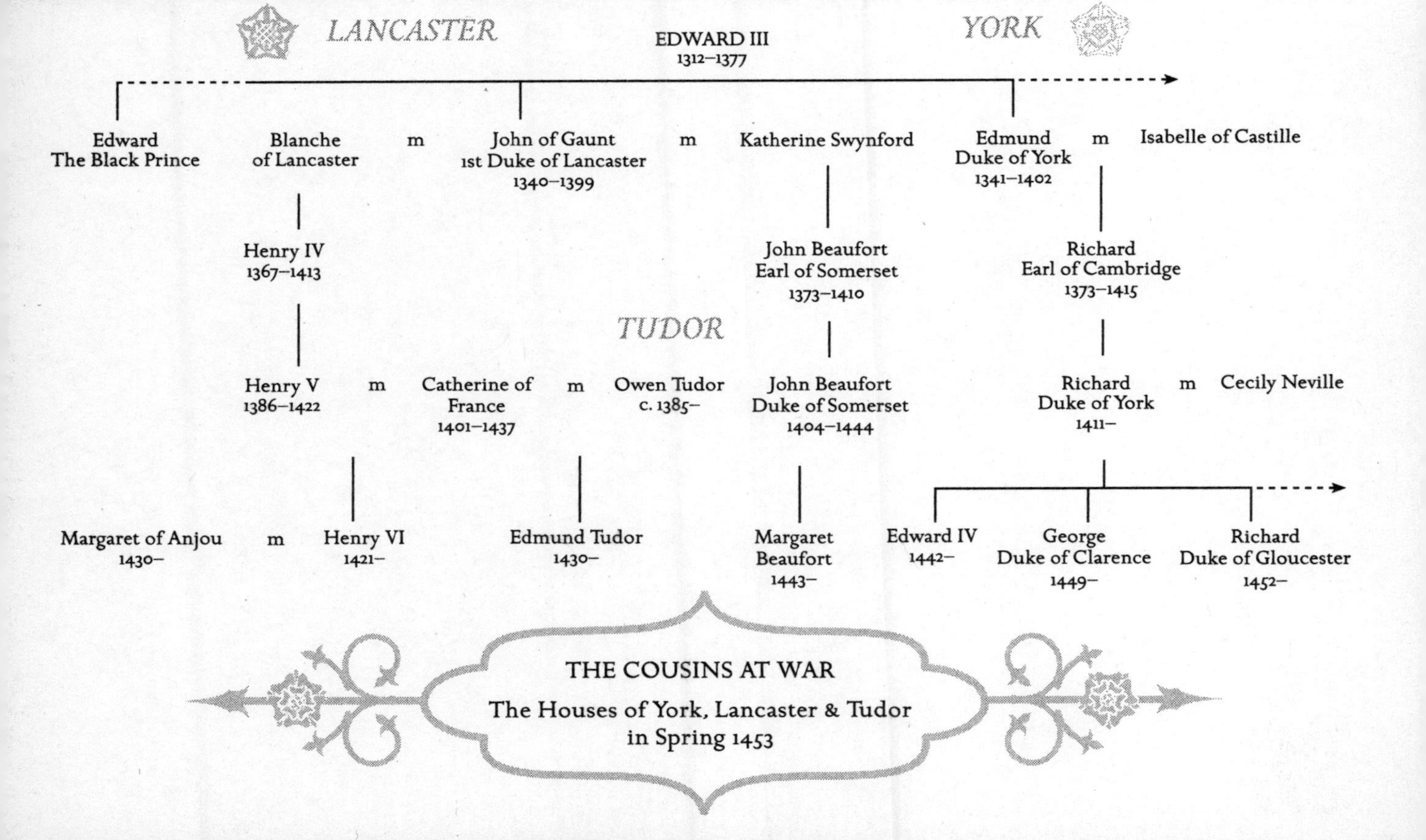
LANCASTER
EDWARD III
1312–1377
YORK
Edward
The Black Prince
Blanche
of Lancaster
m
John of Gaunt
1st Duke of Lancaster
1340–1399
m
Katherine Swynford
Edmund
Duke of York
1341–1402
m
Isabelle of Castille
Henry IV
1367–1413
John Beaufort
Earl of Somerset
1373–1410
Richard
Earl of Cambridge
1373–1415
TUDOR
Henry V
1386–1422
m
Catherine of
France
1401–1437
m
Owen Tudor
c. 1385–
John Beaufort
Duke of Somerset
1404–1444
Richard
Duke of York
1411–
m
Cecily Neville
Margaret of Anjou
1430–
m
Henry VI
1421–
Edmund Tudor
1430–
Margaret
Beaufort
1443–
Edward IV
1442–
George
Duke of Clarence
1449–
Richard
Duke of Gloucester
1452–
THE COUSINS AT WAR
The Houses of York, Lancaster & Tudor
in Spring 1453

Battles of
The Cousins' War
Lancaster victories
York victories
Skye
Inverness
Aberdeen
Dundee
Stirling
Glasgow
Edinburgh
Hedgeley Moor
1464
Carlisle
Hexham
1464
NORTH SEA
Isle of Man
Lancaster
IRISH SEA
Towton
1461
York
Preston
Ferrybridge
1461
Wakefield
1460
Lincoln
Caernarfon
Chester
Blore Heath
1459
Shrewsbury
Losecote Field
1470
Ludford Bridge
1459
Bosworth
1485
Aberystwyth
Northampton
1460
Mortimer's Cross
1461
Edgecote Moor
1469
St. Alban's
1455, 1461
Ipswich
Fishguard
Tewkesbury
1471
Barnet
1471
Swansea
Cardiff
LONDON
Bristol
Dover
Winchester
Taunton
Lewes
Calais
Southampton
Hastings
Exeter
Chichester
Plymouth
Dorchester
FRANCE
Penzance
ENGLISH CHANNEL

SPRING 1453

The light of the open sky is brilliant after the darkness of the inner rooms. I blink and hear the roar of many voices. But this is not my army calling for me, this whisper growing to a rumble is not their roar of attack, the drumming of their swords on shields. The rippling noise of linen in the wind is not my embroidered angels and lilies against the sky, but cursed English standards in the triumphant May breeze. This is a different sort of roar from our bellowed hymns, this is a howl of people hungry for death: my death.

Ahead of me, and towering above me as I step over the threshold from my prison into the town square, is my destination: a wood stack, with a stepladder of rough staves leaning against it. I whisper: 'A cross. May I have a cross?' And then, louder: 'A cross! I must have a cross!' And some man, a stranger, an enemy, an Englishman, one of those that we call 'goddams' for their unending blaspheming, holds out a crucifix of whittled wood, roughly made, and I snatch it without pride from his dirty hand. I clutch it as they push me towards the wood pile and thrust me up the ladder, my feet scraping on the rough rungs as I climb up, higher than my own height, until I reach the unsteady platform hammered into the top of the bonfire, and they turn me, roughly, and tie my hands around the stake at my back.

It all goes so slowly then that I could almost think that time itself has frozen and the angels are coming down for me. Stranger things have happened. Did not the angels come for me when I was herding sheep? Did they not call me by name? Did I not lead an army to the relief of Orléans? Did I not crown the Dauphin and drive out the English? Just me? A girl from Domrémy, advised by angels?

They light the kindling all around the bottom, and the smoke eddies and billows in the breeze. Then the fire takes hold and a hot cloud shrouds me, and makes me cough, blinking, my eyes streaming. Already it is scalding my bare feet. I step from one foot to another, foolishly, as if I hope to spare myself discomfort, and I peer through the smoke in case someone is running with buckets of water, to say that the king that I crowned has forbidden this; or the English, who bought me from a soldier, now acknowledge that I am not theirs to kill, or that my church knows that I am a good girl, a good woman, innocent of everything but serving God with a passionate purpose.

There is no saviour among the jostling crowd. The noise swells to a deafening shriek: a mixture of shouted blessings and curses, prayers and obscenities. I look upwards to the blue sky for my angels descending, and a log shifts in the pyre below me, and my stake rocks, and the first sparks fly up and scorch my jacket. I see them land and glow like fireflies on my sleeve, and I feel a dry scratching in my throat and I cough from the smoke and whisper like a little girl: 'Dear God, save me, Your daughter! Dear God, put down Your hand for me. Dear God, save me, Your maid . . .'

There is a crash of noise and a blow to my head and I am sitting, bewildered, on the floorboards of my bedroom, my hand to my bruised ear, looking around me like a fool and seeing nothing. My lady companion opens my door and, seeing me, dazed, my prayer stool tipped over, says irritably: 'Lady Margaret, go to bed. It is long past your bedtime. Our Lady does not value the prayers of disobedient girls. There is no merit in exaggeration. Your mother wants you up early in the morning, you can't stay up all night praying, it is folly.'

She slams the door shut and I hear her telling the maids that one of them must go in now and put me to bed and sleep beside me to make sure I don't rise up at midnight for another session of prayer. They don't like me to follow the hours of the church, they stand between me and a life of holiness, because they say I am too young and need my sleep. They dare to suggest that I am showing off, playing at piety, when I know that God has called me and it is my duty, my higher duty, to obey Him.

But even if I were to pray all night, I wouldn't be able to recapture the vision that was so bright, just a moment ago; it is gone. For a moment, for a sacred moment, I was there: I was the Maid of Orléans, the holy Joan of France. I understood what a girl could do, what a woman could be. Then they drag me back to earth, and scold me as if I were an ordinary girl, and spoil everything.

'Our Lady Mary guide me, angels come back to me,' I whisper, trying to return to the square, to the watching crowds, to the thrilling moment. But it has all gone. I have to haul myself up the bedpost to stand, I am dizzy from fasting and praying, and I rub my knee where I knocked it. There is a wonderful roughness on the skin, and I put my hand down and pull up my nightgown to see both knees, and they are the same: roughened and red. Saints' knees, praise God, I have saints' knees. I have prayed so much, and on such hard floors, that the skin of my knees is becoming hard, like the callus on the finger of an English longbow-man. I am not yet ten years old; but I have saints' knees. This has got to count for something, whatever my old lady governess may say to my mother about excessive and theatrical devotion. I have saints' knees. I have scuffed the skin of my knees by continual prayer, these are my stigmata: saints' knees. Pray God I can meet their challenge and have a saint's end too.

I get into bed, as I have been ordered to do; for obedience, even to foolish and vulgar women, is a virtue. I may be the daughter of a man who was one of the greatest of English commanders in France, one of the great Beaufort family, and so heir to the throne of Henry VI of England, but still I have to obey my lady governess and my mother as if I were any other ordinary girl. I am highly placed in the kingdom, cousin to the king himself – though dreadfully disregarded at home, where I have to do as I am told by a stupid old woman who sleeps through the priest's homily, and sucks sugared plums through grace. I count her as a cross I have to bear, and I offer her up in my prayers.

These prayers will save her immortal soul – despite her true deserts – for, as it happens, my prayers are especially blessed. Ever since I was a little girl, ever since I was five years old, I have known myself to be a special child in the sight of God. For years I thought this was a unique gift, sometimes I would feel the presence of God near me, sometimes I would sense the blessing of Our Lady. Then, last year, one of the veteran soldiers from France, begging his way back to his parish, came to the kitchen door when I was skimming the cream, and I heard him ask the dairymaid for something to eat, for he was a soldier who had seen miracles: he had seen the girl they called the Maid of Orléans.

'Let him come in!' I commanded, scrambling down from my stool.

'He's dirty,' she replied. 'He's coming no closer than the step.'

He shuffled into the doorway, swinging a pack to the floor. 'If you could spare some milk, little lady,' he whined. 'And perhaps a crust of bread for a poor man, a soldier for his lord and his country—'

'What did you say about the Maid of Orléans?' I interrupted. 'And miracles?'

The maid behind me muttered under her breath, and raised her eyes, and cut him a crust of dark rye bread and poured a rough earthenware mug of milk. He almost snatched it from her hand and poured it down his throat. He looked for more.

'Tell me,' I commanded.

The maid nodded to him that he must obey me, and he turned and bowed. 'I was serving with the Duke of Bedford in France when we heard of a girl who was riding with the French,' he said. 'Some thought her a witch, some thought her in league with the devil. But my doxy . . .' The maid snapped her fingers at him and he choked down the word. 'A young woman I happened to know, a French young woman, told me that this girl Joan from Domrémy had spoken to angels and promised to see the French prince crowned and on the throne of France. She was only a maid, a girl from the country, but she said that angels spoke to her and called her to save her country from us.'

I was entranced. 'Angels spoke to her?'

He smiled ingratiatingly. 'Yes, little lady. When she was a girl no older than you.'

'But how did she make people listen to her? How did she make them see she was special?'

'Oh, she rode a great white horse, and she wore men's clothes, even armour. She had a banner of lilies and angels, and when they brought her to the French prince, she knew him among all his court.'

'She wore armour?' I whispered wonderingly, as if it was my life unfolding before me, and not the story of a strange French girl. What could I be, if only people would realise that the angels spoke to me, just as they did to this Joan?

'She wore armour and she led her men in battle.' He nodded. 'I saw her.'

I gestured to the dairymaid. 'Get him some meat and small ale to drink.' She flounced off to the buttery and the strange man and I stepped outside the dairy and he dropped to a stone seat beside the back door. I stood waiting, as she dumped a platter at his feet, and he crammed food into his mouth. He ate like a starving dog, without dignity, and when he was done and draining his mug I returned to the inquiry. 'Where did you first see her?'

'Ah,' he said, wiping his mouth on his sleeve. 'We were set for siege before a French town called Orléans, certain to win. We always won in those days, before her. We had the longbow, and they didn't, we just used to slice them down, it was like aiming at the butts for us. I was a bowman.' Then he paused as if ashamed at stretching the truth too far. 'I was a fletcher,' he corrected himself. 'I made the arrows. But our bowmen won every battle for us.'

'Never mind that, what about Joan?'

'I am telling about her. But you have to understand that they had no chance of winning. Wiser and better men than she knew they were lost. They lost every battle.'

'But she?' I whispered.

'She claimed she heard voices, angels talking to her. They told her to go to the French prince – a simpleton, a nothing – to go to him and make him take his throne as king and then drive us from our lands in France. She found her way to the king and told him he must take up his throne and let her lead his army. He thought she might have the gift of prophecy, he didn't know – but he had nothing to lose. Men believed in her. She was just a country girl, but she dressed as a man at arms, she had a banner embroidered with lilies and angels. She sent a messenger to a church and there they found an old crusader sword exactly where she said it would be – it had been hidden for years.'

'She did?'

He laughed and then coughed and spat phlegm. 'Who knows? Perhaps there was some truth in it. My dox . . . my woman friend thought that Joan was a holy maid, called by God to save France from us English. Thought she couldn't be touched by a sword. Thought she was a little angel.'

'And what was she like?'

'A girl, just a girl like you. Small, bright-eyed, full of herself.'

My heart swelled. 'Like me?'

'Very like you.'

'Did people tell her what to do all the time? Tell her she knew nothing?'

He shook his head. 'No, no, she was the commander. She followed her own vision of herself. She led an army of more than four thousand and fell on us when we were camped outside Orléans. Our lords couldn't get our men forwards to fight her; we were terrified of the very sight of her. Nobody would raise a sword against her. We all thought she was unbeatable. We went on to Jargeau and she chased after us, on the attack, always on the attack. We were all terrified of her. We swore she was a witch.'

'A witch or guided by angels?' I demanded.

He smiled. 'I saw her at Paris. There was nothing evil about her. She looked like God Himself was holding her up on that big horse. My lord called her a flower of chivalry. Really.'

'Beautiful?' I whispered. I am not a pretty girl myself, which is a disappointment to my mother; but not to me, for I rise above vanity.

He shook his head and said exactly what I wanted to hear. 'No, not pretty, not a pretty little thing, not girlish; but the light shone from her.'

I nodded. I felt that at that very moment, I understood – everything. 'Is she fighting still?'

'God bless you for a little fool, no: she's dead. Dead, what – about twenty years ago.'

'Dead?'

'The tide turned for her after Paris, we threw her back from the very walls of the city but it was a close thing – think of it! She nearly took Paris! And then in the end a Burgundy soldier pulled her off her white horse in a battle,' the beggar said matter-of-factly. 'Ransomed her to us, and we executed her. We burned her for heresy.'

I was horrified. 'But you said she was guided by the angels!'

'She followed her voices to her death,' he said flatly. 'But they examined her and said she was a virgin indeed. She was Joan the Maid in truth. And she saw true when she thought we would be defeated in France. I think we are lost now. She made a man of their king and she made an army out of their soldiers. She was no ordinary girl. I don't expect to see such a one again. She was burning up long before we put her on the pyre. She was ablaze with the Holy Spirit.'

I took a breath. 'I am such a one as her,' I whispered to him.

He looked down at my rapt face and laughed. 'No, these are old stories,' he said. 'Nothing to a girl like you. She is dead and will be soon forgotten. They scattered her ashes so no-one could make her a shrine.'

'But God spoke to her, a girl,' I whispered. 'He did not speak to the king, nor to a boy. He spoke to a girl.'

The old soldier nodded. 'I don't doubt she was sure of it,' he said. 'I don't doubt she heard the voices of angels. She must have done. Otherwise she couldn't have done what she did.'

I heard my governess's shrill call from the front door of the house and I turned my head for a moment as the soldier picked up his pack and swung it round on his back.

'But is this true?' I demanded with sudden urgency as he started to walk in a long, loping stride towards the stable yard and the gate to the road.

'Soldiers' tales,' he said indifferently. 'You can forget them, and forget her, and God knows, nobody will remember me.'

I let him go, but I did not forget Joan, and I will never forget Joan. I pray to her by name for guidance and I close my eyes and try to see her. Ever since that day, every soldier that comes to the door of Bletsoe begging for food is told to wait, for little Lady Margaret will want to see him. I always ask them if they were at Les Augustins, at Les Tourelles, at Orléans, at Jargeau, at Beaugency, at Patay, at Paris? I know her victories as well as I know the names of our neighbouring villages in Bedfordshire. Some of the soldiers were at these battles, some of them even saw her. They all speak of a slight girl on a big horse, a banner over her head, glimpsed where the fighting was the fiercest, a girl like a prince, sworn to bring peace and victory to her country, giving herself to the service of God, nothing more than a girl, nothing more than a girl like me: but a heroine.

Next morning, at breakfast, I learn why I was banned from praying through the night. My mother tells me to prepare for a journey, a long journey. 'We are going to London,' she says calmly. 'To court.'

I am thrilled at the thought of a trip to London but I take care not to exult like a vain proud girl. I bow my head and whisper: 'As you wish, Lady Mother.' This is the best thing that could happen. My home at Bletsoe, in the heart of the county of Bedfordshire, is so quiet and dull that there is no chance for me to resist the perils of the world. There are no temptations to overcome, and no-one sees me but servants and my older half-brothers and -sisters and they all think of me as a little girl, of no importance. I try to think of Joan, herding her father's sheep at Domrémy, who was buried like me, among miles of muddy fields. She did not complain of being bored in the country, she waited and listened for the voices to summon her to greatness. I must do the same.

I wonder if this command to go to London is the voice I have been waiting for, calling me to greatness now. We will be at the court of the good King Henry VI. He must welcome me as his nearest kin, I am all but his cousin, after all. His grandfather and my grandfather were half-brothers, which is a very close connection when one of you is king and the other is not, and he himself passed a law to recognise my family, the Beauforts, as legitimate though not royal. Surely, he will see in me the light of holiness that everyone says is in him. He must claim me as both kin and kindred spirit. What if he decides I shall stay at court with him? Why not? What if he wants to take me as his advisor, as the Dauphin took Joan of Arc? I am his second cousin and I can almost see visions of the saints. I am only nine years old but I hear the voices of angels and I pray all night when they let me. If I had been born a boy I would be all but the Prince of Wales now. Sometimes I wonder if they wish I had been born a boy and that is why they are blind to the light that shines within me. Could it be that they are so filled with the sin of pride in our place that they wish I was a boy, and ignore the greatness that is me, as a holy girl?

'Yes, Lady Mother,' I say obediently.

'You don't sound very excited,' she says. 'Don't you want to know why we are going?'

Desperately. 'Yes, if you please.'

'I am sorry to say that your your betrothal to John de la Pole must be ended. It was a good match when it was made when you were six; but now you are to dissent from it. You will face a panel of judges who will ask you if you wish your betrothal to be ended and you will say "Yes". Do you understand?'

This sounds very alarming. 'But I won't know what to say.'

'You will just consent to the end of your betrothal. You will just say "Yes".'

'What if they ask me if I think it is the will of God? What if they ask me if this is the answer to my prayers?'

She sighs as if I am tiresome. 'They won't ask you that.'

'And then what will happen?'

'His Grace, the king, will appoint a new guardian, and, in turn, he will give you in marriage to the man of his choice.'

'Another betrothal?'

'Yes.'

'Can I not go to an abbey?' I ask very quietly, though I know what her answer will be. Nobody regards my spiritual gifts. 'Now I am released from this betrothal can I not go now?'

'Of course you can't go to an abbey, Margaret. Don't be stupid. Your duty is to bear a son and heir, a boy for our family, the Beauforts, a young kinsman to the King of

England, a boy for the House of Lancaster. God knows, the House of York has boys enough. We have to have one of our own. You will give us one of our own.'

'But I think I have a calling . . .'

'You are called to be mother of the next heir of Lancaster,' she says briskly. 'That is an ambition great enough for any girl. Now go and get ready to leave. Your women will have packed your clothes, you just have to fetch your doll for the journey.'

I fetch my doll and my own carefully copied book of prayers too. I can read French of course and also English, but I cannot understand Latin or Greek and my mother will not allow me a tutor. A girl is not worth educating, she says. I wish that I could read the gospels and prayers in Latin, but I cannot, and the handwritten copies in English are rare and precious. Boys are taught Latin and Greek and other subjects too; but girls need only be able to read and write, to sew, to keep the household accounts, to make music and enjoy poetry. If I were an abbess I would have access to a great library and I could set clerks to copy all the texts that I wanted to read. I would make the novices read to me all day. I would be a woman of learning instead of an untaught girl, as stupid as any ordinary girl.

If my father had lived, perhaps he would have taught me Latin. He was a great reader and writer; at least I know that much about him. He spent years in captivity in France when he studied every day. But he died just days before my first birthday. My birth was so unimportant to him that he was in France on campaign, trying to restore his fortune, when my mother was brought to bed, and he did not come home again until just before my first birthday, and then he died; so he never knew me and my gifts.

It will take us three days to get to London. My mother will

ride her own horse but I am to ride pillion behind one of the grooms. He is called Wat and he thinks himself a great charmer in the stables and kitchen. He winks at me as if I would be friendly to a man such as him, and I frown to remind him that I am a Beaufort and he is a nobody. I sit behind him, and I have to take tight hold of his leather belt, and when he says to me; 'Right and tight? Righty tighty?' I nod coldly, so as to warn him that I don't want him talking to me all the way to Ampthill.

He sings instead, which is just as bad. He sings love songs and hay-making songs in a bright tenor voice and the men who ride with us, to protect us from the armed bands who are everywhere in England these days, join in with him and sing too. I wish my mother would order them to be silent, or at least command them to sing psalms; but she is happy, riding out in the warm spring sunshine, and when she comes alongside me she smiles and says: 'Not far now, Margaret. We will spend tonight at Abbots Langley and go on to London tomorrow. Are you not too tired?'

I am so unprepared by those who should care for me that I haven't even been taught how to ride, and I am not allowed even to sit on a horse of my own and be led, not even when we arrive in London and hundreds of people in the streets and markets and shops gawp at the fifty of our household as we ride by. How am I to appear as the heroine who will save England if I have to jog behind Wat, seated pillion, my hand on his belt, like some village slut going to a goose fair? I am not at all like an heir to the House of Lancaster. We stay at an inn, not even at court, for the Duke of Suffolk, my guardian, was terribly disgraced and is now dead, so we cannot stay in his palace. I offer up to Our Lady the fact that we don't have a good London house of our own, and then I think that She too had to make do with a common inn at Bethlehem, when surely Herod must have had spare rooms in the palace. There must have been more suitable arrangements than a stable, surely? Considering who She was. And so I try to be resigned, like Her.

At least I am to have London clothes before we go to court for me to renounce my betrothal. My Lady Mother summons the tailors and the sempstresses to our inn and I am fitted for a wonderful gown. They say that the ladies of the court are wearing tall, conical headdresses, so high that a woman has to duck to get under a seven-foot doorway. The queen, Margaret of Anjou, loves beautiful clothes and is wearing a new colour of ruby red made from a new dye; they say it is as red as blood. My mother orders me a gown of angelic white by way of contrast, and has it trimmed with Lancaster red roses to remind everyone that I may be only a girl of nine years old but I am the heiress of our house. Only when the clothes are ready can we take a barge downriver to declare my dissent against my betrothal, and to be presented at court.

The dissent is a tremendous disappointment. I am hoping that they will question me and that I might stand before them, shy but clear-spoken, to say that I know from God Himself that John de la Pole is not to be my husband. I imagine myself before a tribunal of judges amazing them like Baby Jesus at the synagogue. I thought I might say that I had a dream which told me that I was not to marry him for I have a greater destiny: I am chosen by God Himself to save England! I am to be Queen of England and sign my name Margaret Regina: *Margaret R.* But there is no opportunity for me to address them, to shine. It is all written down before we arrive and all I am allowed to say is, 'I dissent', and sign my name, which is only Margaret Beaufort, and it is done. Nobody even asks me for my opinion on the matter.

We go to wait outside the presence chamber and then one of the king's men comes out and calls 'Lady Margaret Beaufort!' and everyone looks around and sees me. I have a moment, a really wonderful moment, when I feel everyone looking at me and I remember to cast down my eyes, and despise worldly vanity, and then my mother leads the way into the king's presence chamber.

The king is on his great throne with his cloth of estate suspended over the chair and a throne almost the same size beside him for the queen. She is fair-haired, and brown-eyed, with a round pudding face and a straight nose. I think she looks beautiful and spoilt, and the king beside her looks fair and pale. I can't say I see any great light of holiness at this first inspection. He looks quite normal. He smiles at me as I come in and curtsey, but the queen looks from the red roses at the hem of my gown to the little coronet that holds my veil, and then looks away as if she does not think much of me. I suppose, being French, she does not understand who I am. Someone should have told her that if she does not have a baby then they will have to find another boy to be their heir for the House of Lancaster and it could well be mine. Then I am sure she would have paid me more attention. But she is worldly. The French can be terribly worldly, I have observed it from my reading. I am sure she would not even have seen the light in Joan the Maid. I cannot be surprised that she does not admire me.

Next to her is a most beautiful woman, perhaps the most beautiful woman I have ever seen. She is wearing a gown of blue with a silver thread running through which makes it shimmer like water. You would think her scaled like a fish.

She sees me staring at her, and she smiles back at me, which makes her face light up with a warm beauty like sunlight on water on a summer's day.

'Who is that?' I whisper to my mother, who pinches my arm to remind me to be silent, 'Jacquetta Rivers. Stop staring,' my mother snaps, and pinches my arm again to recall me to the present. I curtsey very low and I smile at the king.

'I am giving your daughter in wardship to my dearly loved half-brothers, Edmund and Jasper Tudor,' the king says to my mother. 'She can live with you until it is time for her to marry.'

The queen looks away and whispers something to Jacquetta, who leans forwards like a willow tree beside a stream, the veil billowing around her tall headdress, to listen. The queen does not look much pleased by this news, but I am dumbfounded. I wait for someone to ask me for my consent so that I can explain that I am destined for a life of holiness, but my mother merely curtseys and steps back and then someone else steps forwards and it all seems to be over. The king has barely looked at me, he knows nothing about me, no more than he knew before I walked in the room, and yet he has given me to a new guardian, to another stranger. How can it be that he does not realise that I am a child of special holiness as he was? Am I not to have the chance to tell him about my saints' knees?

'Can I speak?' I whisper to my mother.

'No, of course not.'

Then how is he to know who I am, if God does not hurry up and tell him? 'Well, what happens now?'

'We wait until the other petitioners have seen the king, and then go in to dine,' she replies.

'No, I mean, what happens to me?'

She looks at me as if I am foolish not to understand. 'You

are to be betrothed again,' she says. 'Did you not hear, Margaret? I wish you would pay attention. This is an even greater match for you. You are first going to be the ward, and then the wife of Edmund Tudor, the king's half-brother. The Tudor boys are the sons of the king's own mother, Queen Catherine of Valois, by her second marriage to Owen Tudor. There are two Tudor brothers, both great favourites of the king, Edmund and Jasper. Both half-royal, both favoured. You will marry the older one.'

'Won't he want to meet me first?'

'Why would he?'

'To see if he likes me?'

She shakes her head. 'It is not you they want,' she says. 'It is the son you will bear.'

'But I'm only nine.'

'He can wait until you're twelve,' she says.

'I am to be married then?'

'Of course,' she says, as if I am a fool to ask.

'And how old will he be?'

She thinks for a moment. 'Twenty-five.'

I blink. 'Where will he sleep?' I ask. I am thinking of the house at Bletsoe, which does not have an empty set of rooms for a hulking young man and his entourage, nor for his younger brother.

She laughs. 'Oh, Margaret. You won't stay at home with me. You will go to live with him and his brother, in Lamphey Palace, in Wales.'

I blink. 'Lady Mother, are you sending me away to live with two full-grown men, to Wales, on my own? When I am twelve?'

She shrugs, as if she is sorry for it, but that nothing can be done. 'It's a good match,' she says. 'Royal blood on both sides of the marriage. If you have a son, his claim to the throne will be very strong. You are cousin to the king and your husband is the king's half-brother. Any boy you have will keep Richard of York at bay for ever. Think of that, don't think about anything else.'

AUGUST 1453

My mother tells me that the time will pass quickly; but of course it does not. The days go on for ever and ever, and nothing ever happens. My half-brothers and -sisters from my mother's first marriage into the St John family show no more respect for me now that I am to be married to a Tudor than when I was to be married to a de la Pole. Indeed, now they laugh at me going to live in Wales, which they tell me is a place inhabited by dragons and witches, where there are no roads, but just huge castles in dark forests where water witches rise up out of fountains and entrance mortal men, and wolves prowl in vast man-eating packs. Nothing changes at all until one evening, at family prayers, my mother cites the name of the king with more than her usual devotion, and we all have to stay on our knees for an extra half hour to pray for the health of the king, Henry VI, in this, his time of trouble; and beg Our Lady that the new baby, now in the royal womb of the queen, will prove to be a boy and a new prince for Lancaster.

I don't say 'Amen' to the prayer for the health of the queen, for I thought she was not particularly pleasant to me, and any child that she has will take my place as the next Lancaster heir. I don't pray against a live birth for that would be ill-wishing, and also the sin of envy; but my lack of enthusiasm in the prayers will be understood, I am sure, by Our Lady, who is Queen of Heaven and understands all about inheritance and how difficult it is to be one of the heirs to the throne, but a girl. Whatever happens in the future, I could never be queen, nobody would accept it. But if I have a son he would have a good claim to be king. Our Lady Herself had a boy, of course, which was what everyone wanted, and so became Our Lady Queen of Heaven and could sign her name Mary Regina: *Mary R.*

I wait till my half-brothers and -sisters have gone ahead, hurrying for their dinner, and I ask my mother why we are praying so earnestly for the king's health, and what does she mean by a 'time of trouble'? Her face is quite strained with worry. 'I have had a letter from your new guardian, Edmund Tudor today,' she says. 'He tells me that the king has fallen into some sort of a trance. He says nothing, and he does nothing, he sits still with his eyes on the ground and nothing wakens him.'

'Is God speaking to him?'

She gives a little irritated sniff. 'Well, who knows? Who knows? I am sure your piety does you great credit, Margaret. But certainly, if God is speaking to the king then He has not chosen the best time for this conversation. If the king shows any sign of weakness then the Duke of York is bound to take the opportunity to seize power. The queen has gone to parliament to claim all the powers of the king for herself, but they will never trust her. They will appoint Richard, Duke of York, as regent instead of her. It is a certainty. Then we will be ruled by the Yorks and you will see a change in our fortunes for the worse.'

'What change?'

'If the king does not recover, then we will be ruled by Richard of York in place of the king, and he and his family will enjoy a long regency while the queen's baby grows to be a man. They will have years to put themselves into the best positions in the church, in France, and in the best places in England.' She bustles ahead of me to the great hall, spurred on by her own irritation. 'I can expect to have them coming to me, to have your betrothal overturned. They won't let you be betrothed to a Tudor of Lancaster. They will want you married into their house, so your son is their heir, and I will have to defy them if the House of Lancaster is to continue through you. And that will bring Richard of York down on me, and years of trouble.'

'But why does it matter so much?' I ask, half-running to keep up with her down the long passageway. 'We are all royal. Why do we have to be rivals? We are all Plantagenets, we are all descended from Edward III. We are all cousins. Richard, Duke of York, is cousin to the king just as I am.'

She rounds on me, her gown releasing the scent of lavender as it sweeps the strewing herbs on the floor. 'We may be of the same family but that is the very reason why we are not friends, for we are rivals for the throne. What quarrels are worse than family quarrels? We may all be cousins; but they are of the House of York and we are of the House of Lancaster. Never forget it. We of Lancaster are the direct line of descent from Edward III by his son, John of Gaunt. The direct line! But the Yorks can only trace their line back to John of Gaunt's younger brother Edmund. They are a junior line, they are not descended from Edward's heir, they descend from a younger brother. They can only inherit the throne of England if there is no Lancaster boy left. So – think, Margaret! – what do you think they are hoping for when the King of England falls into a trance, and his child is yet unborn? What d'you think they dream, when you are a Lancaster heir but only a girl, and not even married yet? Let alone brought to bed of a son?'

'They would want to marry me into their house?' I ask, bewildered at the thought of yet another betrothal.

She laughs shortly. 'That; or, to tell the truth, they would rather see you dead.'

I am silenced by this. That a whole family, a great house like York, would wish for my death is a frightening thought. 'But surely the king will wake up? And then everything will be all right. And his baby could be a son. And then he will be the Lancaster heir, and everything will be all right.'

'Pray God the king wakes soon,' she says. 'But you should pray that there is no baby to supplant you. And pray God we get you wedded and bedded without delay. For no-one is safe from the ambitions of the House of York.'

OCTOBER 1453

The king dreams on, smiling in his waking sleep. In my room, alone, I try sitting, as they say he does, and staring at the floorboards, in case God will come to me as He has come to the king. I try to be deaf to the noises of the stable yard outside my window, and the loud singing from the laundry room where someone is thumping cloths on a washboard. I try to let my soul drift to God, and feel the absorbing peace that must wash the soul of the king so that he does not see the worried faces of his counsellors, and is even blind to his wife when she puts his new-born baby son in his arms and tells him to wake up and greet the little Prince Edward, heir to the throne of England. Even when in temper, she shouts into his face that he must wake up or the House of Lancaster will be destroyed.

I try to be entranced by God, as the king is, but someone always comes and bangs on my door or shouts down the hall for me to come and do some chores, and I am dragged back to the ordinary world of sin again, and I wake. The great mystery for England is that the king does not wake, and while he sits, hearing only the words of angels, the man who has made himself

Regent of England, Richard, Duke of York, takes the reins of government into his own hands, starts to act like a king himself, and so Margaret, the queen, has to recruit her friends and warn them that she may need their help to defend her baby son. The warning alone is enough to generate unease. Up and down England men start to muster their forces and consider whether they would do better under a hated French queen with a true-born baby prince in her arms, or to follow the handsome and beloved Englishman, Richard of York, to wherever his ambition may take him.

SUMMER 1455

It is my wedding day – come at last. I stand at the door of the church in my best gown, the belt high and tight around my ribcage and the absurdly wide sleeves drowning my thin arms and little hands. My headdress is so heavy on my head that I droop beneath the wire support, and the tall, conical height. The sweep of the scarf from the apex veils my pale resentment. My mother is beside me to escort me to my guardian Edmund Tudor, who has decided – as any wise guardian would, no doubt – that my best interests will be served by marriage to him: he is his own best choice as caretaker of my interests.

I whisper to my mother. 'I am afraid,' and she looks down at me. My head is only up to her shoulder. I am twelve years old; but still a little girl, my chest as flat as a board, my body hairless beneath my thick layers of rich clothes. They had to pack my bodice with linen to give the impression of breasts. I am a child sent out to do a woman's duty.

'Nothing to be afraid about,' she says bluntly.

I try again. 'I thought I would be a virgin like Joan of Arc,' I say to her. I put my hand on her sleeve to tug at her attention.

'You know I did. I always did. I wanted to go to a convent. I still want to go. I may have a calling. It might be God's will. We should take advice. We could ask the priest. We could ask him now, before it is too late. What if God wants me for His own? Then it would be blasphemy if I married.'

She turns to me, and takes my cold hand in hers. 'Margaret,' she says seriously, 'you must know that you could never choose your own life. You are a girl: girls have no choice. You could never even choose your own husband: you are of the royal family. A husband would always have been chosen for you. It is forbidden for one of royal blood to marry their own choice. You know this too. And finally, you are of the House of Lancaster. You cannot choose your allegiance. You have to serve your house, your family, and your husband. I have allowed you to dream, and I have allowed you to read; but the time has come to put aside silly stories and silly dreams and do your duty. Don't think you can be like your father and run away from your duty. He took a coward's way out, you cannot.'

This sudden reference to my father shocks me. She never speaks of her second husband, my father, except in the vaguest and most general terms. I am about to ask, how did he run away, what was his coward's way out? when the doors of the church open, and I have to walk forwards and take the hand of my new husband, and stand before a priest and swear to be a wife. I feel his big hand take mine and I hear his deep voice answer the questions, where I just whisper. He pushes a heavy ring of Welsh gold on my finger and I have to hold my fingers together like a little paw to keep it on. It is far too big for me. I look up at him, amazed that he thinks such a marriage can go ahead, when his ring is too big for my hand and I am only twelve and he is more than twice my age: a man, tempered by fighting and filled with ambition. He is a hard man from a power-seeking family. But I am still a child longing for a spiritual life, praying that people will see that I am special. This is yet another of the many things that nobody seems to care about but me.

I am to start married life in the palace of Lamphey, Pembrokeshire, which is in the heart of horrible Wales. I have no time to miss my mother and my family in the first months for everything is so different that I have to learn completely new ways. Most of my time is spent with the servants and the women attendants in the castle. My husband and his brother storm in and out like rain. My lady governess has come with me, and my own maidservant, but everyone else is a stranger. They all speak Welsh and stare at me when I try to ask them for a glass of small ale or a jug of water for washing. I so long for a friendly face from home that I would even be glad to see Wat, the groom.

The castle stands in desolate countryside. Around me is nothing but high mountains and sky. I can see the rain clouds coming like a wet curtain, half an hour before they pour down on the grey slate roofs and rain-streaked walls. The chapel is a cold and neglected building and the priest is very poor in his attendance; he does not even notice my exceptional piety. I often go there to pray and the light streams through the western window onto my bowed head, but nobody even notices. London is a nine-day arduous journey away, my old home is as far. It can take ten days for a letter to come from my mother, but she hardly ever writes. Sometimes I feel that I have been stolen from a battlefield and held to ransom in an enemy land, like my father. Certainly I could not feel more foreign and lonely.

Worst of all, I have not had a vision since my wedding night.

I spend every afternoon on my knees, when I close my privy chamber door and pretend to be sewing. I spend every evening in the damp chapel. But nothing comes to me. Not a vision of the stake, not the battles, not even the flicker of a banner of angels and lilies. I beg Our Lady for a vision of Joan the Maid; but She grants me nothing, and in the end, sitting back on my heels, I begin to fear that I was holy only when I was a virgin; I am nothing special as a wife.

Nothing in the world could compensate me for this loss. I was raised to know myself as the daughter of a great man and an heir of the royal family, but my own private glory was that I knew that God spoke to me, directly to me, and that he sent me the vision of Joan the Maid. He sent me an angel in the guise of a beggar to tell me all about her. He appointed William de la Pole as my guardian so that he – having seen Joan – would recognise the same holiness in me. But then God, for some reason, forgot all about this sensible plan, and let me fall into the keeping of a husband who takes no interest in my holiness; and by roughly consummating the marriage vows, takes my virginity and visions in one awful night. Why I should be chosen by God and then neglected by Him, I cannot understand. It is not for me to question the will of God, but I have to wonder: why did He choose me in the first place if it was just to leave me here, abandoned in Wales? If He were not God, then one would think it very badly planned. It is not as if there is anything I can do here, and for sure, nobody sees me as a living light. It is even worse than Bletsoe, where at least people complained that I was excessively holy. Here they don't even notice and I am afraid that I am hidden under a bushel and there is nothing I can do to reveal myself as a beacon for the world.

My husband is handsome and brave, I suppose. I hardly see him or his brother during the day, as they are constantly riding out to keep the king's peace against dozens of local uprisings. Edmund is always in the lead, Jasper, his brother, at his shoulder like a shadow. They even walk at the same pace, Edmund striding forwards, Jasper just behind, in step. They are only a year apart in age. I thought them twins when I first saw them together. They have the same unfortunate ginger hair and long thin noses, they both stand tall and lean now but I think they will run to fat in later life, which must be quite soon. When they talk they can finish each other's sentences and they laugh all the time at private jokes. They hardly ever speak to me, and they never tell me what is supposed to be so funny. They are utterly fascinated by weapons and can spend the entire evening talking about the stringing of a bow. I cannot see the use of either of them in God's will.

The castle is in a constant state of alert because warring parties and bands of armed and disaffected soldiers come by all the time and raid the nearby villages. Just as my mother feared when the king first fell into his trance, there is unrest everywhere. Worse here than anywhere else, of course since it is half-savage already. And it made no real difference when the king recovered, though the common people were told to rejoice, for now he has fallen ill again, and some people are saying that this is how it will always be: we will live with a king who cannot be relied on to stay awake. This is obviously a disadvantage. Even I can see that.

Men are taking arms against the king's rule, first complaining of the taxes raised to fight the unending French wars, and now complaining that the wars are over but we have lost everything we won under the king's braver father and grandfather. Everyone hates the queen, who is French herself, of course, and everyone whispers that the king is under the cat's-paw in this marriage, and that a French woman rules the country and that it would be better if we were ruled by the Duke of York.

Everyone who has a grievance against his neighbour takes this chance to pull down his fences or poach his game, or steal his timber, and then there is a fight and Edmund has to go out and make rough and ready justice. The roads are dangerous to travel because of roaming companies of soldiers that were formed in France and are now in the habit of forage and kidnap. When I ride out behind a servant into the little village that clusters around the walls of the castle, I have to take an armed guard with me. I see the white faces and hollow eyes of hunger, and nobody smiles at me, though you would think they would be glad that the new lady of the palace is taking an interest. For who will intercede for them on earth and in heaven if not I? But I can't understand what they say to me as they all speak Welsh, and if they come too close the servants lower their pikes and order them back. Clearly, I am not a light for the common people in the village, any more than I am in the palace. I am twelve – if people cannot see that I am a light in a dark world now, when are they going to see it? But how will anyone see anything here in miserable Wales, where they can see nothing for the mud?

Edmund's brother Jasper is supposed to live a few miles away at Pembroke Castle; but he is rarely there. He is either at the royal court, trying to hold together the irritable accord between the York family and the king, in the interests of the peace of England; or he is with us. Whether he is riding out to visit the king, or coming home, his face grave with worry that the king has slipped into his trance again, he always manages to find a road which passes by Lamphey, and come for his dinner.

At dinner, my husband Edmund talks only to his brother Jasper. Neither of them say so much as one word to me; but I have to listen to the two of them worrying that Richard, Duke of York, will make a claim on the throne on his own account.

He is advised by Richard Neville, the Earl of Warwick, and these two, Warwick and York, are men of too vast an ambition to obey a sleeping king. There are many who say that the country cannot even be safe in the hands of a regent, and if the king does not wake, then England cannot survive the dozen years before his son is old enough to rule. Someone will have to take the throne; we cannot be governed by a sleeping king and a baby.

'We can't endure another long regency, we have to have a king,' Jasper says. 'I wish to God you had married and bedded her years ago, at least we would be ahead of the game now.'

I flush and look down at my plate, heaped with overcooked and unrecognisable bits of game. They hunt better than they farm in Wales, and every meal brings some skinny bird or beast to the table in butchered portions. I long for fast days when we have only fish, and I impose extra fast days on myself to escape the sticky mess of dinner. Everyone stabs what they want with their dagger from a common plate, and sops up the gravy with a hunk of bread. They wipe their hands on their breeches, and their mouths on their coat-cuffs. Even at the high table we are served our meat on trenchers of bread that are eaten up at the end of the meal, there are no plates laid on the table. Napkins are obviously too French, they count it a patriotic duty to wipe their mouths on their sleeves, and they all bring their own spoons as if they were heirlooms, tucked inside their boots.

I take a little piece of meat and nibble at it. The smell of grease turns my stomach. Now they are talking, in front of me as if I were deaf, of my fertility and the possibility that if the queen is driven from England, or her baby dies, then my son will be one of the king's likely heirs.

'You think the queen will let that happen? You think Margaret of Anjou won't fight for England? She knows her duty better than that,' Edmund says with a laugh. 'There are even those who say that she was too determined to be stopped by a sleeping husband. They say she got the baby without the king. Some say she got a stable boy to mount her rather than leave the royal cradle empty and her husband dreaming.'

I put my hands to my hot cheeks. This is unbearable, but nobody notices my discomfort.

'Not another word,' Jasper says flatly. 'She is a great lady and I fear for her and her child. You get an heir for yourself, and don't repeat gossip to me. The confidence of York with his quiver of four boys grows every day. We need to show them there is a true Lancaster heir in waiting, we need to keep their ambitions down. The Staffords and the Hollands have heirs already, where's the Tudor-Beaufort boy?'

Edmund laughs shortly and reaches for more wine. 'I try every night,' he says. 'Trust me. I don't skimp my duty. She may be little more than a child herself, with no liking for the act, but I do what I have to.'

For the first time, Jasper glances over to me, as if he is wondering what I make of this bleak description of married life. I meet his gaze blankly with my teeth gritted. I don't want his sympathy. This is my martyrdom. Marriage to his brother in this peasant palace in horrible Wales is my martyrdom; and I offer it up, and I know that God will reward me.

Edmund tells his brother nothing more than the truth. Every single night of our life, he comes to my room, slightly unsteady from the wine at dinner that he throws down his throat like a sot. Every night, he gets into bed beside me, and takes a handful of my nightgown as if it were not the finest Valenciennes lace hemmed by my little-girl stitches, and holds it aside so he can push himself against me. Every night I grit my teeth and say not one word of protest, not even a whimper of pain, as he takes me without kindness or courtesy, and every night, moments later, he gets up from my bed and throws on his gown and goes without a word of thanks or farewell. I say nothing, not one word, from beginning to end, and neither does he. If it were lawful for a woman to hate her husband I would hate him as a rapist. But hatred would make the baby malformed, so I make sure I do not hate him, not even in secret. Instead, I slide from the bed the minute he has gone and kneel at the foot of it, still smelling his rancid sweat, still feeling the burning pain between my legs, and I pray to Our Lady who had the good fortune to be spared all this by the kindly visit of the bodiless Holy Ghost. I pray to Her to forgive Edmund Tudor for being such a torturer to me, her child, especially favoured by God. I, who am without sin; and certainly without lust. Months into marriage I am as far away from desire as I was when I was a little girl; and it seems to me that there is nothing more likely to cure a woman of lust than marriage. Now I understand what the saint meant when he said that it was better to marry than to burn. In my experience, if you marry, you certainly won't burn.

SUMMER 1456

One long year of loneliness and disgust and pain, and now I have another burden to bear. Edmund's old nursemaid becomes so impatient for another Tudor boy that she comes to me every month to ask if I am bleeding, as if I were a favourite mare at stud. She is longing for me to say 'no' for then she can count on her fat old fingers and see that her precious boy has done his duty. For months I can disappoint her and see her wizened old face fall, but at the end of June I can tell her that I have not bled, and she kneels down in my own privy chamber and thanks God and the Virgin Mary that the House of Tudor will have an heir and that England is saved for the House of Lancaster.

At first I think she is a fool, but after she has run to tell my husband Edmund and his brother Jasper, and they have both come to me like a pair of excited twins, and shouted their well wishes, and asked me if I would like anything special to eat, or if they should send for my mother, or whether I should like to gently walk in the courtyard, or to rest, I see that to them, this conception is indeed a first step towards greatness, and could be the saving of our house.

That night, as I kneel to pray, at last I have a vision again. I have a vision as clear as if I were in my waking life, but the sun is as bright as in France, not Welsh grey. It is not a vision of Joan going to the scaffold, but a miraculous vision of Joan as she was called to greatness. I am with her in the fields near her home, I can feel the softness of the grass under my feet and I am dazzled by the brightness of the sky. I hear the bells tolling the Angelus, and they ring in my head like voices. I hear the celestial singing, and then I see the shimmering light. I drop my head to the rich cloth of my bed and still the blazing light burns the inside of my eyelids. I am filled with conviction that I am seeing her calling and I am being called myself. God wanted Joan to serve Him and now He wants me. My hour has come and my heroine, Joan, has shown me the way. I tremble with desire for holiness and the burning behind my eyes spreads through my whole body and burns, I am sure, in my womb where the baby is growing into the light of life and his spirit is forming.

I don't know how long I kneel in prayer. Nobody interrupts me and I feel as if I have been in the sacred light for a whole year when I finally open my eyes in wonder, and blink at the dancing candle flames. Slowly, I rise to my feet, hauling myself up the bedpost, weak at the knees with my sense of the divine. I sit on the side of my bed in a state of wonder, and puzzle at the nature of my calling. Joan was called to save France from war and to put the true King of France on his throne. There must be a reason that I saw myself in her fields, that all my life I have dreamed of her life. Our lives must march in step. Her story must speak to me. I too must be called to save my country, as she was summoned to rescue hers. I have been called to save England from danger, from uncertainty, from war itself, and put the true King of England on his throne. When Henry the king dies, even if his son survives, I know it will be the baby now growing in my womb who will inherit. I know it. This baby must be a son – this is what my vision is telling me. My son will inherit the throne of England. The horror of war with France will be ended by the rule of my son. The unrest in our country will be turned into peace by my son. I shall bring him into the world, and I shall put him on the throne, and I shall guide him in the ways of God that I shall teach him. This is my destiny: to put my son on the throne of England, and those who laughed at my visions and doubted my vocation will call me My Lady, the King's Mother. I shall sign myself Margaret Regina: Margaret the queen.

I put my hand to my belly that is still as flat as a child's. 'King,' I say quietly. 'You are going to be King of England,' and I know that the baby hears me and knows that his destiny and that of all England is given to me by God, and is in my keeping.

My knowledge that the baby in my womb is to be king and that everyone will curtsey to me supports me through the early months, though I am sick every morning and weary to my soul. It is hot, and Edmund has to ride out through the fields where the men are making hay, to hunt down our enemies. William Herbert, a fierce Yorkist partisan, thinks to make Wales his own while there is a sleeping king and no-one to call him to account. He marches his men through our lands and collects our taxes under the pretext that he is ruling Wales for the regency of York. Indeed, it is true that he has been appointed by his good friend the Earl of Warwick to rule Wales; but long before that, we Tudors were put here by the king, and here we stay doing our duty, whether our king is awake or not. Both Herbert and we Tudors believe ourselves to be the only rightful rulers of Wales, properly appointed; but the difference is that we are right and he is wrong. And God smiles on me, of course.

Edmund and Jasper are in a state of constant muted fury at the incursions of Herbert and the Yorkists, writing to their father Owen who is in turn riding out with his men, harrying York lands, and planning a concerted campaign with his boys. It is as my mother predicted. The king is of the House of Lancaster; but he is fast asleep. The regent is of the House of York and he is only too lively. Jasper is away much of the time, brooding over the sleeping king like a poor hen with addled eggs. He says that the queen has all but abandoned her husband in London, seeking greater safety for herself in the walled city of Coventry which she can hold against an army, and thinks that she will have to rule England from there, and avoid the treachery of the City of London. He says that the London merchants and half of the southern counties are all for York because they hope for peaceful times to make money, and care nothing for the true king and the will of God.

Meanwhile every lord prepares his men and chooses his side, and Jasper and Edmund wait only till the end of haymaking, and then muster the men with their scythes and bill hooks and march out to find William Herbert and teach him who commands Wales. I go down to the gate of the castle to wave them farewell and bid them Godspeed. Jasper assures me that they will defeat Herbert within two days and capture Carmarthen Castle from him, and that I can look for them to come home in time for the harvest; but two days come and go and we have no news of them.

I am supposed to rest every afternoon and my lady governess is ordered by my mother to take a renewed interest in my health, now I am carrying a child that could be a royal heir. She sits with me in the darkened rooms to make sure that I do not read by the light of a smuggled candle, or get down on my knees to pray. I have to lie on my bed and think of cheerful things to make the baby strong and blithe in his spirits. Knowing I am making the next king, I obey her, and try to think of sturdy horses and beautiful clothes, of the magic of the joust and of the king's court, and the queen in her ruby gown. But one day there is a commotion at my door and I sit up, and glance at my lady governess who, far from watching over me as the vessel preparing to bear the next king, is fast asleep in her chair. I get up and patter over to my door and open it myself and there is our maid Gwyneth, white-faced, with a letter in her hand. 'We can't read it,' she says. 'It's a letter for someone. None of us can read.'

'My lady governess is asleep,' I say. 'Give it to me.'

Stupidly, she hands it over though it is addressed to my lady governess, and marked for her eyes alone. I break Jasper Tudor's seal and open it. He has written from Pembroke Castle.

Edmund wounded and captured by William Herbert. Held prisoner at Carmarthen. Prepare for attack as best you can there, while I go to rescue him. Admit no strangers; there is plague.

Gwyneth looks at me. 'What does it say?' she asks.

'Nothing,' I say. The lie comes to my mouth so swiftly that it must be put there by God to help me, and therefore it does not count as a lie at all. 'He says that they are staying on a few days in Pembroke Castle. He will come back later.'

I close the door in her face and I go back to my bed and lie down. I put my hand on my fat belly that has grown bigger and now curves beneath my gown. I will tell them the news later tonight, I think. But first I must decide what to say and what to do.

I think, as always, what would Joan of Arc do, if she were in my place? The most important thing would be to make sure that the future king is safe. Edmund and Jasper can look after themselves. For me, there is nothing more important than ensuring that my son is safe behind defensible walls, so when Black Herbert comes to sack the Tudor lands at least we can keep my baby safe.

At the thought of William Herbert marching his army against me, I slide down to my knees to pray. 'What am I to do?' I whisper to Our Lady, and never in my life would I have been more glad of a clear reply. 'We can't defend here, there isn't even a wall that goes all round, and we don't have the fighting men. I can't go to Pembroke if there is plague there, and anyway, I don't even know where Pembroke is. But if Herbert attacks us here how shall we be safe? What if he kidnaps me for ransom? But if we try to get to Pembroke, then what if I am ill on the road? What if travelling is bad for a baby?'

There is nothing but silence. 'Our Lady?' I ask. 'Lady Mary?'

Nothing. It is a quite disagreeable silence.

I sigh. 'What would Joan do?' I ask myself. 'If she had to make a dangerous choice? What would Joan do? If I were Joan, with her courage, what would I do?'

Wearily, I rise to my feet. I walk over to my lady governess and take a pleasure in shaking her awake. 'Get up,' I say. 'You have work to do. We are going to Pembroke Castle.'

AUTUMN 1456

Edmund does not come home. William Herbert does not even demand a ransom for him, the heir to the Tudor name, and father of my child. In these uncertain times nobody can say what Edmund is worth and besides, they tell me he is sick. He is held at Carmarthen Castle, a prisoner of the Herberts, and he does not write to me, having nothing to say to a wife who is little more than a child, and I do not write to him, having nothing to say to him either.

I wait, alone in Pembroke Castle, preparing for siege, admitting no-one from the town for fear they are carrying the sickness, knowing I may have to hold this castle against our enemies, not knowing where to send for help for Jasper is constantly on the move. We have food and we have arms and we have water. I sleep with the key to the drawbridge and the portcullis under my pillow; but I can't say that I know what I should do next. I wait for my husband to tell me; but I hear nothing from him. I wait for his brother to come. I wish his father would ride by and rescue me. But it is as if I have walled myself in and am forgotten. I pray for guidance from Our

Lady who also faced troubled times when she was with child; but no Holy Ghost appears to announce to the world that I am the Lord's vessel. It seems that there is to be no annunciation for me at all. Indeed, the servants, the priest, and even my lady governess are rapt in their own misfortunes and worries as the news of the king's strange sleep and the struggle of power between his queen and the country's regent alerts every scoundrel to the opportunity of easy pickings to be made in a country without government, and Herbert's friends in Wales know that the Tudors are on the run, their heir captured, his brother missing, and his bride all alone at Pembroke Castle, sick with fear.

Then, in November, I get a letter addressed to me, to Lady Margaret Tudor, from my brother-in-law, Jasper. It is the first time in his life he has ever written to me, and I open it with shaking hands. He does not waste many words.

Regret to tell you that your husband, my dearly beloved brother Edmund, is dead of the plague. Hold the castle at all costs. I am coming.

I greet Jasper at the castle gate, and at once see the difference in him. He has lost his twin, his brother, the great love of his life. He jumps down from his horse with the same grace that Edmund had, but now there is only the noise of one pair of boots ringing iron-tipped heels on the stone. For the rest of his life he will listen for the clatter of his brother and hear nothing. His face is grim, his eyes hollowed with sadness. He takes my hand as if I am a grown lady, and he kneels and offers up his hands, in the gesture of prayer, as if he is swearing fealty. 'I have lost my brother, and you, your husband,' he says. 'I swear to you, that if you have a boy, I will care for him as if he were my own. I will guard him with my life. I will keep him safe. I will take him to the very throne of England, for my brother's sake.'

His eyes are filled with tears and I am most uncomfortable to have this big, fully grown man on his knees before me. 'Thank you,' I say. I look round in my discomfiture but there is no-one to tell me how to raise Jasper up. I don't know what I am supposed to say. I notice he doesn't promise anything to me if I have a girl. I sigh and clasp my hands around his, as he seems to want me to do. Really, if it were not for Joan of Arc, I would think that girls are completely useless.

JANUARY 1457

I go into confinement at the start of the month. They put up shutters on my bedroom windows to close out the grey winter light. I can't imagine that a sky which is never blue and a sun which never shines can be thought so distracting that a woman with child should be shaded from it; but the midwife insists that I go into darkness for a month before my time, as the tradition is, and Jasper, pale with worry, says that everything must be done to keep the baby safe.

The midwife thinks that the baby will come early. She feels my belly and says that he is lying wrongly but he may turn in time. Sometimes, she says, babies turn very late. It is important that they come out head first, I don't know why. She does not mention any details to Jasper but I know that he paces up and down outside my chamber every day. I can hear the floorboards creak as he tiptoes north and south, as anxious as a loving husband. Since I am in confinement I can see no man, and that is a great relief. But I do wish I could come out to church. Father William, here at Pembroke, was moved to tears by my first confession. He said he had never met a young woman of more piety. I was glad at last to find someone who understands me. He is allowed to pray with me if he sits one side of the screen and I the other, but it is not nearly as inspiring as praying before a congregation, where everyone can see me.

After a week, I start to have terrible pain in the very bones of my body when I am walking the narrow confines of the chamber, and Nan the midwife and her fellow crone whose name sounds something like a squawk, and who speaks no English at all, agree that I had better go to bed and not walk any more, not even stand. The pain is so bad I could almost believe that the bones are breaking inside me. Clearly, something has gone wrong, but nobody knows what it is. They ask the physician but since he cannot lay a hand on me, nor do more than ask me what I think might be the matter, we get no further forwards. I am thirteen years old, and small for my age. How am I to know what is going wrong with the baby in my body? They keep asking me, does it really feel as if my bones are breaking inside me? And when I say yes, then they look at one another as if they fear it must be true. But I can't believe that I will die in childbirth. I can't believe that God will have gone to all this trouble to get me here in Wales, with a child who might be king in my womb, only to have me die before he is even born.

They speak of sending for my mother, but she is so far away and the roads are so dangerous now that she cannot come, and besides, she would know no better than them. Nobody knows what is wrong with me, and now they remark that I am too young and too small to be with child at all, which is rather belated advice, and no comfort to me now I am so close to the birth. I have not dared to ask how the baby is actually going to come out of my belly. I fear very much that I am supposed to split open like a small pod for a fat pea, and then I am certain to bleed to death.

I had thought the pain of waiting was the worst pain I could endure, but that was only until the night when I wake to an agony as if my belly were heaving up and turning over inside me. I scream in shock and the two women bounce up from their trestle beds and my lady governess comes running, and my maid, and in a moment the room is filled with candles and people fetching hot water and firewood and among it all, nobody is even looking at me though I can feel a sudden flood pour out of me, and I am certain that it is blood and I am bleeding to death.

They fly at me and give me a lathe to bite on, and a sacred girdle to tie around my heaving belly. Father William has sent the Host in the Monstrance from the chapel and they put it on my prie dieu so I can fix my eyes on the body of the Lord. I have to say I am much less impressed by crucifixion now that I am in childbirth. It is really not possible that anything could hurt more than this. I grieve for the suffering of Our Lord, of course. But if He had tried a bad birth He would know what pain is.

They hold me down on the bed but let me heave on a rope when the pains start to come. I faint once for the agony of it, and then they give me a strong drink which makes me giddy and sick, but nothing can free me from the vice which has gripped on my belly and is tearing me apart. This goes on for hours, from dawn till dusk, and then I hear them muttering to each other that the timing of the baby is wrong, it is taking too long. One of the midwives says to me that she is sorry but they are going to have to toss me in a blanket to make the baby come on.

'What?' I mutter, so confused with pain that I don't know what she means. I don't understand what they are doing as they help me off the bed and bid me lie on a blanket on the floor. I think perhaps they are doing something which will relieve the gripping pain which makes me cry out until I think I can bear no more. So I lie down, obedient to their tugging hands and then the six of them gather round and lift the blanket between them. I am suspended like a sack of potatoes, and then they pull the blanket all at once and I am thrown up and drop down again. I am only a small girl of thirteen, they can throw me up into the air, and I feel a terrible flying and falling sensation and then the agony of landing and then they fling me up again. Ten times they do this while I scream and beg them to stop and then they heave me back into the bed and look at me as if they expect me to be much improved while I hang over the side of the bed and vomit between sobs.

I lie back for a moment and for a blessed moment the worst of it stops. In the sudden silence I hear my lady governess say, very clearly: 'Your orders are to save the baby if you have to choose. Especially if it is a boy.'

I am so enraged at the thought of Jasper ordering my own lady governess to tell my midwives that they should let me die if they have to choose between my life or that of his nephew that I spit on the floor and cry out: 'Oh, who says so? I am Lady Margaret Beaufort of the house of Lancaster . . .' But they don't even hear me, they don't turn to listen to me.

'That's the right thing to do,' Nan agrees. 'But seems hard on the little maid . . .'

'It is her mother's order,' my lady governess says, and at once I don't want to shout at them any more. My mother? My own mother told my lady governess that if the baby and I were in danger then they should save the baby?

'Poor little girl. Poor poor little girl,' Nan says, and at first I think she is speaking of the baby, perhaps it is a girl after all. But then I realise she is speaking of me, a girl of thirteen years, whose own mother has said that they can let her die as long as a son and heir is born.

It takes two days and nights for the baby to make his agonising way out of me, and I do not die, though there are long hours when I would have done so willingly, just to escape the pain. They show him to me, as I am falling asleep, drowning in pain. He is brown-haired, I think, and he has tiny hands. I reach out to touch him but the drink and the pain and the exhaustion flood over me like darkness and I faint away.

When I wake, it is morning and one of the shutters is opened, the yellow winter sun is shining in the little panes of glass, and the room is warm with the banked-up fire glowing in the fireplace. The baby is in his cradle, swaddled tight on his board. When the nursemaid hands him to me I cannot even feel his body, he is wrapped so tight in the swaddling bands that are like bandages from head to toe. She says he has to be strapped to his board so his arms and legs cannot move, so his head is kept still, to make sure that his young bones grow straight and true. I will be allowed to see his feet and his hands and his little body when they unwrap him to change his clout, which they will do at midday. Until then I can hold him while he sleeps, like a stiff little doll. The swaddling cloth is wrapped around his head and chin to keep his neck straight, and it finishes with a little loop on the top of his head. The poor women use the loop to hook their babies up on a roof beam when they are cooking, or doing their work, but this boy, who is the newest baby in the House of Lancaster, will be rocked and carried by a team of nursemaids.

I lie him down on the bed beside me, and gaze at his tiny face, his little nose, and the smiling curves of his rosy eyelids. He is not like a living thing, but more like a little stone carving of a baby as you find in a church, placed beside his stone-dead mother. It is a miracle to think that such a thing has been made, has grown, has come into the world; that I made him, almost entirely on my own (for I hardly count Edmund's drunken labours). This tiny little object, this miniature being, is the bone of my bone and the flesh of my flesh and he is of my making, all of my making.

After a little while he wakes, and starts to cry. For such a small object the cry is incredibly loud and I am glad the nursemaid comes in at a run and takes him from the room to the wet nurse. My own small breasts ache to suckle him, but I am bound up as tight as my swaddled baby, the two of us are strapped tight to do our duty: a baby who must grow straight, and a young mother who may not feed her child. His wet nurse has left her own baby at home, so that she can come and take up her position in the castle. She will eat better than she has ever eaten in her life before, and she is allowed a good ration of ale. She does not even have to care for my baby, she just has to make milk for him, as if she were a dairy cow. He is brought to her when he needs feeding and the rest of the time he is cared for by the maids of the nursery. She does a little cleaning, washing his clouts and linen, and helps in his rooms. She does not hold him except at feeding time. He has other women to do that. He has his own rocker to sleep by his cradle, his own two nursemaids to wait on him, his own physician comes once a week, and the midwives will stay with us until I am churched and he is christened. He has a larger entourage than me, and I suddenly realise that this is because he is more important than me. I am Lady Margaret Tudor, born a Beaufort, of the

House of Lancaster, cousin to the sleeping King of England. But he is both a Beaufort and a Tudor. He has royal blood on both sides. He is Earl of Richmond, of the House of Lancaster, and has a claim, after the king's son, Prince Edward, to the throne of England.

My lady governess comes into the room. 'Your brother-in-law Jasper asks you to agree to his name for the baby,' she says. 'He is writing to the king and to your mother to tell them he is going to call him Edmund Owen, for the baby's father and his Tudor grandfather.'

'No,' I say. I am not going to name my baby, who cost me so much pain, after a man who caused me nothing but pain. Or his stupid father. 'No, I won't call him Edmund.'

'You can't call him Edward,' she says. 'The king's son is Prince Edward.'

'I am going to call him Henry,' I say, thinking of the sleeping king who might wake for a boy of the House of Lancaster called Henry, though he slept through the birth of the prince called Edward. 'Henry is a royal name for England, some of our best and bravest kings have been called Henry. This boy will be Henry Tudor.' I repeat the name proudly: 'Henry Tudor.' And I think to myself, when the sleeping King Henry VI is dead, then this baby will be Henry VII.

'He said Edmund Owen,' she repeats, as if I might be deaf as well as stupid.

'And I say Henry,' I say. 'And I have called him this already. This is his name. It is decided. I have named him in my prayers. He is all but baptised Henry already.'

She raises her eyebrows at my ringing emphasis. 'They won't like it,' she says, and she goes out of the room to tell my brother-in-law Jasper that the girl is being stubborn and will not name her son for her dead husband, but has chosen her own name for him and will not be dissuaded.

I lie back against the pillows again and close my eyes. My boy will be Henry Tudor, whatever anyone says.

SPRING 1457

I have to stay in my rooms for another six weeks after the birth of my boy, before I can go to the chapel and be cleansed of the sin of childbirth. When I come back to my rooms the shutters are down and the dark drapes have been taken away. There is wine in jugs and small cakes on plates, and Jasper has come to visit me, and congratulate me on the birth of my child. The nursemaids tell me that Jasper visits the baby in his nursery every day, as if he were the doting father himself. He sits by the cradle if the baby is asleep, he touches his cheek with his finger, he cups the tightly wrapped head in his big hands. If the baby is awake, Jasper watches him feed, or he stands over them when they unwrap the swaddling and admires the straight legs and the strong arms. They tell me that Jasper begs them to leave the swaddling off for a moment more so he can see the little fists and the fat little feet. They think it unmanly for him to hang over the cradle, and I agree; but all the Tudors only please themselves.

He smiles at me tentatively, and I smile back. 'Are you well, sister?' he asks.

'I am,' I say.

'They tell me it was a difficult birth for you.'

'It was.'

He nods. 'I have a letter from your mother for you, and she also wrote to me.'

He hands me one sheet of paper, folded square and sealed with my mother's Beaufort crest of the portcullis. I lift the seal carefully and read her letter. She has written in French and she commands me to meet her at Greenfield House in Newport, Gwent. That is all. She sends me no words of affection or inquiry after my son, her own grandson. I remember that she told them if it was a choice between a boy and me, then they should let me die, and I ignore her coldness and turn to Jasper. 'Does she tell you why I am to go to Newport? For she does not trouble herself to explain to me.'

'Yes,' he says. 'I am to take you with an armed escort and your baby is to stay here. You are to meet with Humphrey, the Duke of Buckingham. It is his house.'

'Why am I to see him?' I ask. I have a distant memory of the duke, who heads one of the great wealthy families of the kingdom. We are cousins of some sort. 'Is he to be my new guardian? Can't you be my guardian now, Jasper?'

He looks away. 'No. It's not that.' He tries to smile at me but his eyes are soft with pity. 'You are to be married again, my sister. You are to be married to the Duke of Buckingham's son, as soon as your year of mourning is finished. But the contract of marriage and the betrothal is to take place now. You are to marry the duke's son: Sir Henry Stafford.'

I look at him and I know my face is horrified. 'I have to marry again?' I blurt out, thinking of the agony of childbirth and the likelihood that it will kill me another time. 'Jasper, can I refuse to go? Can I stay here with you?'

He shakes his head. 'I am afraid not.'

MARCH 1457

A parcel, taken from one place to another, handed from one owner to another, unwrapped and bundled up at will is all that I am. A vessel, for the bearing of sons, for one nobleman or another: it hardly matters who. Nobody sees me for what I am: a young woman of great family with royal connections, a young woman of exceptional piety who deserves – surely to God! – some recognition. But no, having been shipped to Lamphey Castle in a litter, I now ride to Newport on a fat cob, seated behind a manservant, unable to see anything of the road ahead of me and glimpsing muddy fields and pale pasture-lands only through the jogging ranks of the men at arms. They are armed with lances and cudgels and are wearing the badge of the Tudor crest at their collars. Jasper is leading the way on his warhorse, and has warned them to be prepared for ambush from Herbert's men, or trouble on the road from bands of thieves. Once we get closer to the sea there is also the danger of a marauding party of pirates. This is how I am protected. This is the country I live in. This is what a good king, a strong king, should prevent.

We ride under the portcullis of Greenfield House and the gate slams shut behind us. We dismount in the courtyard before the house and my mother comes out to greet me. I have not seen her for almost two years, not since my wedding day, when she told me there was nothing to fear. Now as she comes towards me and I kneel for her blessing I realise that she will see from my face that I know she was lying to me that day, for I have faced the very fear of death itself, and learned that she was prepared to sacrifice me for a grandson. There was nothing to fear for her – so she was right about that. But there was much to fear for me.

'Margaret,' she says quietly. She puts her hand on my head for a blessing and then raises me up and kisses me on both cheeks. 'You've grown! And you are looking well!'

I long for her to hold me and hug me and tell me that she has missed me, but that would be to wish for a different sort of mother, and then I would have been a different girl. Instead she looks at me with cool approval and then turns, as the door of the house opens, and the duke comes out.

'Here is my daughter,' she says. 'Lady Margaret Tudor. Margaret, this is your kinsman the Duke of Buckingham.'

I make a low curtsey. This is a duke most particular about his position; they say that he took his order of precedence to parliament to get a ruling on who should walk behind him. He raises me up and kisses me on both cheeks. 'You are welcome,' he says. 'But you must be cold and tired from your journey. Come inside.'

The house is furnished with a luxury that I had almost forgotten, having spent these years in exile at Lamphey and Pembroke. Thick tapestries warm the stone walls, and the wooden beams above are gilded and brightly painted. Everywhere the duke's crest is picked out in new gold. The rushes on the floor are fresh and sweet so that every room is scented lightly with herbs and lavender, and in every great stone fireplace there are blazing logs and a lad going round with a basket to bring in more firewood. Even the firewood boy wears the duke's livery; they say that he has a small army always dressed and armed at his command. The boy even has boots. I think of the barefoot slovenliness of my husband's home and I feel a little better about this betrothal if it is going to take me into a house that is kept clean, with servants who are properly dressed.

The duke offers me a glass of small ale, which is mulled hot and sweet, to warm me from the chill of travelling. As I am sipping it, Jasper comes into the room with another older man, greying hair at his temples, lines in his face; he must be forty if he is a day. I look to Jasper to introduce this stranger, and when I see his grave face I realise. With a little gasp of shock I understand that this old man is Henry Stafford, and that I am before my new husband. He is not a boy of my age like John de la Pole, my first betrothed. He is not a young man like Edmund – and God knows he was too old and too hard for me. No, this time they have picked out a man old enough to be my father, old enough to be my grandfather, my ancestor. He is forty years old, fifty years old, probably sixty. I realise I am staring, and I quite fail to curtsey until my mother says sharply, 'Margaret!' and I mumble, 'Excuse me,' and sink down in a gesture of humility, to yet another man, who will make me live with him wherever he chooses, and will make another heir to the Lancaster line on me, whether I like it or not.

I see that Jasper is scowling down at his boots; but he raises his head to greet my mother with his usual courtesy and bows to the duke.

'I see you have kept my daughter safe through these most troubled times,' my mother says to him.

'I will keep the whole principality safe if I can,' he replies. 'At last we seem to be gaining ground. I have recaptured the castles that the York party took, and William Herbert is on the run, in hiding. If he stays within Wales I will catch him. We Tudors are well loved here, someone will betray him to me.'

'And then?' the Duke of Buckingham asks him. 'What then?'

Jasper shrugs. He knows it is not a question about the fate of William Herbert, nor even of Wales. It is the question that every Englishman asks himself these days: what then? How can we go on with a court so unpopular it dare not even live in London? How can we go on with a king who slips away into dreams without warning, and leaves a queen hated by so many? How can we face the future when their heir is just one little weak boy? How can we be safe when the kingdom slides into the keeping of our enemies: the House of York?

'I have tried to reason with Richard of York, and his advisor the Earl of Warwick,' Jasper says. 'You know how hard I have tried to persuade them to work with the queen. I have talked and talked with the queen. But she is terrified of them and fearful that they will attack her and her son at the next illness of the king. And in their turn, they fear that she will destroy them when the king is well enough to do her bidding. I can't see a resolution.'

'If they could be sent from the country?' Buckingham suggests. 'One of them to Calais? Perhaps we could send York to Dublin?'

Jasper shrugs. 'I wouldn't sleep easy in my bed at night knowing that they were off our coasts with their own armies,' he says. 'From Calais they command the narrow seas; no southern port would be safe. From Dublin, Richard of York could raise an army and come against us. And the Irish love York like a king already.'

'Perhaps the king will stay well this time,' my mother suggests hopefully.

I realise how gravely ill His Grace has become from the awkward silence that greets this remark. 'Perhaps,' the duke says.

They waste no time on courtship between Henry Stafford and me. They waste no time on giving us even a moment to meet. Why should they? This is a matter for the lawyers and the officers of the household who manage the wealth. It would not matter if Henry Stafford and I hated each other on sight. It matters not at all that I do not want to marry, that I am afraid of the wedding, afraid of consummating the marriage, afraid of childbirth, afraid of everything about being a wife. Nobody even asks if I have lost my childhood sense of vocation, if I still want to be a nun. Nobody cares what I think at all. They treat me like an ordinary young woman, bred for wedding and bedding, and since they do not ask me what I think, nor observe what I feel, there is nothing that gives them pause at all.

They draw up the contracts and we sign them. We go to the chapel and before witnesses and before the priest we swear to marry each other in January so that I have a year to mourn my first marriage, which brought me so little joy and ended so soon. I will be fourteen years old and he will be not exactly forty, but still an old man to me: thirty-three years old.

After the betrothal we go back to the house and my mother and I sit in the solar, where there is a fire burning, with our ladies around us, listening to the musicians play. I draw my stool a little closer to her so that we can speak privately for once.

'Do you remember what you said before I was married to Edmund Tudor?' I ask her.

She shakes her head and glances away as if she would avoid this conversation. I am very sure she does not want to be reproached for telling me there was nothing to fear, when she instructed my own lady governess to let me die. 'No, I don't remember,' she says quickly. 'It feels like years ago.'

'You said that I could not take the coward's way out, my father's way out.'

She flinches from me even naming the man who has been buried in silence for so long. 'Did I?'

'Yes.'

'I can't imagine what I was thinking of.'

'So what did he do?'

She turns away with a false laugh. 'Have you waited all this time to ask me to explain a silly thing I said at the church door?'

'Yes.'

'Oh, Margaret, you are so . . .' She breaks off, and I wait to hear what I am that makes her toss her head like this and frown. 'You are so very serious.'

'Yes.' I nod. 'That is true. I am very serious, Lady Mother. I would have thought you would have known that by now. I have always been a serious person, a studious person. And you said something about my father that I think I have a right to understand. I take it seriously.'

She gets up and walks to the window, looking out as if admiring the dark evening. She shrugs her shoulders at the awkwardness of this daughter, her only Beaufort child. Her lady in waiting looks up at her in case she needs anything and I see the glance that passes between them. It is as if I am known to be a difficult girl, and I flush with embarrassment.

'Oh,' sighs my mother. 'It's such a long time ago now,' she

says. 'How old are you now? Thirteen? For heaven's sake, it is twelve years ago.'

'Then you can tell me. I am old enough to know. And if you don't, then someone is bound to tell me something. You surely don't want me to ask the servants?'

The flush that comes to her face tells me that she does not want me to ask the servants, that they have been warned never to discuss this matter with me. Something happened twelve years ago that she wanted to forget, that she wanted me never to know. Something shameful happened.

'How did he die?' I ask.

'By his own hand,' she says quickly and quietly. 'If you must know. If you insist on knowing his shame. He left you and he left me and he died by his own hand. I was with child, a baby that I lost. I lost a baby in my shock and my grief, a baby that might have been a son for the House of Lancaster; but he didn't think about that. It was days before your first birthday, he didn't care enough for either of us even to wait to see you into your second year. And that is why I have always told you that your future lies in your son. A husband can come and go, he can leave on his own account. He can go to war or get sick or kill himself; but if you make your son your own, your own creation, then you are safe. A boy is your guardian. If you had been a boy I would have poured my life into you. You would have been my destiny.'

'But since I was a girl you did not love me, and he did not wait to see my birthday?'

She looks at me honestly and repeats the dreadful words. 'Since you were a girl, of course not. Since you were a girl you could only be the bridge to the next generation; you could be nothing more than the means by which our family gets a boy.'

There is a short silence while I absorb my mother's belief in my unimportance. 'I see. I see. I am lucky to be valued by

God, since I am not valued by you. I was not valued by my father.'

She nods as if it does not matter much. Still she does not understand me. She will never understand. She will never think that I am worth the effort of understanding. To her I am, as she so frankly tells me, a bridge.

'So why did my father kill himself?' I return to her first revelation. 'Why would he do such a thing? His soul will have gone to hell. They must have told a string of lies to get him buried in holy ground.' I correct myself. 'You must have told a string of lies.'

My mother comes back and sinks onto the bench by the warm fire. 'I did what I could to protect our good name,' she says quietly. 'As anyone of a great name would do. Your father came back from France with stories of victory, but then people started to whisper. They said he had done nothing of any value, indeed he had taken the troops and money that his commander Richard of York – the great hero – needed to hold France for England. Richard of York was making progress but your father set it back. Your father set siege to a town but it was the wrong town, owned by the Duke of Brittany, and he had to return it to them. We nearly lost the alliance with Brittany through his folly. That would have cost the country dear, but he did not think of it. He set a tax to raise money in the defeated areas of France, but it was illegal; and worse, he kept all the revenue for himself. He said he had a great campaign plan; but he led his men round in circles and then brought them home again without either victory or plunder, so they were bitter against him, and said that he was a false lord to them. He was dearly loved by our king, but not even the king could pretend that he had done well.

'There would have been an inquiry in London about his conduct; he escaped that shame only by his death. There might even have been an excommunication from the Pope. They would have come for your father and accused him of treason, and he would have paid with his life on the block, and you would have lost your fortune, and we would have been attainted and ruined; he spared us that, but only by running away into death.'

'An excommunication?' I am more horrified by this than anything else.

'People wrote ballads about him,' she says bitterly. 'People laughed at his stupidity and marvelled at our infamy. You cannot imagine the shame of it. I have shielded you from it, from the shame of him, and I get no thanks for it. You are such a child you don't know that he is notorious as the great example of his age of the change of fortune, of the cruelty of the wheel of fortune. He could not have been born with better prospects and better opportunities; but he was unlucky, fatally unlucky. In his very first battle in France, when he rode out as a boy, he was captured, and he was left in captivity for seventeen years. It broke his heart. He thought that nobody cared enough to ransom him. Perhaps that is the lesson that I should have taught you – never mind your studies, never mind your nagging for books, for a tutor, for Latin lessons. I should have taught you never to be unlucky, never to be unlucky like your father.'

'Does everyone know?' I ask. I am horrified at the shame I have inherited, unknowingly. 'Jasper, for instance? Does Jasper know I am the daughter of a coward?'

My mother shrugs. 'Everyone. We said that he was exhausted by campaigning, and died of his service to the king. But people will always gossip about their betters.'

'And are we an unlucky family?' I ask her. 'Do you think I have inherited his bad luck?'

She will not answer me. She gets to her feet and smoothes

the skirt of her gown as if to brush away smuts from the fire, or to sweep away ill fortune.

'Are we unlucky?' I ask. 'Lady Mother?'

'Well, I am not,' she says defensively. 'I was born a Beauchamp, and after your father's death I married again and changed my name from his. Now I am a Welles. But you might be unlucky. The Beauforts may be. But perhaps you will change the luck,' she says indifferently. 'You were lucky enough to have a boy, after all. Now you have a Lancaster heir.'

They serve dinner very late; the Duke of Buckingham keeps court hours and is not troubled by the cost of candles. At least the meat is better cooked and there are more side dishes of pastries and sweetmeats than at Pembroke Castle. I see that at this table where everything is so beautiful, Jasper's manners are positively courtly, and I understand for the first time that he lives as a soldier when he is in his border castle on the very frontiers of the kingdom, but he is a courtier when he is in a great house. He sees me watching him and he winks at me as if we two share the secret of how we manage our lives when we do not have to be on our best behaviour.

We eat a good dinner and afterwards there is an entertainment, some fools, a juggler, and a girl who sings. Then my mother nods to me and sends me to bed as if I were a child still, and before the grand company I can do nothing but curtsey for her blessing and go. I glance at my future husband as I leave. He is looking at the girl singer with his eyes narrowed, a little smile on his mouth. I don't mind walking out after I see that look. I am more sick of men, all men, than I dare to acknowledge to myself.

Next day, the horses are in the stable yard and I am to be sent back to Pembroke Castle until my year of mourning is finished and I can be married again to the smiling stranger. My mother comes to bid me farewell, and watches the manservant lift me onto the pillion saddle behind Jasper's master of horse. Jasper himself is riding ahead with this troop of guards. The rear file are waiting for me.

'You will leave your son in the care of Jasper Tudor when you marry Sir Henry,' my mother remarks, as if this arrangement has just occurred to her this minute, as I am leaving.

'No, he will come with me. Surely he will come with me,' I blurt out. 'He must come with me. He is my son. Where should he be, but with me?'

'It's not possible,' she says decidedly. 'It is all agreed. He is to stay with Jasper. Jasper will care for him and keep him safe.'

'But he is my son!'

My mother smiles. 'You are little more than a child yourself. You cannot look after an heir to our name, and keep him safe. These are dangerous times, Margaret, you should understand that by now. He is a valuable boy. He will be safer if he is at some distance from London, while the Yorks are in power. He will be safer in Pembroke than anywhere else in the country. Wales loves the Tudors. Jasper will guard him as his own.'

'But he is *my* own! Not Jasper's!'

My mother comes closer and puts her hand on my knee. 'You own nothing, Margaret. You yourself are the property of your husband. Once again I have chosen a good husband for you, one near to the crown, kinsman to the Nevilles, son of the greatest duke in England. Be grateful, child. Your son will be well cared for, and then you will have more, Stafford boys this time.'

'I nearly died last time,' I burst out, careless of the man seated before me on the horse, his shoulders squared, pretending not to listen.

'I know,' my mother says. 'And this is the price of being a woman. Your husband did his duty and died. You did yours and survived. You were lucky this time; he was not. Let's hope you take your luck onwards.'

'What if I am not so lucky next time? What if I have the Beaufort luck and next time the midwives do as you ordered them, and let me die? What if they do as you command and drag a grandson out of your daughter's dead body?'

She does not even blink. 'The baby should always be saved in preference to the mother. That is the advice of the Holy Church, you know that. I was only reminding the women of their duty. There is no need to make everything so personal, Margaret. You make everything into your own tragedy.'

'I think it is my tragedy, if you are telling my midwives to let me die!'

She all but shrugs as she steps back. 'These are the chances that a woman faces. Men die in battle; women die in childbirth. Battle is more dangerous. The odds are with you.'

'But what if the odds are against me, if I am unlucky? What if I die?'

'Then you will have the satisfaction of knowing that you made at least one son for the House of Lancaster.'

'Mother, before God,' I say, my voice shaking with tears, 'I swear that I have to believe that there is more for me in life than being wife to one man after another, and hoping not to die in childbirth!'

She shakes her head, smiling at me as if my sense of outrage is like a little girl shouting over her toys. 'No, truly, my dear, there is nothing more for you,' she says. 'So do your duty with an obedient heart. I will see you in January, at your wedding.'

I ride back to Pembroke Castle in a surly silence and none of the signs of the coming spring down the greening lanes give me any pleasure at all. I turn my head away from the wild daffodils that make the high meadows a blaze of silver and gold, and I am deaf to the insistent, joyous singing of the birds. The lapwing soaring blunt-winged over a ploughed field and calling out his sharp whistle means nothing to me, for everything means nothing to me. The snipe diving downwards making a sound like a roll of drums does not call to me. My life will not be dedicated to God, will not be special in any way. I shall sign myself Margaret Stafford – I won't even be duchess. I shall live like a hedge sparrow on a twig until the sparrowhawk kills me, and my death will be unnoticed and unmourned by any. My mother herself has told me that there is nothing in my life that is worth doing, and the best I can hope is to avoid an early death in childbirth.

Jasper spurs on ahead as soon as he sees the high towers of Pembroke, and so greets me at the castle gates with my baby in his arms, beaming with joy. 'He can smile!' he exclaims before the horses even come to a standstill. 'He can smile. I saw it. I leaned over his cradle to pick him up, and he saw me, and he smiled. I am sure it was a smile. I did not think he would smile so early. But it was a smile for sure. Perhaps he will smile at you.'

We both wait expectantly, looking into the dark blue eyes of the little baby. He is still strapped up as if ready for the coffin, only his eyes can move, he cannot even turn his head. He is swaddled into immobility.

'Perhaps he will smile later,' Jasper says consolingly. 'There! Did he then? No.'

'It doesn't matter, since I am to leave him within a year anyway, since I have to go and marry Sir Henry Stafford. Since I now have to give birth to Stafford boys, even if I die in the trying. Perhaps he has nothing to smile about, perhaps he knows he is to be an orphan.'

Jasper turns with me towards the front door of the castle, walking beside me, my baby resting comfortably in his arms. 'They will let you visit him,' he says consolingly.

'But you are to keep him. I suppose you knew. I suppose you all planned this together. You, and my mother, and my father-in-law, and my old husband-to-be.'

He glances down at my tearful face. 'He is a Tudor,' he says carefully. 'My brother's son. The only heir to our name. You could choose no-one better to care for him than me.'

'You are not even his father,' I say irritably. 'Why should he stay with you, and not with me?'

'Lady Sister, you are little more than a child yourself, and these are dangerous times.'

I round on him and stamp my foot. 'I am old enough to be married twice. I am old enough to be bedded without tenderness or consideration. I am old enough to face death in the confinement room and be told that my own mother – my own mother – has commanded them to save the child and not me! I think I am a woman now. I have a babe in arms and I have been married and widowed and now betrothed again. I am like a draper's parcel to be sent about like cloth, and cut to the pattern that people wish. My mother told me that my father died by his own hand and that we are an unlucky family. I think I am a woman now! I am treated as a woman grown when it suits you all, you can hardly make me a child again!'

He nods as if he is listening to me and considering what I have to say. 'You have cause for complaint,' he says steadily. 'But this is the way of the world, Lady Margaret, we cannot make an exception for you.'

'But you should!' I exclaim. 'This is what I have been saying since my childhood. You should make an exception for me. Our Lady speaks to me, the holy Joan appears to me, I am sent to be a light to you. I cannot be married to an ordinary man and sent away to God knows where again. I should be given a nunnery of my own and be an abbess! You should do this, Brother Jasper, you command Wales. You should give me a nunnery, I want to found an order!'

He holds the baby close, and turns away from me a little. I think he is moved to tears by my righteous anger, but then I see his face is flushed and his shoulders are shaking because he is laughing. 'Oh, my lord,' he says. 'Forgive me, Margaret, but oh, my lord. You are a child, a child, you are a baby like our Henry here, and I shall care for both of you.'

'Nobody shall care for me,' I shout. 'For you are all mistaken about me, and you are a fool to laugh at me. I am in the care of God and I am not going to marry anyone! I am going to be an abbess.'

He catches his breath, his face still bright with laughter. 'An abbess. Certainly. And will you be dining with us tonight, Reverend Mother?'

I scowl at him. 'I shall be served in my rooms,' I say crossly. 'I shall not dine with you. Possibly I shall never dine with you again. But you can tell Father William to come to me. I will have to confess trespassing against those who have trespassed against me.'

'I will send him,' Jasper says kindly. 'And I will send the best of the dishes to your room. And tomorrow I hope you will meet me in the stable yard and I will teach you to ride on your own. A lady of your importance should have her own horse, she should ride a beautiful horse well. When you go back to England I think you should go on your own fine horse.'

I hesitate. 'I cannot be tempted by vanity,' I warn him. 'I am going to be an abbess and nothing will divert me. You shall see. You will all see. You shall not treat me as a thing for trading and selling. I shall command my own life.'

'Certainly,' he says pleasantly. 'It is very wrong that you

should feel we think of you like that, for I love and respect you, as I promised I would. I shall find you an expensive horse and you will look beautiful on his back and everyone will admire you, and it can all mean nothing to you at all.'

I sleep in a dream of white-washed cloister walls and a great library where illuminated books are chained to the desks and I can go every day and study. I dream of a tutor who will lead me through Greek and Latin and even Hebrew, and that I will read the Bible in the tongue which is closest to the angels, and I will know everything. In my dream, my hunger for learning and my desire to be special is quieted, soothed. I think that if I could be a scholar I could live in peace. If I could wake every day to the discipline of the offices of the day, and spend my days in study, I think I would feel that I was living a life that was pleasing to God and to me. I would not care whether people thought I was special, if my life was truly special. It would not matter to me that people could see me as pious, if I could truly live as a woman scholar of piety. I want to be what I seem to be. I act as if I am specially holy, a special girl; but this is what I really want to be. I really do.

In the morning, I wake and dress, but before I go for my breakfast I go to the nursery to see the baby. He is still in his cradle, but I can hear him cooing, little quiet noises like a duckling quacking to itself on a still pond. I lean over his cradle to see him, and he smiles. He does. There is an unmistakable recognition in his dark blue eyes, and the funny, gummy triangular grin which makes him at once less like a pretty doll, and tremendously like a little person.

'Why, Henry,' I say, and the little beam widens, as if he knows his name, as if he knows my name, as if he knows me as his mother, as if he believes we are lucky and that we have everything to play for, as if we might have a life which is filled with promise, in which I have more to hope for than the meanest survival.

He beams for a moment longer and then something distracts him. I can see a surprised look cross his face and in moments he is choking and crying and his rockers come forwards and brush me aside to take him out of the cradle and carry him off to the wet nurse. I let them take him, and I go down to the great hall to tell Jasper that Baby Henry has smiled at me too.

Jasper waits for me in the stable yard. A big dark horse is standing beside him, its large head bowed, its tail swishing. 'Is he for me?' I ask. I try not to sound anxious but he is, undoubtedly, a very large horse indeed, and I have only ridden little ponies when led by the master of horse, or pillion behind a groom on long journeys.

'This is Arthur,' Jasper says gently. 'And he is big. But he is very calm and steady and a good horse for you to learn to ride. He was my father's warhorse, but he is too old now for jousting. Yet he is afraid of nothing, and he will carry you safely anywhere you command.'

The horse raises his head and looks at me and there is something so trustworthy about the steady darkness of his gaze that I step forwards and hold out my hand. The big head comes down, the wide nostrils sniff at my glove, then gently, he lips at my fingers.

'I shall walk beside you, and Arthur will go quietly,' Jasper promises me. 'Come here and I will lift you up into the saddle.'

I go to him and he lifts me up and helps me to sit astride. When I am safely in the saddle he pulls down the hem of my gown so it falls evenly on either side of the horse and covers my boots. 'There,' he says. 'Now keep your legs still, but gently pressed against him. That way he knows you are there, and you hold yourself steady. Take up the reins.'

I lift them and Arthur's big head comes up, alerted by my touch. 'He won't go off, will he?' I ask nervously.

'Only when you give him a gentle kick, to tell him you are ready. And when you want him to stop, you make a gentle pull on the reins.' Jasper reaches up and moves my hands so the reins are threaded through my fingers. 'Just let him walk two steps forwards so you know that you can make him start and stop.'

Tentatively, I give a little kick with both heels, and I am startled by the first big rolling stride forwards, and I pull on the reins. Obediently, he stops at once. 'I did it!' I say breathlessly. 'He stopped for me! Did he? Did he stop because I told him?'

Jasper smiles up at me. 'He will do anything for you. You just have to give him a clear signal so he knows what it is that you want him to do. He served my father loyally. Edmund and I learned to joust on him, and now he will be your tutor. Perhaps he will live long enough and Baby Henry will learn to ride on him. Now walk him out of the stable yard and into the courtyard before the castle.'

More confidently, I give Arthur the signal to start and this time I let him go on. His huge shoulders move forwards but his back is so broad that I can sit firmly and steadily. Jasper walks at his head but he does not touch the rein. It is me, and me alone, who makes the horse walk to the courtyard and then through the gate, and then out to the road that leads down to Pembroke.

Jasper strolls beside me as if he is out to take the air. He does not look up at me, nor glance at the horse. He gives the impression of a man walking beside a perfectly competent horsewoman; he is just there for company. Only when we have gone some distance down the road does he say: 'Would you like to turn him around now, and head for home?'

'How does he turn?'

'You turn his head by pulling it gently round. He will know what you mean. And you give him a little squeeze with your leg to tell him to go on walking.'

I do no more than touch the rein and the big head turns and Arthur circles around and heads for home. It is easy to walk back up the hill and then I steer him through the courtyard and to the stables and without telling, he goes to stand beside the mounting block, and waits for me to get off.

Jasper helps me down and then slips me a heel of bread to give to the horse. He shows me how to keep my hand flat so Arthur can find his titbit with his gentle lips, and then he shouts for a stable boy to take the horse away.

'Would you like to ride again tomorrow?' he asks. 'I could come out with you on my horse, they could go side by side and we could go further. Perhaps down to the river.'

'I should like that,' I say. 'Are you going to the nursery now?'

He nods. 'He is usually awake about now. They will let me undo the swaddling and he can kick for a bit. He likes it when he is free.'

'You do like him very much, don't you?'

He nods, shyly. 'He is all I have left of Edmund,' he says. 'He is the last of us Tudors. He is the most precious thing in the castle. And who knows? One day he might be the most precious thing in Wales, even in England itself.'

In Henry's nursery I see that Jasper is a welcome and regular visitor. He has his own chair where he sits and watches the baby being slowly unwrapped from the swaddling bands. He does not flinch from the smell of the dirty clout nor turn his head away. Instead, he leans forwards and inspects the baby's bottom carefully for any signs of redness or soreness, and when they tell him they have greased the baby with the oil from the sheep fleeces as he ordered, he nods and is satisfied. Then when the baby is cleaned they put a warm woollen blanket on Jasper's knees and he lies the baby on his back, and tickles his little feet and blows on his bare tummy, and the baby kicks and squirms with joy at his freedom.

I watch this like a stranger, feeling odd and out of place. This is my baby but I don't handle him easily like this. Awkwardly, I go to kneel beside Jasper so I can take one of the little hands and look at the tiny fingernails and the creases in the fat little palm, the exquisite little lines around his plump wrist. 'He is beautiful,' I say wonderingly. 'But are you not afraid of dropping him?'

'Why would I drop him?' Jasper asks. 'If anything, I am most likely to spoil him with too much attention. Your lady governess says a child should be left alone and not played with every day.'

'She'd say anything which meant she could sit longer over her dinner or sleep in her chair,' I say acidly. 'She persuaded my mother that I should not have a tutor for Latin because she knew it would make more work for her. I won't have her tutoring him.'

'Oh no,' Jasper says. 'He'll have a proper scholar. We'll get someone from one of the universities, Cambridge probably. Someone who can give him a good grounding in everything he'll need to know. The modern subjects as well as the classics: geography and mathematics as well as rhetoric.'

He leans forwards and plants a smacking kiss on Henry's warm little belly. The baby gurgles with pleasure and waves his little hands.

'He's not likely to inherit, you know,' I remind him, denying my own belief. 'He doesn't need the education of a prince. There is the king on the throne and Prince Edward to come after him, and the queen is young, she can easily have more children.'

Jasper hides the baby's face with a little napkin and then whisks it away. The baby gives a little shout of surprise and delight. Jasper does it again, and again, and again. Clearly, the two of them could play this game all day.

'He may never be more than a royal cousin,' I repeat. 'And then your care of him and his education will all have gone to waste.'

Jasper holds the baby close to him, warmed in his blanket. 'Ah no. He is precious on his own account,' he says to me. 'He is precious as my brother's child and the grandson of my father, Owen Tudor, and my mother, God bless her, who was Queen of England. He is precious to me as your child – I don't forget your sufferings as you gave birth to him. And he is precious as a Tudor. As for the rest – we will learn the future as God wills. But if they ever call for Henry Tudor, then they will find that I have kept him safe and prepared him so that he is ready to rule.'

'Whereas they will never call for me, and I won't be fit for anything but to be a wife, if I am even alive,' I say irritably.

Jasper looks at me and does not laugh. He looks at me and it is as if, for the first time in my life, someone has seen me, and understood me. 'You are the heir whose blood line gives Henry his claim to the throne,' he says. 'You, Margaret Beaufort. And you are precious to God. You know that, at least. I have never known a woman more devout. You are more like an angel than a girl.'

I glow, the way a lesser woman would blush if someone praised her beauty. 'I didn't know you had even noticed.'

'I have, and I think you have a real calling. I know that you can't be an abbess, of course not. But I do think you have a calling to God.'

'Yes, but Jasper, what good is it being devout, if I am not to be an example to the world? If all that they will allow for me is a marriage to someone who hardly cares for me at all, and then an early death in childbed?'

'These are dangerous and difficult times,' he says thoughtfully, 'and it is hard to know what one should do. I thought that my duty was to be a good second to my brother, and to hold Wales for King Henry. But now my brother is dead, it is a constant battle to hold Wales for the king, and when I go to court the queen herself tells me that I should be commanded by her and not by the king. She tells me that the only safety for England is to follow her and she will lead us to peace and alliance with France, our great enemy.'

'So how do you know what to do?' I ask. 'Does God tell you?' I think it most unlikely that God would speak to Jasper, whose skin is so very freckled, even now in March.

He laughs. 'No. God does not speak to me, so I try to keep the faith with my family, with my king, and with my country in that order. And I prepare for trouble and hope for the best.'

I draw close to speak to him quietly. 'Do you think that Richard of York would dare to take the king's throne, if the king were to be ill for very long?' I ask. 'If he does not get better?'

He looks bleak. 'I would think it a certainty.'

'So what am I to do if I am far from you and a false king takes the throne?'

Jasper looks consideringly at the baby. 'Say that our King Henry dies and then the prince, his son.'

'God forbid.'

'Amen. Say that they die the one after the other. On that day this baby is the next in line to the throne.'

'I know that well enough.'

'Do you not think that this might be your calling? To keep this child safe, to teach him the ways of kingship, to prepare him for the highest task in the land – to see him ordained as king and take the holy oil on his breast and become more than a man, a king, a being almost divine?'

'I dreamed of it,' I tell him very quietly. 'When he was first conceived. I dreamed that to carry him and give birth to him was my vocation, as to bring the French king to Rheims was Joan's. But I have never spoken of it to anyone but God.'

'Say you were right,' Jasper goes on, his whisper binding a spell around us both. 'Say that my brother did not die in vain, for his death made this boy the Earl of Richmond. His seed made this boy a Tudor and so half-nephew to the King of England. Your carrying him made him a Beaufort and next in direct line to the King of England. Say this is your destiny, to go through these difficult times and bring this boy to the throne. Do you not think this? Do you not feel it?'

'I don't know,' I say hesitantly. 'I thought I would have a higher calling than this. I thought I would be a mother superior.'

'There is no more superior mother in the world,' he said smiling at me. 'You could be the mother of the King of England.'

'What would they call me?'

'What?' He is distracted by my question.

'What would they call me if my son was King of England but I was not crowned as a queen?'

He thinks. 'They would probably call you "Your Grace". Your son would make your husband a duke, perhaps? Then you would be "Your Grace".'

'My husband would be a duke?'

'It's the only way you could be a duchess. As a woman you could hold no title in your own right, I don't think.'

I shake my head. 'Why should my husband be ennobled, when it will be me who has done all the work?'

Jasper chokes back a laugh. 'What title would you have?'

I think for a moment. 'Everyone can call me "My Lady, the King's Mother",' I decide. 'They can call me "My Lady, the King's Mother", and I shall sign my letters "Margaret R".'

'"Margaret R"? You would sign yourself "Margaret Regina"? You would call yourself a queen?'

'Why not?' I demand. 'I shall be the mother of a king. I shall be all-but Queen of England.'

He bows with mock ceremony. 'You shall be My Lady, the King's Mother, and everyone will have to do whatever you say.'

SUMMER 1457

We do not speak of my destiny again, nor of the future of England. Jasper is too busy. He is gone from the castle for weeks and weeks at a time. In the early summer he comes back with his force in tatters and his own face bruised, but smiling. He rode down and captured William Herbert and the peace of Wales is restored, and the rule of Wales is again in our hands. Wales is held by a Tudor for the House of Lancaster, once more.

Jasper sends Herbert to London as a proclaimed traitor, and we hear that he is tried for treason and held in the Tower. I shudder at that, thinking of my old guardian, William de la Pole, who had been in the Tower when I, a little girl, had been forced to declare myself free of him.

'It doesn't matter,' Jasper tells me, hardly able to speak for yawning over dinner. 'Forgive me, sister, I am exhausted. I shall sleep for all of tomorrow. Herbert won't go to the block as he deserves. The queen herself warned me that the king will pardon and release Herbert, and he will live to attack us again. Mark my words. Our king is an expert at forgiveness. He will forgive the man who raises a sword against him. He will forgive the man who raises England against him. Herbert will be released, and in time he will come back to Wales and he and I will fight all over again for the same handful of castles. The king forgives the Yorks and thinks they will live with him in charity. This is a mark of his greatness, really, Margaret – you strive for sainthood and it must run in your family, for I think he has it. He is filled with the greatest of kindness and the greatest of trust. He cannot bear a grudge, he sees every man as a sinner striving to be good and he does what he can to help him. You cannot help but love and admire him. It is a mark of his enemies that they take his mercy as a licence to go on as they wish.' He pauses. 'He is a great man; but perhaps not a great king. He is beyond us all. It just makes it very hard for the rest of us. And the common people only see weakness where there is greatness of spirit.'

'But he is well now, surely? And the court is back in London. The queen is living with the king again and you hold Wales for him. He may stay well, their son is strong, they might have another child. Surely the Yorks will settle themselves to live as great men, under a greater king. They must know that this is their place?'

He shakes his head and spoons himself another bowl of stewed beef and a slice of manchet bread. He is hungry; he has been riding with his men for weeks. 'Truly, Margaret, I don't think the Yorks can settle. They see the king, they do their best sometimes to work with him; but even when he is well he is weak, and when he is ill, he is entranced. If I were not his man, bound heart and soul, I would find it hard to be loyal to him. I would be filled with doubt as to what comes next. I cannot in my heart blame them for hoping to control what comes next. I never doubt Richard of York. I think he knows and loves the king, and knows that he is of the royal line but not a king ordained. But Richard Neville, the Earl of Warwick, I would trust no further than I could see an arrow flight. He is so accustomed to ruling all the north, he will never see why he cannot rule a kingdom. Both of them, thank God, would never touch an ordained king. But every time the king is ill it leaves the question: when will he get better? And what shall we do until he is better? And the question nobody asks out loud: what shall we do if he never gets better at all?

'Worst of all is that we have a queen who is a law to herself. When the king is gone, we are a ship without a tiller and the queen is the wind that can blow in any direction. If I believed that Joan of Arc was not a holy girl but a witch, as some say, I would think she had cursed us with a king whose first loyalty is to his dreams and a queen whose first loyalty is to France.'

'Don't say it! Don't say it!' I object to the slight on Joan and put my hand quickly on his, to silence him. For a moment we are hand-clasped, and then gently he moves his hand from under mine, as if I may not even touch him, not even like this, like sister and brother.

'I speak to you now, trusting that it all goes no further than your prayers,' he said. 'But when you are married, this January, I will talk to you only of family business.'

I am hurt that he should take his hand from my touch. 'Jasper,' I say quietly. 'From this January, I will have nobody in the world that loves me.'

'I will love you,' he says quietly. 'As a brother, as a friend, as the guardian of your son. And you can always write to me and I can always reply to you, as a brother and a friend and the guardian of your son.'

'But who will talk to me? Who will see me as I am?'

He shrugs. 'Some of us are born to a solitary life,' he says. 'You will be married but you may be very much alone. I shall think of you: you in your grand house in Lincolnshire with

Henry Stafford while I live here without you. The castle will seem very quiet and very strange without you here. The stone stairs and the chapel will miss your footstep, the gateway will miss your laughter, and the wall will miss your shadow.'

'But you will keep my son,' I say, jealous as always.

He nods. 'I will keep him, even though Edmund and you are lost from me.'

JANUARY 1458

True to their word, my mother, Sir Henry Stafford, and the Duke of Buckingham come to Pembroke Castle in January, despite snow and freezing fog to fetch me for my wedding. Jasper and I are beside ourselves trying to get in enough wood for big fires in every chamber, and to wrest enough meat from a hungry winter countryside to prepare a wedding feast. In the end we have to reconcile ourselves to the fact that there can be no more than three meat dishes and two sweetmeat courses, and that there are very few crystallised fruits and only a few marchpane dishes. It won't be what the duke expects; but this is Wales in mid-winter, and Jasper and I are united by a sort of rebellious pride that we have done what we can and if it is not good enough for His Grace and my mother, then they can ride back to London where the Burgundian merchants arrive with a new luxury every day for those rich and vain enough to waste their money.

In the end they hardly notice the poor fare for they stay for only two days. They have brought me a fur hood and gloves for the journey and my mother agrees that I can ride Arthur for some of the way. We are to leave early in the morning, to catch as much as we can of the short winter daylight, and I have to be ready and waiting in the stable yard so as not to disoblige my new family and my silent husband-to-be. They will take me first to my mother's house for our wedding, and then my new husband will take me to his house at Bourne in Lincolnshire, wherever that is. Another husband, another new house, another new country, but I never belong anywhere and I never own anything in my own right.

When everything is ready I run back upstairs and Jasper comes with me to the nursery for me to say goodbye to my son. Henry has grown out of his swaddling bands and even out of his cradle. He now sleeps in a little bed with high bars on either side. He is so near to walking alone that I cannot bear to leave him. He can stand, endearingly bow-legged, clinging onto a prayer seat or a low stool, then he eyes the next safe haven and flings himself towards it, taking one staggering step and collapsing on the way. If I am ready to play with him, he will take my hands, and with me bent double to support him, walk the length of the room and back again. When Jasper comes into the nursery, Henry crows like a cockerel, for he knows that Jasper will go up and down, and up and down, like an obedient beast turning the threshing wheel, tirelessly holding Henry's little hands, while he pit-pats forwards on his fat little feet.

But the magic moment when he walks alone has not yet happened, and I was praying he would do it before I have to leave. Now he will take his first step without me. And every step thereafter, I know. Every step of his life, and me not there to see him walk.

'I will write to you the moment he does it,' Jasper swears to me.

'And write to me if you can make him eat meat,' I say. 'He can't live his life on gruel.'

'And his teeth,' he promises me. 'I will write you as each new one comes in.'

I pull at his arm and he turns towards me. 'And if he is ill,' I whisper. 'They will tell you to spare me worry. But it won't spare me worry if I think he is ill but nobody would tell me. Swear you will write to me if he is ill at all, or if he has a fall or any sort of accident.'

'I swear,' he says. 'And I will keep him as safe as I can.'

We turn towards the high-sided bed where Henry is holding the rail and beaming up at us. For a moment I catch a glimpse of the two of us reflected in the little lattice panes of the window behind him. I am nearly fifteen and Jasper will be twenty-seven next birthday. In the darkened glass we look like the parents of our boy, we look like the handsome young parents of a beloved heir. 'I will come to visit him as soon as I am allowed,' I say miserably.

My baby Henry does not know that I have come to say goodbye. He holds up his arms to be lifted up. 'I will bring you news of him whenever I am in England,' Jasper promises.

He leans down and picks up our boy. Henry clings to him and puts his little face against Jasper's neck. I step back and look at the both of them, trying to hold the picture of this boy of mine and his guardian, so that I can see it on my eyelids when I pray for them. I know I will see them at every office of prayer, five times a day. I know that my heart will ache for them both all through the day, every day, and at night, when I cannot sleep for longing for both of them.

'Don't come down to see me off,' I say anguished. 'I will tell them that someone came and called you away. I can't bear it.'

He looks at me, his face strained. 'Of course I will come down and I will bring your son,' he says bleakly. 'It would look most odd if I did not bid you farewell as your brother-in-law and the guardian of your son. You are betrothed now, Margaret, you must take care how you look to the world and how things appear to your future husband.'

'You think I am going to consider him today, of all days?' I burst out. 'When I have to leave you, when I have to say goodbye to my son? You think I care what he thinks of me when my heart is breaking?'

But Jasper nods. 'This day and every day. Consider him carefully. He will own all your property, all your land. Your good name is in his keeping, your son's inheritance will be decided by him. If you cannot be a loving wife' – he lifts his hand to stop me arguing – 'then be at least a wife of whom he can make no complaint. His family is one of the greatest in the land. He will inherit a fortune. If he dies, some of that will come to you. Be a wife of whom he can make no complaint, Margaret. That is the best advice I can give to you. You will be his wife, that is to be his servant, his possession. He will be your master. You had better please him.'

I don't step towards him, and I don't touch him. After that time at dinner when I put my hand on his and he took his hand away I have never touched him. I may be a girl of fourteen, but I have my pride; and besides, some things are too powerful for words. 'At least let me tell you this once that I don't want to marry him, and I don't want to leave here,' I say flatly.

Over my son's round head Jasper smiles at me, but his eyes are dark with pain. 'I know,' he says. 'And I can tell you that I shall be filled with grief when you are gone. I will miss you.'

'You love me as a sister,' I insist, daring him to contradict me.

He turns away, takes one step, and then comes back to me. Henry gurgles and reaches his arms out to me, thinking this is a game. Jasper stops short – just half a pace away from me, close enough for me to feel his warm breath on my cheek, close enough for me to step towards him, into his arms, if I only dared. 'You know I can't speak,' Jasper says tightly. 'You will be Lady Stafford within a week. Go with the knowledge that I will think of you every time I lift your boy from his bed, every time I kneel for my prayers, every time I order my horse, every hour of every day. There are words that cannot in honour be said between the Earl of Pembroke and Lady Stafford, so I will not say them. You will have to be satisfied with this.'

I rub my eyes hard and my fists come away wet with tears. 'But this is nothing,' I say fiercely. 'Nothing to what I would say to you. Not at all what I want to hear.'

'As it should be. This way you have nothing to confess, neither to a priest nor a husband. And neither do I.' He pauses. 'Now go.'

I lead the way down the stairs to the courtyard of the castle where the horses are waiting. My betrothed gets down heavily from his saddle and lifts me on to my horse, and murmurs again that it is a long way and I might like to ride pillion, or take a litter, and I say, once more, that I have learned to ride, that I like to ride, and that Arthur, the horse that Jasper gave me, will carry me steadily and safely all day.

The guards are mounted, they line up and dip their banners to the Earl of Pembroke, with the little Earl of Richmond, my boy, in his arms. Sir Henry throws him a casual salute. Jasper looks at me and I look back at him for one unflinching moment, and then I turn my horse's head and I ride away from Pembroke, the castle and its earl. I do not turn my head to see if he is looking after me; I know that he is.

We go to my mother's house at Bletsoe and I am married in the little chapel with my half-sisters in attendance. This time, I do not ask my mother if I can be spared the wedding and she does not reassure me with false promises. I look sideways at my new husband and think that though he is twice my age perhaps he will be kinder to me than a younger man would be. As I kneel at the altar for my wedding blessing I pray with all my heart that he is so old as to be impotent.

They give us a wedding feast and put us to bed and I kneel at the foot of the bed and pray for courage, and that his strength may fail him. He comes into the room before I am finished and takes off his gown, letting me see him naked, as if there is no awkwardness at all. 'What are you praying for?' he asks, bare-chested, bare-arsed, just utterly gross and shocking and yet he speaks as if he did not know it.

'To be spared,' I blurt out, and at once clap my hand to my mouth in horror. 'I am so sorry, I beg your pardon. I meant to be spared from fear.'

Amazingly, he shows no flare of temper. He does not even seem to be angry. He laughs as he gets into bed, still naked. 'Poor child,' he says. 'Poor child. You have nothing to fear from me. I will try not to hurt you, and I will always be kind to you. But you must learn to mind your tongue.'

I flush scarlet with misery and get into the bed. He gently pulls me towards him and puts his arm around me and holds me to his shoulder as if it were the most natural thing in the world. No man has ever held me before, and I am rigid with fear at his touch and at the smell of him. I am waiting for the rough lunge that Edmund always made, but nothing happens. He does not move and his quiet breathing makes me think he is asleep. Little by little I dare to breathe, and then I feel myself rest into the softness of the bed and the fineness of the linen. He is warm and there is something comforting about his bulk and quietness, lying beside me. He reminds me of Arthur the horse, so strong and large and gentle. I realise that God has answered my prayers and that my new husband must be so old at thirty-three as to be completely impotent. Why else would he lie still and quiet, his hand just gently stroking my back? Lady Mother be praised! He is unmanned, and lying beside him feels like being safe and warm and even beloved. He does not move, he makes no noise but a quiet sigh, and as my anxiety slips away, I fall asleep in his arms.

SUMMER 1459

I have been married a year and a half before I see my brother-in-law Jasper again and as I wait for him, in the hall of our grand manor in Lincolnshire, I feel strangely embarrassed, as if I am ashamed of the easy comfort of my life with my husband, Sir Henry. I expect Jasper will find me much changed, and I know that I am changed. I am less haunted than the girl who swore she did not want to marry anyone, I am far happier than the girl who railed against her mother for saying there was no future for her but wedding and bedding. In the past eighteen months I have learned that my husband is not impotent, but on the contrary very kind and very gentle to me. His tenderness and sweetness have taught me tenderness in return, and I would have to admit to being a happy and satisfied wife.

He gives me much freedom in our life together, he allows me to attend chapel as often as I wish, I command the priest and the church that adjoins our house. I have ordered the services to run to the daily order of a monastery, and I attend most of them, even the offices of the night on holy days, and he makes no objection. He gives me a generous allowance and encourages me to buy books, I am starting to create my own library of translations and manuscripts, and occasionally he sits with me in the evenings and reads to me from the gospel in Latin and I follow the words in an English translation that he has had copied for me, which I am slowly coming to understand. In short, this man treats me more as his young ward than his wife, and provides for my health, my education and my religious life.

He is kind and considerate for my comfort, and he makes no complaint that a baby has not yet been conceived, and he does his duty gently.

And so, waiting for Jasper, I feel strangely ashamed, as if I have found a safe haven and ignobly run away from the danger and fears of Wales. Then I can see the cloud of dust on the road, hear the hoofbeats and the clatter of the arms, and Jasper and his men rattle into the stable yard. He is with fifty mounted horsemen, all of them carrying weapons, all of them grim-faced as if ready for a war. Sir Henry is at my side as we step forwards to greet Jasper, and any hope that I had that he might have taken my hand, or kissed my lips, vanishes when I see that Sir Henry and Jasper are anxious to talk to each other and neither of them need me there at all. Sir Henry grasps Jasper's elbows in a hard embrace. 'Any trouble on the road?'

Jasper slaps him on the back. 'A band of brigands wearing the white rose of York but nothing more,' he says. 'We had to fight them off and then they ran. What's the news around here?'

Sir Henry grimaces. 'The county of Lincolnshire is mostly for York, Hertfordshire, Essex and East Anglia for him or for his ally Warwick. South of London, Kent is half-rebel as usual. They suffer so much from the French pirates and the blockade of trade that they see the Earl of Warwick in Calais as their saviour and they will never forgive the French queen for her birth.'

'Will I get to London unscathed, d'you think? I want to go the day after tomorrow. Are there many armed bands raiding the highway? Should I ride cross-country?'

'As long as Warwick stays in Calais, you will only face the usual rogues. But they say he could land at any time, and then he would march to meet York at Ludlow and your paths could cross on the way. Better send scouts ahead of you and keep a party following behind. If you meet Warwick you will find yourself pitched into battle, perhaps the first of a war. Are you going to the king?'

They turn and walk into the house together and I follow, the mistress of the house only in name. Sir Henry's household servants always have everything prepared. I am little more than a guest.

'No, the king has gone to Coventry, God bless and keep him, and he will summon the York lords to meet with him there and acknowledge his rule. It is their test. If they refuse to go then they will be indicted. The queen and the prince are with the king for their own safety. I am commanded to invest Westminster Palace and hold London for the king. I am to be ready for a siege. We are preparing for war.'

'You'll get no help from the merchants and the City lords,' my husband warns him. 'They are all for York. They cannot do business while the king cannot keep the peace, and that's all they think of.'

Jasper nods. 'That's what I heard. I will overrule them. I am ordered to recruit men and build ditches. I will turn London into a walled town for Lancaster, whatever the citizens want.'

Sir Henry takes Jasper into an inner room, I follow, and we close the door behind us so that they can speak privately. 'There are few in the whole country who could deny that York has just cause,' my husband says. 'You know him yourself. He is loyal to the king, heart and soul. But while the king is ruled by the queen and while she conspires with the Duke of Somerset there will be no peace and no safety for York nor any of his affinity.' He hesitates. 'No peace for any of us in truth,' he adds. 'What Englishman can feel safe if a French queen commands everything? Will she not hand us over to French?'

Jasper shakes his head. 'But still she is Queen of England,' he says flatly. 'And mother to the Prince of Wales. And the chief lady of the House of Lancaster, our house. She commands our loyalty. She is our queen, whatever her birth, whatever friends she keeps, whatever she commands.'

Sir Henry smiles his crooked smile, which I know, from a year of his company, means that something strikes him as overly simple. 'Even so, she should not rule the king,' he says. 'She should not advise him instead of his council. He should consult York and Warwick. They are the greatest men of his kingdom, they are leaders of men. They must advise him.'

'We can deal with the membership of the royal council when the threat from York is over,' Jasper says impatiently. 'There is no time to discuss it now. Are you arming your tenants?'

'I?'

Jasper shoots a shocked look at me. 'Yes, Sir Henry, you. The king is calling on all his loyal subjects to prepare for war. I am recruiting men. I have come here for your tenants. Are you coming with me to defend London? Or will you march to join your king at Coventry?'

'Neither,' my husband says quietly. 'My father is calling up his men, and my brother will ride with him. They will muster a small army for the king and I would think that is enough from one family. If my father orders me to accompany him, I will go, of course. It would be my duty as his son. If York's men come here I will fight them as I would fight anyone marching over my fields. If Warwick tries to ride roughshod over my land I will defend it; but I won't be riding out this month on my own account.'

Jasper looks away, and I blush with shame to have a husband who stays by the fireside when the call to battle is heard. 'I am sorry to learn it,' Jasper says shortly. 'I took you for a loyal Lancastrian. I would not have thought this of you.'

My husband glances towards me with a little smile. 'I am afraid my wife also thinks the less of me, but I cannot, in conscience, go out and kill my own countrymen to defend the right of a young, foolish Frenchwoman to give her husband bad advice. The king needs the best of men to advise him and York and Warwick are the best of men, proven true. If he makes them into his enemies then York and Warwick may march against him, but I am sure that they intend to do no more than force the king to listen to them. I am certain they will do nothing more than insist on being in his council and having their voices heard. And since I think that is their right, how can I, in conscience, fight against them? Their cause is just. They have the right to advise him and the queen has not. You know that as well as I.'

Jasper leaps to his feet in a swift, impatient movement. 'Sir Henry, in honour, you have no choice. You must fight because your king has called on you, because the head of your house has called on you. If you are of the House of Lancaster, you follow the call.'

'I am not a hound to yelp at the hunting horn,' my husband says quietly, not at all stirred by Jasper's raised voice. 'I don't give tongue to order. I don't bay for the chase. I will go to war should there ever be a cause I think worth dying for – and not before. But I do admire your, er . . . martial spirit.'

Jasper flushes to the roots of his ginger hair at the older man's tone. 'I think this is no laughing matter, sir. I have been fighting for my king and for my house for two years, and I must remind you that it has cost me dear. I lost my own brother at the walls of Carmarthen, the heir to our name, the flower of our house, Margaret's husband who never saw his son . . .'

'I know, I know, and I am not laughing. I too have lost a brother, remember. These battles are a tragedy for England, no laughing matter. Come, let us go in to dine and forget our differences. I pray that it will not come to a fight, and so must you. We need peace in England if we are to grow strong and rich again. We conquered France because the people were divided among themselves. Let us not lose our way, as they did, let us not be our own worst enemies in our own country.'

Jasper would argue; but my husband takes him by his arm and leads him to the great hall where the men are already seated, ten to a table, waiting for their dinners. When Jasper comes in his men hammer the table with the hilts of their daggers as applause, and I think it a great thing that he is such a commander, and so beloved of his men. He is like a knight errant from the stories; he is their hero. My husband's servants and retainers merely bow their heads and doff their caps in silent respect as he goes by. But no-one has ever cheered Henry Stafford to the rafters. No-one ever will.

We walk through the deep rumble of male noise to the high table and I see Jasper glance over at me as if he pities me for marrying a man who will not fight for his family. I keep my eyes down. I think that everyone knows I am the daughter of a coward, and now I am the wife of a coward, and I have to live with shame.

As the server of the ewery pours water over our hands and pats them with the napkin, my husband says kindly, 'But I have distracted you from the great interest for my wife: the health of her son. How is young Henry? Is he well?'

Jasper turns to me. 'He is well and strong. I wrote you that his back teeth were coming through, they gave him a fever for a few days but he is through that now. He is walking and running. He is speaking a lot, not always clearly, but he chatters all the day. His nursemaid says that he is wilful, but no more than befits his position in the world and his age. I have told her not to be too severe with him. He is Earl of Richmond, he should not have his spirit broken, he has a right to his pride.'

'Do you tell him of me?' I ask.

'Of course I do,' he says with a smile. 'I tell him that his mother is a great lady in England and will come and see him soon, and he says "Mama!" just like that.'

I laugh at his impression of a two-year-old's fluting voice. 'And his hair?' I say. 'Is it coming through red like Edmund's?'

'Ah no,' Jasper says with a disappointment that I don't share. 'We did not breed true in that, as it turns out. His hair is in ringlets and brown, like a bright bay horse. His nursemaid thinks he will go more fair in the summer when he is out in the sunshine, but he won't be a brass-head like us Tudors.'

'And does he like to play? And does he know his prayers?'

'He plays with his bat and his ball, he will play all day if someone will throw a ball for him. And he is learning the Lord's Prayer and his catechism. Your friend Father William sees him every morning for prayers, and his nursemaid sets him at the foot of his bed every night, and makes him stay there. He is ordered to pray for you by name.'

'Do you have playmates for him?' my husband asks. 'Children from the neighbouring houses?'

'We are very isolated in the castle,' Jasper replies. 'There are no families of his breeding nearby. There are no suitable companions for a boy such as him. He is Earl of Richmond, and kinsman to the king. I cannot let him play with children from the village, and besides, I would be afraid of illness. He plays with his nursemaids. I play with him. He does not need any others.'

I nod. I don't want him playing with village children who might teach him rough ways.

'Surely, he needs to be with children of his own age,' my husband demurs. 'He will need to match himself against other lads, even if they are from the village and from cottages.'

'I will see when the time comes,' Jasper says stiffly. 'He needs no companions but those I give him, for now.'

There is an awkward silence. 'And does he eat well?' I ask.

'Eats well, sleeps well, runs about all day,' Jasper says. 'He is growing well too. He will be tall, I think. He has Edmund's shape: long and lean.'

'We will go and visit him as soon as it is safe to travel,' my husband promises me. 'And Jasper, you are sure you can keep him safe there?'

'There is not a Yorkist left in Wales who could raise enough troops to take Pembroke village, let alone my castle,' Jasper assures us. 'William Herbert is the king's man now, he has turned his coat completely since his pardon, he is a Lancaster man now. Wales is safer than England for a Lancaster boy. I hold all the key castles and patrol the roads. I will keep him safe, as I promised. I will always keep him safe.'

Jasper stays with us only two nights, and in the days he rides out among our tenants and musters as many men as will go with him to march to London to defend it for the king. Few of them are willing to go. We may be of the House of Lancaster; but everyone who lives close enough to London to hear the gossip of the court knows better than to lay down his life for a king that they have heard is half-mad, and a queen who is a Frenchwoman and a virago as well.

On the third day, Jasper is ready to ride away again, and I have to say goodbye to him. 'You seem happy at any rate,' he says to me quietly in the stable yard as his men saddle up and mount onto their saddles.

'I am well enough. He is kind to me.'

'I wish you could persuade him to play his part,' Jasper says.

'I do what I can, but I doubt he will listen to me. I know he should serve, Jasper, but he is older than me and thinks he knows better.'

'Our king could be fighting for his very right to rule,' Jasper says. 'A true man would be at his side. One of the House of Lancaster should not wait to be summoned, let alone ignore the call.'

'I know, I know, I will tell him again. And you tell Baby Henry that I will come and see him as soon as the roads are safe to travel.'

'There will be no peace and safety for travel until York and Warwick submit to their rightful king!' Jasper says irritably.

'I know that,' I say. 'But for Sir Henry . . .'

'What?'

'He is old,' I say with all the wisdom of a sixteen-year-old. 'He does not understand that God gives us a moment sometimes, and we have to seize it. Joan of Arc knew that, you know it. Sometimes God gives us a moment of destiny and we have to hear the call and rise to it.'

Jasper's smile warms his face. 'Yes,' he says. 'You are right, Margaret. That is how it is. Sometimes there is a moment and you have to answer it. Even if some think you are nothing more than a foolish hound to the hunting horn.'

He kisses me as a brother-in-law should do, gently on the mouth, and he holds my hands for a moment. I close my eyes and feel myself sway, dizzy at his touch, and then he lets me go, turns his back on me and swings into the saddle.

'Is our old horse Arthur still carrying you well?' he asks, as if he does not want either of us to notice he is leaving me again, and riding into danger.

'Yes,' I say. 'I ride out on him most days. Go with God, Jasper.'

He nods. 'God will protect me. For we are in the right. And when I am in the very heat of battle I know that God will always protect the man who serves his king.'

Then he wheels his horse and rides at the head of his men, south to London, to keep the palace of Westminster safe from our enemies.

AUTUMN 1459

I hear nothing of Jasper until one of our tenants who was persuaded to follow him comes back to his home in the middle of September, strapped on his own little pony, one arm a suppurating stump, his face white, and the smell of death on him. His wife, a girl only a little older than me, screams in terror and faints as they bring him to their door. She cannot nurse him, she does not know what to do with these rotting remains of the young man she married for love, so they bring him up to the manor for better care than they can manage in his dirty cottage. I turn a spare room in the dairy into a sick room, and I wonder how many more will come home wounded from Jasper's hastily recruited band. Jasper's volunteer tells my husband that Warwick's father, the Earl of Salisbury, was marching his army of men to meet with the Duke of York at Ludlow when two of our lords, Dudley and Audley, prepared an ambush for him at Market Drayton, on the road to Wales. Our force was double the size of Salisbury's army, our man John said that the York soldiers went down on their knees and kissed the ground of the field, thinking it would be their deathbed.

But the York army played a trick, a trick that Salisbury could play since his men would do anything for him – fall back, stand, attack – so he commanded them to withdraw, as if giving up the fight. Our cavalry rode them down, thinking they were chasing a runaway force, and found that they were the ones who were caught, just as they were wading through the brook. The enemy turned and stood, fast as a striking snake and our men had to fight their way uphill through ground that became more and more churned as they tried to charge the horses through it, and drag our guns upwards. The York archers could shoot downhill into our men, and their horses died under them, and they were lost in the mud and the mess and the hail of arrows and shot. John said that the river was red with blood of the wounded and the dying, and men who waded through to escape the battle were dyed red.

Night fell on a battlefield where we had lost the cause, and our men were left in the fields to die. The York commander Salisbury slipped away before the main body of our army could come up, and deceitfully left his cannon in the field and paid some turncoat friar to shoot them off all night. When the royal army thundered up at dawn, ready for battle, expecting to find the Yorks standing on the defensive with their cannon, ready to massacre the traitors, there was no-one there but one drunk hedge-friar, hopping from firing pan to firing pan, who told them that their enemy had run off to Ludlow, laughing about their victory over the two Lancaster lords.

'So, battle has been met,' my husband says grimly. 'And lost.'

'They didn't engage the king himself,' I say. 'The king would have won, without a doubt. They just met two of our lords, not the king in command.'

'Actually, they faced nothing more than one threadbare friar,' my husband points out.

'Our two lords would surely have won if the forces of York had fought fairly,' I insist.

'Yes, but one of those lords is now dead, and the other is captured. I think we can take it that our enemies have won the first round.'

'But there will be more fighting? We can regroup? When Joan failed to take Paris she didn't surrender . . .'

'Ah, Joan,' he says wearily. 'Yes, if we take Joan as our example we should go on to the death. A successful martyrdom beckons. You are right. There will be more battles. You can be sure of that. There are now two powers marching around each other like cocks in a pit, seeking advantage. You can be sure that there will be a fight, and then another, and then another, until one or the other is sickened by defeat or dead.'

I am deaf to his scathing tone. 'Husband, will you go now to serve your king? Now that the first battle has been fought, and we have lost. Now that you can see that you are badly needed. That every man of honour has to go.'

He looks at me. 'When I have to go, I will,' he says grimly. 'Not before.'

'Every true man in England will be there but you!' I protest hotly.

'Then there will be so many true men that they won't need a faint-heart like me,' says Sir Henry, and walks from the sick chamber where Jasper's volunteer is dying, before I can say more.

There is coldness between Sir Henry and me after this, and so I don't tell him when I receive a crumpled piece of paper from Jasper with his spiky ill-formed writing that says simply:

Don't fear. The king himself is taking the field. We are marching on them – J

Instead, I wait till we are alone after dinner and my husband is fingering a lute without making a tune, and I ask: 'Have you any news from your father? Is he with the king?'

'They are chasing the Yorks back to their castle at Ludlow,' he says, picking out a desultory little melody. 'My father says there are more than twenty thousand turned out for the king. It seems that most men think that we will win, that York will be captured and killed, though the king in his tender heart has said he will forgive them all if they will surrrender.'

'Will there be another battle?'

'Unless York decides he cannot face the king in person. It is one sort of sin to kill your friends and cousins; quite another to order your bowmen to fire at the king's banner and him beneath it. What if the king is killed in battle? What if York brings his broadsword down on the king's sanctified head?'

I close my eyes in horror at the thought of the king, all but a saint, being martyred by his own subject who has sworn loyalty to him. 'Surely, the Duke of York cannot do it? Surely he cannot even consider it?'

OCTOBER 1459

As it turned out, he could not.

When the army of York came face to face with their true king on the battlefield, they found that they could not bring themselves to attack him. I was on my knees for all of the day that the York forces drew up behind their guns and carts and looked down the hill to Ludford Bridge and the king's own banners. They spent the day parlaying, as I spent the day wrestling with my prayers, and in the night, their sinful courage collapsed beneath them and they ran away. They ran like the cowards they were and in the morning the king, a saint, but thank God not a martyr, went among the ranks of the York common soldiers, abandoned in their lines by their commanders, and forgave them and kindly sent them home. York's wife, the Duchess Cecily, had to wait before the town cross in Ludlow as the king's mob poured in, hungry for plunder, the keys to the castle in her hand, her two little boys George and Richard trembling on either side of her. She had to surrender to the king and take her boys into imprisonment, not knowing where her husband and two older sons had fled. She must have been shamed to her soul. The great rebellion of the House of York and Warwick against their divinely appointed king was ended in a brawl of looting in York's own castle, and with their duchess in prison clutching her little traitorous boys who wept for their defeat.

'They are cowards,' I whisper to the statue of Our Lady in my private chapel. 'And You punished them with shame. I prayed that they would be defeated and You have answered my prayers and brought them low.'

When I rise from my knees, I walk out from the chapel a little taller, knowing that my house is blessed by God, is led by a man as much a saint as a king, and that our cause is just and has been won without so much as an arrow being loosed.

SPRING 1460

'Except that it is not won,' my husband observes acidly. 'There is no settlement with York nor answer to his grievances. Salisbury, Warwick, and the two older York boys are in Calais, and they won't be wasting their time there. York has fled to Ireland and he too will be gathering his forces. The queen has insisted that they all be arraigned as traitors, and now she is demanding lists of every able-bodied man in every county of England. She thinks she has the right to summon them directly to her army.'

'Surely she means only to ask the lords to call up their own men as usual?'

He shakes his head. 'No, she is going to raise troops in the French way. She thinks to command the commons directly. Her plan is to have lists of young men in every county and raise them herself, to her standard, as if she were a king in France. No-one will stand for it. The commons will refuse to go out for her – why should they, she's not their liege lord – and the lords will see it as an act against them, undermining their power. They will suspect her of going behind their backs to their own tenants. Everyone will see this as bringing French tyranny to England. She will make enemies from her natural allies. God knows, she makes it hard to be loyal to the king.'

I take his gloomy predictions to confession and tell the priest that I have to confess the sin of doubting my husband's judgement. A careful man, he is too discreet to enquire about my doubts – after all, it is my husband who owns the chapel and the living and pays for the chantries and masses in the church; but he gives me ten Hail Marys and an hour on my knees in remorseful prayer. I kneel, but I cannot be remorseful. I am starting to fear that my husband is worse than a coward. I am starting to fear the very worst of him: that he has sympathies with the York cause. I am beginning to doubt his loyalty to the king. My rosary beads are still in my hand when I acknowledge this thought to myself. What can I do? What should I do? How should I live if I am married to a traitor? If he is not loyal to our king and our house, how can I be loyal to him as a wife? Could it be possible that God is calling me to leave my husband? And where would God want me to go, but to a man who is heart and soul loyal to the cause? Would God want me to go to Jasper?

Then, in July, everything my husband had warned about the Calais garrison becomes terribly true, as York launches a fleet, lands in Sandwich, halfway to London, and marches on the capital city, without a shot being fired against him, without a door slammed shut. God forgive the men of London, they fling open the gates for him and he marches in to acclaim, as if he is freeing the City from a usurper. The king and the court are at Coventry, but as soon as they hear the news, the call goes out across the country that the king is mustering and summoning all his affinity. York has taken London; Lancaster must march.

'Are you going now?' I demand of my husband, finding him in the stable yard, checking over the harness and saddles of his horses and men. At last, I think, he sees the danger to the king and knows he must defend him.

'No,' he replies shortly. 'Though my father is there, God keep him safe in this madness.'

'Will you not even go to be with your father in danger?'

'No,' he says again. 'I love my father, and I will join him if he orders me; but he has not commanded me to his side. He will unfurl the standard of Buckingham, he doesn't want me under it, yet.'

I know that my anger flares in my face and I meet his glance with hard eyes. 'How can you bear not to be there?'

'I doubt the cause,' he says frankly. 'If the king wants to retake London from the Duke of York, I imagine he only has to go to the City and discuss terms. He does not need to attack his own capital, he has only to agree to speak with them.'

'He should cut York down like a traitor and you should be there!' I say hotly.

He sighs. 'You are very quick to send me into danger, wife,' he remarks with a wry smile. 'I must say, I would find it more agreeable if you were begging me to stay home.'

'I beg you only to do your duty,' I say proudly. 'If I were a man I would ride out for the king. If I were a man I would be at his side now.'

'You would be a very Joan of Arc, I am sure,' he says quietly. 'But I have seen battles and I know what they cost, and right now, I see it as my duty to keep these lands and our people in safety and peace while other men scramble for their own ambition, and tear this country apart.'

I am so furious I cannot speak, and I turn on my heel and walk away to the loosebox where Arthur, the old warhorse, is stabled. Gently he brings his big head down to me and I pat his neck and rub behind his ears and whisper that he and I should go together, ride to Coventry, find Jasper, who is certain to be there, and fight for the king.

10 JULY 1460

Even if Arthur and I had ridden out, we would have got there too late. The king had his army dug in outside Northampton, a palisade of sharpened stakes before them to bring down the cavalry, their newly forged cannon primed and ready to fire. The Yorks, led by the boy Edward, Earl of March, the traitors Lord Fauconberg and Warwick himself in the centre, came on in three troops in the pouring rain. The ground churned into mud under the horses' hooves and the cavalry charge got bogged down. God rained down on the rebels and they looked likely to sink in the quagmire. The boy Edward of York had to dig deep to find the courage to lead his men through ground which was a marsh, against a hail of Lancaster arrows. He would surely have failed and his young face would have gone down in the mud; but the leader on our right, Lord Grey of Ruthin, turned traitor in that moment, and pulled the York forces up over the barricade and turned on his own house in bitter hand-to-hand fighting which pushed our men back toward the River Nene, where many drowned, and let Warwick and Fauconberg come on.

In victory they were merciless. They let the common men go, but anyone in armour was killed without offer of ransom. Worst of all, they marched into our camp and found the king's own tent, His Grace inside, sitting thoughtfully, as peaceful as if he were praying in his own chapel, waiting for them to capture him as the great prize of the battle.

Terribly, treasonously, they take him.

Two nights later my husband comes to me in my chamber as I am dressing for dinner. 'Leave us,' he says abruptly to my lady in waiting, and she glances at me, and then seeing the darkness in his face, flicks out of the room.

'My father is dead,' he says, without preparation. 'I have just had word. England has lost a great duke in the mud of Northampton, and I have lost a dear father. His heir, my nephew, little Henry Stafford, has lost his grandfather and protector.'

I gasp as if the air has been knocked out of me. 'I am sorry. I am so sorry, Henry.'

'They cut him down in a muddy field while he was trying to get to his horse,' he continues, sparing me nothing. 'He, and the Earl of Shrewsbury, Lord Beaumont, Lord Egremont, dear God, the list is endless. We have lost a generation of noblemen. It seems that the rules of war are changed and there is no capture and ransom in England any more. There is no offer of surrender. It is the rule of the sword and every battle must be to the death. It is the rule of savagery.'

'And the king?' I breathe. 'They have not dared to hurt him?'

'The king is captive, and they have taken him as their prisoner to London.'

'Prisoner?' I cannot believe my ears.

'As good as.'

'And the queen?'

'Missing with her son.'

'Missing?'

'Not dead. I believe run away. In hiding. What a country this is becoming. My father . . .'

He swallows his grief and turns to look out of the window. Outside the trees are rich and fat and green and the fields beyond are turning golden. It is hard to imagine a field of churned mud and my father-in-law, that vain aristocrat, clubbed down while running away.

'I shall not dine in the hall tonight,' my husband says tightly. 'You can go in, or be served in your rooms as you like. I will have to ride to Northampton and fetch his body home. I shall leave at dawn.'

'I am sorry,' I say again, weakly.

'There will be hundreds of sons making the same journey,' he says. 'All of us riding with broken hearts, all of us thinking of vengeance. This is what I feared would come, this is what I have dreaded. It is not very bright and honourable as you have always thought it; it is not like a ballad. It is a muddle and a mess, and a sinful waste, and good men have died and more will follow.'

I hide my fears from my husband till he leaves for the journey on the high road south, but of course I am in utter terror for Jasper's safety. He will have been where the fighting was the worst, there is no doubt in my mind that anyone going to the king's tent will have had to get past Jasper. He cannot be alive if the king has been captured. How can he still live, when so many are dead?

I get my answer even before my husband returns home again.

Sister, I have taken a very great lady and her son to safety and they are in hiding with me. I will not tell you where, in case this letter falls into traitors' hands. I am safe and your son is safe as I left him. The lady will be safe with me until she can get away. It is a reverse for us, but it is not over, and she is full of courage and ready to fight again. J

It takes me a moment to realise that he has the queen in safe-keeping, that he spirited her from the battle and has her in hiding in Wales. Of course, the king may be imprisoned, but while she is still free we have a commander, while her son is free we have an heir to the throne. Jasper has guarded our cause, has guarded the most precious heart of our cause, and there is no doubt in my mind that she will be safe with him. He will have her in hiding at Pembroke or Denbigh Castle. He will keep her close, I don't doubt, and she will be grateful for his protection. He will be like a knight errant to her, he will serve her on bended knee and she will ride behind him, her slim hands on his belt. I have to go to the chapel and confess to the priest that I am filled with the sin of jealousy but I don't say exactly why.

My husband comes home in sombre mood having buried his father, and delivered up his nephew to his new guardian. Little Henry Stafford, the new Duke of Buckingham, is only five years old, poor child. His father died fighting for Lancaster when he was only a baby, and now he has lost his grandfather too. My husband is stunned at this blow to his house, but I cannot sympathise; for who should be blamed for our defeat, but him and all those who chose to stay at home, though their queen summoned them and we were in the utmost danger? My father-in-law died because he was defeated in the battle. Whose fault is that but that of the son who would not ride beside him? Henry tells me that the Duke of York entered London with the king riding alongside him, as his prisoner, and was greeted by a stunned silence. The citizens of London turn out to be only half-hearted traitors, and when York put his hand on the marble throne to claim kingship for himself, there was no support for him.

'Well, how could there be?' I ask. 'We have a king already. Even the faithless men of London know that.'

My husband sighs as if he is tired of my convictions, and I notice how weary and old he looks, a deep groove between his eyebrows. Grief sits heavy on him with the responsibility for his house. If our king is a prisoner, and our power is thrown down, then someone will take the little duke from us and have him as their ward for the profit of his lands. If my husband were great with either Lancaster or York he might have had a say in the disposition of his nephew, the future head of our family. If he had exerted himself he would now be one of the great men. But since he chose to stay home, he is of no account to anyone. He has made himself as nothing. The great decisions of the world will be made without him, and he cannot even guard his own, as he said he would.

'They have put together an agreement.'

'What agreement?' I ask him. 'Who has agreed?'

He throws his travelling cape to one of the household men. He drops into a chair and beckons a pageboy to pull off his boots. I wonder if he is ill, he looks so grey and weary. Of course he is very old to have made such a great journey, he is thirty-five years old. 'The king is to keep the throne till his death, and then the next king is to be York,' he says shortly. He glances at my face and then looks away. 'I knew you wouldn't like it. There's no need to trouble yourself, it probably won't hold.'

'The Prince of Wales is to be robbed of his rights?' I can hardly frame the words, I am so shocked. 'How can he be Prince of Wales and not become king? How can anyone think that they can pass over him?'

Henry shrugs. 'You are all to be robbed, you who were in the line of succession. You, yourself, are no longer of the ruling house now. Your son is no longer related to a king, nor is he one of the heirs to the throne. It will be York; York, and his line. Yes,' he repeats to my stunned face. 'He has won for his sons what no-one would give to him. It is York's sons who will come after the king. The new royal line is to be the House of York. The Lancasters are to be the royal cousins. That is what they have agreed. That is what the king has sworn to follow.'

He rises up in his stockinged feet and turns for his rooms.

I put a hand on his arm. 'But this is just what Joan saw!' I exclaim. 'When her king was put aside, and his inheritance given to another. This is just what she saw when she took her king to be crowned in Rheims, despite a blasphemous agreement that he should not be crowned. She saw that the order of God was put aside and she fought for the true heir. This is what inspired her to be great. She saw the true heir and she fought for him.'

He cannot muster his usual smile for me. 'And so what? Do you think you can take Edward, Prince of Wales, to London and have him crowned despite his defeat, despite this agreement? Will you lead a beaten army? Will you be England's Joan?'

'Someone has to be,' I cry out passionately. 'The prince cannot be robbed of the throne. How could they agree to this? How could the king agree to this?'

'Who knows what he thinks, poor soul?' my husband says. 'Who knows what he understands now, or even if he can stay awake? And if he goes to sleep or even dies and York takes the throne, at least York will be able to hold the country to peace.'

'That's not the point!' I shout at him. 'York is not called by God. York is not of the senior line from Edward III. York is not of the royal house – we are! I am! My son is! This is *my* destiny that the king is giving away!' I give a shaking sob. 'I was born for this, my son was born for this! The king cannot make us into royal cousins, we were born to be the royal line!'

He looks down at me and his brown eyes are for once not kindly, but dark with anger. 'Enough,' he growls. 'You are a stupid young woman of, what? – only seventeen years old, and you understand nothing, Margaret. You should be silent. This is not a ballad or a tale, this is not a romance. This is a disaster that is costing the men and women of England every day. This is nothing to do with Joan of Arc, nothing to do with you, and God Himself knows, nothing to do with Him.'

He pulls away from me and he goes, treading carefully up the stairs to his room. He is stiff from his long ride and he hobbles, bow-legged. I watch him go with hatred, my hand over my mouth to stifle my sobs. He is an old man, an old fool. I know the will of God better than him, and He is, as He has always been, for Lancaster.

WINTER 1460

I am right in this, and my husband, for all that he is my husband and set over me, is wrong, and this is proved at Christmastide when the Duke of York, who is supposed to be so clever, so brilliant in battle, is caught outside his own castle walls of Sandal, with a small guard, among them his son Edmund, the Earl of Rutland, and both York and his boy are brutally killed by our forces. So much for the man who would be king and would claim the royal line!

The queen's army takes his hacked body and makes mock of him, and beheads the corpse and sticks his head above the gates of York with a paper crown on his head, so he can view his kingdom before the crows and buzzards peck out his dead eyes. This is a traitor's death, and with it die the hopes of York, for who is left? His great ally the Earl of Warwick has only useless daughters, and the three remaining boys of York, Edward, George, and Richard, are too young to lead an army on their own account.

I do not exult over my husband, for we have settled to living quietly together and are celebrating Christmas with our tenants, retainers, and servants, as if the world were not trembling with uncertainty. We do not speak of the divided kingdom, and though he has letters from merchants and tradesmen in London he does not tell me their news, nor that his family are constantly urging him to revenge the death of his father. And though he knows that Jasper writes to me from Wales, he does not ask of his newly won castle of Denbigh, and how Jasper so bravely reclaimed it.

I send my son Henry a little cart on wooden wheels, that he can pull along, for his Christmas present, and my husband gives me a shilling to send to him for fairings. In return I give him a silver sixpence to send to the little Duke of Buckingham, Henry Stafford, and we do not speak of the war, or of the queen's march south at the head of five thousand murderous, dangerous Scots, stained like eager huntsmen with the blood of the rebel York, or of my belief that our house has triumphed again, and will come to victory next year, as it must since we are blessed by God.

SPRING 1461

I think, like everyone else of any sense, that with the death of the Duke of York the wars are over. His son Edward is only eighteen years old, and all alone on the borders of Wales, where all the men follow Jasper and the House of Lancaster. His mother, the Duchess Cecily, knowing that this is her final defeat, wearing black in her widowhood, sends her two younger sons George and Richard into hiding in Flanders, with the Duke of Burgundy. Duchess Cecily must fear the arrival of the queen in London, at the head of her army of wild men, demanding vengeance for this second failed rebellion. Her oldest son she cannot save, Edward will most probably die in the borders of Wales, hopelessly outnumbered, fighting for his dead father's lost cause.

My brother-in-law Jasper will be defending his own, his father Owen Tudor marches with him. They cannot fail against an army led by a boy, who has just lost his brother, his father and commander, as Jasper confirms:

We will have to kill the cub to scotch the family. Thank God that the lion is gone. My father and I are mustering against the new Duke of York, young Edward, and will meet him within days. Your son is safe in Pembroke Castle. This should be easily done. Fear nothing.

'I think there may be another battle,' I say tentatively to my husband Henry when he comes to my bedroom. I am seated at the fireside. He drapes his gown on the end of the bed and slides between the sheets. 'Your bed is always so comfortable,' he remarks. 'Do you have better sheets than me?'

I giggle, distracted for a moment. 'I shouldn't think so. It is your steward of the household who orders everything. My sheets came with me from Wales, but I can tell him to put them on your bed, if you think them finer.'

'No, I like to enjoy them here, with you. Let's not talk of the troubles of the country.'

'But I have had a letter from Jasper.'

'Tell me of it in the morning.'

'I think it is important.'

He sighs. 'Oh, very well. What does he say?'

I hand him my note, and he glances at it. 'Yes. I knew this. I heard that they were mustering in Wales. Your old enemy William Herbert has changed his coat again.'

'Never!'

'He will wear a white rose once more, and fight alongside the York boy. He was not a friend to Lancaster for long. It must rile Jasper that Herbert rides out against him once more.'

'Herbert is quite without honour!' I exclaim. 'And after the king himself pardoned him!'

My husband shrugs. 'Who knows why a man chooses one side or another? I hear from my cousin, who is with the queen's forces, that they will mop up the remnants of the York threat and then come to London in victory.'

'Can we go to court, when she gets to London?' I ask.

'A celebration feast?' he asks wryly. 'Certainly there will be work for me in parliament. Half of England will be designated traitors and fined of their lands. The other half will be paid them as reward for their part in murder.'

'And we will be neither,' I say sullenly.

'I would rather not have the lands of a man accused of treason because he tried to give good advice to his king,' my older husband says quietly. 'And you may be well assured that half of the lands will be returned to their owners when the king returns to his power and issues pardons. He will forgive all his enemies and return them to their homes. His allies will find their service to him is ill-rewarded. There is neither profit nor true honour in following this king.'

I fold my lips together to stop my retort. He is my husband. What he says must be the rule in our household. He is my lord under God. There is no point in disagreeing with him aloud. But in my heart I name him a coward.

'Come to bed,' he says gently. 'Why would you care either way as long as you and your son are safe? And I keep you safe, Margaret. I keep the war away from our lands and I don't widow you for a second time by riding off to glory. Come to bed and smile for me.'

I go to bed with him as it is my duty, but I don't smile.

Then I get the worst news possible. The worst news, and it comes from Jasper. I had thought him invincible; but he is not, he is not. I had thought it impossible for Jasper to lose. But terribly, it turns out that he can.

Sister, we are defeated, and my father is dead. He went to the scaffold with a joke, not believing they would do it; but they took his head off and set it on a stake at Hereford.

I am going to fetch your boy from Pembroke and I will take him with me to Harlech Castle. We will be safer there. Don't fear for me, but I think our cause is lost for a generation, perhaps for ever. Margaret, I have to tell you the worst: there was a sign from God here at Mortimer's Cross, and it was not for our house. God showed us the three suns of York in the sky above the battlefield and the one son of York in command on the field below laid utter waste to us.

I saw it. It was without doubt. Above his army there were three brilliant suns, each as bright as the other. They beamed through the mist, three of them, and then they came together as one and shone down on his standard. I saw it with my own eyes, without doubt. I don't know what it means, and I will go on fighting for my cause until I understand. I still trust that God is with us, but I know for a certainty that He was not with us this day. He shone the light of His countenance on York. He blessed the three sons of York. I will write again as soon as we are safe at Harlech. J

My husband is away in London, and I have to wait days before he comes home and I can tell him that Jasper says the war is finished and we are lost. As I greet him in the stable yard he shakes his head at my babble of anxious news. 'Hush, Margaret. It is worse than you know. Young Edward of York has claimed the throne and they have lost their minds and made him king.'

This silences me completely. I glance around the yard as if I would keep it secret. 'King?'

'They have offered him the throne and say that he is the true king and heir. He need not wait for the death of King Henry.

He has claimed the throne and says he'll drive our king and queen out of England and then have a coronation, take the crown and be ordained. I have come home only to gather my men. I am going to have to fight for King Henry.'

'You?' I ask incredulously. 'At last?'

'Yes. Me, at last.'

'Why would you ride out now?'

He sighs. 'Because it is no longer a subject trying to bring his king to account, where I might find my mind divided, where a subject should advise his king against evil council. Now it is nothing but rebellion, open rebellion, and the posing of a false king against the true. This is a cause I must follow. It was not a cause that called me until now. York is fighting for treason now. I must fight against treason.'

I bite my tongue on the reproach that if he had gone before, we might not have got to this terrible pass.

'There has to be a Stafford in the field, fighting for his king. Our standard has to be there. Before it was my poor brother, then it was my honoured father, who gave his life in this brew of wars. Now it is me who has to stand beneath the Stafford banner, perhaps half-hearted, perhaps uncertain, but I am the senior Stafford, and I have to go.'

I have little interest in his reasons. 'But where is the king?'

'The queen has him safely with her. There was a battle at St Albans, and she won and took him back into her keeping.'

'The York army was defeated?' I ask, bewildered. 'But I thought they were winning?'

He shakes his head. 'No, it was little more than a scrap in the town centre of St Albans between Warwick's men and those fighting for the queen, while Edward of York marched in triumph on London. But Warwick had the king with him, and after the Yorks ran away, they found the king, sitting under an oak tree, where he had been watching the fighting.'

'He was unhurt?' I ask.

'Yes, he had been well-guarded throughout the battle by two lords of York: Lord Bonville and Sir Thomas Kyriell. They kept him safely. He was as quiet as a child. They handed him over to the queen and now he is with her, and their son.'

'And is he . . .' I hesitate to choose the word. 'Is he in his right mind?'

'So they say. For the time being.'

'So what is the matter? Why look like that?'

'A story that was doing the rounds of the taverns in London. Perhaps all untrue. I hope so.'

'A story about what?'

'They say that the lords who guarded the king and kept him safe through the battle, York lords, were taken before the queen and her son, little Prince Edward, seven years old.'

'And?'

'They say that she asked the little prince what should be done with the York lords, Lord Bonville and Sir Thomas Kyriell, who had guarded his father during the battle, and kept him safe, and handed him back with honour, in safety, to his own people. And the prince said – take off their heads. Just like that. So they beheaded the two of them on his word, the word of a boy of seven, and then they knighted him for his courage. Margaret of Anjou's son has learned the trade of war indeed. How will he ever rule a country at peace?'

I hesitate and look at my husband's grimace. 'That sounds very bad.'

'They say that the son is as vicious as the mother. All of London is for York now. Nobody wants such a boy as Prince Edward on the throne.'

'What happens next?'

He shakes his head. 'It must be the last battle. The king and the queen are reunited, and at the head of their army. Young

Edward of York and his father's friend Warwick are marching on them. It is no longer an argument about who should advise the king. It is now a battle about who should be king. And finally, I will have to defend my king.'

I find that I am shaking. 'I never thought you would go to war,' I say, my voice trembling. 'I always thought you would refuse to go. I never thought you would go to war.'

He smiles as if it is a bitter jest. 'You thought me a coward and now you cannot rejoice in my courage? Well, never mind. This is the cause that my father died for, and even he only rode out at the last possible moment. Now I find that in my turn, I will have to go. And I too have left it to the last possible moment. If we lose this battle, then we will have a York king and his heirs on the throne for ever; and your house will be a royal house no more. It is not a question of the rights of the cause, but simply on which side I was born. The king must be the king, I have to ride out for that. Or your son will no longer be three steps from the throne; but a boy without a title, without lands, and without a royal name. You and I will be traitors in our own lands. Perhaps they will even give our lands to others. I don't know what we might lose.'

'When will you go?' I ask tremulously.

His smile is without humour or warmth. 'I am afraid I will have to go now.'

EASTER 1461

When they woke in the morning it was to the silence and eerie whiteness of a world of blowing snow. It was bitterly cold. The blizzard started at dawn and the snow whirled around the standards all day. The Lancaster army, commanding the height of the long ridge near to the village of Towton, ideally placed on the heights, peered down into the valley below them, where the York army was hidden by the swirling flakes. It was too wet for the cannon to fire, and the swirling snow blinded the Lancaster archers, and their bow strings were damp. They fired blindly, aiming in hope down the hill, into snowflakes, and time and again a volley of arrows hammered back at them as the York archers found their targets clearly silhouetted against the light sky.

It was as if God had ordered the Palm Sunday weather to make sure that it was man against man, hand-to-hand fighting, the most bitter battle of all of the battles of the war, on the field they called Bloody Meadow. Rank after rank of conscripted Lancaster soldiers dropped beneath the storm of arrows, before their commanders allowed them to charge.

Then they dropped their useless bows and drew their swords, axes and blades, and thundered down the hill to meet the army of the eighteen-year-old boy who would be king, trying to hold his men steady against the shock of the downhill charge.

With a roar of 'York!' and 'Warwick! À Warwick!' they pushed forwards and the two armies struck and held. For two long hours, while the snow churned into red slush under their feet, they locked together like a plough grinding through rocky ground. Henry Stafford, riding his horse downhill into the thick of it, felt a stab to his leg and felt his horse stagger and fall beneath him. He flung himself clear but found himself lying across a dying man, his eyes staring, his bloody mouth mumbling for help. Stafford pushed himself up and away, ducked down to avoid a swing from a battle axe, and forced himself to stand and draw his sword.

Nothing in the jousting ring or the cock-fighting pit could have prepared him for the savagery of this battlefield. Cousin against cousin, blinded by snow and maddened with the killing rage, the strongest of men stabbed and clubbed, kicked and stamped on fallen enemies, and the weaker men tore themselves away and started to run, stumbling and falling in heavy armour, often with a chain-mailed rider coming behind them, mace swinging to smash off their heads.

All day, in snow which whirled around them like feathers in a poultry shop, the two armies thrust and stabbed and pushed one another, going nowhere, without hope of victory, as if they were trapped inside a nightmare of pointless rage. A man falling was replaced by a reserve who would step on his body to reach up for a killer stab. Only when it started to grow dark, in the eerie white-skied twilight of spring snow, did the Lancastrian front rank started to yield ground. The first falling back was pressed hard, and they dropped back again, until those at the sides felt their fear rise greater than their rage and one by one started to break away.

At once, they gained relief, for the York men also disengaged and stepped back. Stafford, sensing a lull in the battle, rested for a moment on his sword and looked around him.

He could see the front line of the Lancaster army starting to peel away, like unwilling haymakers, heading early for home. 'Hi!' he shouted. 'Stand. Stand for Stafford! Stand for the king!' but their pace only quickened, and they did not look back.

'My horse,' he shouted. He knew that he must get after them, and halt their retreat before they started to run in earnest. He slipped his dirty sword into its scabbard and started a stumbling run towards his horse lines, and as he ran he glanced to his right and then froze in horror.

The Yorks had not dropped back for a breath and a rest, as so often happened in battle, but had broken from the fight to run as fast as they could to their own horse lines to get their horses, and the men who had been on foot, savagely pressing the Lancaster men at arms, were now mounted and riding down on them, maces swinging, broadswords out, lances pointed down at throat height. Stafford leaped over a dying horse and threw himself face down on the ground behind it as the whistle of the ball of a mace swung through the air just where his head had been. He heard a grunt of fear and knew his own voice. He heard a thunder of hooves, a cavalry charge coming towards him, and he felt himself contract like a frightened snail, against the belly of the groaning horse. Above him, a rider jumped the horse and man in one leap and Stafford saw the hooves beside his face, felt the wind as they went over, flinched against the splash of mud and snow, clung to the dying horse without pride.

When the thunder of the first rush of cavalry was past him,

cautiously he raised his head. The York knights were like huntsmen, riding down the Lancaster men at arms who were running like deer towards the bridge over Cock Beck, the little river at the side of the meadow, their only escape. The York foot soldiers, cheering on the riders, raced beside them to head off the running enemy, before they could reach the bridge. In moments, the bridge became a mass of struggling, fighting men, Lancastrians desperate to get across and away, York soldiers pulling them back, or stabbing them in the back as they scrambled over their fallen comrades. The bridge creaked as the soldiers surged back and forth, the horses pushing onwards, forcing men over the guard rails into the freezing river, trampling the others underfoot. Dozens of men seeing the knights coming on with their great double-edged swords swinging like scythes on either side of their horses' heads, seeing the war horses rear up and bring down their great iron-shod hooves on men's heads, simply jumped into the river where soldiers were still struggling, some thrashing against the weight of their armour, others locked on each other's heads and shoulders, forcing them down to drown in the icy, reddened waters.

Stafford staggered to his feet, horrified. 'Get back! Regroup!' he shouted; but knew that no man would listen to him, and then he heard, above the screams of the battle, the timbers of the bridge shiver and groan.

'Clear the bridge! Clear the bridge!' Stafford fought his way, pushing and shoving, towards the bank to shout at the men, still stabbing and hacking though they could all feel the bridge start to sway under the shifting load. The men cried out warnings but they still fought, hoping to make an end and break away, and then the rails of the bridge went outwards, and the timber supports cracked, and the whole structure went down, throwing men, enemies, horses and corpses all as one into the water.

''Ware bridge!' Stafford shouted on the river bank, then as the enormity of the defeat started to sink in, ''Ware bridge!' he said more softly.

For a moment, as the snow fell around him and the men in the fast flowing water went down and came up shouting for help and were then pulled down again by the weight of their armour, it was as if everything had gone very quiet, and he was the only man alive in the world. He looked around and could not see another man standing. There were some clinging to the timbers and still hacking at each other's grasping fingers, there were some drowning before him, or being swept away in the bloodstained flood; on the battlefield the men on the ground lay still, slowly disappearing under the falling snow.

Stafford, chilled in the cold air, felt the snow fall cleanly on his sweaty face, put out his tongue like a child and felt the flake rest and then melt in the warmth of his mouth. Out of the whiteness another man walked slowly, like a ghost. Wearily, Stafford turned and dragged his sword from the scabbard and readied himself for another fight. He did not think he had the strength to hold up his heavy sword, but he knew he must find from somewhere the courage to kill another fellow countryman.

'Peace,' the man said in a voice drained of emotion. 'Peace, friend. It's over.'

'Who's won?' Stafford asked. Beside them the river was rolling corpses over and over in the flood. In the field all around them men were getting to their feet or crawling to their lines. Most of them were not moving at all.

'Who cares?' the man said. 'I know I have lost all my troop.'

'You are wounded?' Stafford asked as the man staggered.

The man took away his hand from his armpit. At once blood gushed out and splashed to the ground. A sword had stabbed him in the underarm joint of his armour. 'I will die, I think,' he said quietly and now Stafford saw that his face was as white as the snow on his shoulders.

'Here,' he said. 'Come on. I have my horse near. We can get to Towton, we can get you strapped up.'

'I don't know if I can make it.'

'Come on,' Stafford urged. 'Let's get out of this alive.' At once, it seemed tremendously important that one man, this one man, should survive the carnage with him.

The man leaned against him and the two of them hobbled wearily uphill towards the Lancaster lines. The stranger hesitated, gripped his wound, and choked on a laugh.

'What is it? Come on. You can make it! What is it?'

'We're going uphill? Your horse is on the ridge?'

'Yes, of course.'

'You're for Lancaster?'

Stafford staggered under his weight. 'Aren't you?'

'York. You are my enemy.'

Embracing each other like brothers the two men glared at each other for a moment and then both brokenly laughed.

'How would I know?' the man said. 'Good God, my own brother is on the other side. I just assumed you were for York, but how could any man tell?'

Stafford shook his head. 'God knows what I am, or what will happen, or what I will have to be,' he said. 'And God knows that a battle like this is no way to resolve it.'

'Have you fought before in these wars?'

'Never, and if I can, I never will again.'

'You'll have to come before King Edward and surrender yourself,' the stranger said.

'King Edward,' Stafford repeated. 'That's the first time I have heard the boy of York called king.'

'This is the new king,' the man said certainly. 'And I will ask him to forgive you and release you to your home. He will be merciful, though if it were the other way round and you took me to your queen and to your prince, I swear I would not survive them. She kills unarmed prisoners – we don't. And her son is a thing of horror.'

'Come on then,' Stafford said, and the two of them fell into line with the Lancaster soldiers waiting to beg pardon of the new king and promise never to raise arms against him again. Before them were Lancaster families that Stafford had known all his life, among them Lord Rivers and his son Anthony, their heads bowed, silent under the shame of defeat. Stafford cleaned his sword while he waited, and readied himself to offer it up. It was still snowing, and the wound in his leg was throbbing as he walked slowly up to the crest of the ridge where the empty pole for the royal standard still stood at the peak with the Lancaster standard bearers dead all around it and the York boy standing tall.

My husband does not come back from the war like a hero. He comes quietly, with no stories of battle and no tales of chivalry. Twice, three times, I ask him what it was like, thinking that it might have been like Joan's battles: a war in the name of God for the king ordained by God, hoping that he might have seen a sign from God – like the three suns over the York victory – something that would tell us that God is with us despite the setback of defeat. But he says nothing, he will tell me nothing, he behaves as if war is not a glorious thing at all, as if it is not the working out of God's will by ordeal.

All he will tell me, briefly, is that the king and the queen got safely away with the prince, the head of my house, Henry Beaufort, with them. They have fled to Scotland and will, no doubt, rebuild their shaken army, and that Edward of York must have the luck of the hedgerow rose of his badge, for he fought in grief and mist at Mortimer's Cross, uphill in snow at Towton, and won both battles, and is now crowned King of England by public acclaim.

We spend the summer quietly, almost as if we are in hiding. My husband may have been pardoned for riding out against the new King of England but no-one is likely to forget that we are one of the great families of the Lancaster connection, and that I am the mother of a boy in line to the lost throne. Henry goes up to London to gather news, and brings me back a beautifully copied manuscript of *The Imitation of Christ* in French that he thinks I might translate into English, as part of my studies. I know he is trying to keep my mind from the defeat of my house, and the despair of England, and I thank him for his consideration, and start to study; but my heart is not in it.

I wait for news from Jasper but I imagine he is lost in the same sorrow that greets me on waking, every morning, before I am even fully awake. Every day I open my eyes and realise with such a sick pang in my heart, that my cousin the king is in exile – who knows where? – and our enemy is on his throne. I spend days on my knees but God sends me no sign that these days are only to test us, and that the true king will be restored. Then, one morning, I am in the stable yard, when a messenger comes riding in, muddy and travel-stained, on a little Welsh pony. I know at once that he brings me word, at last, from Jasper.

As usual, he is brusque.

William Herbert is to be given all of Wales, all my lands and my castles as prize for turning his coat back to York. The new king has made him a baron also. He will hunt me down as I hunted him, and I doubt that I will get a pardon from a tender king as he did. I will have to leave Wales. Will you come and fetch your boy? I will meet you at Pembroke Castle within the month. I won't be able to wait longer than that. J

I round on the stable lad. 'Where is my husband, where is Sir Henry?'

'He is riding the fields with his land steward, my lady,' the boy says.

'Saddle my horse, I must see him,' I say. They bring Arthur from his stall and he catches my impatience and tosses his head while they fiddle with the bridle and I say: 'Hurry, hurry.' As soon as he is ready, I am in the saddle and riding out towards the barley fields.

I can see my husband riding the margins of the field, talking to his land steward, and I kick Arthur into a rolling canter and come up to him in a rush that makes his own horse sidle and curvet in the mud.

'Steady,' my husband says, drawing rein. 'What's the matter?'

In reply, I thrust the letter at him, and wave the land steward out of earshot. 'We have to fetch Henry,' I say. 'Jasper will meet us at Pembroke Castle. He has to go. We have to go there.'

He is infuriatingly slow. He takes the letter and reads it, then he turns his horse's head for home and reads it again, as he rides.

'We have to leave at once,' I say.'

'As soon as it is safe to do so.'

'I must fetch my son. Jasper himself tells me to fetch him!'

'Jasper's judgement is not of the best, as perhaps you can now see, since his cause is lost and he is running away to France or Brittany or Flanders and leaving your son without a guardian.'

'He has to!'

'Anyway, he is going. His advice is not material. I will muster a suitable guard and if the roads are safe enough, I will go and fetch Henry.'

'*You* will go?' I am so anxious for my son that I forget to hide the scorn in my voice.

'Yes. I, myself. Did you think me too decrepit to ride to Wales in haste?'

'There may be soldiers on the way. William Herbert's army will be on the road. You are likely to cross their path.'

'Then we shall have to hope that my ancient years and grey hairs protect me,' he says with a smile.

I don't even hear the joke. 'You have to get through,' I say, 'or Jasper will leave my boy alone at Pembroke, and Herbert will take him.'

'I know.'

We come into the stable yard and he has a quiet word with Graham, his master of horse, and next thing all the men at arms are tumbling from our house and from the stable yard, and the chapel bell is tolling to call the tenants to muster. It is all done at such speed and efficiency that for the first time I see that my husband has command of his men.

'Can I come too?' I ask. 'Please, husband. He is my son. I want to bring him safely home.'

He looks thoughtful. 'It will be a hard ride.'

'You know I am strong.'

'There might be danger. Graham says that there are no armies near here; but we are going to have to cross most of England and nearly all of Wales.'

'I am not afraid, and I will do as you order.'

He pauses for a moment.

'I beg you,' I say. 'Husband, we have been married three and a half years and I have never asked you for anything.'

He nods. 'Oh, very well. You can come too. Go and pack your things. You can bring only a saddle bag, and tell them to put a change of clothes up for me. Tell them to pack provisions for fifty men.'

If I commanded the house, I would do it myself, but I am still served as a guest. So I get off my horse and go to the groom of the servery and tell him that his master, and I, and the guard, are going on a journey and we will need food and drink. Then I tell my maid and Henry's servant to pack a bag for us both and I go back to the stable yard to wait.

They are ready within the hour, and my husband comes out of the house with his travelling cloak carried on his arm. 'D'you have a thick cloak?' he asks me. 'No, I thought not. You can have this and I will use an old one. Take it, strap it to your saddle.'

Arthur is steady as I mount him, as if he knows that we have work to do. My husband draws up his horse beside mine. 'If we see an army, then Will and his brother will ride away with you. You are to do as they order. They are commanded to ride with you for home, or for the nearest house of safety, as fast as they can. Their task is to keep you safe, you are to do as they say.'

'Not if it is our army,' I point out. 'What if we meet the queen's army on the road?'

He grimaces. 'We won't see the queen's army,' he says shortly. 'The queen could not pay for an archer, let alone a troop. We will not see her again until she can make an alliance with France.'

'Well anyway, I promise,' I say. I nod at Will and his brother. 'I will go with them when you tell me I must.'

My husband nods, his face grim, and then turns his horse so he is at the head of our little guard – about fifty mounted men armed with nothing but a handful of swords and a few axes – and leads us west for Wales.

❦

It takes us more than ten days of hard riding every day to get there. We go west on poor roads, skirting the town of Warwick and going cross country wherever we can, for fear of meeting an army: any army, friend or foe. Every night we have to go to a village, an ale house or an abbey and find someone who can guide us for the next day. This is the very heart of England and many people know no further than their parish boundaries. My husband sends scouts a good mile ahead of us with orders that if there is any sign of outriders from any army, they are to gallop back to warn us and we will turn off the road and get into hiding in the forest. I cannot believe that we must hide, even from our own army. We are Lancaster, but the Lancaster army that the queen has brought down on her country is out of all control. Some nights the men have to sleep in a barn while Henry and I beg hospitality in a farmhouse. Some nights we take a room at an inn on the road, one night in an abbey where they have dozens of guest rooms and are used to serving small armies of men marching from one battle to another. They don't even ask us which lord we serve, but I see that there is no gold and silver on show in the church. They will have buried their treasures in some hiding place and are praying for peaceful times to come again.

We don't go to the big houses nor to any of the castles that we can sometimes see on the hills overlooking the road, or sheltered by great woods. The victory of York has been so complete that we don't dare advertise that we are riding to save my son, an heir to the House of Lancaster. I understand now what Henry my husband tried to tell me before, that the country is blighted not only by war, but by the constant threat of war. Families who have been friends and neighbours for years avoid each other in fear, and even I, riding towards land that belonged to my first husband, whose name is still beloved, am fearful of meeting anyone who might remember me.

On the road, when I am exhausted and aching in every bone in my body, I learn that Henry Stafford cares for me, without ever making a fuss over me, or suggesting that I am a weak woman, and should not have come. He lifts me down from my horse when we take a rest, and he sees that I have wine and water. When we stop for dinner he gets my food himself, even before he is served, and then he spreads out his own cloak for my bed, and covers me up and makes me rest. We are lucky with the weather and it does not rain on our journey, and he rides beside me in the mornings and teaches me the songs that the soldiers sing: bawdy songs for which he invents new words for me.

He makes me laugh with his nonsense songs, and he tells me of his own childhood, as a younger son of the great House of Stafford and how his father meant him for the church until he begged to be excused. They would not release him from their plan until he told the priest that he feared he was possessed by the devil, and they were all so anxious about the state of his soul that they gave up the idea of the priesthood for him.

In return, I tell him how I wanted to be a saint, and how glad I was when I found I had saints' knees, and he laughs out loud at that and puts his hand over mine on my reins, and calls me a darling child, and his very own.

I had thought him a coward when he would not go to war and when he came back so silent from the battlefield; but I was wrong. He is a very cautious man and he believes whole heartedly in nothing. He would not be a priest for he could not give himself wholly to God. He was glad that he was not born the oldest, for he did not want to be duke and head of such a great house. He is of the House of Lancaster, but he dislikes and fears the queen. He is enemy to the House of York, but he thinks highly of Warwick and admires the courage of the boy of York, and surrendered his sword to him. He would not dream of going into exile like Jasper, he likes his home too much. He does not align himself with any lord but he thinks for himself, and I see now what he means when he says he is not a hound to yelp when the huntsman blows the horn. He considers everything in the light of what might be right, and what would be the best outcome for himself, for his family, his affinity and even for his country. He is not a man to give himself easily. Not like Jasper. He is not a man for these times of passion and hot temper.

'A little caution.' He smiles at me as Arthur splashes stolidly through the great river crossing of the Severn, the gateway to Wales. 'We have been born into difficult times where a man or even a woman has to choose their own way, has to choose their loyalties. I think it is right to go carefully and to think before acting.'

'I have always thought one should do the right thing,' I say. 'And nothing but that.'

'Yes, but then you wanted to be a saint.' He smiles. 'Now you are the mother of a child, now you have to consider not only what is the right thing to do, but if it is likely to keep you and your son safe. You will want to keep your son safe more than anything in the world. The safety of your son may matter to you more than the will of God.'

For a moment I am puzzled by this. 'But it must be the will of God that my son is safe,' I say. 'My son is without sin, and he is of the royal line. He is of the only true royal house. God must want him to be safe to serve the House of Lancaster. What I wish and what God wishes must be the same.'

'Do you really think God, in his heaven with all the angels, there from the beginning of time and looking towards the Day of Judgement, really looks down on all the world and sees you and little Henry Tudor and says that whatever you choose to do is His will?'

It sounds like blasphemy somewhere. 'Yes, I do,' I say uncertainly. 'Jesus Christ Himself promised that I am as precious as the lilies of the field.'

'And so you are,' he says with a smile, as if comforting me with a story.

That silences me and makes me think for the rest of the ride. 'So, do you think there are many men like you, who have not given their hearts to one side or another?' I ask as he helps me down from the saddle in the yard of a dirty little inn, on the road to Cardiff, that evening.

He pats Arthur's dark neck. 'I think most men will choose to follow the house that can promise them peace and safety,' he says. 'There is loyalty to the king, of course; no-one can deny that King Henry is crowned King of England. But what if he is not fit to rule? What if he is ill again and can do nothing? What if he is commanded by the queen? What if she is ill advised? How can it be a crime to want the next heir in his place? If that claimant was of the royal line also? If he was as close as a cousin? If he has as good a claim to the throne as Henry?'

I am so weary that I lean back against Arthur's big comfortable shoulder, and then my husband draws me to him and holds me. 'Don't you worry about this now,' he says. 'The main thing is that we get your boy and make sure he is safe. Then you can consider who God and you would prefer to rule the kingdom.'

On the tenth morning of our journey, travelling now on tiny, stony lanes through high, mountainous country, my husband says to me, 'We should be there by midday,' and I gasp at the thought of seeing my boy again so soon. We send scouts ahead to the castle to see if it is safe to approach. It looks as if everything is quiet. We wait out of sight, and my husband points out to me that the gates of the castle are open, and the drawbridge down, and as we watch a girl comes out with a flock of geese and calls them down to the river.

'Looks safe enough,' my husband says cautiously and gets off his horse and helps me down and the two of us go to the other side of the river. The geese are swimming on the water, some are dabbling their yellow beaks in the mud, the girl is seated on the bank, fiddling about with some lace.

'Girl, who is the master of the castle?' my husband asks her.

She jumps at the sound of his voice and scrambles to her feet and bobs a curtsey. 'It was the Earl of Pembroke but he ran away to the wars,' she says, her accent so strong I can hardly make out what she is saying.

'Anyone taken the castle since he left?'

'Nay, we're just hoping he'll come back. D'you know where he is, sir?'

'I don't know. Is the little lad in the castle nursery?'

'The little earl? Yes, he's there. I keep the hens too and I send in a good new-laid egg for him every morning.'

'Do you?' I am unable to silence my delight. 'Does he have a fresh-laid egg for his breakfast every day?'

'Oh yes,' she says. 'And they say he likes a slice of roast chicken too for his dinner.'

'How many men at arms?' my husband interrupts.

'A hundred,' she says. 'But three times that rode out with Jasper Tudor and didn't come back. They say it was a terrible defeat. They say that God set three suns in the sky to curse our boys, and now the three sons of York will curse our country.'

My husband spins a coin across the river to her and she catches it with snatching hands. We go back to where our men are hidden by the turn in the road and we mount up. My husband orders them to unfurl our standard and to go forwards at slow walk and halt when he gives the word. 'We don't want a flight of arrows as our welcome,' he says to me. 'You and Will and Stephen go to the rear of the ride, just to be safe.'

I am desperate to ride into the castle that was once my home; but I do as he orders me, and we go slowly forwards until we hear the shouted challenge from the castle walls and at the same time we hear the roar of the chain and the great portcullis comes clanging down. My husband and his standard bearer ride up to the gate and shout our name to the officer on the walls of the castle, and then the portcullis creaks up and we ride into the courtyard.

Arthur goes at once to the old mounting block and I dismount without help and I let his reins go. He heads at once for his old stall, as if he were still Owen Tudor's battle horse. The stable lad exclaims to see him, and I go quickly to the front door and the groom of the household flings it open before me, recognises me though I have grown taller, bows to me and says: 'My lady.'

'Where is my son?' I ask. 'In his nursery?'

'Yes,' he says. 'I will have them bring him to you.'

'I'll go up,' I say, and without waiting I run up the stairs and burst into his nursery.

He is eating his dinner. They have laid a table for him with a spoon and a knife and he is seated at the head of the table and they are waiting on him as they should, as an earl should be served. He turns his little head as I come in, and he looks at me without recognition. His curly hair is brown, like a bright bay horse as Jasper said, his eyes are hazel. His face is baby-round still; but he is not a baby any more, he is a boy, a little boy of four years old.

He climbs down from his chair, he has to use the rungs of the chair as steps, and comes towards me. He bows, he has been well taught. 'Welcome, madam, to Pembroke Castle,' he says. He has the slightest lilt of a Welsh accent in his clear, high voice. 'I am the Earl of Richmond.'

I drop to my knees so my face is level with his. I so long to snatch him into my arms; but I have to remember that to him I am a stranger.

'Your Uncle Jasper will have told you about me,' I say.

His face lights up with joy. 'Is he here? Is he safe?'

I shake my head. 'No, I am sorry. I believe he is safe; but he is not here.'

His little mouth trembles. I am so afraid that he will cry, I put my hand out to him but at once he straightens up and I see his little jaw square as he holds back tears. He nips his lower lip. 'Will he come back?'

'I am sure of it. Soon.'

He nods, he blinks. One tear rolls down his cheek.

'I am your mother, Lady Margaret,' I say to him. 'I have come to take you to my home.'

'You are my mother?'

I try to smile but I give a little choke. 'I am. I have ridden for nearly two weeks to come to you to make sure you are safe.'

'I am safe,' he says solemnly. 'I am just waiting for my Uncle Jasper to come home. I can't come with you. He told me to stay here.'

The door behind me opens and Henry enters quietly. 'And this is my husband, Sir Henry Stafford,' I say to my little son.

The boy steps away from the table and bows. Jasper has taught him well. My husband, hiding his smile, bows solemnly in return.

'Welcome to Pembroke Castle, sir.'

'I thank you,' my husband says. He glances at me, taking in the tears in my eyes and my flushed face. 'Is everything all right?'

I make a helpless gesture with my hand as if to say – yes, everything is all right, except my son treats me as a polite stranger and the only person he wants to see is Jasper who is an attainted traitor and in exile for life. My husband nods as if he can understand all of this, and then turns to my son. 'My men have ridden all the way from England, and they have extremely fine horses. I wonder if you would like to see them in their harness before the horses are put into the fields?'

Henry brightens at once. 'How many men?'

'Fifty men at arms, a few servants and scouts.'

He nods. This is a boy who was born into a country at war and was raised by one of the greatest commanders of our house. He would rather inspect a troop than eat his dinner.

'I should like to see them. I will get my jacket.' He goes into his private chamber and we can hear him calling for his nursemaid to fetch his best jacket as he is going to inspect his mother's guard.

Henry smiles at me. 'Nice little fellow,' he says.

'He didn't recognise me.' I am holding back tears but the quaver in my voice betrays me. 'He has no idea who I am. I am a complete stranger to him.'

'Of course, but he will learn,' Henry says soothingly. 'He will come to know you. You can be a mother to him. He is only four, you have missed only three years, you can start again with him now. And he has been well-raised and well-educated.'

'He is Jasper's boy through and through,' I say jealously.

Henry draws my hand through his arm. 'And now you will make him yours. After he has seen my men, you show him Arthur and tell him that he was Owen Tudor's battle horse, but that you ride him now. You'll see, he will want to know all about it and you can tell him stories.'

I take a seat in silence in the nursery as they prepare him for bed. The mistress of the nursery is still the woman that Jasper appointed when my son was born, she has cared for him all his life, and I find myself burning with envy at her easy way with him, at the companionable way she hauls him to her knee and strips off his little shirt, at the familiar way that she tickles him as she pulls on his nightshirt and scolds him for wriggling like a Severn eel. He is deliciously at ease with her; but now and then he remembers that I am there and shoots me a little shy smile, as a polite child at a stranger.

'Would you like to hear him say his prayers?' she asks me, as he goes through to his bedroom.

Resentfully, in second place, I follow her to see him kneel at the foot of his tester bed, fold his hands together and recite the Lord's Prayer and the prayers for the evening. She hands me a badly transcribed prayer book and I read the collect for the day and the prayer for the evening and hear his soprano 'Amen'. Then he crosses himself and rises up and goes to her for her blessing. She steps back and gestures to him that he should kneel to me. I see his little mouth turn down; but he kneels before me, obediently enough, and I put my hand on his head and say: 'God bless you and keep you, my son.' Then he rises up and takes a great run and a leap into his bed and bounces until she folds back the sheet and tucks him up and bends and kisses him in one thoughtless gesture.

Awkwardly, a stranger in his nursery, uncertain of my welcome, I go to his bedside and lean over him. I kiss him. His cheek is warm, the smell of his skin like a new-baked bread roll, firm as a warm peach.

'Goodnight,' I say again.

I step back from the bed. The woman moves the candle away from the curtains, and pulls up her chair to the fire. She is going to sit with him till he sleeps, as she does every night, as she has done every night since his birth. He has gone to sleep with the creak of the treadles of her rocking chair and the reassuring sight of her beloved face in the firelight. There is nothing for me to do here, he has no need of me at all. 'Goodnight,' I say again, and I go quietly from his room.

I close the outer door of his presence chamber and pause at the head of the stone stairs. I am just about to go down in search of my husband when I hear a door above me, high up in the tower, quietly open. It is a door that goes out to the roof where Jasper used to sometimes go to gaze up at the stars, or during troubled times, look out across the country for an enemy army. My first thought is that Black Herbert has got someone into Pembroke Castle and he is coming down the stairs with his knife drawn, ready to let in his troop through the sally port. I press myself back against Henry's bedroom door, ready to fling myself into his room and lock the door behind me, I must keep him safe. I can raise the alarm from his bedroom window. I would lay down my life for him.

I hear a quiet footstep, and then the closing of the roof door, and then the turning of the key, and I hold my breath so that there shall be no sound but another quiet step, as whoever it is comes silently down the spiral stone stairs of the tower.

And at once, as if I could recognise him by his footstep, I know it is Jasper, and I step out from the shadow and say quietly, 'Jasper, oh Jasper!' and he takes the last three steps in a bound and has his arms around me and is holding me tightly to him and my arms are around his broad back and we are gripping each other as if we cannot bear to let each other go. I pull myself back so I can look up at him and at once his mouth comes down on mine and he kisses me, and I am shot through with such desire and such longing that it is like being at prayer when God answers in flame.

That thought of prayer makes me pull away from him and gasp, and he releases me at once.

'I am sorry.'

'No!'

'I thought you would be at dinner or in the solar. I meant to come to you and your husband quietly.'

'I was with my boy.'

'Was he pleased to see you?'

I make a little gesture. 'He is more concerned with you. He is missing you. How long have you been here?'

'I have been in the area for nearly a week. I didn't want to come to the castle for fear of Herbert's spies. I didn't want to bring him down on us. So I have been hiding out in the hills, waiting for you to come.'

'I came as soon as I could. Oh, Jasper, do you have to go away?'

His arm is around my waist again, and I cannot stop myself leaning against him. I have grown taller, my head rests against his shoulder. I feel as if I fit him, as if his body were a piece of fretwork, hammered to interlock with mine. I feel as if I will ache all my life if we are not fitted together.

'Margaret, my own love, I have to go,' he says simply. 'There is a price on my head, and bad blood between Herbert and me. But I will be back. I will go to France or Scotland and recruit for the true king, and I will return with an army. You can be sure of it. I will come back and this will be my castle once more, when Lancaster is on the throne again and we have won.'

I find I am clinging to him, and I unclench my hands from where I am holding his jacket, step back and force myself to let him go. The space that I make between us, no more than a foot or so, is an unbearable void.

'And you, are you well?' His direct blue eyes scan my face, run frankly down my body. 'No child?'

'No,' I say shortly. 'It doesn't seem to happen. I don't know why.'

'He treats you well?'

'He does. He lets me have the chapel as I wish it, and he lets me study. He gives me an allowance from my lands that is generous. He even gets me books, he helps me with Latin.'

'A treat indeed,' he says solemnly.

'Well, it is for me,' I say defensively.

'And how will he stand with King Edward?' he asks. 'Are you in any danger?'

'I think not. He rode out for King Henry at Towton . . .'

'He went to war?'

I nearly giggle. 'He did; and I don't think he liked it much. But he has been pardoned and his pardon should cover me. We'll take Henry home with us and live quietly. When the true king comes into his own again, we will be ready. I doubt that York will trouble himself with us. Surely he has greater enemies? Sir Henry does not play a big part in the affairs of the world, he likes to stay at home, quietly. Surely, he has made himself so unimportant that nobody will bother with us?'

Jasper grins, a young man born to play a part in the great affairs of the world and quite incapable of staying at home quietly. 'Perhaps. At any rate, I am glad he will keep you and the boy safe while I am away.'

I cannot resist stepping forwards and taking hold of the lapel of his jacket again so I can look up earnestly into his face. His arm comes around my waist and holds me closer. 'Jasper, how long will you be gone?'

'As soon as I can muster an army that can retake Wales for the king, I'll be back,' he promises me. 'These are my lands and my cause. My father died for them, my brother died for them, I won't let their deaths be in vain.'

I nod. I can feel the heat of his body through his jacket.

'And don't you let them persuade you that York is the true king,' he warns me in an urgent whisper. 'Bow your knee and bend your head and smile but know always that Lancaster is the royal house and while the king is alive we have a king. While Prince Edward is alive we have a Prince of Wales, and while your son is alive we have an heir to the throne. Stay true.'

'I do,' I whisper. 'I always will. There will never be anyone for me but . . .'

A clattering sound from lower down the well of the stair startles us both and reminds me that I should be at dinner. 'Will you come to eat with us?' I ask.

He shakes his head. 'I'd rather not be seen. The moment Herbert knows I am here he will have the castle surrounded and I don't want you and the boy exposed to danger. I'll get some food sent up to the nursery, and I will meet you and your husband in the solar after dinner, and tomorrow morning I leave.'

I tighten my grip on him. 'So soon? You won't go so soon? I have hardly seen you! Henry will want to see you!'

'I have to go and the longer I stay, the more danger you are in, and the more likely I am to be caught. Now that the boy is in your keeping I can leave him with a clear conscience.'

'And you can leave me?'

He smiles his crooked smile. 'Ah, Margaret, all the time I have known you, you have been the wife of another man. I am a courtly lover, as it turns out. A troubadour to a distant mistress. I don't ask for more than a smile and to be in your prayers. I love from afar.'

'But this is going to be very far,' I say childishly.

Silently, he puts a gentle finger to my cheek and wipes away a single tear.

'How shall I live without you?' I whisper.

'I can't do anything to dishonour you,' he says gently.

'Really, Margaret, I could not. You are my brother's widow and your son carries a great name. I have to love and serve you, and for now, I serve you best by going away and mustering an army to take your son's lands back into my keeping, and to defeat those who would deny his house.'

The trumpet call, which announces that dinner is ready to be served, echoes up the stone well of the stair, making me jump.

'Go on,' Jasper says. 'I will see you and your husband in the solar later. You can tell him I am here.'

He gives me a little push and I start down the stairs. As I look back I see that he has gone into the nursery. I realise that he trusts Henry's nurse with his life, and he has gone to sit beside my sleeping boy.

Jasper joins us in the solar after dinner. 'I shall leave early tomorrow,' he says. 'There are men here that I can trust to take me to Tenby, I have a ship waiting there. Herbert is looking for me in the north of Wales, he can't get here in time, even if he hears of me.'

I glance at my husband. 'Can we ride with you and see you leave?' I ask.

Jasper politely waits for my husband to rule.

'As you wish,' Sir Henry says levelly. 'If Jasper thinks it safe. It might help the boy to see you safely away, he is likely to pine for you.'

'It's safe enough,' Jasper says. 'I had thought Herbert was on my tail but he has taken a false scent.'

'At dawn then,' my husband says pleasantly. He rises to his feet and puts out a hand to me. 'Come, Margaret.'

I hesitate. I want to stay by the fireside with Jasper. He will go tomorrow and we will have no time alone together at all. I wonder that my husband does not see this, does not understand that I might want some time alone with this friend of my childhood, this guardian of my son.

His weary smile would have told me – if I had been looking at him – that he understood this completely, and much more. 'Come, wife,' he says gently, and at that bidding Jasper gets to his feet and bows over my hand, so I have to go to bed with my husband, and leave my dearest friend, my only friend, sitting alone over the fire for his last evening in the home that we used to share.

In the morning I see a different child in my boy Henry. His face is bright with happiness, he is his uncle's little shadow, he follows him like an enthusiastic puppy. His manners are still beautiful, perhaps even better when he knows that his guardian is watching him, but there is a joy in every movement when he can look up and see Jasper's approving smile. He serves him like a pageboy, standing behind him proudly holding his gloves, stepping forwards to take the reins of the great horse. Once, he stops a groom bringing a whip: 'Lord Pembroke doesn't like that whip,' he says. 'Get the one with the plaited end,' and the man bows and runs to obey.

Jasper and he walk side by side to inspect the guard who have assembled to ride with us to Tenby. Henry walks just as Jasper does, his hands clasped behind his back, his eyes intent on the faces of the men, though he has to look up as they tower above him. He stops, just as Jasper does, from time to time to remark on a well-honed weapon, or on a well-groomed horse. To see my little boy inspecting the guard, the very mirror of the great commander who is his uncle, is to watch a prince serving his apprenticeship.

'What does Jasper think his future will be?' my husband wonders in my ear. 'For he is training a little tyrant here.'

'He thinks he will rule Wales as his father and grandfather did,' I say shortly. 'At the very least.'

'And what at the most?'

I turn my head and I don't answer, for I know the extent of Jasper's ambition in the regal bearing of my son. Jasper is raising an heir to the throne of England.

'If they had weapons, or even boots, this would be a little more impressive,' my husband the Englishman remarks quietly in my ear; and for the first time I notice that many of the guard are indeed barefoot, and many of them have only sickles or coppicing hooks. They are an army of country men, not professional soldiers. Most of Jasper's battle-hardened, well-equipped guard died under the three suns of Mortimer's Cross, the rest of them at Towton.

Jasper reaches the end of the line of soldiers, and snaps his fingers for his horse. Henry turns and nods to the groom as if to tell him to hurry. He is to ride before his uncle and from the confident way that Jasper swings up into the big saddle and then bends down to offer Henry his hand, I can tell that they have done this often. Henry stretches up to reach Jasper's big hand, and is hauled up to sit before him. He nestles back into his uncle's firm grip and beams with pride.

'March on,' Jasper says quietly. 'For God and the Tudors.'

I think that Henry will cry when we get to the little fishing port of Tenby and Jasper swings him down to the ground and then jumps down beside him. For a moment Jasper kneels, and his copper head and Henry's brown curls are very close. Then Jasper straightens up and says, 'Like a Tudor, eh, Henry?' and my little boy looks up to his uncle and says, 'Like a Tudor, sir!' and solemnly the two of them clasp hands. Jasper claps him on the back so hard as to nearly knock him off his little feet, and then turns to me.

'Godspeed,' Jasper says to me. 'I don't like long farewells.'

'Godspeed,' I say. My voice is trembling and I don't dare to add more before my husband and the men of the guard.

'I'll write,' Jasper says. 'Keep the boy safe. Don't spoil him.'

I am so irritated by Jasper telling me how to care for my own son that I can hardly speak for a moment, but then I bite my lip. 'I will.'

Jasper turns to my husband. 'Thank you for coming,' he says formally. 'It is good to hand Henry over in safety, to a guardian I can trust.'

My husband inclines his head. 'Good luck,' he says quietly. 'I will keep them both safe.'

Jasper turns on his heel and is about to walk away when he checks, turns back to Henry and sweeps him up for a quick, hard hug. When he puts the little boy gently down, I see that Jasper's blue eyes are filled with tears. Then he takes the reins of his horse, and leads it carefully and quietly onto the ramp to the boat. A dozen men go with him, the rest wait with us. I glance at their faces and see their aghast look, as their lord and commander shouts to the master of the ship that he can cast off.

They throw the lines to the ship, they raise the sail. At first it seems as if it is not moving at all, but then the sails flap and quiver and the wind and the force of the tide slides the ship from the little stone quayside. I step forwards and put my hand on my little son's shoulder, he is trembling like a foal. He does not turn his head at my touch, he is straining his eyes to see the last possible sight of his guardian. Only when the ship is a little distant dot at sea does he take a shuddering breath and drop his head and I feel his shoulders heave with a sob.

'Would you like to ride before me?' I ask him quietly. 'You can sit up before me like you did with Jasper.'

He looks up at me. 'No thank you, my lady,' he says.

I devote myself to my son in the following weeks that we spend at Pembroke Castle. An armed band, little better than brigands, is threatening the road to England and my husband decides that we are safer waiting at Pembroke for them to move on, than to ride out and risk meeting them. So I sit with little Henry when he takes his lessons from the tutor that Jasper has employed, I ride with him in the morning, I watch him as he jousts at the little quintain that Jasper had built for him in the field behind the stables. We ride to the river together and we go out in a fishing boat and have the servants build a fire on the beach so we can eat our catch roasted on sticks. I give him toys and a book and a new pony of his own. I personally transcribe his prayers for the day into English, in a better translation from the Latin. I play catch and cards with him. I sing nursery rhymes with him and I read to him in French. I put him to bed and spend the evening planning what he might like to do the next day. I wake him in the morning with a smile. I never discipline him – I let his tutor do that. I never send him to change his clothes or scold him for getting dirty – I let his nurse do that. To him I am a perfect playmate, always happy always ready for a game, happy to let him name the game, happy to let him win, and every night he kneels at his bedside in prayer and I kneel beside him. And every night, whatever we have done during the day, however carefree he seems to have been, he prays God to send his Uncle Jasper home to him so that they can be happy again.

'Why do you still miss Jasper so much?' I ask him, as I tuck him up. I make sure my voice is light, almost indifferent.

His little face brightens against the white linen pillow. He beams at the thought of his uncle. 'He is my lord,' he says simply. 'I am going to ride out with him when I am big enough. We are going to bring peace to England and when that is done we are going on crusade together. We will never be parted. I shall swear fealty to him and be the son that he does not have. He is my lord. I am his man.'

'But I am your mother,' I remark. 'I am here to take care of you now.'

'Jasper and I love you,' he says cheerfully. 'We say you are our guiding light. And we always pray for you, and for my father Edmund too.'

'But I am here now,' I insist. 'And Edmund never even saw you. He hardly counts, it is not the same at all. Jasper is in exile, I am the only one here now.'

He turns his little head, his eyelids are drooping, dark eyelashes brushing his pink cheeks. 'My uncle, Lord Pembroke, is glad to have you at his castle,' he says quietly. 'We are both glad to welcome . . .'

He is asleep. I turn and find my husband leaning silently against the stone doorway. 'Did you hear that?' I ask him. 'All he thinks about is Jasper. He prays for me as he does for his father who was dead before he was born. I am as distant as the queen to him.'

My husband puts out an arm to me and I am glad for the comfort. I rest my head on his chest and feel him hold me.

'He's a bright boy,' he says soothingly. 'You have to give him time to get to know you. He has lived with Jasper for so long that the man fills his world. He has to learn about you. It will come. Be patient. And besides, it is no disadvantage to be as the queen to him. You are his mother, not his nursemaid. Why not be his guiding light, the one who commands him? He has learned from Jasper to adore you from afar. He understands that. Why would you want to be anything else?'

AUTUMN 1461

We are wakened by the clanging of the tocsin, and I jump out of bed, throw on a gown and run to the nursery. My boy is pulling on his breeches and shouting for his boots. The mistress of the nursery looks up as I come in. 'My lady? D'you know what it is?'

I shake my head and look out of the window. The portcullis is coming down with a speedy clatter, the guards and the grooms of the stables are spilling out of their living quarters and shouting. Among the men I see my husband moving quietly and steadily towards the guard tower that overlooks the gate.

'I'm going down,' I say.

'I'll come! I'll come!' my son pipes. 'I need my sword.'

'You don't need your sword,' I say. 'But you can come if you promise to stay with me.'

'May I come with the little earl, please, m'lady?' his nurse asks. I know she thinks that I won't be able to make him stay beside me, and I flush with irritation; but I nod and the three of us run down the stone stairs, across the yard, and up the narrow stairs to the tower where my husband and the captain of the guard are looking over the battlements to where the flag of William Herbert is fluttering over a small army of his men, trotting along the road.

'God be with us,' I whisper.

Henry drags his nurse to the furthest corner of the tower where he can look down on the drawbridge being hauled up.

My husband smiles at me. 'I doubt we are in danger,' he says gently. 'I have no doubt that Herbert has been given this castle, and perhaps the earldom too. He has only come to claim his own. We are his unexpected guests.'

'What will we do?'

'Hand it over to him.'

'Hand it over to him?' I am so shocked at my husband's traitorous plan that I stare at him, my mouth agape. 'Just give him the keys? Of Jasper's castle? Just open the doors and invite him to dine?'

'He might ask us to dine,' my husband corrects me. 'If, as I think, that this is his castle now.'

'You cannot intend to just let him in.'

'Of course I do,' he says. 'If King Edward has given him the castle and the command of Wales then we are behaving as loyal citizens should by giving William Herbert his own and rendering to Caesar his due.'

'This castle belongs to us Tudors,' I spit at him. 'To Jasper, and in his absence to me and Henry. This is Henry's home, this is my castle.'

My husband shakes his grey head. 'No, my dear. You are forgetting that there is a new king on the throne and he will have made new grants and allowances. Lancaster no longer holds the throne, nor Wales, not even Pembroke Castle. For all that this was your home, it will have been given to one of proven loyalty to York. I had thought perhaps William Hastings or Warwick, but as we see, William Herbert is the lucky man.' He glances over the castle wall. They are nearly within hailing distance.

'Jasper would have raised a siege,' I say bitterly. 'Jasper would have defended his own. He would have died rather than hand over our castle to such as Herbert. He would not surrender like a woman. He would have fought. Herbert is a traitor and I won't admit him to Jasper's castle.'

My husband looks at me, and he is no longer smiling. 'Margaret, you see for yourself what Jasper would have done. You see for yourself what choice he made. He saw that the battle was lost and he left the castle, and he left your son, and he left you. He left you without a backward glance. He told you he didn't like long goodbyes and he ran away to secure his own safety, far away. He told me himself that he expected Herbert to come and claim Pembroke, and that he expected us to yield. He told me that he would be glad if we stayed to hand over Pembroke to Herbert and make sure that the servants were safe. Anything like a siege would be to waste our lives for nothing. Anything else and we might as well have run away as he did. The battle is lost, it was lost at Towton, and Jasper knew it and ran away.'

'He didn't run away,' I say hotly.

'He's not here now, is he?' my husband observes. He leans out over the battlements and shouts: 'Hi! Sir William!'

The big man at the front of his men pulls up his horse and dips his standard. 'I am William, Lord Herbert. Who calls me? Is that you, Sir Henry Stafford?'

'The same. I am here with my wife Lady Margaret and her son, the Earl of Richmond.'

'And Jasper Tudor, the traitor, the former Earl of Pembroke?'

Henry pulls at my hand and I bend down to listen to his whisper. 'My uncle is still Earl of Pembroke, isn't he? Why does that bad man say the former earl?'

'We will never call him that,' I swear. 'In our prayers he will always be the Earl of Pembroke to us. It is just the Yorks who think differently. They are all liars.'

'Jasper Tudor is gone away,' Sir Henry shouts back. 'You have my word of honour that he is not in the castle nor nearby.'

'I have been granted the castle and the command of Wales by King Edward, God save him!' Herbert bellows up. 'Will you open the gates and admit me to my own?'

'I will,' Sir Henry says cheerfully, and nods to the captain of the guard. Two men go running and I watch, disbelieving, as the portcullis is cranked up and the drawbridge dropped down, and the red dragon standard of the Tudors, smartly as a traitor, drops down the flagpole and disappears from sight as if it had not fluttered over the castle for all the time that I have known it.

William Herbert tips a salute to the soldiers at the gate and rides into the castle that is now his own, with a merry flourish, and dismounts on my mounting block as if it had been standing there, all these years, just waiting for him.

I am speechless with rage at dinner that night; but my husband and Lord Herbert talk of the new king, of the likelihood of an invasion from France, of the danger of a Scots army marching down on England, as if these were our enemies and not our saviours. I find myself hating my husband for his easy good manners, and I keep my eyes on my plate, and I speak only in reply to a direct question. Indeed, Lord Herbert says almost nothing to me until I rise from the table to withdraw, and then he glances at my husband and says: 'I would speak with both of you about young Henry Tudor. Shall we talk in the solar after dinner?'

'Of course,' my husband says, answering for me and so preventing a refusal. 'I am sure Lady Margaret will have some good wine and fruit waiting for us when we join her there.'

I bow my head and leave them to their drink and their amiable chat, and then wait in my chair by the fireside. I don't have to worry alone for long. The two of them come into the room, now talking about the hunting, and my husband is praising the game that can be hunted near the castle, as if it had not been preserved and guarded by Jasper, as if it were not the inheritance of my son and this man were not an interloper, a poacher if he takes our game.

'I'll be brief,' Lord Herbert says, putting himself before the fire and warming his backside as if the logs were his to burn. 'I am to have custody of the boy Henry and he will live with me. The king will confirm that I am to be his guardian after Christmas.'

My head flies up but my husband does not even look surprised.

'You will live here?' he asks, as if this is all that matters.

'Raglan,' Sir William says shortly. 'It's a better building, and my wife likes it. Henry will be brought up with our children with an education befitting his station. You will be welcome to visit him any time you wish.'

'That's gracious,' my husband says when I am still silent. 'I am sure Lady Margaret is grateful.' His admonitory look towards me prompts me to say something grateful; but I cannot.

'He should stay in my keeping,' I say flatly.

Lord Herbert shakes his head. 'That would never have been allowed, my lady. Your son is heir to an enormous fortune and name. Someone would be bound to bid for him and take him as his ward. In many ways you are lucky it is me. I don't expect you to see it right now, but if a Neville had taken him as their ward he would have had to go far away among strangers.

With me, he can stay in Wales, he can keep his own servants about him, he can be in the country that he knows. My wife is a tender-hearted woman, he will be brought up with my children. He could have done a lot worse.'

'He is my son!' I exclaim. 'He is a Lancaster boy, he is heir to—'

'We're grateful,' my husband says, silencing me.

Lord Herbert looks at me. 'Your son's family connections are a mixed blessing, my lady,' he says. 'I wouldn't boast of them overmuch if I were you. His cousin, the former king, is in exile and plotting with the enemies of our country. His guardian and the head of his house, Jasper Tudor, is in exile with a price on his head as a named traitor. His grandfather was beheaded for treason. I myself captured his father, and your own father's end was less than glorious. I would be glad that he is to be raised in a loyal York household if I were you.'

'She is grateful,' my husband says again. He steps across to me and holds out a peremptory hand. I have to rise to my feet and hold hands with him as if we were in agreement. 'We will tell Henry when he wakes in the morning, and we will go back to our own house in England, as soon as the guards and the horses can be ready.'

'Stay,' says Sir William pleasantly. 'Stay till the boy is accustomed, stay as long as you wish. We can hunt some of those deer that Jasper has taken such trouble to preserve.' He laughs, and my husband, the turncoat, laughs with him.

We ride back to our house in Lincolnshire in stony silence, and when we reach home I devote myself to prayer and to my studies. My husband, after a few quizzical remarks that earn him no reply, after asking me if I would like to take a trip to

London with him – as if I would go to the City which has celebrated shame! – turns his attention to running our great estates and to his trade in London. The new king's determination to keep the peace means more work for local gentry and my husband finds that he is commanded to root out self-serving and corrupt local officers who have thrived under the lackadaisical rule of King Henry. The law courts now have to be open to give justice to all, and not just to those who can bribe the court officers. The new King Edward summons a parliament and tells them that it is his determination to live of his own and not burden the country with heavy taxation. He commands that the roads be made safe and that private armies be reduced. He orders that brigands and criminals be brought to justice and that the casual violence of the ale house and the highway be controlled. Everyone welcomes these changes and foresees a time of greater prosperity and peace for England, with this glorious son of York guiding it into the ways of peace. Everyone is delighted with the reforms and the improvements. Everyone seems to be in love with the handsome son of York. Everyone but me.

This King Edward is a young man of nineteen, just a year older than me, surviving the death of his father as I have done, dreaming of greatness as I do – and yet he has put himself at the head of his house's army and led them to the throne of England; while I have done nothing. It is he who has been a Joan of Arc for England; not me. I cannot even hold my son in my own keeping. This boy, this Edward that they call the sweet rose of England, the fair herb of England, the white flower, is fabled to be handsome and brave and strong – and I am nothing. He is adored by women, they sing his praises, his looks and his charms; I cannot even be seen at his court. I am known to nobody. I am a flower that wastes its sweetness on the desert air, indeed. He has never even seen me. No-one has written a single, solitary ballad about me, no-one has drawn my likeness. I am wife to a man of no ambition, who will not ride out to war until he is forced to go. I am mother to a son in my enemy's keeping, and I am the distant love of a defeated man in exile. I spend my days – which get shorter all the time as the evenings draw in on this most miserable year – on my knees, and I pray to God to let this dark night pass, to let this cold winter pass, and to throw down the House of York and let the House of Lancaster come home.

AUTUMN 1470

It is not one dark winter, it is nearly ten winters before God releases me and my house from the misery of defeat in our days, and exile in our own country. For nine long years I live with a husband with whom I share nothing but our new house at Woking in the country. House, land and interest we share and yet I am lonely, longing for my son, raised by my enemy that I have to pretend is my friend. Together, Stafford and I conceive no child, which I think is the fault of the midwives at the birth of my son Henry, and I have to endure my husband's generous acceptance that I will not give him an heir. He does not reproach me, and I have to bear his kindness as best I can. We both have to endure the power of the Yorks, who wear the ermine collar of monarchy as if they were born to it. Edward, the young king, marries a nobody in the first years of his reign and most people think she enchanted him by witchcraft with the help of her witch mother Jacquetta, the great friend of our queen who has turned her coat and now rules the York court. My husband's nephew, the little duke Henry Stafford, is snatched up by the greedy siren Elizabeth, who calls herself queen. She takes him from us, his family, and betrothes him to her own sister, Katherine Woodville, a girl born and bred only to raise hens in Northampton, and so the Woodville girl becomes the new duchess and head of our house. My husband does not protest against this kidnap of our boy, he says it is part of the new world and we have to become accustomed. But I do not. I cannot. I will never become accustomed.

Once a year I visit my boy in the ostentatious luxury of the Herbert household and see him grow taller and stronger, see him at ease in among the Yorks, beloved of Anne Devereux, the wife of Black Herbert, see him affectionate and comfortable with their son William, his dearest friend, his playmate and his companion in his studies, and gentle with their daughter Maud, who clearly they have picked out for him as a wife, without a word to me.

Every year I visit faithfully, and speak to him of his Uncle Jasper in exile, and of his cousin the king imprisoned in the Tower of London, and he listens, his brown head inclined to me, his brown eyes smiling and obedient. He listens for as long as I speak, politely attentive, never disagreeing, never questioning. But I cannot tell if he truly understands even one word of my earnest sermon: that he must hold himself in waiting, that he is to know that he is a boy chosen for greatness, that I, his mother, heiress to the Beauforts and to the House of Lancaster, nearly died in giving birth to him, that the two of us were saved by God for a great purpose, that he was not born to be a boy glad of the affection of such as William Herbert. I do not want a girl like Maud Herbert as my daughter-in-law.

I tell him he must live with them like a spy, he must live with them like an enemy in their camp. He must speak politely but wait for his revenge. He must bend the knee to them but dream of the sword. But he will not. He cannot. He lives with them like an open-hearted boy of five, then six, then seven; he lives with them until he is thirteen, he grows into a young man under their care, not mine. He is a boy of their making, not mine. He is like a beloved son to them. He is not a son to me, and I will never forgive them for this.

For nearly nine years I whisper poison in his little ear against the guardian that he trusts, and against his guardian's wife that he loves. I can see him flourishing in their care, I can see him growing under their tuition. They hire masters of swordsmanship, of French, of mathematics, of rhetoric for him. They spare no fee that would teach him skills or encourage him to learn. They give him the education of their own son, the two boys study side by side as equals. I have no cause to complain. But I stifle a silent howl of resentment and anger that I can never release: that this is my boy, that this is an heir to the throne of England, that this is a boy of Lancaster – what in the name of God is he doing, flourishing and happy, in a house of York?

I know the answer to this. I know just what he is doing in one of the loyal houses of York. He is growing into a Yorkist. He loves the luxury and comfort of Raglan Castle, I swear he would prefer it to the holy plainness of my new home at Woking, if he had ever been allowed to see my home. He warms to the gentle piety of Anne Devereux, my demand that he know every collect of the day and honour every saint's day is too much for him, I know it is. He admires the courage and dash of William Herbert, and while he loves Jasper still, and writes to tell him so, boyish letters filled with boasting and affection, he is learning to admire his uncle's enemy and adopt him as a very model of a chivalrous, honourable knight and landlord.

And worst of all for me, he thinks of me as a woman who cannot reconcile herself to defeat, I know he thinks this. He thinks I am a woman who saw my king driven from his throne, and my husband killed and my brother-in-law run away, and he thinks that it is disappointment and failure that has made me seek solace in religion. He thinks I am a woman seeking consolation in God for the failure of her life. Nothing I can do can convince him that my life in God is my power and glory. Nothing I can do can convince him that I do not see our cause as lost, I don't see myself as defeated, I don't believe, not even now, that York will hold the throne, I think we will return, I think we will win. I can say this to him, I can say it over and over again; but I have no evidence to support my conviction, and the embarrassed smile, and the way he bows his head to me and murmurs, 'Lady Mother, I am sure you are right,' tells me, as clearly as if he loudly contradicted me, that he thinks I am wrong and mistaken and – worse than that – irrelevant.

I am the woman who gave him birth, but I lived with him only for the first year of his life. Now he sees me once a year, and rarely more, and I spoil my time with him by trying to persuade him to be faithful to a cause which was lost nearly ten years ago. No wonder he does not cleave to me. Every year I must seem more of a fool.

And I cannot help myself. God knows, if I could reconcile myself to living with a man who is the embodiment of mediocrity, in a country under a usurper – with a queen so much my inferior in every way! – observing my God only as a once-a-day deity in my evening prayers, I would do so. But I cannot. I want a husband with the courage and determination to play his part in the rule of the country, I want my country ruled by my true king, and I have to pray to God for this in the five services of the day. It is how I am, I cannot deny myself.

William Herbert is King Edward's man through and through, of course. In his house, my son, my own son, the flower of the House of Lancaster, learns to speak of the usurper with respect, to admire the so-called ravishing beauty of his hastily married wife, the commoner Elizabeth, and to pray for an heir for their accursed house. She is fertile as a stable cat, but every year she manages to give birth only to a girl. The joke is on her, for they say she married him by enchantment and comes from a long line of women who dabble in magic. Now all she can make are little witches for the burning, she cannot give him a prince, and her magical skills do not seem to help.

Indeed, if they had conceived an heir early on, then perhaps our story would be a different one; but they do not, and slowly but surely the notorious York disloyalty begins to split the self-aggrandising House of York against itself. Their great advisor and mentor, the Earl of Warwick, turns against the boy he helped to the throne, and the second son George, Duke of Clarence, turns against the brother he proclaimed as his king. Together they make an alliance as a pair of opportunists.

Envy, the family poison of York, flows through George's veins like their second-rate blood. As Warwick grows away from the first York boy that he made king, the second York boy creeps closer, dreaming of the same favour, and Warwick begins to think he might play the same trick again: this time replacing a pretender king with a new pretender. Warwick marries his daughter Isobel to George and easily, like the serpent in Eden, Warwick tempts George, Duke of Clarence, to abandon his brother's cause and dream of usurping the usurper's throne. They snatch the new king as if he were the crown at the top of the maypole and hold him prisoner – and I think that a way is open to me.

I know all Yorkists are ambitious and disloyal in their very cradles. But the division in their house can only serve mine. I play my own hand in the middle of these plots. When the Yorks took everything, they stole my son's title of Earl of Richmond, and George, Duke of Clarence, took it as his own. I send a message to George, through his confessor and mine, and promise my friendship and loyalty, if he will return the title of Earl of Richmond to my son. I indicate to him that the support of my house can be commanded by me; he knows, without my boasting of it, how many men I could muster. I indicate to him that if he will return the title to my son, he can name his price, and I will back him against his brother the king.

I keep this from my husband, and I think it has been done cleverly in secret until it becomes clear, as Edward escapes from his false friend and his false brother and returns in triumph to London, that we have fallen from the favour of the York court. The title Earl of Wiltshire should have come to my husband; but King Edward passes over him and instead honours his younger brother John, who is made Earl of Wiltshire for his ostentatious loyalty to Edward. It seems we are not to rise under this new king. We are tolerated but not favoured. It is an injustice but it cannot be challenged. My husband will be nothing but 'Sir' till the end of his days. He can give me no title but 'Lady'. I shall never be a countess. He says nothing, and by his very silence I guess that he has heard of my meddling offer of friendship to George of Clarence, and blames me for disloyalty to him and to King Edward, and indeed, he is right.

But then – and who could have predicted it? – everything changes again. Queen Margaret, our precious Queen Margaret, in desperate exile in France, running out of money and lost without soldiers, agrees to an alliance with the snake Warwick, her old enemy, formerly our greatest adversary. Amazingly, she lets her precious son Edward, Prince of Wales, marry Warwick's younger daughter Anne, and the two parents agree to invade England together, to give the young people a bloodbath for a honeymoon and put the Lancaster son and the Warwick girl on the throne of England.

The end for York comes as swift as sunset, Warwick and George land together, and march north. William Herbert calls out his men to join with the king, but before they can meet with the main force of York, Herbert sights the enemy outside Banbury, at Edgecote Hill. He did nothing more than his duty when he took my son with him that day, but I will never forgive him. As a nobleman should, he took his ward into battle to give him a taste of violence and a lesson in real fighting, as he should, as he should; but this is my son, my precious son, my only son. Even worse – I cannot bear to think it, but it is true – my son first put on his armour, first took a lance in his hand and then rode out to fight for York, against a Lancaster army. He fought for our enemy, at the side of our enemy, against our own house.

It was over quickly, as God's will is sometimes done in battle. The York troops were overpowered and Warwick took a feast of prisoners, including William Herbert himself. Warwick, already stained in blood, already a turncoat, did not add uncertainty to his crimes. He had Herbert beheaded on the spot, and my son's guardian died that day, perhaps as my son watched.

I am glad of it. I never had a moment of pity for him. He took my son from me and then he raised him so well that Henry loved him as a father. I never forgave him for either, and I was glad to hear he was dead.

'We have to fetch Henry,' I say to my husband, Sir Henry, as the news comes to us in snippets of gossip and gales of rumour. 'God knows where he is. If Warwick has him, he will surely keep him safe; but if Warwick had him surely he would have sent us a message? Perhaps my boy is in hiding, or perhaps he is injured—' I break off. The rest of my sentence, 'perhaps he is dead', is as clear as if it were written on the air between us.

'We'll get news soon,' my husband says calmly. 'And be sure that if he were dead or injured we would have heard straight away. See, we have the news of Herbert's death quick enough.'

'We have to fetch Henry,' I repeat.

'I will go,' he says. 'You can't come with me, the roads will be filled with men running from the battle and those seeking plunder. Warwick has brought danger and turmoil back into York's England. God knows where this will all end. You will have to stay here. I will even have to leave you with an extra guard in case any of the armed bands come through this way.'

'But my son . . .'

'Herbert will have told him what to do in the event of the battle going against them. He will have appointed someone to take care of him. I'll go first to Lady Herbert and see what news she has, then I'll go to Edgecote. Trust me, I will find your boy.'

'And when you find him, bring him here.'

He hesitates. 'Depends who his new guardian is to be. We can't just take him.'

'But who will decide that now? If York is defeated?'

He smiles. 'Lancaster, I suppose. You have victory, remember? Your house will now decide everything. Warwick will put King Henry back on the throne just as he took him off, then I imagine Warwick will rule the country until the prince is of age, and possibly thereafter.'

'We have won?' I ask uncertainly. With my son missing and his guardian dead, it does not feel like victory, it feels like more danger.

'We have won,' my husband says and there is no gladness in his voice at all. 'At any rate, Lancaster has won and that is us, once more, apparently.'

On the very morning that my cautious husband is about to set out, we have a letter in Jasper's familiar scrawl.

I have our boy, he was safe with Lady Herbert, staying with her late husband's family. I will bring him to London to present him to our king. Will you meet us there, with our king on his throne again, at court? England is ours again and your prayers are answered, thank God.

It is like a dream, a dream as bright as those I used to have as a child when I prayed myself into visions. We are in the Stafford barge sailing down the Thames, the rowers keeping their pace with the low thudding of the drum, my boy gazing at the people on the river bank who cheer to see our standards flying, and to glimpse my boy in the prow of the boat, a prince in waiting. We go past Westminster and I look at the low buildings that huddle down by the river's edge. Somewhere in the sanctuary of the abbey is the former queen, Elizabeth Woodville, the King of York's famously beautiful wife, hiding from her enemies and wondering if she will ever see her husband again. She is thrown down and alone, and I am up high. I wonder if she is looking out from those dark little windows, if her eyes are on my standard even now. I shiver, as if I could feel a baleful glance on me; but I shrug it off. I am the chosen daughter of God, of His chosen house. She can stay there till she rots for all I care, and her beautiful daughters with her.

From the prow of the boat, my son Henry turns back to me with a shy smile and I say: 'Wave to them, wave at your people. They are glad to see our family back in honour, back in power. Show them that you are glad to be here.'

He makes a little gesture and then he steps back to where I am seated under the Stafford canopy, the red rose of Lancaster embroidered overall.

'Lady Mother, you were right all along,' he says shyly. 'I must beg your pardon. I did not understand.'

I put my hand to my heart to feel it thud. 'Right about what?'

'We are a great family and the King Henry is the true king. I didn't know. When you told me it, I didn't understand. But I understand now.'

'I am guided by God,' I say earnestly. 'I look beyond the fleeting days, to the wisdom of God. Will you be guided by me in the future?'

He gives a solemn little bow. 'I shall be your son and your liegeman,' he says formally.

I turn my head so he cannot see the triumph in my face. Henry the King has won England, and I have won my son. Thirteen years old and he swears fealty to me. He is mine for life! I feel the tears well up into my eyes. 'I accept your service,' I say quietly. Then the barge noses up to the pier, the gangplank is run aboard and Henry my son shows his beautiful Herbert manners and gives me a hand to help me ashore, and we walk through the garden where everyone is smiling in joy that the country has come to its senses and we can all be in our rightful places again. And here is our king, back on his throne, his face so bright with happiness that I hardly see the five years of pallor from his imprisonment. Here is the royal canopy over his head, embroidered with the red rose of Lancaster in full bloom, here are his courtiers around him. It is as if I were a child again and he about to assign me to the Tudors as my guardians. It is as if my childhood joys have come back to me again and the world can start anew.

And here is my son, my boy, his short-cropped hair as bright as a chestnut mane, his shoulders broad, grown taller yet again, standing beside his Uncle Jasper, a handsome boy from a handsome family. We are restored. England is returned to its senses, Jasper is Earl of Pembroke once more, my son is in my keeping.

'You see?' I demand of him quietly. 'You see now? I was keeping my faith to this king, my cousin, and here he is restored to his throne. God has me in His special keeping, as He has you. I knew that the York reign would be short, I knew that we would all be restored to our true places.' I glance past my son and see that the king has nodded to Jasper to bring him forwards. 'Go,' I prompt him. 'The king wants you, his cousin.'

My son gives a little jump, but then straightens his shoulders and goes forward to the throne with an air of real grace and quiet confidence. He carries himself so well that I cannot stop myself whispering to my husband, Sir Henry: 'See how he walks?'

'Both feet,' my husband commends wryly. 'One after the other. Miraculous.'

'Like a nobleman, like a prince,' I correct him. I lean forwards to listen.

'And this is young Henry Tudor, my cousin?' the king asks Jasper.

Jasper bows. 'My brother Edmund's son and his mother is now Lady Margaret Stafford.'

Henry kneels before the king who leans down and puts his hand on the brown curly head in his royal blessing.

'There,' I say to my husband. 'The king himself favours Henry. I expect the king can foretell he will have a great future. He will know that this is a special boy. He has the vision of a saint, he will see the grace in Henry, as I do.'

The storm, which blew away the little boat of the usurper Edward and his runaway companions after their defeat at Edgecote Hill, blows around the coast for almost all the winter. Our lands are flooded both in Surrey and elsewhere, and we have to lay out on ditching and even build dykes against the rising rivers. The tenants are late with their rents and the crops are sodden in the fields. My husband is pessimistic about the state of the country, as if the loss of the usurper House of York brings rain and discontent.

The news gets out that the former queen, Elizabeth Woodville, who turns out to be so beloved of her king that he ran away and left her, is going to give birth to another child, even though she is in sanctuary in Westminster, on holy ground. Even this final act of grossness and folly is forgiven by our sainted king, who refuses to have her taken from her place of hiding, and instead sends her midwives and ladies to care for her. The attention that this woman attracts continues to amaze me. I managed to give birth to my boy Henry with no more than two midwives and they under instruction to let me die. Elizabeth Woodville has to have midwives and physicians and her own mother in attendance, when she is in hiding for treason.

She continues to attract admiration, even though nobody can see her fabled beauty. They say that the citizens of London and the farmers of Kent keep her supplied with food, and that her husband is in Flanders, raising an army to rescue her. The thought of her, revelling in all this attention, makes me grit my teeth. Why cannot people see that all she has done, in all her life, is use a pretty face, or the snare of her body or worse, to capture a king. This is neither noble nor holy – and yet people speak of her as beloved.

The worst news of all is that she has a boy. He cannot inherit the throne since his father has so thoroughly abandoned it; but a York son born just now is bound to have an influence on gullible people, who will see the hand of destiny in giving the York family an heir in prison.

If I were the king I don't think I would be so very scrupulous about respecting the laws of sanctuary for such a person. How can a woman who is widely regarded as a witch invoke the protection of the Holy Church? How can a baby claim sanctuary? How shall a treasonous family live untouchable in the very heart of London? Our king is a saint, but he should be served by men who can take worldly decisions; and Elizabeth Woodville and her mother Jacquetta, whom I now know to be truly a most notorious and proven witch and a turncoat, should be bundled onto a ship and sent off to Flanders and let them weave their magic and practise their beauty over there, where they are likely to be better appreciated among foreigners.

My childish stunned regard for Elizabeth Woodville's mother Jacquetta quickly changed when I learned what sort of woman she was, and when I saw her bump her daughter upwards to the throne. There is no doubt in my mind that the grace and beauty which caught my eye when I was a little girl at the court of King Henry was a mask over a most sinful nature. She allowed her daughter to stand at the roadside when the young king rode by and she was one of the few witnesses at their secret wedding. She became chief lady in waiting and leader of the York court. No woman with any sense of loyalty or honour could do any of these things. She, who had served Margaret of Anjou, how could she bow the knee to her light-minded daughter? Jacquetta had been a royal duchess with the English army in France and then she was widowed and married her husband's squire, at most shocking speed. Our kindly king forgave her lustful indiscretion so her husband, Richard Woodville, could call himself Lord Rivers, taking his title as a tribute to the pagan traditions of her family, who sprang from streams and name a water goddess as their ancestor. Since then, scandal and rumours of dealing with the devil have followed her as waters flow downhill. And this is the woman whose daughter thought she should be Queen of England!

No wonder he is shamefully dead and they are cast down to little more than prison. She should use her black arts and fly away, or summon the river and swim to safety.

SPRING 1471

I say nothing of these thoughts of mine to Sir Henry, who is so gloomy through the dark, wintry days of January and February that one would think he was mourning the exile of his king. One evening at dinner I ask him if he is well, and he says that he is much worried.

'Is Henry safe?' I ask at once.

His weary smile reassures me. 'Of course, I would have told you if I had any bad news from Jasper. The two of them are at Pembroke I don't doubt, and we can visit them when the roads are clear of all this rain, if there is no more trouble.'

'Trouble?' I repeat.

Sir Henry glances at the server of wine who stands behind us and then looks down the great hall where the servants and tenants on the nearest tables can overhear our speech. 'We can talk later,' he says.

We wait till we are alone in my bedroom, with the hot spiced wine served, and the servants gone for the night. He sits before the fireside and I see that he looks weary and older than his forty-five years.

'I am sorry for your unease,' I say; but he is of an age when a man makes a nonsense out of a nothing, and if my boy Henry is well, and our king on the throne, then what trouble need we fear? 'Please tell me your worries, husband. Perhaps we can put them to naught.'

'I have a message from a man loyal to York, who thinks that I too am loyal to York,' he says heavily. 'It's a summons.'

'A summons?' I repeat stupidly. For a moment I think he means to serve as a justice, and then I realise he means that York is recruiting again. 'Oh, God spare us! Not a summons to rebel?'

He nods.

'A secret plot of York and they have come to you?'

'Yes.' He sighs. For a moment I lose my fear and am tempted to giggle. His correspondent cannot know my husband very well if he thinks he is a Yorkist. And not well at all if he thinks he will arm to command, and joyously ride out to war. My husband makes a most reluctant soldier. He is not made of heroic stuff.

'Edward is planning to invade and take back his kingdom,' he says. 'We will have the wars starting again.'

Now I am alarmed. I grip my chair. 'It's not his kingdom.'

My husband shrugs. 'Whoever has the right of it, Edward will fight for it.'

'Oh no,' I say. 'Not again. He cannot hope to come against our king. Not now that he has just been restored. He has been back on his throne – what? – five months?'

'My friend who wrote me to turn out for Edward said more,' my husband goes on. 'My friend is not just Edward's man, he is a friend of George, Duke of Clarence.'

I wait. Surely, George of Clarence cannot have turned his coat. He has staked everything on being his brother's enemy. He is in thrall to Warwick, married to his daughter, standing in line for the throne only second to our Prince of Wales. He is a key member of the court, a most beloved cousin of our king. He has burned his boats with his brother, he cannot go back. Edward would never have him back. 'George?' I ask.

'He is to join his brother again,' my husband tells me. 'The three sons of York are to be reunited.'

'You must send this at once to the king, and to Jasper.' I insist. 'They have to know, they have to be prepared.'

'I have sent messages to both Wales and the court,' my husband says. 'But I doubt I am telling either of them anything that they don't already know. Everyone knows that Edward is arming and raising an army in Flanders – he would be bound to come again to reclaim his throne. And the king . . .' He breaks off. 'I don't think the king cares for anything any more but his own soul. I truly think he would be glad to surrender his throne if he could go into a monastery and spend his days in prayer.'

'God has called him to be king,' I say firmly.

'Then God will have to help him,' my husband replies. 'And I think he will need all the help he can get if he is to hold off Edward.'

The king's need for help is spelled out for us when my cousin, the Duke of Somerset, Edmund Beaufort, announces he is coming for a visit. I send to the town of Guildford and even to the coast for delicacies for the table and His Grace sits down to a small banquet every day of his visit. He thanks me for my hospitality when we are by the fire in my presence chamber, my husband Sir Henry out of the room for a moment. I smile and bow my head; but I don't think for a moment that he has come to stay for the pleasure of oysters from the Sussex coast or potted cherries from Kent.

'You have entertained me royally,' he says, tasting a sugared plum. 'These are from your orchards?'

I nod. 'Last summer's crop,' I say, as if I care one way or another for household things. 'It was a good year for fruit.'

'A good year for England,' he says. 'Our king back on the throne, and the usurper driven away. Lady Margaret, I swear, we cannot let these scoundrels back into the country again to drive our good king from the throne!'

'I know it,' I say. 'Who should know better than I, his cousin, whose son was given into the charge of traitors? And now I have him restored to me like Lazarus from death.'

'Your husband commands much of Sussex and his influence goes into Kent,' the duke presses on, disregarding Lazarus. 'He has an army of tenants who would turn out for him if he commanded. It might be that the York fleet will land on your shores. We have to know that your husband will stand loyal to his king and that he will call his tenants out to defend us. But I am afraid that I have reason to doubt him.'

'He is a man who loves peace above all,' I say lamely.

'We all love peace,' my cousin asserts. 'But sometimes a man has to defend his own. We all have to defend the king. If York makes it back to England with an army of Flanders mercenary soldiers and defeats us again, we will none of us be safe in our lands, in our titles, or' – he nods at me – 'in our heirs. How would you like to see young Henry brought up in yet another York household? His inheritance used by a York guardian? Married to a York girl? Don't you think that Elizabeth Woodville as queen, restored to her throne, will turn her greedy grey eyes on your son and his inheritance? She took your little nephew the Duke of Buckingham and married him to her own sister Katherine for profit – a shocking mismatch. Don't you think she will take your son for one of her endless daughters if she comes back to power?'

I stand and walk to the fireplace. I look down at the flames and wish for a moment that I had the Sight to foretell the future like the York queen. Does she know that her husband is coming to save her, to rescue her and his new baby son from their prison? Can she tell if they will succeed or fail? Can she whistle up a storm to blow them onshore as they say she whistled one up to blow him safely away?

'I wish I could promise you my husband's sword and fortune and tenantry at your service,' I say quietly. 'Everything I can do to persuade him to ride out for the king, I do already. I make it clear to my own tenants that I would be pleased to see them form into bands for their true king. But Sir Henry is slow to act, and reluctant to act. I wish I could promise you more, cousin. I am ashamed that I cannot.'

'Does he not realise that you stand to lose everything? Your son's title and wealth will be taken from him again?'

I nod. 'Yes, but he is much influenced by the London traders and his business friends. And they are all for York because they believe Edward makes peace throughout the land, and because he makes the courts of law work so that a man can have justice. My husband is influenced too by the greater men among his tenants, and by the other noblemen in the area. They don't all think as they should. They favour York. They say he brought peace and justice to England and that since he has gone there has been trouble and uncertainty. They say he is young and strong and commands the country and that our king is frail and ruled by his wife.'

'I can't deny that,' my cousin says briskly. 'But Edward of York is not the true king. He could be a very Daniel bringing judgement, he could be Moses bringing fine laws, and he would still be a traitor. We have to follow the king, our king, or be traitors ourselves.'

The door opens and my husband comes in, all smiles. 'I am

sorry,' he says. 'There was trouble in the stable, some fool tipped over a brazier and they were running around putting out the fire. I just went down to check that it was thoroughly out. Don't want our honoured guest to be burned in his bed!' He smiles pleasantly at the duke and in that moment, in his smiling, honest warmth, in his lack of fearfulness, in his confident sense of his own rightness – I think that we both know that Sir Henry is not going to ride out for the king.

Within days we have the news that Edward of York has made landfall, not where anyone expected him, but in the north of England where the witch's wind blew him to safe harbour, and he has marched on York and asked them to open their gates to him, not on his own account as king, but so that he can take up his dukedom again. The city, persuaded like a set of fools, lets him in and at once the York supporters flock to their leader and his traitorous ambition is plain. George, the turncoat Duke of Clarence, is among them. It has taken some time; but even stupid George finally realises that his future as a York boy would be brighter with a York king on the throne, and suddenly, he loves his brother above any other, and declares that his loyalty to the true king and to his father-in-law Warwick was a great mistake. I suppose from this that my son has lost his earldom for ever, as everything will belong to the York boys again and no pleading messages from me to George, Duke of Clarence, will make him give Henry's title back. All at once everything is golden daylight and the three suns of York are the dawn over England. In the fields the hares are fighting and leaping and it seems as if the whole country has gone as mad as hares this March.

Amazingly, Edward gets to London without a single obstacle

in his path, the gates are thrown open for him by the adoring citizens, and he is reunited with his wife, as if he had never been chased from his own land, running for his life.

I take to my chamber and pray on my knees when I hear this news from Somerset's hard-riding messenger. I think of Elizabeth Woodville – the so-called beauty – with her baby son in her arms, and her daughters all around her, starting up as the door is thrown open and Edward of York strides into the room, victorious as he always is. I spend two long hours on my knees but I cannot pray for victory and I cannot pray for peace. I can only think of her running into his arms, knowing that her husband is the bravest and most able man in the kingdom, showing him her son, surrounded by their daughters. I take up my rosary and pray again. The words are for the safety of my king; but I cannot think of anything but my jealousy that a woman, far worse born than me, far worse educated than me, without doubt less beloved by God than me, should be able to run to her husband with joy and show him their son and know he will fight to defend him. That a woman such as her, clearly not favoured by God, showing no signs of grace (unlike me), should be Queen of England. And that, by some mystery – too great for me to understand – God should have overlooked me.

I come out of my chamber and find my husband in the great hall. He is seated at the top table, his face grave. His steward, standing beside him, is putting one sheet of paper after another before him for his signature. His clerk beside him is melting wax and pressing in the seal. It takes me only a moment to recognise the commissions of array. He is calling up his tenants. He is going to war, at last he is going to war. I feel my heart lift like a lark at the sight, God be praised, he is owning his duty and going to war at last. I step up to the table, my face glad.

'Husband, God bless you and the work you are finally doing.'

He does not smile back at me, he looks at me wearily and his eyes are sad. His hand keeps moving, signing Henry Stafford, time after time, and he hardly glances down at his pen. They come to the last page, the clerk drips wax, stamps the seal and hands it in its box back to his chief secretary.

'Send them at once,' Henry says.

He pushes back his chair and steps off the little dais to stand before me, takes my hand and tucks it in his arm and walks me away from the clerk who is gathering up the papers to take to the stables for the waiting messengers.

'Wife, I have to tell you a thing which will trouble you,' he says.

I shake my head. I think he is about to tell me that he is going to war with a heavy heart for fear of leaving me and so I rush to reassure him that I fear nothing when he is doing God's work. 'Truly husband, I am glad . . .' He stills me with a gentle touch on my cheek.

'I am calling up my men not to serve King Henry; but to serve King Edward,' he says quietly.

At first I hear the words but they make no sense to me. Then I am so frozen with horror that I say nothing. I am so silent that he thinks I have not heard him.

'I will serve King Edward of York, not Henry of Lancaster,' he says. 'I am sorry if you are disappointed.'

'Disappointed?' He is telling me he has turned traitor and he thinks I may be disappointed?

'I am sorry for it.'

'But my cousin himself came to persuade you to war . . .'

'He did nothing but convince me that we have to have a strong king who will put an end to war, now and for ever, or he and his sort will go on until England is destroyed. When he told me that he would fight for ever I knew that he would have to be defeated.'

'Edward is not born to be king. He is not a bringer of peace.'

'My dear, you know that he is. The only peace we have known in the last ten years was when he was on the throne. And now he has a son and heir, so please God the Yorks will hold the throne for ever and there will be an end to these unending battles.'

I wrench my hand away from his grip. 'He is not born royal,' I cry. 'He is not sacred. He is a usurper. You are calling out your tenants and mine, *my* tenants from *my* lands to serve a traitor. You would have my standard, the Beaufort portcullis, unfurled on the York side?'

He nods. 'I knew you would not like it,' he says resignedly.

'I would rather die than see this!'

He nods as if I am exaggerating, like a child.

'And what if you lose?' I demand. 'You will be known as a turncoat who supported York. Do you think they will call Henry – your stepson – to court again, and give him back his earldom? Do you think Henry the king will bless him as he did before, when everyone knows you have shamed yourself, and shamed me?'

He grimaces. 'I think it is the right thing to do. And, as it happens, I think York will win.'

'Against Warwick?' I ask him scornfully. 'He can't beat Warwick. He didn't do so well last time, when Warwick chased him out of England. And the time before that when Warwick took him prisoner. He is Warwick's boy, not his master.'

'He was betrayed last time,' he said. 'He was alone without his army. This time he knows his enemies, and he has summoned his men.'

'Say you win then,' I say, the words tumbling out in my distress. 'Say you put Edward on my family's throne. What happens to me? What happens to Henry? Will Jasper have to go into exile again, thanks to your enmity? Will my son and his uncle be driven out of England by you? Do you want me to go too?'

He sighs. 'If I serve Edward and he is glad of my service then he will reward me,' he says. 'We might even get Henry's earldom back from him. The throne will no longer run in your family, but Margaret, dear little wife, to be honest with you: your family does not deserve to own it. The king is sick, to tell the truth, he is mad. He is not fit to run a country, and the queen is a nightmare of vanity and ambition. Her son is a murderer: can you think what we will suffer if he ever gets the throne? I cannot serve such a prince and such a queen. There *is* no-one but Edward. The direct line is . . .'

'Is what?' I spit.

'Insane,' he says simply. 'Hopeless. The king is a saint and cannot rule and his son is a devil and should not.'

'If you do this, I will never forgive you,' I swear. The tears are running down my face and angrily I brush them away. 'If you ride out to defeat my own cousin, the true king, I will never forgive you. I will never call you "husband" again, you will be as if you were dead to me.'

He releases my hand as if I am a bad-tempered child. 'I knew you would say that,' he says sadly. 'Though I am doing what I think best for us both. I am even doing what I think best for England, which is more than many men can say in these troubled times.'

APRIL 1471

The summons comes from Edward the usurper in London and my husband rides out at the head of his army of tenants to join his new lord. He is in such a hurry to go that half the men are not yet equipped and his master of horse stays behind to see that the sharpened staves and newly forged swords are loaded in carts to follow the men.

I stand in the stable yard and watch the men falling into line. Many of them have served in France, many of them have marched out before for English battles, this is a generation of men accustomed to warfare, inured to danger and familiar with cruelty. For a moment I understand my husband's yearning for peace but then I remember that he is backing the wrong king and I fire up my anger again.

He comes from the house, wearing his best boots and the thick travelling cape that he gave to me when we rode to see my boy. I was glad of his kindness then; but he has disappointed me since. I am hard-faced as I look at him, and I despise his hangdog expression.

'You will forgive me if we win and I can bring your boy home to you,' he suggests hopefully.

'You will be on opposing sides,' I say coldly. 'You will be fighting on one side and my brother-in-law and my boy on the other. You ask me to hope that my brother-in-law Jasper is defeated or killed. For that is the only way that my boy will need a new guardian. I cannot do that.'

He sighs. 'I suppose not. Will you give me your blessing, anyway?'

'How can I bless you when you are cursed in your choice?' I demand.

He cannot maintain his smile. 'Wife, will you pray for my safety at least while I am gone?'

'I shall pray that you see sense and change sides in the very middle of the battle,' I say. 'You could do that and make sure you were on the victorious side. I would pray for your victory then.'

'That would be quite without principle,' he remarks mildly. He kneels to me and takes my hand and kisses it and I stubbornly do not touch his head with my other hand in blessing. He rises up and goes to the mounting block. I hear him grunt with the effort of stepping onto it and swinging into the saddle, and for a moment I feel pity that a man, not young any more, who so dislikes leaving his home, should be forced out on a hot spring day to battle.

He turns his horse and raises his hand to me in salute. 'Goodbye, Margaret,' he says. 'And I say "God bless you" to you, even if you won't say it to me.'

I think it is unkind of me to stand there with my hands by my side and a frown on my face. But I let him go without a blown kiss, without a blessing, without a command to come back safely. I let him go without a word or a gesture of love for he is going out to fight for my enemy and so he is my enemy now.

I hear from him within a few days. His second squire comes back in a rush because he forgot the gussets for his coat of mail. He brings the will that my husband has scribbled in haste, thinking battle will be joined at once. 'Why? Does he think he will die?' I ask cruelly when the man hands it to me for safe-keeping.

'He is very low in his spirits,' he answers me honestly. 'Shall I take a message back to cheer him?'

'No message,' I say, turning away. No man who fights under the banner of York against the interests of my son will have a message of hope from me. How can I? My prayer must be that York fails and is defeated. My prayer must be for my husband's defeat. I will pray that he is not killed, but in all honesty, before my God, I can't do more than that.

I spend that night, all the night, on my knees praying for the victory of my House of Lancaster. The servant said that they were gathering outside London and would march to meet our forces that are mustering in thousands, somewhere near Oxford. Edward will march out his troops along the great west road and the armies will meet somewhere on the way. I expect Warwick to win for our king, even with both York boys, George of Clarence, and Richard of Gloucester, fighting alongside their older brother. Warwick is the more experienced commander, he taught the York boys everything they know about warfare. And Warwick has the greatest force. And Warwick is in the right. Our king, an ordained monarch, a saintly man, is held a prisoner in the Tower of

London by order of the York usurper. How can God allow his captor to have victory? My husband may be there, in the armies of York. But I have to pray for his defeat. I am for Lancaster, I am for my king, I am for Jasper, and I am for my son.

I send to Guildford every day for news, expecting riders to come from London with word of a battle; but no-one knows what is happening until one of our men comes back, riding a stolen horse, ahead of all the others to tell me that my husband Henry is wounded and near to death. I hear him out, standing alone in the stable yard until someone thinks to send for one of my ladies and she clasps my arm to hold me up, while the man tells me of a battle of shifting fortunes and confusion. There was thick mist, the line of the army swung about, the Earl of Oxford changed his coat, or so someone said, there was a panic when he attacked our side, and Edward came out of the mist in a charge like the devil himself, and the Lancaster forces broke before him.

'I will have to go to him and fetch him home,' I say. I turn to his steward. 'Get a cart ready so we can bring him home, and put a feather bed in it and everything he will need. Bandages, I suppose, and physic.'

'I will fetch the physician to go with you,' he says. I take it as a reproach that I have never been much of a nurse or a herbalist. 'And the priest,' I say. I see him flinch and I know that he is thinking that his master may need the last rites, that he may be near death as we speak. 'And we'll go at once,' I say. 'This day.'

I ride ahead of the slow wagon, but it is a hard long ride and I get to Barnet as the dusk of the spring evening closes down on the muddy road. All along the way there are men begging for help to get home, or lying down in the hedgerow and dying for lack of friends or family or someone to care for them. Sometimes we are crowded off the road by an armed troop hurrying after the main armies to join with them. I see hideous sights, a man with half his face cut away, a man tying his shirt over his belly to stop his lights from spilling out. A pair of men clinging to each other like drunkards, trying to help each other home with only three feet between the two of them. I ride along the road, cutting across the fields wherever I can to avoid the straggle of dying men, trying not to look at the men who stagger towards me, trying not to see the scatter of equipment and bodies all around me, as if the fields were growing strange and terrible crops.

There are women here, like crows, bending over the dying men and rifling through their jackets, looking for money or jewels. Sometimes a loose horse comes trotting towards mine, whinnying for company and for reassurance. I see a few knights who have been pulled down and killed on the ground, and one whose suit of armour protected him so well that he died inside it, his face smashed to pulp against the helmet. When a looter pulls the helmet upwards the head comes with it too, and the slop of brains spills out through the visor. I keep a grip on my rosary and I say 'Hail Mary' over and over again to keep myself in the saddle and the vomit at the back of my mouth. My horse walks warily as if he too is repelled at the smell of blood, and knows this is dangerous ground. I had no idea that it would be this bad. I had no idea that it would be like this.

I cannot believe that it was like this for Joan of Arc. I thought of her always on a white horse with a banner of lilies and angels above her head, clean. I never thought of her riding through carnage, though she must have done so, as I am doing. If this is the will of God it takes a strange and terrible shape. I did not know that the God of Battles was vile like this. I never knew that a saint could summon torment like this. It is like riding through the valley of the shadow of death, and we go like harbingers of death ourselves, for we give away no water though men imploringly reach towards me, pointing to their bloodstained mouths, where their teeth are all knocked out. We dare not stop and give to one, for that would bring them all down on us, so the master of the horse goes ahead with a whip and shouts, 'Clear the way for Lady Margaret Stafford', and the wounded shuffle out of our way and shield their heads from the lash.

An outrider comes back to us and says that they have found my husband lodged in an inn at Whetstone, and we follow him as he leads us down the muddy lanes to the little village. The inn is nothing more than a village ale house with two rooms for passing travellers. I am reluctant to get down from my horse, fearful of being on the ground with the walking dead. But I dismount and go in. I am very afraid that my husband will be horribly maimed, like the men on the road, or hacked by a battle axe; but I find him lying on a settle in the back room, with a scarf tied tight around his belly. The growing red on the scarf tells me he is still bleeding. He turns his head as I come in and manages to smile at the sight of me. 'Margaret, you shouldn't have come.'

'I am safe enough, and I have the wagon following to bring you home.'

His face lights up at the very mention of our home. 'I should be glad to see my home. There were moments when I thought I would never see it again.'

I hesitate. 'Was it very bad? Has York won?'

'Yes.' He nods. 'We had a great victory. We went uphill in the mist at them, and there were twice our number. Nobody but York would have dared to do it. I think he is invincible.'

'So it's over?'

'No. The Lancaster queen has landed her army somewhere in Devon. Every man who could march has fallen in and Edward is going as fast as he can to cut her off, and stop her getting to reinforcements in Wales.'

'In Wales?'

'She will be going to Jasper,' he says. 'She will know her ally Warwick is dead and this army defeated, but if she can get to Jasper and his Welsh levies she can fight on.'

'So Edward could still be defeated and all this' – I am thinking of the men scrambling south down the road, crying out in their pain – 'all this will have been for nothing.'

'All this is always for nothing,' he says. 'Don't you understand that yet? Every death is a pointless death, every battle should have been avoided. But if Edward can defeat the queen, and imprison her along with her husband, then it will indeed be over.'

I hear the physician's horse and I go to let him in. 'Shall I stay and help you?' I ask, without much enthusiasm for the work.

'You go,' Henry says. 'I don't want you to see this.'

'What is your wound?'

'A sword slash across my belly,' he says. 'You go and have them set you up a camp in the field behind this inn. There are no beds to be had in here. And make sure they post a guard over you and your possessions. I wish you hadn't come.'

'I had to come,' I say. 'Who else?'

He gives me his crooked smile. 'I am glad to see you,' he says. 'I was so sick with fear the night before battle that I even made my will.'

I try to smile in sympathy but I am afraid he can tell that I think he is a coward as well as a traitor.

'Oh well,' he says. 'What's done is done. Now you go, Margaret, and ask the innkeeper what he can find for your dinner.'

I don't do as my husband bids me. Of course I don't. While he is lying in a dirty inn being served by our physician as a wounded hero, injured in the cause of York, the Queen of England will be marching as fast as she can towards my son and my only true friend, Jasper, certain that they will be arming and mustering their men to ride with her. I call the lad who rides before me, who is young and faithful and will go fast. I give him a note addressed to Jasper and command him to ride west as fast as he can and find some men marching under the banner of Lancaster who will be going towards Wales, to join the armies that Jasper will be recruiting. I tell him to approach them as a friend and order them to give the letter to the earl with the promise of a reward. I write:

Jasper, my husband has turned his coat and is our enemy. Write to me privately and at once what are your fortunes and that my boy is safe. Edward has won his battle here at Barnet and is marching to find you and the queen. He has the king in the Tower and has secured London. He knows the queen has landed and he guesses she is headed for you. God bless and keep you safe. God keep my son safe, guard him with your life.

I have no sealing wax or seal with me and so I fold it over

twice. It does not matter if anyone reads it. It will be the reply that will tell so much. Then, and only then, do I go to find someone who can make me some dinner and find me a bed for the night.

SUMMER 1471

It was not easy getting my husband safely home, though he did not complain and begged me to ride ahead. But I did my duty as a wife to him, though he had failed in his duty to me. It was not easy getting through the summer when finally we learned of what had happened when the queen's forces met Edward. They were outside Tewkesbury and the queen and her new daughter-in-law, Anne Neville, Warwick's youngest daughter, took sanctuary in a nunnery and waited for news, as every other woman in England waited for news.

It was a long, hard battle, evenly matched between men exhausted by forced marches in hot sunshine. Edward won, damn him to the hell that he deserves, and the prince, our Prince of Wales, died on the battlefield, like a flower cut down in the harvest. His mother, Queen Margaret of Anjou, was taken prisoner, Anne Neville with her, and Edward of York returned to London like a conqueror. He left behind him a battlefield drenched in blood. Even the churchyard at Tewkesbury had to be scrubbed out and reconsecrated after he let his soldiers in among the Lancaster men who were hiding there to claim sanctuary. Nothing is sacred to York, not even the house of God. My cousin, the Duke of Somerset, Edmund Beaufort, who came to our house to ask my husband to ride beside him, was dragged out of the sanctuary of Tewkesbury Abbey and cut down in the market place: a traitor's death.

Edward came into London in a triumphal procession, Queen Margaret of Anjou in his train, and the same night our king, the true king, the only king, King Henry of Lancaster, died in his rooms at the Tower. They gave out that he was ill, that he was weak with ill health. I knew in my heart that he died a martyr on the blade of the York usurpers.

I excused myself to my husband for all of June and I went to the nuns at Bermondsey Abbey. I spent four weeks on my knees praying for the soul of my king, and for the soul of his son, and for his defeated widow. I prayed for vengeance on the House of York and on Edward, and I prayed that he would lose his son too, and that his wife – the relentlessly successful, beautiful, and now triumphant – Elizabeth would know the agony of losing a boy, as our queen had done. I could only bear to go home when I heard God whisper to me, in those dark nights of my prayer, that I would have vengeance, that if I would be patient and wait and plan, then I would triumph. Then, at last, I could return home, and smile at my husband, and pretend to be at peace.

Jasper held out in Wales until September, and then he wrote to me that he thought both he and Henry would be safer out of the country. If Edward could make war on men in sanctuary, on a saint himself, helpless in his private rooms, then he could certainly murder my son for no greater crime than his name and his inheritance. The true Prince of Wales died at

Tewkesbury, God bless him; and this puts me still closer to the Lancaster throne, and Henry is my son and heir. If in future years men look for a Lancaster claimant to the usurped throne of England, they could call on Henry Tudor. This is his destiny and his danger, and I see both coming to him. York is predominant, nothing can destroy him now. But Henry is young and has a claim to the throne. We must keep him safe and prepare him for war.

I go to my husband's room and note his comfortable arrangements. He has a well-made bed, his jug of small ale on a table at his side, his books in their box, his writing paper for memoranda on his writing desk: everything around him that he could wish. He is seated in his chair, strapped tight around his belly, the pain making him grey and older than his years. But his smile to me is cheerful as always.

'I have heard from Jasper in Wales,' I say flatly. 'He is going into exile.'

My husband waits for me to say more.

'He will take my son with him,' I volunteer. 'There is no safety in England for a boy who is heir to the Lancaster line.'

'I agree,' my husband says equably. 'But my nephew Henry Stafford is safe enough in the York court. They have accepted his fealty. Shouldn't your Henry approach King Edward and offer to serve him?'

I shake my head. 'They are going to France.'

'To plan invasion?'

'For their own safety. Who knows what will come next? These are troubled times.'

'I would see you spared from trouble,' he says gently. 'I wish you would ask Jasper to avoid trouble and not make it.'

'I don't seek trouble for myself and neither does Jasper. I only ask that you will allow me to ride to Tenby and see them sail. I want to say goodbye to my son.'

He pauses for a moment. This turncoat, this coward, snug in his bed, has the right to command me. I wonder if he dares to forbid me to go, and if I dare to defy him.

'It is to put yourself in danger.'

'I have to see Henry before he leaves. Who knows when it will be safe for him to return? He is fourteen years old, he will be a man before I see him again.'

He sighs, and I know I have won. 'You will ride with a full guard?'

'Of course.'

'And turn back if the roads are closed?'

'Yes.'

'Then you can go to say goodbye to your son. But make no promises to them, nor to the future of the House of Lancaster. Your cause was finally defeated at Tewkesbury. Henry's house was destroyed at Tewkesbury. It is over. Your advice to them should be to seek for a way to return in peace.'

I look at him and I know my face is defiant and cold. 'I know it is over,' I say. 'Who should know better than I? It is my cause that is defeated, the head of my house executed, my husband wounded fighting on the wrong side, and my son going into exile. Who should know better than I that all hope is dead for my country?'

SEPTEMBER 1471: TENBY, WALES

I look disbelievingly over the bright water of the harbour at Tenby. The sunshine sparkles, there is a light wind blowing, it is a day to sail for pleasure, surely not for me to stand here, amid the smell of fish, with my heart breaking.

This tiny village is heart and soul for Jasper, and the fishwives and the men are clattering in their rough wooden pattens down the cobbled street that leads to the quay where the little boat bobs that is waiting to take my son away from me. Some of the women are red-eyed at their lord's exile; but I do not cry. Nobody would know from looking at me that I could weep for a week.

My boy has grown again, he is now as tall as me, a youth of fourteen, starting to thicken around his shoulders, his brown eyes level with mine, and he is pale though his summertime freckles are speckled on his nose like the markings on a warm bird's egg. I stare at him, seeing both the child that has grown to a man, and now the boy who should be king. The glory of majesty has come down to him. King Henry and his son Prince Edward are both dead. This boy, my boy, is heir to the

House of Lancaster. This is no longer my boy, the child in my possession: this is England's rightful king.

'I will pray for you every day and write to you,' I say quietly. 'Make sure that you reply to me, I shall want to know how you are. And make sure you say your prayers and attend to your studies.'

'Yes, Lady Mother,' he says obediently.

'I'll keep him safe,' Jasper says to me. For a moment our eyes meet, but we exchange nothing except a grim determination to get this parting over, to get this exile underway, to keep this precious boy safe. I suppose that Jasper is the only man that I have loved, perhaps he is the only man that I will ever love. But there has never been time for words of love between us, we have spent most of our time saying goodbye.

'Times can change,' I say to Henry. 'Edward looks as if he is secure on the throne now with our king in his grave and our prince dead too, but I don't give up. Don't you give up either, my son. We are of the House of Lancaster, we are born to rule England. I said it before, and I was right. I will be right again. Don't forget it.'

'No, Lady Mother.'

Jasper takes my hand and kisses it, bows, and goes towards the little boat. He throws his few bundles of goods down to the master and then, holding his sword carefully aloft, steps down into the fishing smack. He, who commanded half of Wales, is going away with almost nothing. This is indeed defeat. Jasper Tudor leaves Wales like a convict on the run. I can feel my belly burn with resentment at the York usurpers.

My son kneels before me and I put my hand on his soft, warm head and say, 'God bless you and keep you, my son,' and then he rises up and in just a moment he is gone, light-footed over the dirty cobbles. He jumps down the harbour steps like a deer, and is in the boat, and they are casting off before I can say another word. He is gone before I have advised him how to behave in France, he is gone before I can warn him of the perils of the world. It is too fast, too fast, and too final. He has gone.

They push off from the wall and spread the sails, the wind flutters the canvas and they reef it in tightly. There is a creaking noise as the mast and the sheets take the strain and then the boat starts to move, slowly at first, and then more quickly away from the harbour wall. I want to shout, 'Come back!' I even want to shout, 'Don't leave me! Don't leave without me!' like a child. But I cannot call them back to danger, and I cannot run away myself. I have to let him go, my son, my brown-headed son, I have to let him go across the sea into exile; not even knowing when I will see him again.

I come home, dulled by the journey and my constant muttered prayers on every step of the way, my back aching from the jolting of the horse and my eyes dry and sore, to find the physician once again in attendance on my husband. It is a long journey and I am exhausted by the road, and wearied by grief at the loss of my son. Every step of the way I have wondered where he is now, and when I shall see him, indeed if I shall see him ever again. I cannot find it in myself even to pretend an interest when I see the physician's horse in the stable and his servant waiting in the hall. Since we came home from the battle of Barnet, one nurse or another – or the physician or the apothecary or the barber surgeon – have been constant presences in our house. I assume that he has come to deal with my husband's usual complaint of pain from his wound. The slash across his belly has long healed leaving a ridged scar, but he likes to make much of it, talking of his suffering in the wars, and the moment when the sword came down, the dreams he still has at night.

I am accustomed to ignoring his complaints, or suggesting a soothing drink and going to bed early, so when the groom of the bedchamber stops me as I walk into the hall, all I can think is that I am longing to wash and change out of my dirty clothes. I would brush past him but he is urgent, as if something were really wrong. He says the apothecary is grinding herbs in our still room, the physician is with my husband; perhaps I should prepare myself for bad news. Even then, as I sit in the chair and snap my fingers for the pageboy to pull off my riding boots, I am barely listening. But the man goes on fretting. Now they think that the wound went deeper than we realised, and is unhealed, perhaps bleeding into his belly. He has never eaten well since the battle, his groom reminds me mournfully – but still he eats far more than me, who fasts every saint's day and every Friday. He cannot sleep except for snatches of rest – but still he sleeps more than me, who gets up twice in the night, every night, for my prayers. In short it is something and nothing as usual. I wave at him to leave, and tell him I will come at once, but still he hovers around me. This is not the first time that they have run around my husband, thinking him near to death, and found that he had eaten too ripe fruit or drunk too much wine, and I am very sure it will not be the last.

I have never reproached him for sacrificing his health to put a usurper on the throne, and I have nursed him with care as a good wife should: no fault can be laid at my door. But he knows I blame him for the defeat of my king, and he will know that I will blame him for the loss of my son too.

I brush the groom to one side and go to wash my face and hands and change my travel-stained gown, and so it is nearly an hour before I go to my husband's rooms and enter quietly.

'I am glad you are come at last, Lady Margaret, for I don't think he has long,' the physician says softly to me. He has been waiting for me, in the antechamber to my husband's bedroom.

'Long?' I ask. My mind is so filled with my son, my ears listening for the sound of a storm which could blow them off course, or even – please God spare him – sink the little boat, that I don't understand what the man means.

'I am sorry, Lady Margaret,' he says, thinking me stupid with wifely concern. 'But I am afraid I can do no more.'

'No more?' I repeat again. 'Why, what is the matter? What are you saying?'

He shrugs. 'The wound goes deeper than we thought, and he cannot take food at all now. I fear his stomach was severed inside, and has not healed. I am afraid he has not long to live. He can only drink small ale and wine and water, we cannot feed him.'

I look at him uncomprehendingly and then I brush past him, open the door to my husband's bedroom and stride inside. 'Henry?'

His face is ashen on the pillow, grey against the white. His lips are dark. I see how thin and gaunt he has become in the few weeks that I have been absent.

'Margaret,' he says, and he tries to smile. 'I am so glad you are come home at last.'

'Henry . . .'

'Is your boy safely away?

'Yes,' I say.

'That's good, that's good,' he says. 'You will be glad to know that he is safe. And you can apply for his return later, you know. They will not be ungenerous to you, when they know about me . . .'

I pause. It is suddenly clear to me that he means I will be a widow, applying for favour to the king whose service has cost the life of my husband.

'You have been a good wife,' he says kindly. 'I would not have you grieve for me.'

I press my lips together. I have not been a good wife, and we both know it.

'And you should marry again,' he says, his breath coming short. 'But this time, choose a husband who will serve you in the wider world. You need greatness, Margaret. You should marry a man high in the favour of the king, this king, the York king; not a man who loves his hearth and his fields.'

'Don't speak of it,' I whisper.

'I know I have disappointed you,' he continues in his rasping voice. 'And I am sorry for it. I was not suited to these times.' He smiles his crooked, sad smile. 'You are. You should have been a great commander, you should have been a Joan of Arc.'

'Rest,' I say weakly. 'Perhaps you will get better.'

'No, I think I am done for. But I bless you, Margaret, and your boy, and I think you will bring him home safely again. Surely, if anyone can do it, then you will. Make peace with the Yorks, Margaret, and you will be able to bring your boy home. That's my last word of advice for you. Forget your dreams of kingship for him, that's all over, you know. Settle to seeing him safe home, that's the best thing for him, and for England. Don't bring him home for another battle. Bring him home for peace.'

'I will pray for you,' I say quietly.

'Thank you,' he says. 'I think I will sleep now.'

I leave him to sleep and I go out quietly, closing the door behind me. I tell them to call me if he gets any worse, or if he asks for me, and I go to the chapel and get to my knees on the hard stone floor before the altar. I don't even use a kneeler, and

I pray to God to forgive me for my sins to my husband, and to receive him into His holy kingdom where there is no war and no rival kings. It is only when I hear the bell start to toll over and over in the tower above my head that I realise it is dawn, and I have been on my knees all the night, and that my husband of thirteen years died without asking for me.

Only a few weeks later, with masses being said daily for my husband's soul in our little chapel, a messenger wearing a black ribboned hat comes from my mother's house to say that she has died, and I understand that now I am all alone in the world. The only family I have left is Jasper in exile, and my son with him. I am orphaned and widowed and my child is far away from me. They were blown off course, and instead of landing in France as we had planned, they landed in Brittany. Jasper writes to me that this is luck running our way at last, for the Duke of Brittany has seen them and promises them safety and hospitality in his dukedom, and that they will perhaps be safer in Brittany than in France where Edward is certain to make a peace treaty, since all he wants now is peace, and cares nothing for the honour of England. I reply at once.

> *My dear brother Jasper, I write to tell you that my husband, Sir Henry Stafford, has died of his wounds and so I am now a widow. I apply to you as the head of the Tudor house to advise me what I should do.*

I pause. I write: 'Shall I come to you?' And then I cross it out and throw away the piece of paper. I write: 'May I come to see my son?' Then I write: 'Please, Jasper . . .'

In the end I write, 'I await your advice', and I send it by messenger.

Then I wait for the reply.

I wonder if he will send for me? I wonder if at last he will say that we can be together, with my boy?

WINTER 1471–2

I wear black for my husband and my mother, and I close down much of the house. As a widow I won't be called on to entertain my neighbours, not in this first year of my loss; and even though I am a great lady of the House of Lancaster I won't be summoned to court, nor will this new king, this blanched rose king and his fecund wife, visit me in the twelve months of my mourning. I need not fear the honour of their favour. I expect they want to forget all about me, and the House of Lancaster. Especially, I doubt that she, who is so much older than him – thirty-four now! – would want him to meet me in the first year of my widowhood when he would see the twenty-eight-year-old heiress of the House of Lancaster, in possession of her fortune, ready to marry again. Perhaps he would regret choosing a nobody.

But no message comes from Jasper summoning me, calling me from the safety of England to the danger and challenge of life with him in Brittany. Instead, he writes that the Duke of Brittany has promised to give him and Henry protection. He does not tell me to come to him. He does not see that this is our chance, our only chance, and I understand his silence very well. He has dedicated his life to my son, to raising him to his name and his lands. He is not going to jeopardise this by marrying me, and having all three of us in exile together. He has to keep me, holding Henry's inheritance, managing his lands and pursuing his interests, in England. Jasper loves me, I know that; but it is, as he says, courtly love, from afar. He doesn't seem to mind how far.

My dowry lands revert to me, and I start to gather the information about them, and to summon the stewards so that they can explain to me the profits that can be made from them. At least my husband kept them in good heart, he was a good landlord, if no leader of men. A good English landlord, if no hero. I do not grieve for him as a wife, as Anne Devereux has grieved for her husband William Herbert. She promised him she would never remarry; she swore she would go to her grave hoping to meet him in heaven. I suppose they were in some sort of love, though married by contract. I suppose they found some sort of passion in their marriage. It is rare: but not impossible. I do hope that they have not given my son ideas about loving his wife; a man who is to be king can only marry for advantage. A woman of sense would always only marry for the improvement of her family. Only a lustful fool dreams every night of a marriage of love.

Sir Henry may have hoped for more than dutiful affection from me; but my love was given over to my son, to my family and to my God, long before we ever met. I wanted a celibate life from childhood and neither of my husbands seduced me from my vocation. Henry Stafford was a man of peace rather than passion, and in his later years he was a traitor. But, in all honesty, now he is gone, I find I miss him, more than I would have imagined.

I miss his companionship. The house felt somehow warmer

when he was home; and he was always at home, like a beloved dog at the fireside. I miss his quiet, dry humour, and his thoughtful common sense. And in the first months of my widowhood, I brood on his words of advice that I should reconcile myself to the son of York on the throne and his son in the royal cradle. Perhaps the wars are indeed over, perhaps we are finally defeated, perhaps it is my task in life to learn humility: to live without hope. I, who modelled myself on a fighting virgin, will perhaps have to learn to become a defeated widow. Perhaps this is God's hard will for me, and I should learn to obey.

For a moment, for a moment only, prowling around my quiet house, alone in my dark dress, I wonder if I might leave England altogether, and, uninvited, join Jasper and my son in Brittany. I could take a fortune big enough to keep us for a year or two. I could marry Jasper and we could live as a family, and even if we never reclaimed the throne for Henry we could form our own household and live as royal exiles.

It is a dream that I allow myself for no more than a longing heartbeat. To live with my boy, and watch him grow, is a joy that God has not granted me. If I were to marry a man for love, it would be the first time in a life that has seen two loveless unions. Passion between a man and a woman is not the road that has been marked out for me. I know that God wants me to serve my son and my house in England. To run away to Brittany like a gipsy woman to be with the two of them would be to surrender any chance of getting my son's inheritance restored to him, his title restored to him, and he himself safely returned to his place in the highest circles of the land. And I have to observe that Jasper chooses Henry's cause over Henry's mother.

Even if my husband's dying advice proves right, and there is no future for Henry as King of England, then I still have to claim his earldom, and try to get his lands returned to him. This is the road I have to take now. If I am to serve my family and serve my son, I will have to place myself in the court of York, whatever I think of Edward and his enchanting queen. I will learn to smile at my enemies. I will have to find myself a husband who has influence with them, who can take me to the highest place in the land, but still has the sense to think for himself, and serve his own ambition and mine.

APRIL 1472

I take a month to consider the court of York, the court of hedge-rose usurpers, and wonder which of the men favoured by the king would be most likely to protect me and my lands and bring my son home in safety. William, now ennobled as Lord, Hastings, the king's best friend and companion, has a wife already, and is in any case heart and soul for Edward. He would never consider a stepson's interest against the king he loves. He would never turn his coat against York, and I have to marry a man who is prepared to be true to my cause. At the very best, I want a husband who is ready to turn traitor. The queen's brother, Sir Anthony Woodville, the new Earl Rivers, would be of interest, except that he is notoriously loyal and loving to his sister. Even if I could bear to marry into the upstart family of a queen who found her husband by standing at the roadside like a whore, I could not turn any of her family against her and against their darling baby boy. They stick together like the brigands they are. The Rivers run together, everyone says it. Always downhill, of course.

I consider the king's brothers. I don't think I am looking too high. After all, I am the heiress to the House of Lancaster, it would make sense for York to approach me and heal the wounds of the war through marriage. George, the next brother to the king, the practised turncoat, is already married to Warwick's eldest daughter Isobel, who must rise up every morning to regret her father's ambition in pairing her with this vain fool; but Richard, the younger brother, is still free. He is nearly twenty years old, so there would be eight years between us, but worse matches have been made. All that I hear of him is that he is faithfully loyal to his brother; but once married to me, with an heir to the throne as his stepson, how could any young man resist treasonous ambition, especially a York?

But the fact that I cannot have Edward the King just eats into me, day after day, as I consider the men I could marry. If only Edward had not been entrapped by the beautiful Elizabeth Woodville, he would have made the perfect match for me now. The York boy, and the Lancaster heiress! Together we could have healed the wounds of our country and made my son the next king. By marrying we would have unified our houses and put an end to rivalry and war. I care nothing for his good looks as I am devoid of vanity and lust, but the rightness of being his wife and becoming Queen of England haunts me like a lost love. If it were not for Elizabeth Woodville and her shameless capture of a young man, it could be me at his side now, Queen of England, signing my letters: Margaret R. They say that she is a witch and captured him with spells and married him on May Day – whatever the truth of that, I can clearly see how she has circumvented the will of God by seducing the man who could have made me queen. She must be a woman beyond wickedness.

But it is pointless to mourn, and anyway Edward would be a hard husband to respect. How could one bear to obey a man constantly bent on pleasure? What might he command a wife to do? What vices might he embrace? If he bedded a woman, what dark and secret pleasures might he insist on? It makes me shudder to think of Edward naked. I hear he is quite without morals. He bedded his upstart wife and wedded her (probably in that order) and now they have a handsome strong son to claim the throne that rightfully belongs to my boy, and no chance of her dying in childbed while she is guarded by her mother, who is without doubt a witch. No chance for me at all unless I can creep close to the throne through his young brother Richard. I would not stand in the road and try to tempt him like his brother's wife did; but I might make a proposal that would interest him.

I send my steward, John Leyden, to London with instructions to befriend and dine with the head of Richard's household. He is to say nothing, but see how the land lies. He must see if the young prince has a betrothal in mind, discover if he would be interested in my land holdings in Derbyshire. He is to whisper in his ear that a Tudor stepson whose name commands all of Wales is a boy worth fathering. He is to wonder aloud if Richard's heart-felt fidelity to his brother might waver so far as to marry into the enemy house, if the terms were right. He is to see what the young man might take as a price for the wedding. He is to remind him that though I am eight years his senior, I am still slim and comely and not yet thirty years old; some would say that I am pleasing. Perhaps I could be even seen as beautiful. I am no golden-haired whore of his brother's choosing; but I am a woman of dignity and grace. For one moment only I think of Jasper's hand on my waist on the stair at Pembroke and his kiss on my mouth before we drew back.

My steward is to emphasise that I am devout, and that no woman in England prays with more fervour or goes on more pilgrimages, and that though he may think this is nothing (after all, Richard is a young man and from a foolish family), to have a wife who has the ear of God, whose destiny is guided by the Virgin herself, is an advantage. It is something to have a woman leading your household who has had saints' knees from childhood.

But it is all for nothing. John Leyden comes home on his big bay cob and shakes his head at me as he dismounts before the front door of the house at Woking.

'What?' I snap without further greeting, though he has ridden far, and his face is red from the heat of May. A page runs towards him with a foaming tankard of ale and he buries his face in it as if I am not waiting, as if I do not thirst and fast all Friday, every week, and on holy days too.

'What?' I repeat.

'A word in private,' he says.

So I know that it is bad news and I lead the way, not to my private rooms where I don't want a hot sweaty man drinking ale, but to the chamber on the left of the great hall where my husband used to do the business of his lands. Leyden closes the door behind him and finds me before him, my face hard. 'What went wrong? Did you botch it?'

'Not I. It was a botched plan. He is married already,' he says, and takes another draught.

'What?'

'He has snapped up the other Warwick heiress, the sister of Isobel that is married to George. He has married Anne Neville, the widow of the Prince of Wales, Edward the Prince of Wales that was. He that died at Tewkesbury.'

'How could he?' I demand. 'Her mother would never let such a thing happen. How would even George let it happen? Anne is heiress to the Warwick estates! He's not likely to let his younger brother have her! He won't want Richard sharing the Warwick fortune! Their lands! The loyalty of the north!'

'Didn't know,' my steward gurgles from the bottom of his tankard. 'They say that Richard went to George's house, found Lady Anne there in hiding, took her away, hid her himself, and married her without even permission from the Holy Father. At any event, the court is in uproar at Richard taking her to wife; but he has her, the king will forgive him, and there is no new husband for you, my lady.'

I am so furious that I don't dismiss him but stride from the room, leaving him there with his ale in his hand like a dolt. To think that I was considering young Richard and all the time he was courting and capturing a Warwick girl, and now the York family and the Warwick family are all nicely tied in together and I am excluded. I feel as offended as if I had proposed to him myself, and been rejected. I was truly preparing to lower myself to marry one of the House of York – and then I find that he has taken young Anne to bed and it is all over.

I go to the chapel and drop down on my knees to take my complaints to Our Lady, who will understand how insulting it is to be overlooked, and for such a weak thing as Anne Neville. I pray with irritation for the first hour but then the calm of the chapel comes to me, the priest comes in for the evening prayers, and the familiar ritual of the service soothes me. As I whisper the prayers and run my rosary beads through my fingers, I wonder who else might be the right age, and unmarried and powerful at the court of York, and Our Lady in her particular care for me sends me a name as I say 'Amen'. I rise to my feet and leave the chapel with a new plan. I think I have the very man who would turn his coat to the winning colours and I whisper his name to myself: Thomas, Lord Stanley.

Lord Stanley is a widower born loyal to my house of Lancaster, but never very certain in his preference. I remember Jasper complaining that at the battle of Blore Heath, Stanley swore to our queen, Margaret of Anjou, that he would be there for her, with his two thousand men, and she waited and waited for him to come and take the victory for her, and while she was waiting for him, York won the battle. Jasper swore that Stanley was a man who would take out all his affinity in battle array – an army of many thousands of men – and then sit on a hill to see who was going to win before declaring his loyalty. Jasper said he was a specialist of the final charge. Whichever was the victor, they were always grateful to Stanley. This is a man that Jasper would despise. This is a man that I would have despised. But now it may be that this is the very man I need.

He turned his coat after the battle of Towton to become a York, and rose high in favour with King Edward. He is now steward of the royal household, as close to the king as it is possible to get, and is rewarded with great lands in north-west England that would make a fine match with my own lands, and might make a good inheritance for my son Henry in the future, though Stanley has children and a grown son and heir of his own already. King Edward seems to admire and trust him, though my suspicion is that the king is (and not for the first time) mistaken. I would not trust Stanley further than I could watch him, and if I did, I would still keep an eye on his brother. As a family they have a tendency to divide and join opposing sides to ensure that there is always one who wins. I know him as a proud man, a cold man, a man of calculation. If he were on my side I would have a powerful ally. If he were Henry's stepfather I might hope to see my boy home in safety and restored to his titles.

Without mother or father to represent me, I have to apply to him myself. I am twice widowed, and a woman of nearly thirty years. I think it is time that I might take my life into my own keeping. Certainly, I know that I should have waited for a full year of mourning before I approached him; but once I had thought of him, I was afraid that the queen would snap him up in a marriage to benefit her family if I left him too long, and besides, I want him working to get Henry home at once. I am not a lady of leisure who has years to mull over plans. I want things done now. I don't have the queen's ill-gotten advantages of beauty and witchcraft – I have to do my work with honesty and speed.

And in any case, his name came into my mind when I was on my knees in chapel. Our Lady Mother Herself guided me to him. The will of God is that I should find in him a husband for me, and an ally for my son. I think I will not trust John Leyden this time. Joan of Arc did not find a man to do her work for her, she rode out in her own battles. So I write to Stanley myself, and propose a marriage between ourselves in as simple and as honest terms as I can manage.

I have some nights of worry that I will disgust him by being so blunt about my plans. Then I think of Elizabeth Woodville waiting for the King of England under an oak tree, as if she just happened to be by the roadside, a hedge-witch casting her spells, and I think that my way at least is an honourable offer and not a begging for an amorous glance and a sluttish strutting of her well-worn wares. Then at last he writes in reply. The steward of his household will meet mine in London and if they can agree on a marriage contract, he will be delighted to be my husband at once. It is as simple and as cold as a bill of sale. His letter is as cool as an apple in a store. We have an agreement; but even I note that it does not feel much like a wedding.

The stewards, and then the bailiffs, and then finally the lawyers meet. They wrangle, they agree, and we are to be married in June. It is no little decision for me – for the first time in my life I have my own lands in my own hands as a widow; once I am a wife, everything becomes Lord Stanley's property.

I have to struggle to reserve what I can from the law that rules that a wife has no rights, and I keep what I can, but I know I am choosing my master.

JUNE 1472

We meet only the day before the wedding, in my house – now his house – at Woking, so it is just as well that I find him well-made, with a brown, long face, thinning hair, a proud bearing and dressed richly – the Stanley fortune showing in his choice of embroidered cloth. There is nothing here to make the heart leap; but I want nothing to make my heart leap. I want a man that I can rely on to be false-hearted. I want a man who looks as if he can be trusted, and yet is not trustworthy. I want an ally and a co-conspirator, I want a man who comes naturally to double-dealing, and when I see his straight eyes, and his sideways smile, and his general air of self-importance, I think: here I have one.

I look at myself in the mirror before I go down to him, and I feel once again my fruitless irritation at the York queen. They say she has wide grey eyes but I have only brown. They say she wears the tall, conical hats sweeping with priceless veils that make her appear seven feet tall; and I wear a wimple like a nun. They say she has hair like gold; and mine is brown like a thick mane on a hill pony. I have trained myself in the holy ways, in the life of the spirit, and she is filled with vanity. I am tall like her, and I am slim from fasting on holy days. I am strong and brave and these should be qualities that a man of sense might look for in a woman. For see: I can read, I can write, I have several translations from the French to my credit, I am learning Latin and I have composed a small book of my own prayers, which I have had copied and given to my household commanding them to be read morning and night. There are few such women – indeed is there another woman in the country who can say as much? I am a highly intelligent, highly educated woman, from a royal family, called by God to great office, guided personally by the Maid, and constantly hearing the voice of God in my prayers.

But I am well aware that these virtues count as nothing in the world where a woman like the queen is praised to the skies for the allure of her smile and for the easy fecundity of her cream-fed body. I am a thoughtful, plain, ambitious woman. And today, I have to wonder if this will be enough for my new husband. I know – who should know better than I, who have been disregarded all my life? – that spiritual riches do not count for much in the world.

We dine in the hall before my tenants and servants and so we cannot talk privately till he comes to my chambers after dinner. My ladies are sewing with me and one is reading from the Bible as he comes in and he takes his seat without interrupting her, and listens till she comes to the end of the passage, with his head bowed. So he is a godly man, or at any rate, hoping to pass as one. Then I nod them to stand aside and he and I sit by the fire. He takes the seat where my husband Henry used to sit in the evening, talking of nothing of importance, cracking walnuts and throwing the shells into the hearth; and for a moment, I feel a renewed sense of surprising loss for that comfortable man who had the gift of innocents: being happy in a little life.

'I hope I will please you as a wife,' I say quietly. 'I thought it would be an arrangement which would suit us both equally.'

'I am glad that you thought of it,' he says politely.

I hesitate. 'I believe my advisors made it clear to you that I intend that there should be no issue from our marriage?'

He does not look up at me, perhaps I have embarrassed him by being too blunt. 'I understood that the marriage will be binding but unconsummated. We will share a bed tonight, to complete the contract, but that you regard yourself as celibate as a nun?'

I take a little breath. 'I hope that is agreeable to you?'

'Perfectly,' he says coldly.

For a moment, looking at his down turned face, I wonder if I really want him to agree so readily that he will be my husband but never my lover. Elizabeth the queen, a woman six years older than me, is bedded passionately by her husband, who demonstrates his lust for her with a new baby almost every year. I was infertile with Henry Stafford when I endured his infrequent intimacy; but perhaps I might have had another chance with this husband, himself a father, if I had not ruled it out before we had even met.

'I believe I have been chosen by God for a higher purpose,' I explain, almost as if inviting an argument. 'And that it is His will that I am prepared for it. I cannot be a mistress to a man, and a servant of God.'

'As you wish,' he says, as if he is indifferent.

I want him to understand that this is a calling. I suppose, somehow for some reason, I want him to try to persuade me to be his wife indeed. 'I believe that God chose me to bear the next Lancaster King of England,' I whisper to him. 'And I have dedicated my life to keeping my son in safety and I have sworn a holy vow that I will put him on the throne, whatever it costs me. I will have only one son, I am devoted to his success alone.'

At last he looks up, as if to confirm that my face is shining with holy purpose. 'I think I made it clear to your advisors that you will be required to serve the House of York: King Edward and Queen Elizabeth?'

'Yes. I made it clear to yours that I want to be at court. It is only with the king's favour that I can bring my son home.'

'You will be required to come to court with me, to take up a place in the queen's chamber, to support me in my work as their pre-eminent courtier and advisor, and to be to all appearances a loyal and faithful member of the House of York.'

I nod, not taking my eyes from his face. 'This is my intention.'

'There must be no shadow of doubt or anxiety in their mind from the first day to the last,' he rules. 'You must make them trust you.'

'It will be an honour,' I lie boldly, and I see from the gleam of amusement in his brown eyes that he knows I have steeled myself to come to this point.

'You are wise,' he says so softly that I can hardly hear him. 'I think he is invincible, for now. We will have to cut our coats to suit our cloth, and wait and see.'

'Will he really accept me at his court?' I ask, thinking of the long struggle which Jasper has waged against this king, and that even now Wales is still uneasy under the York rule, and Jasper waiting in Brittany for good times to come, guarding my boy who should be king.

'They are eager to heal the wounds of the past. They are desperate for friends and allies. He wants to believe that you have joined my house and his affinity. He will meet you as my wife,' Lord Stanley replies. 'I have spoken to him of this marriage, of course, and he wishes us well. The queen too.'

'The queen? She does?'

He nods. 'Without her goodwill, nothing happens in England.'

I force a smile. 'Then I suppose I shall have to learn to please her.'

'You will. You and I may have to live and die under York rule. We have to come to terms with them, and – better yet – rise in their favour.'

'Will they let me bring my son home?'

He nods. 'That is my plan. I have not asked for it yet, and I won't for a while; until you are established at court and they start to trust you. You will find them eager to trust and to like people. They are truly charming. You will find them welcoming. Then we will see what we can do for your son, and what rewards he can offer me. How old is he now?'

'He is just fifteen,' I say. I can hear the longing in my voice as I think of my boy growing into manhood unseen. 'His Uncle Jasper has him safely in Brittany.'

'He will have to leave Jasper,' Lord Stanley warns. 'Edward will never reconcile with Jasper Tudor. But I would have thought they would let your son come home, if he was ready to swear loyalty to them, and we gave our word he would cause no trouble, resign his claims.'

'George, Duke of Clarence, has taken my son's title of Earl of Richmond,' I remark jealously. 'My son must come home to his rights. He has to have his title and lands when he comes home. He must come home as the earl that he is.'

'George has to be kept sweet,' Lord Stanley says bluntly. 'But we might buy him off in some way, or make some arrangement. He is as greedy as a boy in the pastry kitchen. He is disgustingly venal. And he is as trustworthy as a cat. We can no doubt bribe him with something from our shared fortune. After all, between the two of us, we are very great landowners.'

'And Richard, the other brother?' I ask.

'Loyal as a dog,' Lord Stanley replies. 'Loyal as a hog. Loyal as the hog of his badge. Heart and soul, Edward's man. He hates the queen, so there is the one small crack in the court, if one wanted to find a fault. But you would be hard put to force the sharpest tip of a dagger in there. Richard loves his brother and despises the queen. William Hastings, the king's great friend, is the same. But what is the use of looking for cracks in a house so staunch? Edward has a handsome, strong boy in the cradle and good reason to hope for more. Elizabeth Woodville is a fecund wife. The Yorks are here to stay and I am working to be their most trusted subject. As my wife you must learn to love them as I do.'

'From conviction?' I ask, as softly as he.

'I am convinced for now,' he says, quiet like a snake.

1482

I learn a new rhythm of life with this new husband, as the years go round, and though he teaches me to be as good a courtier to this royal family as I and mine always were to the true royal house, I never change; I always despise them. We have a great London house, and he rules that we will spend most of the winter months at court, where he waits daily on the king. He is a member of the Privy Council and his advice to the king is always cautious and wise. He is highly regarded for his thoughtfulness and his knowledge of the world. He is particularly careful always to be as good as his word. Having changed sides once in his life, he wants to make sure that the Yorks believe that he will never do it again. He wants to be indispensible: trustworthy as a rock. They nickname him 'the fox' in tribute to his caution; but nobody doubts his loyalty.

The first time he took me to court to present me, as his wife, I was surprised to find that I was more nervous than when I went to court to meet a real monarch. She was nothing but the widow of a country squire; but this usurping queen has dominated my life, and her fortunes have risen unstoppably while mine have struggled. We have been on opposite sides of fortune's wheel and she has risen and risen while I have fallen. She has overshadowed me, she has lived in the palaces that should have been my homes, she has worn a crown that should have been mine. She has been draped in ermine for no better reason than she is beautiful and seductive, whereas those furs are mine by right of birth. She is six years older than me, and she has always been ahead of me. She was on the side of the road when the York king came riding by. The very year that he saw her, fell in love with her, married her and made her his queen was the year that I had to leave my son in my enemy's keeping, live with a husband who I knew who would not father my son, nor fight for my king. While she wore headdresses that grew higher and higher, draped them with the finest lace, commissioned gowns trimmed with ermine, had songs dedicated to her beauty, rewarded winners of tournaments, and conceived a child every year, I went to my chapel and got to my knees and prayed that my son, though raised in my enemy's house, would not become my enemy. I prayed that my husband, though a coward, would not become a turncoat. I prayed that the power of Joan would stay with me and I would find the strength to be constant to my family, my God and myself. All those long years while my son Henry was raised by the Herberts, and I was powerless to do anything but be a good wife to Stafford, this woman spent planning marriages for her family, plotting against her rivals, consolidating her hold over her husband and dazzling England.

Even in the months of her eclipse, when she was in sanctuary and my king was back on the throne and we sailed down the river to the king's court and he recognised my boy as Earl of Richmond, even in that darkness she snatched her moment of triumph, for there she gave birth to her first boy, the baby that we are now to call the Prince of Wales, Prince Edward, and so gave hope to the Yorks.

In everything, even in her moments of apparent defeat, she has triumphed over me, and I must have prayed for nearly twenty years that she should learn the true humility of Our Lady that only comes to those who suffer, and yet I have never seen her improved by hardship.

Now she stands before me, the woman they call the most beautiful in England, the woman who won a throne on her looks, the woman who commands her husband's adoration and the admiration of a nation. I drop my eyes as if in awe. God Himself knows that she doesn't command me.

'Lady Stanley,' she says pleasantly to me as I curtsey low and rise up.

'Your Grace,' I say. I can feel the smile on my face is stretched so hard that my mouth is drying with the effort.

'Lady Stanley, you are welcome to court on your own account, as well as that of your husband who is such a good friend to us,' she says. All the time her grey eyes are taking in my rich gown, my wimple-like headdress, my modest stance. She is trying to read me, and I, standing before her, am trying with every inch of my being to hide my righteous hatred of her, her beauty, and her position. I am trying to look agreeable while I can feel my proud belly turn over with jealousy.

'My husband is happy to serve his king and your house,' I say. I swallow in a dry throat. 'As am I.'

She leans forwards, and in her readiness to hear me I suddenly realise that she wants to believe that I have turned my own coat and am ready to be loyal to them. I see her desire to befriend me, and behind this, her fear that she will never be wholly safe. Only if she has friends in every house in England can she be sure that the houses will not rise against her again.

If she can teach me to love her, then the House of Lancaster loses a great leader: me, the heiress. She must have broken her heart and lost her wits in sanctuary. When her husband had to flee for his life and my king was on the throne she must have been so frightened that now she longs for any friendship: even mine, especially mine.

'I shall be glad to count you among my ladies and my friends,' she says graciously. Anyone would think she was born to be a queen instead of a penniless widow, she has all the style of Margaret of Anjou, and far more charm. 'I am glad to offer you a position at court, as one of my ladies in waiting.'

I picture her as a young widow, standing at the roadside waiting for a lustful king to ride by, and for a moment I fear that my contempt will show in my face. 'I thank you.' I drop my head as I curtsey very low again, and get myself out of her presence.

It is strange for me to smile and bow to my enemy and try to keep the resentment out of my eyes. But over ten years in service to them I learn how to do it so well that no-one knows I whisper to God that He must not forget me in my enemies' house. I learn to pass for a loyal courtier. Indeed, the queen grows fond of me and trusts me as one of her intimate ladies in waiting, who sit with her during the day, dine at her ladies' table at night, dance before the court, and accompany her to her gorgeously furnished rooms. Edward's brother, George, plots against the royal couple, and she clings to us, her ladies, when her husband's family are divided. She has a nasty moment when she is accused of witchcraft and half the court are laughing up their sleeves and the other half crossing themselves when her shadow falls on them. She has me at her side when George goes to his death in the Tower, and I can feel the court shudder with fear at a royal house divided against itself. I hold her hand when they bring news of his death and she thinks that at last she is safe from his enmity. She whispers to me, 'God be praised he is gone,' and all I think is: yes, now he is gone, his title, which once belonged to my son, is free once more. Perhaps I can persuade her to give it back?

When the Princess Cecily was born, I was in and out of the confinement chamber, praying for the queen's safety, and for that of the new baby; and then it was me she asked to stand as godmother to the new princess, and it was I who carried the tiny girl, in my arms, to the font. I, the favourite of all her noble ladies.

Of course, the queen's constant childbearing, almost every year, reminds me of the child I had, but was never allowed to raise. And once a month, through the long ten years, I have a letter from that son, first a youth, and then a man, and then, I realise, a man reaching his majority: a man old enough to make good his claim to be king.

Jasper writes that he has maintained Henry's education; the young man still follows the offices of the church, as I ordered. He jousts, he hunts, he rides, he practises archery, tennis, swimming, all the sports that will keep his body healthy and strong and ready for battle. Jasper has him study accounts of wars and no veteran soldier visits them but Jasper has him talk to Henry about the battle he saw, and how it could have been won, or done differently. He has masters to teach him the geography of England, so that he may know the country where his ships will land, he studies the law and the traditions of his home, so that he may be a just king when his day comes. Jasper never says that teaching a young man in exile from the country that he may never see, preparing him for a battle that may never be joined, is weary work; but as King Edward of England celebrates the twenty-first year of his reign with a glorious Christmas at Westminster Palace, attended by his handsome and strong son, Prince Edward of Wales, we both sense that it is work without purpose, work without chance of success, work without future.

Somehow, over the ten years of my marriage with Thomas Stanley, my son's cause has become a forlorn hope even to me. But Jasper, far away in Brittany, keeps the faith; there is nothing else he can do. And I keep the faith, for it burns inside me that it should be a Lancaster on the throne of England, and my boy is the only Lancaster heir, but for my nephew the Duke of Buckingham, left to us. And the duke is married into the Woodville family and so yoked to York while Henry, my son, keeps the faith, for though he is twenty-five, he has been raised in hope, however faint, and though he is a man grown, he has not yet the independence of thought to tell his beloved guardian Jasper, or me, that he will deny our dream which has cost him his childhood, and still holds him in thrall.

Then, just before the Christmas feast, my husband Thomas Stanley comes to my room in the queen's apartment and says: 'I have good news. I have made an agreement for the return of your son.'

I drop the sacred Bible from my hands and snatch it before it slips from my lap. 'The king has never agreed?'

'He has agreed.'

I am stammering in my joy and relief. 'I never thought he would . . .'

'He is determined on war with France. He doesn't want your boy rattling round on the border as a rival king or a hostage, or whatever. He will let him come home, and he can even have his title. He will be Earl of Richmond.'

I can hardly breathe. 'Praise God,' I say quietly. I long to get to my knees and thank God for sending the king some sense and mercy. 'And his lands?'

'He won't let him have Wales as a Tudor, that's for sure,' Stanley says brutally. 'But he will have to give him something. You might give him something from your dowry lands.'

'He should have his own,' I say, resentful at once. 'I should not have to share my lands. The king should give him his own.'

'He will have to marry a girl of the queen's choosing,' my husband warns me.

'He is not to marry some York makeweight,' I say, instantly irritated.

'He will have to marry whoever she picks out for him,' he corrects me. 'But she has an affection for you. Why don't you talk to her about who you would like? The boy has to marry, but they won't allow him to marry anyone who would strengthen his Lancaster line. It will have to be a York. If you were to put your mind to it, he might have one of the York princesses. There are enough of them, God knows.'

'Can he come at once?' I breathe.

'After the Christmas feast,' my husband says. 'They will need to be reassured, but the main work is done. They trust you, and they trust me, and they believe we would not introduce an enemy into their kingdom.'

It has been so long since we discussed this that I am not sure that he still shares my silent will. 'Have they forgotten that he might be a rival king?' I ask. We are in my own room but still I drop my voice to a whisper.

'Of course he is a rival king,' he says steadily. 'But while Edward the king lives there can be no chance of a throne for him. No-one in England would follow a stranger against Edward. When Edward dies there is Prince Edward, and should anything happen to him, Prince Richard to come after him, beloved boys of a strong ruling house. It is hard to imagine how your Henry could step into a vacant throne. He would have to walk past three coffins. He would have to see the death of a great king and two royal boys. That would be an unlucky set of accidents. Or would he have the stomach to enact such a thing? Would you?'

APRIL 1483: WESTMINSTER

I have to wait till Easter for Henry to come home, though I write to him and to Jasper at once. They start to prepare for his return, dispersing the little court of York opportunists and desperate men who have gathered around them, preparing themselves to part for the first time since Henry's boyhood. Jasper writes to me that he cannot think what he will do with himself without Henry to guide, advise and govern.

> *Perhaps I will go on pilgrimage. Perhaps it is time I considered myself, my own soul. I have lived only for our boy and, far from England as we have been, I had come to think that we would never get home. Now he will return, as he should, but I cannot. I will have lost my brother, my home, you, and now him. I am glad that he can come back to you and take his place in the world. But I shall be very alone in my exile. Truly, I cannot think what I shall do without him.*

I take this letter to Stanley, my husband, where he is working in his day room, papers piled around the table for his assent. 'I think Jasper Tudor would be glad to come home with Henry,' I say cautiously.

'He can come home to the block,' my husband says bluntly. 'Tudor picked the wrong side and clung to it through victory all the way to defeat. He should have sought for pardon after Tewkesbury, when everyone else did; but he was as stubborn as a Welsh pony. I'll use no influence of mine to have him restored, and neither will you. Besides, I think you have an affection for him which I don't share, nor do I admire it in you.'

I look at him in utter amazement. 'He is my brother-in-law,' I say.

'I am aware of that. It only makes it worse.'

'You can't think that I have been in love with him for all these years of absence?'

'I don't think about it at all,' he says coldly. 'I don't want to think about it. I don't want you to think about it. I don't want him to think about it, and especially I don't want the king and that gossip his wife to think about it. So Jasper can stay where he is, we will not intercede for him, and you will have no need to write to him any more. You need not even think of him. He can be dead to us.'

I find I am trembling with indignation. 'You can have no doubt as to my honour.'

'No, I don't want to think about your honour, either,' he repeats.

'Since you have no desire for me yourself, I don't see why you should care one way or the other!' I throw at him.

I cannot anger him. His smile is cold. 'The lack of desire, you will recall, was required by our marriage agreement,' he says. 'Stipulated by you. I have no desire for you at all, my lady. But I have a use for you, as you do for me. Let us stay with this arrangement and not confuse it with words from a romance that neither of us could ever mean to each other. As it happens you are not to my taste as a woman, and God knows what sort of man could raise desire in you. If any. I doubt that even poor Jasper caused more than a chilly flutter.'

I sweep to the door but pause with my hand on the latch to turn back and speak bitterly to him: 'We have been married for ten years, and I have been a good wife to you. You have no grounds for complaint. Have you not the slightest affection for me?'

He looks up from his seat at the table, his quill poised over the silver inkpot. 'You told me when we married that you were given to God and to your cause,' he reminds me. 'I told you I was given to the furtherance of myself and my family. You told me that you wished to live a celibate life, and I accepted this in a wife who brought a fortune, a great name, and a son who has a claim to the throne of England. There is no need for affection here, we have a shared interest. You are more faithful to me for the sake of our cause, than you would ever be for any affection, I know that. If you were a woman who could be ruled by affection you would have gone to Jasper and your son a dozen years ago. Affection is not important to you, nor to me. You want power, Margaret, power and wealth; and so do I. Nothing matters as much as this to either of us, and we will sacrifice anything for it.'

'I am guided by God!' I protest.

'Yes, because you think God wants your son to be King of England. I don't think your God has ever advised you otherwise. You hear only what you want. He only ever commands your preferences.'

I sway as if he has hit me. 'How dare you! I have lived my life in His service!'

'He always tells you to strive for power and wealth. Are you quite sure it is not your own voice that you hear, speaking through the earthquake, wind and fire?'

I bare my teeth at him. 'I tell you that God will have my son Henry on the throne of England and those who laugh now at my visions and doubt my vocation will call me "My Lady, the King's Mother", and I shall sign myself Margaret Regina, *Margaret R* . . .'

There is an urgent tap on the door and the handle is rattled. 'My lord!'

'Come in!' Thomas calls, recognising the voice of his personal secretary.

I step aside as James Peers opens the door and slips in, sketches a bow to me and approaches my husband's writing table. 'It is the king,' he says. 'They are saying he is sick.'

'He was sick last night. Just overeating.'

'He is worse today, they have called more physicians and they are bleeding him.'

'It is serious?'

'It seems so.'

'I'll come at once.'

My husband throws down his pen and strides towards me, where I stand beside the half-open door. He comes close as a lover, and puts his hand on my shoulder to breathe intimately in my ear. 'If he were to be sick, if he were to die, and there were to be a regency and your boy were to return home and serve on the council of regency, then he would be two heartbeats only from the throne and standing beside it. If he were to be a good and loyal servant and attract the notice of men, they might prefer a young man and the House of Lancaster to that of a beardless mother's boy and the House of York. Do you want to stay here and talk about your vocation, and whether you want affection, or do you want to come with me now and see if the York king is dying?'

I don't even answer him. I slip my hand in the crook of his arm and we hurry out, our faces pale with concern for the king that everyone knows we love.

He lingers for days. The agony of the queen is remarkable to see. For all his infidelities to her, and for all his fecklessness with his friends, this is a man who has inspired passionate attachment. The queen is locked in his chamber night and day, physicians go in and out with one remedy after another. The rumours fly around the court like crows seeking a tree in the evening. They say he was chilled by a cold wind off the river when he insisted on fishing at Eastertide. They say that he is sick in his belly from his constant overeating and excessive drinking. Some say that his many whores have given him the pox and it is eating away at him. A few think, like me, that it is the will of God and punishment for treason against the House of Lancaster. I believe that God is making the way straight for the coming of my son.

Stanley takes to the king's rooms where men gather in corners to mutter their fears that Edward, who has been invincible for all his life, may finally have run out of luck. I spend my time in the queen's rooms, waiting for her to come in, to change her headdress and comb her hair. I watch her blank face in the mirror as she lets the maid pin up her hair any way she chooses, I see her white lips moving constantly in prayer. If she were the wife of any other man I would pray for her too from pity. Elizabeth is in agony of fear at losing the man she loves and the one who has stood above us all, unquestionably the greatest man in England.

'What does she say?' my husband asks me as we meet at dinner in the great hall, as subdued as if a funeral pall were laid over us already.

'Nothing,' I reply. 'She says nothing. She is dumbstruck at the thought of losing him. I am certain he is sinking.'

That afternoon the Privy Council is called to the king's bedside. We women wait in the great presence chamber, outside the privy chambers, desperate for news. My husband comes out after an hour, grim faced.

'He swore us to an alliance over his bed,' he says. 'Hastings and the queen: the best friend and the wife. Begged us to work together for the safety of his son. Named his son Edward as the next king, joined the hands of William Hastings and the queen over his bed. Said we should serve under his brother Richard as regent till the boy is of age. Then the priest came in to give him the last rites. He will be dead by nightfall.'

'Did you swear fealty?'

His crooked smile tells me that it meant nothing. 'God, yes. We all swore. We all swore to work peaceably together, swore to friendship unending, so I should think the queen is arming now and sending for her son to come at once from his castle in Wales with as many men as he can muster, armed for war. I should think Hastings is sending for Richard, warning him against the Rivers, calling on him to bring in the men of York. The court will fall apart. Nobody can stand the ascendancy of the Rivers. They are certain to rule England through their boy. It will be Margaret of Anjou all over again, a court run by the distaff. Everyone will be calling on Richard to stop her. You and I must divide and work. I shall write to Richard and pledge fealty to him, while you assure the queen of our loyalty to her and to her family, the Rivers.'

'A foot in each camp at once,' I whisper. It is Stanley's way. This is why I married him, this is the very moment that I married him for.

'My guess is that Richard will hope to rule England till Prince Edward is of age,' he says. 'And then rule England through the boy if he can dominate him. He will be another Warwick. A kingmaker.'

'Or will he be a rival king?' I breathe, thinking as always of my own boy.

'A rival king,' he agrees. 'Duke Richard is a Plantagenet of York, already of age, whose claim to the throne is unquestionable, who does not need a regency nor an alliance of the lords to rule for him. Most people would think him a safer choice for king than an untried boy. Some will see him as the next heir. You must send a messenger to Jasper at once and tell him to keep Henry in safety till we know what will happen next. They cannot come to England till we know who will claim the throne.'

He is about to go but I put a hand on his arm. 'And what do you think will happen next?'

His eyes do not meet mine, he looks away. 'I think the queen and Duke Richard will fight like dogs over the bone that is the little prince,' he says. 'I think they will tear him apart.'

MAY 1483: LONDON

Only four weeks after that hurried conversation I write to Jasper with extraordinary news.

Richard, Duke of Gloucester, the king's own brother, swearing absolute fealty to his nephew Prince Edward, has brought the boy to London and housed him in the king's rooms in the Tower with full honour for his coronation which is to be next month. There was some squabble with the young prince's guardians and Anthony Rivers, his uncle, and Richard Grey, his half-brother, are held by the duke. Elizabeth, the queen, has taken to sanctuary with the rest of her children, swearing that Richard is a false friend and an enemy to her and her own, demanding that her royal son be released to her.

The City is in uproar, not knowing who to believe or whom to trust. Most think that the queen is trying to steal the royal treasure (she has taken as much as she can carry) to defend her own power and family. Her brother is gone with the fleet and has stolen the rest of the treasure of the realm, and is likely to make war on London from the river. Overnight she is an enemy to the kingdom, and even to her own son, since everything is in train for the young prince's coronation and he himself is issuing writs under the joint seal of himself as heir and his uncle as protector. Will the queen's brother bombard her royal son in the Tower? Will she fight him if he is the duke's ward? Will she hide from his coronation?

I will write more as soon as I know more. Stanley says to wait and watch, our time may be now.

Margaret Stanley

JUNE 1483: LONDON.

My husband Lord Stanley is now Duke Richard's trusted advisor, as he was once King Edward's. This is as it should be, he serves the king, and Richard is now the Lord Protector of the king for these short weeks before the boy Edward is crowned. Then Richard must give up everything, throne and power, and the boy will rule as King of England. We will see then who can survive the reign of a child of the Rivers family with the greatest crown in the world on his head, utterly commanded by his mother: a faithless witch in hiding. There are few men who will trust the boy and nobody will trust his mother.

But anyway, what son of the House of York could ever give up power? What child of the House of York could ever bring himself to hand over the throne? Richard surely will not hand the crown and sceptre to the son of a woman who hates him? But whatever doubts we feel, we are all measured for our coronation robes, and they are building the walkway at Westminster Abbey for the royal procession – the widowed Queen Elizabeth must hear the hammering and sawing above her, as she skulks in her sanctuary in the low chambers beside the abbey. The Privy Council went to her in form and demanded that she send her nine-year-old son Richard to join his twelve-year-old brother in the Tower. She could not refuse, and there was no reason for her to refuse, except her own hatred of Duke Richard, and so she had to give way. Now the two royal boys wait in the royal apartments for the coronation day.

I am responsible for the wardrobe for the coronation and I meet with the wardrobe mistress and her maids to see what robes will be provided for the Dowager Queen Elizabeth, the princesses, and the other ladies of court. We must prepare the gowns assuming that the queen will come out of sanctuary for the coronation, and that she will want to be dressed exquisitely as usual. We are supervising the brushing of the queen's ermine robe by the maid of the wardrobe and watching the sempstress sew on a mother-of-pearl button, when the wardrobe mistress remarks that the Duchess of Gloucester, Anne Neville, Richard's wife, has not ordered her gown from the wardrobe.

'Her command must have gone astray,' I observe. 'For she cannot have what she needs to wear for a coronation at her castle at Sherrif Hutton. And she cannot be ordering something to be made, it will never be ready in time.'

She shrugs as she pulls out a robe trimmed with velvet, shakes off the linen cover and spreads it out for me to see. 'I don't know. But I have no order for a gown from her. What should I do?'

'Prepare one for her, in her size,' I say, as if I am not much interested, and I turn the talk to something else.

I hurry home, and I seek out my husband. He is writing out the warrants that will summon every sheriff in England to London to see the young king crowned. 'I am busy. What is it?' he says rudely, as I open the door.

'Anne Neville has not ordered a gown for the coronation. What d'you think of that?'

He thinks as I did, as swiftly as I did. He puts down his pen and beckons me in. I close the door behind me, with a little thrill of joy at conspiring with him. 'She never acts on her own account. Her husband must have ordered her not to come,' he says. 'Why would he do that?'

I don't answer. I know he will be thinking fast.

'She has no gown, so she cannot be coming to the coronation. He will have told her not to come for he must have decided that there will be no coronation,' he says quietly. 'And all this' – he gestures at the piles of paper – 'all this is just to keep us busy and to fool us into thinking that the coronation will happen.'

'Perhaps he has warned her not to come because he thinks London may riot. Perhaps he wants her safe at home.'

'Who would riot? Everyone wants the York prince crowned. There is only one person who would prevent him becoming king, just as there is only one person who would benefit.'

'Duke Richard of Gloucester himself?'

My husband nods. 'What can we do with this precious information? How shall we use it?'

'I'll tell the Dowager Queen,' I decide. 'If she is going to muster her forces she should do it now. She had better get her sons away from Richard's keeping. And if I can persuade the York queen to fight the York regent then there is a chance for Lancaster.'

'Tell her the Duke of Buckingham might be fit for turning,' he says quietly, as I am halfway out of the door. I stop at once. 'Stafford?' I repeat incredulously. This is my second husband's nephew – the little boy who inherited the title when his grandfather died, who was forced into marriage with the queen's sister. He has hated the Rivers family ever since they forced him to marry into them. He cannot abide them. So he was first to back Richard, he was first to his side. He was there when Richard arrested Anthony Rivers. I know he will have loved the humiliation of the man he was forced to call brother-in-law. 'But Henry Stafford cannot bear the queen. He hates her and he hates her sister, his wife Katherine. I know it. I remember when they married him. He would never turn against Richard in their favour.'

'He has his own ambitions,' my husband remarks darkly. 'He has royal blood in his line. He will be thinking that if the throne can be taken from Prince Edward, then it can be taken from Richard too. He would join with the queen, pretending to defend her son, and then take the throne for himself when they have victory.'

I think quickly. The Stafford family, with the exception of my weakly modest husband Henry, has always been extreme in its pride. Stafford backed Richard from spite against the Rivers, now he might indeed stake his own claim. 'I'll tell the queen if you wish,' I say. 'But I would think him utterly untrustworthy. She will be a fool to take him as an ally.'

My husband smiles, more like a wolf than the fox they call him. 'She has not many friends to choose from,' he says. 'I would think she will be glad of him.'

A week after this, at dawn, my husband thumps his fist on my bedroom door and comes in as my maid screams and jumps up from her bed. 'Leave us,' he says brusquely to her, and she scuttles from the room as I sit up in bed and draw my robe around me.

'What is it?' My first fear is that my son is ill, but then I see that Thomas is white as if he has seen a ghost, his hands are shaking. 'What has happened to you?'

'I had a dream.' He sits down heavily on the bed. 'Good God, I had such a dream. Margaret, you have no idea . . .'

'Was it a vision?'

'How would I know? It was like being trapped in hell.'

'What did you dream?'

'I was in a cold and rocky dark place, like some wilderness, nowhere I know. I looked around me, no-one was with me, I was alone, none of my affinity, none of my men, not even my standard, nothing. I was quite alone, not my son, not my brother – not even you.'

I wait for more. The bed shakes with his shudder. 'A monster came towards me,' he says, his voice very low. 'A terrible, terrible thing came towards me, its mouth open to eat me, its breath stinking like hell, its eyes piggy and red, looking from right to left, a monster coming across the country, coming for me.'

'What sort of monster? A serpent?'

'A boar,' he says quietly. 'A wild boar with blood on its tusks and blood on its nostrils, spittle on its mouth, its head down low, tracking me.' He shudders. 'I could hear it snuffle.'

The wild boar is the emblem of Richard, Duke of Gloucester. We both know this. I get out of bed and open the door to make sure that the maid has gone and there is no-one listening outside. I close it tightly, and stir up the embers of the little bedroom fire as if we need heat on this warm June night. I light candles, as if to drive away the darkness of the hunting boar, I touch the cross around my throat with my finger, I make the sign of the cross on myself. Stanley has brought his night terrors in with him, into my room, it is as if the breath of the boar has whispered in with him, as if he will smell us out, even now, even here.

'You think Richard suspects you?'

He looks at me. 'I have done nothing but show him my support. But it was such a dream . . . I can't deny it. Margaret, I woke filled with terror like a child. I woke myself with my scream for help.'

'If he suspects you, he will suspect me,' I say. Stanley's fear is so strong it has me in its grip. 'And I have sent messages to the queen, as we agreed. Could he know I am his enemy?'

'Could your messages have gone astray?'

'I am certain of my man. And she is not a fool. But why else would he doubt you?'

He shakes his head. 'I have done nothing except speak to Hastings, who is loyal to the core. He is desperate to secure the succession of the prince. It is his last act of love for Edward the king. He is deeply afraid that Richard might play false with Prince Edward. He has been frightened of something going wrong ever since Richard took the prince to the Tower. He asked me if I would join with him at a Privy Council meeting to insist that the prince should come out among the people, to visit his mother, to show that he is free in every way. I think he has sent a messenger to the queen to assure her of her safety and ask her to come out of hiding.'

'Does Hastings know that Richard has ordered his own wife to stay home? Does he think Richard might delay the coronation? Prolong his own regency?'

'I told him Anne Neville had no coronation gown, and he swore at once that Richard cannot be truly planning to crown his nephew. It's what we are all starting to think. It's what we're all starting to fear. But I can't see anything worse than Richard delaying the coronation, perhaps for years, perhaps till the boy is twenty-one. Delaying it so that he can rule as regent.' He leaps to his feet and strides barefoot across the room. 'For God's sake, Richard was the most loyal brother Edward could ever have had! He has said nothing but asserted his loyalty to the prince. His own nephew! All his enmity has been directed to the Dowager Queen; not against Edward's son. And he has the boy utterly in his power now. Crowned or not, Prince Edward can only be a puppet king if Richard can keep him from his mother and from his kin.'

'But the dream . . .'

'The dream was of a boar determined on power and death. It was a warning, it must be a warning.'

We are both silent. A log shifts in the fireplace and we both flinch from the sound.

'What will you do?' I ask him.

He shakes his head. 'What would you do? You think that God speaks to you and warns you in dreams. What would you do if you dreamed that the boar was coming for you?'

I hesitate. 'You can't think of running away?'

'No, no.'

'I would pray for guidance.'

'And what would your God say?' he asks with a flare of his usual sarcasm. 'He is usually reliable in advising you to seek power and safety.'

I take my seat on the stool by the fire, looking into the flames as if I were a poor woman telling fortunes, as if I were Queen Elizabeth with her witchcraft skills. 'If Richard were to turn against his nephew, both nephews, and somehow prevent their inheritance, put himself on the throne in their place . . .' I pause. 'They have no powerful defenders any more. The fleet has mutinied against their uncle, their mother is in sanctuary, their Uncle Anthony is under arrest . . .'

'Then what?'

'If Richard were to take the throne and leave his nephews locked in the Tower, do you think the country would rise against him and there would be another war?'

'York against York. It's possible.'

'And in those circumstances there would be a great chance for the House of Lancaster.'

'For your son, Henry.'

'For Henry to be the last one standing when they tear each other to pieces in a fight to the death.'

There is silence in my room. I glance at him, afraid that I may have gone too far.

'There are four lives between Henry and the throne,' he remarks. 'The two York princes: Edward and Richard, Duke Richard himself, and then his son.'

'But they might all fight each other.'

He nods.

'If they choose to destroy themselves, it is no sin for Henry to take the empty throne,' I say firmly. 'And at last, the rightful house takes the throne of England, which is God's will.'

He smiles at my certainty, but this time I am not offended. What matters is that we can see our way, and as long as I know it is the light of God then it does not matter if he thinks it is the blaze of sinful ambition.

'So will you go to the Privy Council meeting today?'

'Yes, it's at the Tower. But I will send a message to Hastings of my fears. If he is going to move against Richard, he had better do so now. He can force Richard to show his hand. He can demand to see the prince. His love for the late king will make him the prince's champion. I can stand back and let him step up the pace. The council is determined that the prince should be crowned. Hastings can demand it. He can bear the brunt of showing Richard that he suspects him. I can set

Hastings on Richard and step back to see what will happen. I can be warned by this, and I can warn Hastings and let him take the danger.'

'But where do you stand?'

'Margaret, I stay loyal to whoever is most likely to triumph, and at the moment, the man with the army of the north at his back, the Tower in his possession, and the rightful king obedient to him and in his keeping: is Richard.'

I wait for the return of my husband from his council meeting, on my knees before my prie dieu. Our dawn conversation has unsettled and frightened me, and I kneel in prayer and think of Joan, who must have known herself to be in danger so many times, and yet rode out on her white horse with her banner of lilies and did not have to fight her battles in secrecy and silence.

I think it is almost a part of my prayer when I hear the march of many feet down the street and the clanking on the cobbles as a hundred pikemen ground their pikes, and then there is a hammering on the big street door of our London house.

I am halfway down the stairs as the porter's boy comes running up to tell the maids to call me. I grab him by the arm. 'Who is it?'

'Duke Richard's men,' he gabbles. 'In his livery, with the master, they've got the lord, your husband. Smacked in the face, blood on his jerkin, bleeding like a pig . . .'

I push him to one side as he is making no sense, and I run down to the cobbled entrance where the gatemen are swinging open the gate and Duke Richard's troop march in, and at the centre of them is my husband, swaying on his feet, blood pouring from a wound to his head. He looks at me and his face is white and his eyes are blank with shock.

'Lady Margaret Stanley?' asks the commander of the guard.

I can hardly drag my eyes from the symbol of the boar on his livery. A tusked boar just as my husband dreamed was coming for him.

'I am Lady Margaret,' I say.

'Your husband is under house arrest and he and you cannot leave here. There will be guards stationed at all doorways and in your house, and at the doors and windows of his chambers. Your household and necessary servants can go about their business but they will be stopped and searched at my command. Do you understand?'

'Yes,' I whisper.

'I am going to search the house for letters and papers,' he says. 'Do you understand this too?'

There is nothing in my rooms that would incriminate either of us. I burn anything dangerous as soon as I have read it, and I never keep a copy of my own letters. All my work for Henry is between me and God.

'I understand. May I take my husband to my closet? He is wounded.'

He gives a grim smile. 'When we marched in to arrest Lord Hastings, your husband dived under the table and nearly took off his own head on a pike-blade. It looks worse than it is.'

'You arrested Lord Hastings?' I ask incredulously. 'On what charge?'

'Madam, we have beheaded him,' he says shortly. He pushes past me into my own rooms, and his men fan out in my yard and take up their positions, and we are prisoners in our own great house.

Stanley and I go to my closet, surrounded by pikemen, and only when they have seen that the window is too small for escape do they step back and close the door on the two of us and we are alone.

Stanley throws his bloodstained jerkin and spoiled shirt to the floor with a shudder, and sits on a stool, stripped to the waist. I pour a jug of water into the ewer and start to wash the cut. It is shallow and long, a glancing blow, not one aimed to kill, but an inch lower and he would have lost an eye. 'What is happening?' I whisper.

'Richard came in at the start of the meeting to determine the order of the coronation, all smiles, asked Bishop Morton to send out for strawberries from his garden, very affable. We started our work on the coronation, the seating, the precedence, the usual things. He went out again, and while he was outside, someone must have brought him some news or a message and he came in a changed man, with a face dark with rage. The troop came in after him like they were overrunning a fort, banging in the door, weapons at the ready. They swung at me, I dropped down, Morton leaped back, Rotherham ducked behind his chair, they took Hastings before he could defend himself.'

'But why? What had been said?'

'Nothing! Nothing had been said. It was as if Richard just unleashed his power. They just grabbed Hastings and took him.'

'Took him where? On what charge? What did they say?'

'They said nothing. You don't understand. It wasn't an arrest. It was a raid. Richard was shouting like a madman that he was under an enchantment, that his arm was failing him, that Hastings and the queen were destroying him by witchcraft . . .'

'What?'

'He pulled up his sleeve and showed us his arm. His sword arm, you know how strong his right arm is. He says it is failing him, he says it is shrivelling away.'

'Dear God, has he run mad?' I pause in wiping the blood, I cannot believe what I am hearing.

'They dragged Hastings out. Not another word. They pulled him outside though he was kicking and swearing and digging in his heels. There was some old lumber lying around from the building work and they just threw down a piece of timber, forced him down on it, and took his head off with one swing.'

'A priest?'

'There was no priest. Do you not hear what I am saying? It was a kidnap and a murder. He had no time even to say his prayers.' Stanley starts to shake. 'Dear God, I thought they were coming after me. I thought I would be next. It was like the dream. The smell of blood and nobody there to save me.'

'They beheaded him before the Tower?'

'As I said, as I said.'

'So if the prince looked out of his window, hearing the noise, he will have seen his father's dearest friend beheaded on a log? The man he called his Uncle William?'

Stanley is silent, looking at me. A trickle of blood runs down his face and he smears it with the back of his hand, turning his cheek red. 'Nobody could have stopped them.'

'The prince will see Richard as his enemy,' I say. 'He can't call him Lord Protector after this. He will think him a monster.'

Stanley shakes his head.

'What is going to happen to us?'

His teeth are starting to chatter. I put down the bowl and wrap a blanket around his shoulders.

'God knows, God knows. We are under house arrest for treason, they suspect us of plotting with the queen and Hastings. Your friend Morton too, and they took Rotherham as well. I don't know how many others. I suppose Richard is going to seize the throne, and has rounded up everyone he thinks might argue.'

'And the princes?'

He is stammering with shock. 'I don't know. Richard could just kill them, like he killed Hastings. He could break into sanctuary and murder the whole royal family: the queen, the little girls, all of them. Today he has shown us that he can do anything. Perhaps they are already dead?'

News comes in snippets from the outside world, carried by housemaids as gossip from the market. Richard declares that the marriage between the queen, Elizabeth Woodville, and King Edward was never valid as Edward was pre-contracted to another lady before he married Elizabeth in secret. He declares all their children bastards and himself as the only York heir. The craven Privy Council, who observe Hastings' headless body being laid to rest beside the king he loved, do nothing to defend their queen and their princes, but there is a general hasty and unanimous agreement that there is only one heir, and it is Richard.

Richard and my kinsman Henry Stafford the Duke of Buckingham, start to put about that King Edward himself was a bastard, the misbegotten son of an English archer on Duchess Cecily while she was with the Duke of York in France. The people hear these accusations – what they make of them God knows – but there is no mistaking the arrival of an army from the northern counties, loyal to no-one but

Richard, and eager for rewards, there is no denying that all the men who might have been loyal to Prince Edward are arrested or dead. Everyone considers their own safety. No-one speaks out.

For the first time in my life, I can think kindly of the woman I have served for nearly ten years, Elizabeth Woodville, who was Queen of England and one of the most beautiful and beloved queens that the country has ever had. Never beautiful to me, never beloved to me except now, fleetingly, in this moment of her utter defeat. I think of her in the damp dimness of the Westminster sanctuary and I think that she will never triumph again, and for the first time in my life I can go on my knees and truly pray for her. All she has in her keeping now are her daughters; the life she revelled in has gone, and her two young sons are held by her enemy. I think of her defeated and afraid, widowed and fearing for her sons, and for the first time in my life I can feel my heart warm towards her: a tragic queen thrown down by no fault of her own. I can pray to Our Lady the Queen of Heaven to succour and comfort Her lost, miserable daughter in these days of her humiliation.

The oldest York girl, Princess Elizabeth, is of marriageable age and is only unmarried at the late age of seventeen years because of the shifting luck of her house. While I am on my knees, praying for the health and safety of the queen, I consider the pretty girl Elizabeth, and think what a wife she would make for my son Henry. The son of Lancaster and the daughter of York would together heal the wounds of England, and resolve the struggle of two generations. If Richard were to die after taking the throne, his heir would be a child, and a sickly Neville child at that, no more able to defend his claim than the York princes, and as easy to throw down as they have been. If my son were to take the throne then, and marry the York princess, the people would cleave to him as a Lancaster heir and the husband of the York heiress.

I send for my doctor, Dr Lewis of Caerleon, a man as interested in conspiracy as medicine. The queen knows him as my physician and she will admit him, knowing he is from me. I tell him to promise her our support, to tell her that Buckingham is ready to be persuaded against Duke Richard, that my son Henry could raise an army in Brittany. And I tell him before anything else to try to discover what plans she has, what her supporters are promising her. My husband may think that she has no hope, but I have seen Elizabeth Woodville come out of sanctuary once before, and take the throne with careless joy, forgetting all about the shame that the Lord had rightly sent her. I tell Lewis he is to say nothing of my husband being under house arrest, but he is to tell her, as a kindly friend, of the murder of Hastings, of the sudden visibility of Richard's ambition, of the bastardising of her sons, of the ruin of her name. He is to tell her with compassion that her cause is lost unless she acts. I have to get her to muster what friends she has, raise what army she can afford, and get her troops into battle against Richard. If I can encourage her into a long and bloody battle then my son can land with fresh troops and take on the exhausted winner.

Lewis goes to her on a day when she will be desperate for a friend: the day that was set for her son's coronation. I doubt that anyone will have warned her that he is not to be crowned at all. Lewis goes through the streets where doors are shut and windows barred and the people don't linger at corners to talk, and then he returns to me almost at once. He is wearing his mask against plague, a long conical mask stuffed with herbs and scented with oils, which gives him a terrifying profile, an inhuman face, a white ghost-face. He removes it only when he is in my room with the door shut behind him, and he bows low.

'She is anxious for help,' he says without preamble. 'She is a desperate woman, I would judge her half-mad with desperation.' He pauses. 'I saw the young Princess of York also . . .'

'And?'

'She was disturbed. She was prophetic.' He gives a little shiver. 'She frightened me, and I am a physician who has seen everything.'

I ignore his boast. 'How did she frighten you?'

'She came at me out of the darkness, her gown soaked with water from the river, trailing behind her like a tail as if she were half-fish. She said that the river had already told her the news I was about to give her mother – that Duke Richard had claimed the throne by right of his legitimacy and that the young princes are proclaimed bastards.'

'She knew that already? They have spies out? I had no idea she could be well informed.'

'It wasn't the queen, she didn't know. It was the girl, and she said the river told her. She said the river told her of a death in the family, and the mother knew at once that it was her brother Anthony and her Grey son. They flung open the windows to listen to the river going by. They were like a pair of water-witches in there. Any man would have been afraid.'

'She says that Anthony Rivers is dead?'

'They both seemed certain of it.'

I make the sign of the cross. Elizabeth Woodville has been accused of working with dark forces before now, but to speak true from the sanctuary of holy ground is surely the devil's work.

'She must have spies working for her, she must be better prepared and armed than we realise. But how could she have got news from Wales before me?'

'She said another thing.'

'The queen?'

'The princess. She said that she was cursed to be the next Queen of England and take her brother's throne.'

We look at each other in stunned incomprehension. 'You are sure?'

'She was terrifying. She complained of her mother's ambition and said it was a curse laid on the family and that she would have to take her brother's throne and that at least would please her mother, though it would disinherit her brother.'

'What could she mean?'

The doctor shrugs. 'She didn't say. She has grown to be a beautiful girl, but she is terrifying. I believed her. I have to say, I believed every word she said. It was like a prophet speaking true. I believe that somehow she will be Queen of England.'

I take a little breath. This is so aligned to my own prayers that it has to be the word of God, though speaking through a most sinful vessel. If Henry were to take the throne and she were to marry him, she would indeed be queen. How else could it come about?

'And there was one other thing,' Lewis says cautiously. 'When I asked the queen what were her plans for the princes in the Tower, Edward and Richard, she said: "It's not Richard".'

'She said what?'

'She said: "It's not Richard".'

'What did she mean?'

'It was then that the princess came in, with her gown all wet from the river and she knew everything: the acclamation for the duke, the disinheriting of the family. Then she said that she would be queen.'

'But did you ask the queen what she meant by "It's not Richard"?'

He shakes his head, this man who has seen everything, but did not have the sense to ask the one key thing. 'Did you not think it might be rather important?' I snap at him.

'I am sorry. The princess coming in was so . . . she was unearthly. And then her mother said that now they were in a dry spell but they would be in flood again. They were terrifying. You know what they say about their ancestry – that they come from a water goddess. If you had been there you would have thought the water goddess about to rise from the Thames itself.'

'Yes, yes,' I say without sympathy. 'I see they were frightening, but did she say anything else? Did the queen speak of her brothers who have got away? Did she say where they are or what they are doing? The two of them have the power to raise half the kingdom.'

He shakes his head. 'She said nothing. But she heard it well enough when I told her that you would help the young princes to escape. She is planning something, I am sure. She was planning it before she realised that Richard is going to take the throne. She will be desperate now.'

I nod and I gesture to him to leave me. I make my way at once to our little chapel to get to my knees. I need the peace of God to clear my mind of this whirl of thoughts. That Elizabeth the princess should know her destiny only confirms my belief that she will be Henry's wife, and he will take the throne. That her mother should say, 'It's not Richard' fills me with deep unease.

What can she mean: 'It's not Richard'? Is it not Richard her son, in the Tower? Or does she merely mean that it is not

Richard, Duke of Gloucester, that she fears? I can't tell and that fool should have asked her. But I suspected something like this. I have been fretting about something like this. I never thought that she would be such a fool as to give up a second son to an enemy who had kidnapped the first. I have known her for ten years, she is not a woman who does not foresee the worst. The Privy Council trooped down to meet her, and lined themselves up to tell her that she had no choice, and then marched away with the little Prince Richard holding the archbishop's hand. But I always thought that she would have prepared for them. I always knew she would do something to get her last free son away to safety. Any woman would do it, and she is determined and clever, and she dotes on her boys. She would never send them into danger. She would never let her youngest son go where her oldest was in danger.

But what has she done? If the second prince in the Tower is not Richard, then who is it? Has she sent some pauper in disguise? Some minor ward who would do anything for her? And worse, if Prince Richard, the legitimate heir to the throne of England, is not in the Tower of London under lock and key, then where is he? If she has hidden him somewhere then he is heir to the York throne, another obstacle to my son's succession. Is she telling me this? Or pretending? Is she tormenting me? Triumphing over me still by telling my thick-witted messenger a riddle to pass on to me? Did she speak her son's name on purpose to laugh at me with her foresight? Or did she just slip up? Is she telling me of Richard, to warn me that whatever happens to Edward, she still has an heir?

I wait for hours on my knees for Our Lady the Queen of Heaven to tell me what this most earthly queen is doing: playing her games, weaving her spells, once again, as ever, before me, triumphing over me even in this moment of her great terror and defeat. But Our Lady does not come to me. Joan does not advise me. God is silent to me, his handmaiden. None of them tell me what Elizabeth Woodville is doing in the hidden sanctuary beneath the abbey, and without their help I know she will come out again to triumph.

No more than a day after this, my lady in waiting comes in with red eyes and says that Anthony, Earl Rivers, the dazzling, chivalrous brother of the queen is dead, executed on Richard's order in Pontefract Castle. She brings the news to me the moment it reaches London. Nobody could have heard more quickly, the official report reaches the Privy Council only an hour after I hear it. It seems that the queen and her daughter told Dr Lewis on the very night that it happened, perhaps at the very moment of his death. And how can that be?

In the morning, my husband meets me at breakfast. 'I am summoned to attend a Privy Council meeting,' he says, showing me a warrant with the seal of the boar. Neither of us looks directly at it, the letter sits on the table between us like a dagger. 'And you are to go to the royal wardrobe and prepare the coronation robes for Anne Neville. The robes for a queen. You are to be lady in waiting to Queen Anne. We are released from house arrest without a word. And we are in royal service again, without a word spoken.'

I nod. I will undertake the work for King Richard that I was doing for King Edward. We will wear the same gowns; but the gown of gold and ermine that was ready for the Dowager Queen Elizabeth, will be cut down for her sister-in-law, the new Queen Anne.

My ladies in waiting and the Stanley men at arms are seated all around us, so my husband and I exchange no more than a small glance of triumph at our own survival. This will be the third royal house that I have served, and each time I have bowed low and thought of my own son as heir. 'I shall be honoured to serve Queen Anne,' I say smoothly.

It is my destiny to smile at the changes of the world and await my reward in heaven, but even I baulk for a moment at the doorway of the queen's chambers when I see little Anne Neville, daughter of the kingmaker Warwick, born well enough, royally married, widowed to nothing, and now risen again to the throne of England itself, standing by the great fireplace in her travelling cloak surrounded by her ladies from the north, like a gipsy encampment from the moors. They see me in the doorway, the steward of her chamber bellows, 'Lady Margaret Stanley!' in an accent no-one living south of Hull could understand, the women shuffle aside, so that I can walk towards her, and I step in and go down to my knees, abase myself to yet another usurper, and hold up my hands in the gesture of fealty.

'Your Grace,' I say to the woman who was picked up from disgrace and poverty by the young Duke Richard because he knew he could claim the Warwick fortune with this most unlucky bride. Now she is to be Queen of England and I have to kneel to her. 'I am so glad to offer you my service.'

She smiles at me. She is pale as marble, her lips pale, her eyelids the palest pink. Certainly, she cannot be well; she puts her hand on the stone of the fireplace and leans against it as if she is weary.

'I thank you for your service, and I would have you serve

as my senior lady in waiting,' she says quietly, a little catch in her breath. 'You will carry my train at my coronation.'

I bow my head to hide my flare of joy. This is to honour my family, this is to have the House of Lancaster one pace from the crown as it is held over an anointed head. I will be just one step behind the Queen of England and – God knows – ready to step up. 'I am glad to accept,' I say.

'My husband speaks so highly of the wisdom of Lord Thomas Stanley,' she says.

So highly that the pikemen nearly sliced off his head and held him for a week under house arrest. 'We have long been in service to the House of York,' I remark. 'You and the Duke have been sadly missed, while you were away from court in the north. I am glad to welcome you home to your capital city.'

She makes a little gesture with her hand and her page brings a stool over so that she can sit before the fire. I stand before her and I watch her shoulders shake as she coughs. This is a woman who is not going to make old bones. This is a woman who is not going to conceive a quiver of heirs for York, not like the fecund Queen Elizabeth. This is a woman who is sick and weak. I doubt she will last five more years. And then? And then?

'And your son, Prince Edward?' I inquire demurely. 'Is he coming to the coronation? Should I order your chamberlain to prepare rooms for him?'

She shakes her head. 'His Grace is not well,' she says. 'He will stay in the north for now.'

Not well? I think to myself. Not well enough to come to the coronation of his own father, is not well at all. He was always a pale boy with his mother's slight build, seldom seen around court; they always kept him away from London for fear of the plague. Has he, perhaps, not outgrown childhood weakness but is going from a frail boy to a sickly adult? Has Duke Richard failed to get himself an heir who will outlive him? Is there now only one strong heartbeat between my son and the throne?

SUNDAY 6 JULY 1483

We are where we planned to be, one step from the crown. My husband follows the king, with the mace of the Constable of England in his grasp, I follow the new Queen Anne, holding her train. Behind me comes the Duchess of Suffolk, the Duchess of Norfolk behind her. But it is I who walk in the footsteps of the queen, and when she is anointed with holy oil I am close enough to smell the heady musk of it.

They have spared no cost for this ceremony. The king is dressed in a gown of purple velvet, a canopy of cloth of gold carried over his head. My kinsman Henry Stafford, the young Duke of Buckingham, is in blue with a cartwheel emblem of solid gold thread dazzling on his cloak. He holds the king's train in one hand, in the other he has the staff of the High Steward of England, his reward for supporting and guiding Duke Richard to the throne. The place for his wife, Katherine Woodville, the dowager queen's sister, is empty. The duchess has not come to celebrate the usurping of her family's throne. She is not with her treasonous husband. He hates her for her family, for her triumph over him when he was young and she was the king's sister-in-law. This is just the first of many times that she can expect humiliation in future.

I walk behind the queen all the day. When she goes in to dine in Westminster Hall, I sit at the table for the ladies as she is served the magnificent dinner. The king's champion himself bows to our table and to me, after he has bellowed his challenge for King Richard. It is a dinner as grand and as self-important as any one of the great occasions of Edward's court. The dining and the dancing goes on till midnight, and after. Stanley and I leave in the early hours of the morning and our barge takes us upriver to our house. As I sit myself in the rear of the barge, my furs gathered around me, I see a small light shining low from a waterside window beneath the dark bulk of the abbey. I know for a certainty it is Queen Elizabeth, queen no more, named as a whore and not even recognised as a widow, her candle shining over the dark waters, listening to her enemy's triumph. I think of her watching me go by in my beautiful barge, rowing away from the king's court, as years ago she watched me row my son towards the king's court. She was in sanctuary then too.

I should revel in my triumph over her; but I shiver and gather my furs around me as if the little pinprick of light was a baleful eye glaring at me over the dark waters. She came out of sanctuary once before to victory. I know she will be planning Richard's downfall, she will be plotting to come out to victory again.

To my brother-in-law Jasper Tudor, and Henry Tudor my son,

I greet you well. I have much news. Richard is crowned King of England and his wife is Queen Anne. We are in high favour and trust. The former Queen Elizabeth has called on her affinity and they are to attack the Tower of London and free the princes as soon as the new royal couple set out on progress, immediately after the coronation. I have promised our support, and Queen Elizabeth trusts me with the secret plans.

Start to recruit your men. If the queen gets her boys out of the Tower she will raise her troops and march on Richard. When either she or Richard win, the victor must turn to find you landed in force, Lancaster rising, and a second battle for him or her to fight against your fresh troops.

I think our time is coming, I think our time is now.

Margaret Stanley

The same day that I send my letter to my son I receive a long letter, delivered in secret, from my old friend Bishop John Morton, released from the Tower into the care of the Duke of Buckingham, at his house at Brecknock.

My dear daughter in Christ,

I have been wrestling with the conscience of the young duke, who has me in his charge as his prisoner; but finds he is captured by me, since I have turned him from his friendship with Richard, now called king. The young duke is struggling with his conscience that he raised Richard to the throne on poor grounds, and that he would have served his God, his country, and himself better if he had either supported the York princes and himself become their protector, or claimed the throne for himself.

He is now ready to turn against Richard, and will join a rebellion against him. As evidence of his good faith, you can call on his men to attack the Tower and get the princes out. I will send you his password under my seal. I think you should meet him and see what alliance you can make in these troubled times. He will be travelling to Brecon after leaving Richard at Worcester, and I have promised him that you will meet him as if by accident on the highway.

I remain your friend,

John Morton, Bishop of Ely

I look up to see one of my ladies in waiting looking at me. 'Are you all right, my lady?' she asks. 'You have gone very pale and now you are flushed.'

'No, I don't feel well at all,' I say. 'Fetch Dr Lewis for me.'

My husband comes to find me in my chapel the night after the coronation. 'I am about to select the men who will join the queen's men in their attack on the Tower, before I leave London with the royal progress,' he says, dropping without ceremony into a seat, giving a cursory nod to the altar where a single candle is burning against the dark, and crossing himself without any show of respect. 'They are drawing their armour and their weapons from the armoury, right now. I have to know your will.'

'My will?' I ask. I don't rise to my feet but turn my head to look at him, my hands still clasped in prayer. 'My will is always God's will.'

'If my men break down the door to the Tower, as I plan they should, if they are first in, as I will order them to be, if they open the princes' door and find them alone but for a couple of attendants, is it your will – or indeed God's will – that they catch them up like lost lambs, and return them to their mother? Or are they to slice off their little heads then and there, and slaughter the servants and then blame it all on them?'

I stare at him. I had not thought he would ever be so blunt. 'These are your orders to your men.' I am playing for time. 'I can't order your men. You must do so. And anyway, someone else might get in before them and do it first.'

'This is your plan to get your son on the throne,' he replies tightly. 'If the princes are dead, then two rival claimants are gone, and your son is two steps closer. If they rejoin their mother then she will be able to turn out all the south of England in her defence. Men will fight for her heirs that would stay home if they were dead. There is no point fighting for Elizabeth Woodville – but it is a glorious cause for the young King Edward and his brother Prince Richard. Those two boys make her twice as strong against Richard – twice as strong against Henry.'

'Obviously the York princes cannot be allowed to claim the throne.'

'Evidently,' my husband replies. 'But do you want to stop them breathing as well?'

I find my praying hands are gripping one another. 'God's will,' I whisper, wishing I could feel the certainty that Joan knew when she rode out to kill or be killed, when she knew that God's will was a hard and bloody road. But Joan did not ride against little boys, innocent boys. Joan never sent killing men into a nursery.

My husband rises from his seat. 'I must go to inspect the muster. What is your wish? I have to order the captains. I can't tell them to wait until God has made up His mind.'

I rise too. 'The little one is only nine years old.'

He nods. 'But he is a prince. War is hard, my lady. What are your commands?'

'This is a most grave, a most grave adventure,' I whisper. I step towards him and put my hand on his arm as if the warmth of his body through his elegantly slashed jacket could comfort me. 'To order the death of two boys, two boys aged only nine and twelve, and them Princes of the Blood . . . Two innocent boys . . .'

He smiles his wolfish smile. 'Oh, say the word and we shall save them from their wicked uncle and their imprisonment and rescue their mother too. Do you want to see the royal family of

York restored with their Prince Edward on the throne as king? For perhaps we can achieve this tonight. Is that your will? Are we to put Prince Edward on the throne? Are we on an errand of mercy?'

I am wringing my hands. 'Of course not!'

'Well, you have to choose. When our men go into the Tower they will either save the boys or slaughter them. The choice is yours.'

I cannot see what else I can do. Joan unsheathed her sword and rode out without fear, without hesitation. I must unsheathe mine. 'They will have to kill them,' I say. My lips are cold but I have to frame the words. 'Obviously, the boys have to die.'

I stand at the little gate which leads from our house to the London street and see the Stanley men slip out into the darkness. My husband has left London on the triumphant coronation progress with the new King Richard and Queen Anne. I am alone. The men are carrying no torches, they run out in silence, lit only by the moon. They are not wearing our livery, their cap badges, hat badges and embossed belts are laid aside. They are wearing nothing that would identify them to our house, and each of them is sworn to say that they were recruited by the queen and serving only her. As soon as they are gone, my husband's brother, Sir William Stanley, writes a warning letter to the Constable of the Tower, Sir Robert Brackenbury, to alert him to the danger of attack. It will be delivered just moments after the attack is launched. 'Always be on both sides, Margaret,' William says to me cheerfully, as he seals the letter with the emblem of our house so that anyone can see our loyalty. 'That's what my brother says. At the very least, always appear to be on both sides.'

Then I have to wait.

I give the appearance of spending an ordinary night. I sit in the great hall before the Stanley household for a little while after dinner, and then I go to my rooms. My maids undress me for bed and I dismiss them, even the girl who sleeps in my room, saying that I may pray through the night. This is normal for me, and causes no comment, and I do pray for a while, and then I put on my thick, warm robe, pull up my chair to the fire and sit and wait.

I think of the Tower of London like a tall fingerpost pointing up to God. The queen's men will enter the precinct through a little sally port that has been left open, my men will follow. The Duke of Buckingham has sent a small band of trained soldiers; they will try the door of the White Tower, the servants have been bribed to leave it open. Our men will slip inside, they may get up the stairs before they are spotted, then they will fight their way, hand-to-hand, to the princes' apartments, break in, and as the boys leap forward, to their freedom, they will plunge their daggers into their bellies. Prince Edward is a brave youth, and trained to arms by his Uncle Anthony, he may well put up a fight, Richard is only nine but he may shout a warning, he could even step before his brother to take the blow, he is a York prince, he knows his duty. But there must be a brief moment of determined slaughter, and then the House of York will be finished, but for Duke Richard, and my son will be two steps closer to the throne. I must be glad of that. I must be hoping for that.

In the early hours of the morning, when the sky is just getting grey, there is a scratch on the door that makes my heart thud, and I hurry to open it. The Captain of the Guard is outside, his black jerkin torn, a dark bruise on the side of his face. I let him in without a word, and pour him a glass of small ale. I gesture that he may sit at the fireside, but I remain standing behind my chair, my hands clenched on the carved wood to stop them trembling. I am as frightened as a child at what I have done.

'We failed,' he says gruffly. 'The boys were better guarded than we thought. The man who should have let us in was cut down while he was fumbling with the bolt. We heard him scream. So we had to ram the door and while we were trying to lift it from its hinges, the Tower guards came out from the courtyard behind us, and we had to turn and fight. We were trapped between the Tower and the guards and had to fight our way out. We didn't even get in to the White Tower. I could hear the doors slamming inside and shouting as the princes were taken deeper into the Tower. Once the alarm was sounded there was no chance we would get to them.'

'Were they forewarned? Did the king know there would be an attack?' And if so, does the king know who is in the plot, I think. Will the boar turn on us again?

'No, it wasn't an ambush. They got the guard out quickly, and they got the door shut, and the queen's spy inside couldn't get it open. But at first, we caught them unawares. I am sorry, my lady.'

'Any captured?'

'We got all our men away. There was one injured of ours, they're seeing to him now, a flesh wound only. And there was a couple of York men down. But I left them where they fell.'

'The Yorks were there, all of them?'

'I saw the queen's brother Richard was there, and her brother Lionel, her son Thomas that was said to be missing, and they had a good guard, well armed. I think there were Buckingham men among them too. They were there in strength, and they put up a good fight. But the Tower was built by the Normans to hold against London. You can hold it against an army for half a year, once you get the door shut. Once we lost the surprise we were beaten.'

'And nobody knew you?'

'We all said we were Yorks, we wore white roses, and I am sure we passed as that.'

I go to my box, heft a purse in my hand and give it to the captain. 'Spread this around the men, and ensure that they don't speak of tonight, even among themselves. It would cost them their lives. It was treason, since it failed. It would be death to a man who boasted he had been there. And no order came from my husband or from me.'

The captain rises. 'Yes, my lady.'

'Did the queen's kin all get safely away?'

'Yes. But her brother swore that they would come again. He shouted aloud so that the boys could hear, that they must be brave and wait, for he would raise the whole of England to free them.'

'Did he? Well, you have done your best, you can go.'

The young man bows and goes from the room.

I go on my knees before the fire. 'Our Lady, if it is Your will that the York boys be spared then send me, Your servant a sign. Their safety tonight cannot be a sign. Surely it cannot be Your will that they live? It cannot be Your will that they inherit? I am Your obedient daughter in every way; but I cannot believe that You would have them on the throne rather than the true Lancaster heir, my son Henry.'

I wait. I wait for a long time. There is no sign. I take it to heart that there is no sign, and so the York boys should not be spared.

I leave London the next day. It suits me not to be seen in the City while they are doubling the guard and asking who attacked the Tower. I decide to take a visit to the cathedral of Worcester. It has long been my wish to visit, it is a Benedictine cathedral, a centre of learning. Elizabeth the queen sends a message which is brought to me as we are saddling up, to say that her kinsmen have gone to ground in London and the countryside nearby, and that they are organising an uprising. I reply to pledge my support and tell her that I am on my way to the Duke of Buckingham to recruit him and his whole affinity to our side in open rebellion.

It is hot weather for travelling but the roads are dry and we make good time. My husband rides back from the court at Worcester to meet me for a night on the road. The new King Richard, happy and confident, greeted with enthusiasm everywhere he goes, grants Lord Stanley leave of absence for a night, assuming that we want to be together as husband and wife. But my lord is anything but loving when he comes into the guest rooms in the abbey.

He spares no time on gentle greetings. 'So they botched it,' he says.

'Your captain tells me it could hardly be done. But he said the Tower wasn't forewarned.'

'No, the king was appalled, it was a shock to him. He had heard of my brother's letter of warning, and that will do us some good. But the princes are to be taken to inner rooms, more easily guarded than the royal rooms, and not allowed out again until he returns to London. Then he will take them away from London. He is going to set up a court for the young royal cousins. The Duke of Clarence's children, his own son, all the York children, will be kept in the north at Sherrif Hutton, and held there, far from any lands where Elizabeth Woodville has any influence. She'll never rescue them from Neville lands, and he will probably marry her to a northern lord who will take her away too.'

'Might he have someone poison them?' I ask. 'To get them out of the way?'

My husband shakes his head. 'He has declared them illegitimate and so they cannot inherit the throne. His own son is going to be invested as Prince of Wales as soon as we get to York. The Rivers are defeated, he just wants to make sure they are not the figurehead of a forlorn hope. Besides, they would be worse for him as dead martyrs than they are as feeble claimants. The ones he really wants dead are the Rivers tribe: the Woodvilles and all their kin, who would rally behind the princes. But the best of them is dead, and the rest will be hunted down. All the country accepts Richard as king and the true York heir. You would have to see it to believe it, Margaret, but every city we go through pours out to celebrate his coronation. Everyone would rather have a strong usurper on the throne than a weak boy, everyone would rather have the king's brother than go through the wars again for a king's son. And he promises to be a good king, he is the picture of his father, he is a York, and beloved.'

'And yet there are many who would rise against him. I should know, I am mustering them.'

He shrugs. 'Yes – you would know better than I. But everywhere we have been, I have seen the people welcome King Richard as the great heir and loyal brother of a great king.'

'The Rivers could yet defeat him. The queen's brothers and her Grey son have secured the support of Kent and Susssex, Hampshire is theirs. Every man who ever served in the royal household would turn out for them. There is always support for my house in Cornwall, and the Tudor name will bring out Wales. Buckingham has tremendous lands and thousands of tenants and my son Henry is promised an army of five thousand from the Duke of Brittany.'

He nods. 'It could be done. But only if you can be certain of Buckingham. You are not strong enough without him.'

'Morton says that he has completely turned Buckingham against Richard. My steward Reginald Bray has spoken with them both. I will know more when I see him.'

'Where are you meeting?'

'By chance, on the road.'

'He will play you,' my husband warns me. 'As he has played Richard. The poor fool Richard even now thinks that Buckingham loves him as a brother. But it turns out that it is always his own ambition at the end of it. He will agree to support your son's claim to the throne, but think to let Tudor do the fighting for him. He will hope that Tudor and the queen will defeat Richard and leave the way open for him.'

'It is lip service for all of us. We are all fighting only for our own cause; all of us promising our loyalty to the princes.'

'Yes, only the boys are quite innocent,' he remarks. 'And Buckingham will be planning their deaths. No-one in England would support his claim if they were still alive. And of course, as High Steward of England, with the Tower in his command, he is better placed than any of us to see them murdered. His servants are inside already.'

I pause as his meaning becomes clear to me. 'You think he would do it?'

'In a moment.' He smiles. 'And when he does it, he could give the orders in the name of the king. It could be made to look like the orders of Richard. He himself would make it look like Richard's doing.'

'Is he planning this?'

'I don't know if he has even thought of it yet. Certainly, someone should make sure it has occurred to him. For sure, someone who wanted the boys dead could do the deed no better way than to make it Buckingham's task.'

There is a rap on the door and my lord's guards admit the steward of the abbey. 'Dinner is served, my lady, my lord.'

'God bless you, my husband,' I say formally. 'I learn so much from studying you.'

'And you,' he says. 'And God bless your meeting with His Grace the duke, may much good come of it.'

I can hear the Duke of Buckingham approaching along the winding dirt road, even before I can see him. He rides with a train as great as a king's, with outriders going ahead and blowing trumpets to warn everyone to clear the highway for the great duke. Even when there is no-one as far as they eye can see, but only a little boy herding sheep under a tree and a small village in the distance, the trumpeters sound the call and the horses, more than a hundred of them, thunder along behind, raising a plume of dust on the summer road that blows like a cloud behind the rippling banners.

The duke is at the forefront of the riders, on a big bay war horse, caparisoned with a saddle of red leather trimmed with golden nails, his personal standard before him, and three men at arms riding around him. He is dressed for hunting but his boots, also red leather, are so fine that a lesser man would have kept them for dancing. His cloak, thrown back over his shoulders, is pinned with a great golden brooch, his hat badge is of gold and rubies. There is a fortune in jewels embroidered on his jerkin and his waistcoat, his breeches are of the most smooth tan broadcloth, trimmed with red leather laces. He was a vain, furious boy when Elizabeth Woodville took him as her ward and humiliated him by marrying him to her sister, and now he is a vain, furious man, not yet thirty years old, taking his revenge on a world which has never, in his mind, shown him enough respect.

I first met him when I married Henry Stafford, and then he was a little boy, spoiled by the indulgent duke, his grandfather. The death of his father and then that of his grandfather gave him the dukedom while he was still a child and taught him to think of himself as born great. Three of his grandparents are descended from Edward III, and so he believes himself to be more royal than the royal family. Now, he considers himself the Lancaster heir. He would consider his claim is greater than that of my son.

He pretends surprise at suddenly seeing my more modest train, though it must be said, I always travel with fifty good men at arms and my own standard and the Stanley colours go before me. He raises his hand to halt his troop. We approach each other slowly, as if to parley, and his young charming smile beams out at me like a sun rising. 'Well met, my lady cousin!' he cries out, and all his troop's banners dip in respect. 'I didn't think to see you so far from your home!'

'I have to go to my house at Bridgnorth,' I say clearly for any spies that might be listening. 'And I had thought you were with the king?'

'I am returning to him now from my house at Brecon,' Buckingham says. 'But do you want to break your journey? There is Tenbury just ahead of us. Would you do me the honour of dining with me?' He casts a casual wave towards his troop. 'I have my kitchen servants with me, and provisions. We could have dinner together.'

'I should be honoured,' I say quietly, and I turn my horse and ride beside him as my outnumbered guard stand aside and then follow the Buckingham troops to Tenbury.

The little inn has a small room with a table and a few stools, adequate for our purpose, and the men rest their horses in lines in the nearby field, and light their own camp fires to roast their meats. Buckingham's cook takes over the meagre kitchen of the inn, and soon has servants running backwards and forwards to kill a couple of chickens and fetch his ingredients from the wagon. Buckingham's steward brings us two glasses of wine from the cellar wagon, and serves them in the duke's own glassware, with his seal engraved at the rim. I note all his worldly extravagance and folly and think, this is a young man who thinks he is going to play me.

I wait. The God I serve is a patient God, and He has taught me that sometimes the best thing to do is to wait, and see what comes. Buckingham has always been an impatient boy, and he can hardly pause for the door to be closed behind his steward before he starts.

'Richard is unbearable. I meant only that he should protect us against the ambition of the Rivers, and I warned him against them for that reason; but he has gone too far now. He has to be pulled down.'

'He is king now,' I observe. 'You warned him early and served him so well that he has become the tyrant that you feared the Rivers would be. And my husband and I myself are sworn to serve him, as are you.'

He waves his hand and spills a little wine. 'An oath of fealty to a usurper is no oath at all,' he says. 'He is not the rightful king.'

'Who is, then?'

'Prince Edward, I suppose,' he says quickly, as if that is not the only question of importance. 'Lady Stanley, you are older and wiser than me, I have trusted your holy judgement for all of my life. Surely you feel that we must free the princes from the Tower and restore them to their state? You were such a loving lady to the Queen Elizabeth. Surely you feel that her boys must be freed, and Prince Edward must take his father's throne?'

'Surely,' I say. 'If he were a legitimate son. But Richard says he is not, you yourself proclaimed him a bastard, and his father a bastard before him.'

Buckingham looks troubled by this, as if it were not he who swore to everyone that Edward had been married before he promised marriage to Elizabeth. 'Indeed, I fear that much is true.'

'And if you put the so-called prince on the throne, you would stand to lose all the wealth and positions you have been given by Richard.'

He waves away the post of High Steward of England as if it were not the greatest honour in the land. 'The gifts of a usurper are not what I want for my house,' he says grandly.

'And I would gain nothing at all,' I remark. 'I would still be lady in waiting to the queen. I would return to the service of the Dowager Queen Elizabeth, having served the Queen Anne – so I would be still in service. And you would have risked everything to restore the Rivers family to power. And we know what a grasping, numerous family they are. Your wife, the queen's sister, would rule you once more. She will repay you for keeping her at home in disgrace. They will all laugh at you again, as they did when you were a little boy.'

His hatred for them flares in his eyes, and he quickly glances away at the fireplace where a little fire licks at the logs. 'She does not dominate me,' he says, irritated. 'Whatever her sister is. Nobody laughs at me.'

He waits, he hardly dares to tell me what he truly wants. The servant comes in with some little pies, and we take them with our wine, thoughtfully, as if we had met together to dine and were savouring the meal.

'I do fear for the lives of the princes,' I say. 'Since the

attempt to free them came so close, I cannot help but think that Richard may send them far away, or worse. Surely he cannot tolerate the risk of them staying in London, a centre for every plot? Everyone must think that Richard will destroy them. Perhaps he will take them to his lands in the north and they will not survive it. Prince Richard has a weak chest, I fear.'

'If he were, God forbid, to kill them in secret, then the Rivers line would be over, and we would be free of them,' the duke says, as if this has occurred to him now, for the first time.

I nod. 'And then, any rebellion that destroyed Richard would leave the throne open for a new king.'

He raises his face from the glow of the fire and looks at me with a bright, open hopefulness. 'Do you mean your son, Henry Tudor? Do you think of him, my lady? Would he take up the challenge and restore Lancaster to the throne of England?'

I don't hesitate for a moment. 'We have done badly enough with York. Henry is the direct Lancaster heir. And he has waited for his chance to return to his country and claim his birthright for all his life.'

'Does he have arms?'

'He can raise thousands,' I promise. 'The Duke of Brittany has promised his support, he has more than a dozen ships, he has more than four thousand men, he has an army at his command. His name alone can turn out Wales, and his Uncle Jasper would be his commander. If you and he were to unite to fight against Richard, I think you would be unbeatable. And if the dowager queen were to summon her affinity, thinking she was fighting for her sons, we could not fail.'

'But when she found out that her sons were dead?'

'As long as she found it out after the battle, it would make no difference to us.'

He nods. 'And then she would just retire.'

'My son Henry is betrothed to marry the Princess Elizabeth,' I remark. 'Elizabeth Woodville would still be mother of the queen, that would be enough for her, if her sons were gone.'

He beams as he suddenly understands my plan. 'And she thinks she has secured you!' he exclaims. 'That your ambitions are one with hers.'

Yes, I think. And you too think that you have secured me, and that I will bring in my son to kill Richard for you. That I will use my precious Henry as a weapon for such a one as you, to give you a safe passage to the throne.

'And if,' he looks pained, 'if, God forbid, your son Henry was to fall in battle?'

'Then you would be king,' I say. 'I have only one son and he is the only heir to my house. No-one could deny that if Henry were dead, then your claim to the throne would be supreme. And if he lives, then you would have his gratitude, and whatever lands you wanted to command. Certainly, I can promise for him, that all the Bohun lands would be restored to you. The two of you would have brought peace at last to England and rid the country of a tyrant. Henry would be king, and you would be the greatest duke. And if he died without issue, you would be his heir.'

He slips from his stool and kneels to me, holds his hands up to me in the old gesture of fealty. I smile down at him, this beautiful young man, as handsome as a player in a masque, mouthing words that surely no-one could believe, offering loyalty where he seeks only his own good. 'Will you take my fealty for your son?' he asks, his eyes shining. 'Will you accept my oath and swear that he will join with me against Richard? Us two together?'

I take his hands in my cool clasp. 'On behalf of my son, Henry Tudor, the rightful King of England, I accept your fealty,' I say solemnly. 'And you, and he, and Elizabeth the

Dowager Queen together will overthrow the Boar and bring joy back to England once more.'

I ride away from Buckingham's dinner feeling oddly unhappy, not at all as a woman in triumph. I should feel exultant: he thinks he has trapped my son into arming and fighting for his rebellion and actually, we have ensnared him. The task I set myself is accomplished; God's will is done. And yet . . . and yet . . . I suppose it is the thought of those two boys in the Tower, saying their prayers and climbing into their big bed, hoping that tomorrow they will see their mother, trusting that their uncle will release them, not knowing that there is a powerful alliance now of myself, my son, and the Duke of Buckingham who wait to hear of their deaths, and will not wait for much longer.

SEPTEMBER 1483

At last I have come into my own. I have inherited the kingdom I dreamed of when I prayed to Joan the Maid and wanted to be her, the only girl to see that her kingdom should rise, the only woman to know, from God Himself, what should be done. My rooms in our London house are my secret headquarters of rebellion; every day messengers come and go with news of arming, asking for money, collecting their weapons and smuggling them secretly out of the City. My table of work, which was once piled with books of devotion for my studies, is now covered with carefully copied maps, and hidden in its drawers are codes for secret messages. My ladies approach their husbands, their brothers or their fathers, swear them to secrecy and bind them to our cause. My friends in the church and in the City and on my lands link one to another and reach out to the country in a web of conspiracy. I judge who shall be trusted and who shall not, and I approach them myself. Three times a day I go down on my knees to pray, and my God is the God of righteous battles.

Dr Lewis goes between me and the Queen Elizabeth almost

daily, as she in her turn draws out those still loyal to the York princes, the great men and loyal servants of the old royal household, and her brothers and her son are everywhere in secret in the counties around London calling out the York affinity, while I summon those who will fight for Lancaster. My steward Reginald Bray goes everywhere, and my beloved friend John Morton as house guest and prisoner is in daily contact with Henry Stafford, the Duke of Buckingham. He tells the duke of our recruiting and reports back to me that the thousands of men that Buckingham can command are secretly arming. To my own people I give the assurance that Henry will marry the Princess Elizabeth of York, and unite the country with his victory. This brings them out for me. But the Yorks and the common people care nothing for my Henry, they are anxious only to set the princes free. They are desperate for the freedom of their boys, they are united against Richard, they would join with any ally, the devil himself, as long as they can free the York boys.

The Duke of Buckingham seems to be true to my plan, though I don't doubt he has one of his own, and promises he will gather up his men and Tudor loyalists through the marches of Wales, cross the Severn, and enter England from the west. At the same time my son is to land in the south and march his forces north. The queen's men will come out of all the southern counties, where her strength lies, and Richard, still in the north, will have to scramble for recruits as he marches south to greet not one but three armies, and choose the place of his death.

Jasper and Henry raise their troops from the prisons and streets of the worst cities in northern Europe. They will be paid fighters and desperate prisoners who are released only to go to war under the Tudor banner. We don't expect them to stand against more than one charge, and they will have no loyalty and no sense of a true cause. But their numbers alone will take the battle. Jasper has raised five thousand of them, truly five thousand, and is drilling them into a force that would strike terror into any country.

Richard, ignorant, far away in York, delighting in the loyalty of that city for their favourite son, has no idea of the plans that we are forming in the very heart of his own capital, but he is astute enough to know that Henry poses a danger. He is trying to persuade King Louis of France into an alliance which would include the handing over of my boy. He is hoping to make a truce with Scotland, he knows that my Henry will be collecting troops, he knows of the betrothal, and that my son is in alliance with the Queen Elizabeth, and he knows that they will either come on the autumn winds this year, or wait for spring. He knows this, and he must fear it. He doesn't know where I stand in this; whether I am the loyal wife of a loyal retainer who he has bought with fees and positions, or whether I am the mother of a son with a claim to the throne. He must watch, he must wait, he must be filled with wondering.

What he doesn't know yet is that a great shadow has fallen over his hopes and his security; what he does not know is that his greatest comrade and his first friend, the Duke of Buckingham, who put him on the throne, who swore fealty to him, who was to be bone of his bone and blood of his blood, another brother as trustworthy as those of the York affinity, is turned against him, and has sworn to bring his destruction. Poor Richard, unknowing, innocent, celebrates in York, revels in the pride and love of his northern friends. What he does not know is that his greatest friend of all, the man he loves as a brother, has become indeed like a brother: as false to him as any envious rivalrous brother of York.

My husband, my lord Thomas Stanley, on a three-day leave from his duties at Richard's court at York, comes to me in the evening, in the hour before dinner and waves my women from the room, without a word of courtesy to them or to me. I raise an eyebrow at his rudeness and wait.

'I have no time for anything but this question,' he snaps. 'The king has sent me on this private errand though God knows he shows little sign of trusting me. I have to be back with him the day after tomorrow, and he eyes me as if he would have me under arrest again. He knows there is a rebellion in the making, he suspects you and therefore me too, but he doesn't know who he can trust. Tell me this one thing: have you ordered the deaths of the princes? And is it done?'

I glance at the closed door, and rise to my feet. 'Husband, why do you ask?'

'Because my land agent today asked me were they dead? My chief of horse asked me had I heard the news? And my vintner told me that half the country believe it is so. Half the country think they are dead and most of them think that Richard did it.'

I conceal my pleasure. 'But really, how would I do such a thing?'

He puts his clenched fist under my face and snaps his fingers. 'Wake up,' he says rudely. 'You are talking to me, not to one of your acolytes. You have dozens of spies, you have a massive fortune at your own command, and now you have the Duke of Buckingham's men to call on, as well as your own guard. If you want it done, it can be done. So is it done? Is it over?'

'Yes,' I say quietly. 'It is done. It is over. The boys are dead.'

He is silent for a moment, almost as if he were saying a prayer for their little souls. Then he asks: 'Have you seen the bodies?'

I am shocked. 'No, of course not.'

'Then how do you know they are dead?'

I draw very close to him. 'The duke and I agreed it should be done, and his man came to me late one night, and told me that the deed was done.'

'How did they do it?'

I cannot meet his eyes. 'He said that he and a couple of others caught them sleeping and pressed them in their bed, smothered them with the mattresses.'

'Only three men!'

'Three,' I say defensively. 'I suppose it would need three . . .' I break off as I see that he is imagining, as I am, holding a ten year old boy and his twelve-year-old brother face down in their beds and then crushing them with a mattress. 'Buckingham's men,' I remind him. 'Not mine.'

'Your orders, and three witnesses to it. Where are the bodies?'

'Hidden under a stair in the Tower. When Henry is proclaimed king he can discover them there, and declare the boys were killed by Richard. He can hold a Mass, a funeral.'

'And how do you know that Buckingham has not played you false? How do you know that he has not spirited them away and they are still alive somewhere?'

I hesitate. Suddenly I feel that I may have made a mistake, giving dirty work to others to do. But I wanted it to be Buckingham's men, and all the blame on Buckingham. 'Why would he do that? It is in his interest that they should be dead,' I say. 'Just as much as ours. You yourself said that. And if the worst comes to the worst, and he has tricked me, and they are alive in the Tower, then someone can kill them later.'

'You put a lot of faith in your allies,' my husband says unpleasantly. 'And you keep your hands clean. But if you don't strike the blow, you don't know if it goes home. I just hope that you have done the job. Your son will never be safe on the throne if there is a York prince somewhere in hiding. He will spend his life looking over his shoulder. There will be a rival king waiting in Brittany for him, just as he was there for Edward. Just as he terrorises Richard. Your precious son will be haunted by fear of a rival, just as he haunts Richard. Tudor will never have a moment's peace. If you have botched this you have given your son over to be dogged by an unquiet spirit and the crown will never sit securely on his head.'

'I do the will of God,' I say fiercely. 'And it has been done. And I won't be questioned. Henry will be safe on his true throne. He will not be haunted. The princes are dead and I am guilty of nothing. Buckingham did it.'

'At your suggestion.'

'Buckingham did it.'

'And you are sure they were both killed?'

I hesitate for a moment as I think of Elizabeth Woodville's odd words: 'It's not Richard'. What if she put a changeling in the Tower for me to kill? 'Both of them,' I say steadily.

My husband smiles his coldest smile. 'I shall be glad to be sure of it.'

'When my son comes into London in triumph and finds the bodies, lays the blame on Buckingham or Richard, and gives them a holy burial, you will see that I have done my part.'

I go to bed uneasy, and the very next day, straight after matins, Dr Lewis comes to my rooms looking strained and anxious. At once I say I am feeling unwell, and send all my women away. We are alone in my privy chamber and I let him take a stool and sit opposite me, almost as an equal.

'The Queen Elizabeth summoned me to sanctuary last night and she was distraught,' he says quietly.

'She was?'

'She had been told that the princes were dead, and she was begging me to tell her that it was not the case.'

'What did you say?'

'I didn't know what you would have me say. So I told her what everyone in the City is saying: that they are dead. That Richard had them killed either on the day of his coronation, or as he left London.'

'And she?'

'She was deeply shocked; she could not believe it. But, Lady Margaret, she said a terrible thing . . .' He breaks off, as if he dare not name it.

'Go on,' I say but I can feel a cold shiver of dread creeping up my spine. I fear I have been betrayed. I fear that this has gone wrong.

'She cried out at first and then she said: "At least Richard is safe".'

'She meant Prince Richard? The younger boy?'

'The one they took into the Tower to keep his brother company.'

'I know that! But what did she mean?'

'That's what I asked her. I asked her at once what she meant and she smiled at me in the most frightening way and said: "Doctor, if you had only two precious, rare jewels and you feared thieves, would you put your two treasures in the same box?"'

He nods at my aghast expression.

'What does she mean?' I repeat.

'She wouldn't say more. I asked her if Prince Richard was not in the Tower when the two boys were killed. She just said that I was to ask you to put your own guards into the Tower to keep her son safe. She would say nothing more. She sent me away.'

I rise from my stool. This damned woman, this witch, has been in my light ever since I was a girl, and now, at this very moment when I am using her, using her own adoring family and loyal supporters to wrench the throne from her, to destroy her sons, she may yet win, she may have done something that will spoil everything for me. How does she always do it? How is it that when she is brought so low that I can even bring myself to pray for her, she manages to turn her fortunes around? It must be witchcraft; it can only be witchcraft. Her happiness and her success have haunted my life. I know her to be in league with the devil, for sure. I wish he would take her to hell.

'You will have to go back to her,' I say, turning to him.

He almost looks as if he would refuse.

'What?' I snap.

'Lady Margaret, I swear, I dread going to her. She is like a witch imprisoned in the cleft of a pine tree, she is like an entrapped spirit, she is like a water goddess on a frozen lake, waiting for spring. She lives in the gloom of sanctuary with the river flowing all the time beside their rooms and she listens to the babble as a counsellor. She knows things that she cannot know by earthly means. She fills me with terror. And her daughter is as bad.'

'You will have to summon your courage,' I say briskly. 'Be brave, you are doing God's work. You have to go back to her and tell her to be of stout heart. Tell her that I am certain that the princes are alive. Remind her that when we attacked the Tower we heard the guards taking them back from the door. They were alive then, why would Richard kill them now? Richard has taken the throne without killing them, why would he put them to death now? Richard is a man who does his own work and he is hundreds of miles away from them now. Tell her I will double my people in the Tower and that I swear to her, on my honour, that I will protect them. Remind her that the uprising will start next month. As soon as we defeat Richard the king, we will set the boys free. Then, when she is reassured, when she is in her first moment of relief, when you see the colour come to her face and you have convinced her – in that moment quickly ask her if she has her son Prince Richard in safety already. If she has him hidden away somewhere.'

He nods, but he is pale with fear. 'And are they safe?' he asks. 'Can I truly assure her that those poor boys are safe and we will rescue them? That the rumours, even in your own household, are false? Do you know if they are alive or dead, Lady Margaret? Can I tell their mother that they are alive and speak the truth?'

'They are in the hands of God,' I reply steadily. 'As are we all. My son too. These are dangerous times, and the princes are in the hands of God.'

That night we hear news of the first uprising. It is mistimed, it comes too early. The men of Kent are marching on London, calling on the Duke of Buckingham to take the throne. The county of Sussex gets up in arms, believing they cannot delay a moment longer, and the men of Hampshire beside them rise up too, as a fire will leap from one dry woodland to another. Richard's most loyal commander, Thomas Howard, the brand new Duke of Norfolk, marches down the west road from London, and occupies Guildford, fighting skirmishes to the west and to the east, but holding the rebels down in their own counties, and sending a desperate warning to the king: the counties of the south are up in the name of the former queen and her imprisoned sons, the princes.

Richard, the battle-hardened leader of York, marches south at the fast speed of a York army, makes his centre of command at Lincoln, and raises troops in every county, especially from those who greeted his progress with such joy. He hears of the betrayal of the Duke of Buckingham when men come from Wales to tell him that the duke is already on the march, going north through the Welsh marches, recruiting men and clearly planning to cross at Gloucester, or perhaps Tewkesbury, to come into the heart of England with his own men and his Welsh recruits. His beloved friend, Henry Stafford, is marching out under his standard, as proudly and as bravely as once he did for Richard; only now he is marching against him.

Richard goes white with rage and he grips his right arm, his sword arm, above the elbow, as if he were shaking with rage, as if to hold it steady. 'A man with the best cause to be true,' he exclaims. 'The most untrue creature living. A man who had everything he asked for. Never was a false traitor better treated; a traitor, a traitor.'

At once he sends out commissions of array to every county in England demanding their loyalty, demanding their arms and their men. This is the first and greatest crisis of his new reign. He summons them to support a York king, he demands the loyalty that they gave to his brother, which they have all promised to him. He warns those who cheered when he took the crown less than sixteen weeks ago that they must now stand by that decision, or England will fall to an unholy alliance of the false Duke of Buckingham, the witch queen, and the Tudor pretender.

It is pouring with rain, and there is a strong wind blowing hard from the north. It is unnatural weather, witch's weather. My son must set sail now, if he is to arrive while the queen's supporters are up, and while Buckingham is marching. But if it is so foul here, in the south of England, then I fear the weather in Brittany. He must come at exactly the right moment to catch the weary victor of the first battle and make them turn and fight again, while they are sick of fighting. But – I stand at my window and watch the rain pouring down, and the wind lashing the trees in our garden – I know he cannot set sail in this weather, the wind is howling towards the south, I cannot believe he will even be able to get out of port.

The next day the rains are worse and the river is starting to rise. It is over our landing steps at the foot of the garden and the boatmen drag the Stanley barge up the garden to the very orchard, out of the swirling flood, fearing that it will be torn from its moorings by the current. I can't believe that Henry can set sail in this, and even if he were to get out of harbour, I can't believe that he could safely get across the English seas to the south coast.

My web of informers, spies and plotters are stunned by the ferocity of the rain, which is like a weapon against us. The roads into London are all but impassable; no-one can get a message through. A horse and rider cannot get from London to Guildford, and as the river rises higher, there is news of flooding and drowning upstream and down. The tides are unnaturally high and every day and night the floods from the river pour down to the inrushing tide and there is a boiling surge of water which wipes out riverside houses, quays, piers and docks. Nobody can remember weather like this, a rain storm which lasts for days, and the rivers are bursting their banks all around England.

I have no-one to talk to but my God, and I cannot always hear His voice, as if the rain is blotting out His very face, and the wind blowing away His words. This is how I know for sure that it is a witch's wind. I spend my day at the window overlooking the garden, watching the river boil over the garden wall and come up through the orchard, lap by lap, till the trees themselves seem to be stretching up to the heavy clouds for help. Whenever one of my ladies comes to my side, or Dr Lewis comes to my door, or any of the plotters in London ask for admittance, they all want to know what is happening: as if I know any more than them, when all I can hear is rain, as if I can foretell the future in the gale-ripped sky. But I know nothing, anything could be happening out there; a waterlogged massacre could be taking place even half a mile away, and none of us would know, we would hear no voices over the sound of the storm, no lights would show through the rain.

I spend my nights in my chapel, praying for the safety of my son and the success of our venture, and hearing no answer from God but only the steady hammer of the torrent on the roof and the whine of the wind lifting the slates above me, until I think that God Himself has been blotted from the heavens of England by the witch's wind, and I will never hear Him again.

Finally, I get a letter from my husband at Coventry.

The king has commanded my presence and I fear he doubts me. He has sent for my son Lord Strange too, and was very dark when he learned that my son is from his home with an army of ten thousand men on the march, but my son has told nobody where he is going, and his servants only swear that he said he was raising his men for the true cause. I assure the king that my son will be marching to join us, loyal to the throne; but he has not yet arrived here at our command centre, in Coventry Castle.

Buckingham is trapped in Wales by the rising of the river Severn. Your son, I believe, will be held in port by the storm on the seas. The queen's men will be unable to march out on the drowned roads and the Duke of Norfolk is waiting for them. I think your rebellion is over, you have been beaten by the rain and the rising of the waters. They are calling it the Duke of Buckingham's Water and it has washed him and his ambition to hell along with your hopes. Nobody has seen a storm like this since the Queen Elizabeth called up a mist to hide her husband's army at the battle of Barnet, or summoned the wind to blow him safely home. Nobody doubts she can do such a thing and most of us only hope she will stop before she washes us all away. But why? Can she be working against you now? And if so, why? Does she know, with her inner sight, what has befallen her boys and who has done it? Does she think you have done it? Is she drowning your son in revenge?

Destroy what papers you have kept, and deny whatever you have done. Richard is coming to London and there will be a scaffold built on Tower Green. If he believes half what he has heard, he will put you on it and I will be unable to save you.

Stanley

OCTOBER 1483

I have been on my knees all night, but I don't know if God can hear me through the hellish noise of the rain. My son sets sail from Brittany with fifteen valuable ships and an army of five thousand men and loses them all in the storm at sea. Only two ships struggle ashore on the south coast and learn at once that Buckingham has been defeated by the rising of the river, his rebellion is washed away by the waters, and Richard is waiting, dry-shod, to execute the survivors.

My son turns his back on the country that should have been his, and sails for Brittany again, flying like a faintheart, leaving me here, unprotected, and clearly guilty of plotting his rebellion. We are parted once more, my heir and I, this time without even meeting, and this time it feels as if it is for ever. He and Jasper leave me to face the king, who marches vengefully on London like an invading enemy, mad with anger. Dr Lewis vanishes off to Wales, Bishop Morton takes the first ship that can sail after the storms and goes to France, Buckingham's men slip from the City in silence and under lowering skies, the queen's kin make their way to Brittany and to the tattered remains of my son's makeshift court, and my husband arrives in London in the train of King Richard, whose handsome face is dark with the sullen rage of a traitor betrayed.

'He knows,' my husband says shortly as he comes to my room, his travelling cape still around his shoulders, his sympathy scant. 'He knows you were working with the queen, and he will put you on trial. He has evidence from half a dozen witnesses. Rebels from Devon to East Anglia know your name and have letters from you.'

'Husband, surely he will not.'

'You are clearly guilty of treason and that is punishable by death.'

'But if he thinks you are faithful . . .'

'I *am* faithful,' he corrects me. 'It is not a matter of opinion but of fact. Not what the king thinks – but what he can see. When Buckingham rode out, while you were summoning your son to invade England, and paying rebels, while the queen was raising the southern counties, I was at his side, advising him, loaning him money, calling out my own affinity to defend him, faithful as any northerner. He trusts me now as he has never done before. My son raised an army for him.'

'Your son's army was for me!' I interrupt.

'My son will deny that, I will deny that, we will call you a liar and nobody can prove anything, either way.'

I pause. 'Husband, you will intercede for me?'

He looks at me thoughtfully, as if the answer could be 'no'. 'Well, it is a consideration, Lady Margaret. My King Richard is bitter, he cannot believe that the Duke of Buckingham, his best friend, his only friend, should betray him. And you? He is astonished at your infidelity. You carried his wife's train at her coronation, you were her friend, you welcomed her to London. He feels you have betrayed him. Unforgiveably. He thinks you as faithless as your kinsman Buckingham; and Buckingham was executed on the spot.'

'Buckingham is dead?'

'They took off his head in Salisbury market place. The king would not even see him. He was too angry with him and he is filled with hate towards you. You said that Queen Anne was welcome to her city, that she had been missed. You bowed the knee to him and wished him well. And then you sent out messages to every disaffected Lancastrian family in the country to tell them the cousins' war had come again, and that this time you will win.'

I grit my teeth. 'Should I run away? Should I go to Brittany too?'

'My dear, how ever would you get there?'

'I have my money chest, I have my guard. I could bribe a ship to take me, if I went down to the docks at London now, I could get away. Or Greenwich. Or I could ride to Dover or Southampton . . .'

He smiles at me and I remember they call him 'the fox' for his ability to survive, to double back, to escape the hounds. 'Yes, indeed, all that might have been possible; but I am sorry to tell you, I am nominated as your gaoler, and I cannot let you escape me. King Richard has decided that all your lands and your wealth will be mine, signed over to me, despite our marriage contract. Everything you owned as a girl is mine, everything you owned as a Tudor is mine, everything you gained from your marriage to Stafford is now mine, everything you inherited from your mother is mine. My men are in your chambers now collecting your jewels, your papers and your money chest. Your men are already under arrest, and your women are locked in their rooms. Your tenants and your affinity will learn you cannot summon them; they are all mine.'

I gasp. For a moment I cannot speak, I just look at him. 'You have robbed me? You have taken this chance to betray me?'

'You are to live at the house at Woking, my house now; you are not to leave the grounds. You will be served by my people, your own servants will be turned away. You will see neither ladies in waiting, servants, nor your confessor. You will meet with no-one and send no messages.'

I can hardly grasp the depth and breadth of his betrayal. He has taken everything from me. 'It is you who betrayed me to Richard!' I fling at him. 'You who betrayed the whole plot. It is you, with an eye to my fortune, who led me on to do this and now profit from my destruction. You told the Duke of Norfolk to go down to Guildford and suppress the rebellion in Hampshire. You told Richard to beware of the Duke of Buckingham. You told him that the queen was rising against him and I with her!'

He shakes his head. 'No. I am not your enemy, Margaret, I have served you well as your husband. No-one else could have saved you from the traitor's death that you deserve. This is the best deal I could get for you. I have saved you from the Tower, from the scaffold. I have saved your lands from sequestration; he could have taken them outright. I have saved you to live in my house, as my wife, in safety. And I am still placed at the heart of things, where we can learn of his plans against your son. Richard will seek to have Tudor killed now, he will send spies with orders to murder Henry. You have signed your son's death warrant with your failure. Only I can save him. You should be grateful to me.'

I cannot think, I cannot think through this mixture of threats and promises. 'Henry?'

'Richard will not stop until he is dead. Only I can save him.'

'I am to be your prisoner?'

He nods. 'And I am to have your fortune. It is nothing between us, Margaret. Think of the safety of your son.'

'You will let me warn Henry of his danger?'

He rises to his feet. 'Of course. You can write to him as you wish. But all your letters are to come through me, they will be carried by my men. I have to give the appearance of controlling you completely.'

'The appearance?' I repeat. 'If I know you at all, you will give the appearance of being on both sides.'

He smiles in genuine amusement. 'Always.'

WINTER 1483–4

It is a long, dark winter that I face, on my own at Woking. My ladies are taken from me, accused of plotting treason, and all of my trusted friends and messengers are turned away, I may not even see them. My household is chosen by my husband – my gaoler – and they are men and women loyal only to him. They look at me askance, as a woman who has betrayed him and his interests, a faithless wife. I am living among strangers again, far from the centre of court life, isolated from my friends, and far – so very far – from my defeated son. Sometimes I fear I will never see him again. Sometimes I fear that he will give up his great cause, settle in Brittany, marry an ordinary girl, become an ordinary young man; not a boy chosen by God for greatness and brought into the world by his mother's agony. He is the son of a woman who was called to greatness by Joan of Arc herself. Can he become a sluggard? A drunkard? A boy who in the pot-houses tells people that he might have been a king but for bad luck and a witch's wind?

I find a way to send him one letter, before Christmas. It is not a letter of goodwill or Christmas cheer. The days are too dark for the exchange of gifts. It has been a bad year for the House of Lancaster. I have no joy to wish anyone. We have long, hard work to do if he is to reach his throne, and Christmas Day is the very day to start again.

My brother-in-law Jasper and my son Henry
I greet you well.
I understand that Elizabeth the false queen and Richard the usurper are talking together about her terms for release from sanctuary.
My wish is that my son Henry should publicly announce his betrothal to Princess Elizabeth of York. This should prevent any other marriage for her, remind her affinity and mine of his claim to the throne, demonstrate their previous support for him, and re-establish his claim to the throne of England.
He should do it on Christmas Day in Rennes cathedral, just as Joan of Arc declared the King of France in Rheims cathedral. This is my command as his mother and the head of his house.
Greetings of the Season.
Margaret Stanley

I have time to meditate on the vanity of ambition and the sin of overthrowing an ordained king in the long winter nights of a miserable Christmas and a cheerless new year, as the impenetrable dark yields slowly to cold grey mornings. I go on my knees to my God and ask him why my son's venture to gain his rightful place in the world was not blessed, why the rain was against him, why the wind blew his ships away, why the God of earthquake, wind and fire could not calm the storm for Henry as He calmed it for Himself in Galilee? I ask Him that if Elizabeth Woodville,

Dowager Queen of England, is a witch as everyone knows, then why should she come out of sanctuary and make an agreement with a usurping king? How can she get her way in the world when my own is blocked and mired? I stretch out on the cold tiles of the chancel steps and give myself up to holy and remorseful grief.

And then it comes to me. In the end, after many long nights of fasting and prayer, I hear an answer. I find that I know why. I come to an understanding.

At last I recognise that the sin of ambition and greed darkened our enterprise, our plans were overshadowed by a sinful woman's desire for revenge. The plans were formed by a woman who thought herself the mother of a king, who could not be satisfied to be an ordinary woman. The fault of the enterprise lay in the vanity of a woman who would be a queen, and who would overturn the peace of the country for her own selfish desire. To know oneself is to know all, and I will confess my own sin and the part it played in our failure.

I am guilty of nothing more than a righteous ambition and a powerful desire to take my rightful place. It is a righteous rage. But Elizabeth Woodville is to blame for everything. She brought war to England for her own vanity and revenge, she it was who came to us filled with desire for her son, filled with pride in her house, puffed up with belief in her own beauty; and I should have refused to ally with her in her sinful ambition. It was Elizabeth's desire for her son's triumph that put us outside the pale of God's patience. I should have seen her vanity and turned from it.

I have been much at fault, I see it all now, and I beg God to forgive me. My fault was to ally with Buckingham, whose vain ambition and ungodly lust for power brought down the rain on us, and with the Queen Elizabeth whose vanity and desire were unsightly in the eyes of God. Also, who knows what she did to call up the rain?

I should have been, as Joan was, a woman riding out alone,

with her own vision. By allying myself with sinners – and such sinners! A woman who was the widow of Sir John Grey. A boy who was married to Katherine Woodville. – I received the punishment for their sins. I was not sinful myself – and God who knows everything, will know this – but I let myself join with them; and I, the godly, shared the punishment of sinners.

It is agony to me, to think that their wrongdoing should destroy the righteousness of my cause, she a proclaimed witch, and the daughter of a witch, and he a peacock for all his short life. I should not have stooped to ally myself with them, I should have kept my own counsel and let them raise their own rebellion and do their own murders, and kept myself free of it all. But as it is, their failure has brought me down, their rain has washed away my hopes, their sin is blamed on me; and here I am, cruelly punished for their crimes.

SPRING 1484

All the winter and all of the spring, I meditate on their wrong-doing, and I find I am glad that the queen is still locked in sanctuary. While I am imprisoned in my own home, I think of her, trapped in the gloomy crypt beside the river, facing her defeat in the darkness. But then, in the spring, I have a letter from my husband.

King Richard and Elizabeth Woodville have come to an accord. She has accepted the writ of parliament that she was never married to the late king, and King Richard has sworn that she and her daughters will be safe to come out of sanctuary. She is going into the keeping of John Nesfield and will live in his manor at Heytesbury in Wiltshire, and the girls are to go to court and serve as ladies in waiting to Queen Anne until marriages can be arranged for them. He knows that your son declared his betrothal to the Princess Elizabeth, but you and your son are disregarded. Elizabeth Woodville seems to have accepted defeat, and she seems reconciled to the deaths of her two sons. She never speaks of either.

And – at this time of reconciliation – I ordered a private search of the Tower so that the bodies of the princes might be found and their deaths blamed on the Duke of Buckingham (and not on you) but the stair where you said they were buried has not been disturbed and there is no sign of them. I have let it be spread about that their bodies were buried and then taken away by a remorseful priest and laid to rest in the deepest waters of the Thames – appropriate, I thought, for sons of the House of Rivers. This seems to conclude the story as well as any other version, and no-one has contradicted this with any more inconvenient details. Your three murderers, if they did the deed at all, are staying quiet.

I shall come to visit you shortly – the court is joyous in its triumph in the fine weather and the newly released Princess Elizabeth of York is the little queen of the court. She is the most charming girl, as beautiful as her mother was, half the court is besotted with her and she will certainly be married very well within the year. A girl so exquisite will be hard to match.

Stanley

This letter irritates me so intensely that I cannot even pray for the rest of the day. I have to take my horse and ride to the end of the parkland and all around the perimeter – the limit of my freedom – hardly seeing the bobbing yellow heads of the daffodils, nor the young lambs in the fields, before I can recover my temper. The suggestion that the princes are not dead and buried, which undoubtedly they are, and his further layering of lies with his exhumation and water-burial in the Thames story – which merely creates further questions – would be enough to enrage me, but to couple it with news of the freedom of Queen Elizabeth and the triumph of her daughter at the court of the man who should be their enemy till death: this shocks me to the core.

How can the queen bring herself to forge an agreement with the man she should accuse of killing her sons? It is a mystery to me, an abomination. And how can that girl go dancing round her uncle's court as if he were not the murderer of her brothers and the gaoler of her girlhood? I cannot comprehend it. The queen is, as she always has been, steeped in vanity and lives only for her own comfort and pleasure. No surprise to me at all that she should settle for a handsome manor and – no doubt – a good pension and a pleasant livelihood. She cannot be grieving for her boys at all, if she will take her freedom from the hands of their murderer.

Heytesbury Manor indeed! I know that house and she will be luxuriously comfortable there, and I don't doubt that John Nesfield will allow her to order anything she wants. Men always fall over themselves to oblige Elizabeth Woodville because they are fools for a pretty face, and though she led a rebellion in which good men died and which cost me everything; it seems that she is to get off scot-free.

And her daughter must be a thousand times worse, to accept freedom under these terms and to go to court and order fine dresses, and serve as lady in waiting to a usurping queen, sitting on the throne that had been her mother's! Words fail me, my prayers fail me, I am stunned into silence by the falseness and the vanity of the York queen and the York princess and the only thing I can think of is how can I punish them for getting free, when I am ruined and imprisoned? It cannot be right, after all we have gone through, that the York queen once again comes out of danger and sanctuary and lives in a beautiful house in the heart of England, raises her daughters and sees them married well among her friends and neighbours. It cannot be right that the York princess is a favourite at the court, the darling of her uncle, the sweetheart of the people, and I thrown down. God cannot really want these women to lead peaceful, happy lives while my son is in exile. It cannot be His will. He must want justice, He must want to see them punished, He must want to see their downfall. He must long for the burning of the brand. He must desire the scent of the smoke of their sacrifice. And, God knows, I would be His willing instrument if He would just put the weapon in my obedient hand.

1484 APRIL

My husband comes to visit me as the king is on a spring progress, travelling to Nottingham where he will make his headquarters this year, readying for the invasion of my son that he knows must come this year, or the next, or the year after. Thomas Stanley rides out on my lands every day, as greedy for the chase as if it were his own game to kill – and then I remember that it is. Everything belongs to him now. He eats well at night and drinks deeply of the rare wines laid down in the cellar by Henry Stafford for me and for my son, and which now belong to him. I thank God that I am not attached to worldly goods, as other women are, or I would look at the march of bottles along the table with deep resentment. But, I thank Our Lady, my mind is fixed on the will of God and the success of my son.

'Does Richard know of Henry's plans?' I ask, one evening before he is utterly sodden with the wine that my cellars are forced to yield to him.

'He has spies all over Henry's little court, of course,' Stanley replies. 'And a spy network which passes news from one end of the country to the other. A fishing boat could not land in Penzance now without Richard learning of it the next day. But your son has grown into a cautious and clever young man. As far as I know, he keeps his counsel and makes plans only with his Uncle Jasper. He takes no-one else into his confidence, Richard never refers to any intelligence from Brittany which is not obvious news. It is clear that they will equip ships and come again, as soon as they are able. But they will be set back by their failure last year. They have lost their sponsor a small fortune, perhaps he will not want to risk another fleet for them. Most people think the Duke of Brittany will have to give them up, and hand them over to France. Once in the power of the French king they could be lost, they could be made. More than that, Richard doesn't know.'

I nod.

'Did you hear that Thomas Grey, Elizabeth Woodville's son, ran from your son's court and was trying to get home to England?'

'No!' I am shocked. 'Why would he do that? Why would he want to leave Henry?'

My husband smiles at me over his wine glass. 'It seems that his mother commanded him to come home and make his peace with Richard, just as she and the girls have done. Doesn't look as if she believes that Richard killed the boys, does it? Doesn't look like she thinks Henry is a horse worth backing any more. Why else would she hope for a full reconciliation with the king? Looks like she wants to sever her ties with Henry Tudor.'

'Who knows what she thinks?' I say irritably. 'She is a fickle woman with no loyalty to anyone but her own interest. And no sense.'

'Your son Henry Tudor caught Thomas Grey on the road, and took him back again,' my husband remarks. 'So now, they are holding him as a prisoner. He is more a hostage than a supporter to their court. It doesn't bode well for the betrothal of your son and the princess though, does it? I assume she will reject the betrothal, just as her half-brother has denied his fealty. That must hurt your cause, as well as humiliating Henry. Looks like the House of York has turned against you.'

'She can't deny her betrothal,' I snap. 'Her mother swore to it, and so did I. And Henry has sworn to it before God in the cathedral at Rennes. She will have to get a dispensation from the Pope himself if she wants to get out of it. And, anyway, why would she want to get out of it?'

My husband's smile grows broader. 'She has a suitor,' he says quietly.

'She has no right to have a suitor, she is betrothed to my son.'

'Yes, but she has all the same.'

'Some grubby page, I daresay.'

He chuckles as if at a private jest. 'Oh no. Not exactly.'

'No nobleman would stoop to marry her. She is declared a bastard, she is publicly betrothed to my son, and her uncle has promised her only a moderate dowry. Why would anyone want her? She is shamed three times over.'

'For her beauty? She is radiant, you know. And her charm – she has the most delightful smile, you really can't look away from her. And she has a merry heart, and a pure soul. She is a lovely girl, a real princess in every way. It is as if she came out of sanctuary and simply came alive in the world. I think he is just simply in love with her.'

'Who is this fool?'

He glows with amusement. 'Her suitor, the one I am telling you about.'

'So who is this love-struck idiot?'

'King Richard himself.'

For a moment I am silenced. I cannot imagine such wickedness, such a ruling of lust. 'He is her uncle!'

'They could get a papal dispensation.'

'He is married.'

'You said yourself that Queen Anne is infertile and unlikely to make old bones. He could ask her to step aside, it wouldn't be unreasonable. He needs another heir, his own son is ill again. He needs another boy to secure his line, and the Rivers are famously fertile. Think of Queen Elizabeth's performance in the marriage bed of England!'

My sour face tells him I am thinking of it. 'She is young enough to be his daughter!'

'As you yourself know, that is hardly an obstacle, but in any case, it isn't true. There are only fourteen years between them.'

'He is the murderer of her brothers, and the destruction of her house!'

'Now you, of all people, know that is not true. Not even the common people believe that Richard killed the boys, now that the queen is reconciled with him, living in the country and the princesses are at his court.'

I rise from the table, I am so disturbed I forget even to say grace. 'He can't intend to marry her, he must mean only to seduce her and shame her, to make her unfit for Henry.'

'Unfit for Henry!' He laughs aloud. 'As though Henry is in a position to choose! As though he is such a catch himself! As though you have not tied him to the princess just as you say she is tied to him.'

'Richard will make her his whore to shame her and her whole family.'

'I don't think so. I think he loves her, truly, I think King Richard is in love with Princess Elizabeth, and it is the first time in his life he has ever been in love. You see him look at her, and he seems just filled with wonder. It is an extraordinary thing to see, as if he had discovered the meaning of life in her. It is as if she were his white rose, truly.'

'And she?' I spit. 'Does she show proper distance, is she a princess in her self-respect? She should think only of her purity and her virtue, if she is a princess and hopes to be queen.'

'She adores him,' he says simply. 'It shows. She lights up when he comes in the room and when she dances she throws him a little private smile and he can't take his eyes off her. They are a couple in love and anyone but a fool would see it is simply that, nothing more – and certainly nothing less.'

'Then she is no better than a whore,' I say, going from the room as I cannot bear to hear another word. 'And I shall write to her mother and give her my sympathy, and my prayers for her daughter who has fallen into shame. But I cannot be surprised at the two of them. The mother is a whore; and it turns out that the daughter is no better.'

I close the door on his mocking laughter and I find to my surprise that I am shaking, and there are tears on my cheeks.

Next day, a messenger comes from the court for my husband and he does not have the courtesy to send it on to me, so I have to go down to the stable yard, like a maid in waiting, to find him calling out his men and ordering them into the saddle. 'What is happening?'

'I am going back to court. I have had a message.'

'I was waiting for you to send the messenger on to me.'

'It was my business. Not yours.'

I close my lips on an undutiful retort. Since he was granted my lands and my fortune he has not hesitated to behave as my master. I submit to his rudeness with the grace from Our Lady and I know that She will make note of it.

'Husband, will you tell me please if there is danger or trouble in the land? I must be allowed an answer to that.'

'There is loss,' he says briefly. 'There is loss in the land. King Richard's son, the little Prince Edward, is dead.'

'God rest his soul,' I say piously, while my head spins with excitement.

'Amen. And so I must go back to court. We will be in mourning. It will strike Richard hard, I don't doubt. Only one child ever born to them, and now he is gone.'

I nod. Now there is only Richard himself between my boy and the throne, there is no other heir but my son. We spoke of the heartbeats that blocked my son's path to the throne, now all the boys of York are dead. It is time for the Lancaster boy. 'So Richard has no heir,' I breathe. 'We serve a childless king.'

My husband's dark eyes are on my face, he smiles as if he is amused by my ambition. 'Unless he marries the York princess,' he teases me gently. 'And they are fertile stock, remember. Her mother gave birth almost every year. Say Elizabeth of York gives him a quiver full of princes and the support of the Rivers family, and the love of the York affinity? He has no son from Anne, what should now stop him putting her aside? She might give him a divorce at once, and retire to a nunnery.'

'Why don't you go back to court?' I ask, too angry to mind my tongue. 'You go back to your faithless master and his York whore.'

'I will go.' He swings up into the saddle. 'But I will leave you with Ned Parton over there.' He gestures to a young man standing beside a big black horse. 'He is my messenger. He speaks three languages, including Breton, should you want to send him to Brittany. He has a safe pass through this country, through France and Flanders, signed by me as Constable of England. You can trust him to send messages to anyone you like, and no-one can stop him or take them from him. King

Richard may appear to be my master, but I don't forget your son and his ambitions, and he is only one step from the throne this morning, and my beloved stepson as always.'

'But which side are you on?' I demand in frustration, as his men mount their horses and raise his banner.

'The winning side,' he says with a short laugh, and thumps his chest in a salute to me, like a soldier, and is gone.

SUMMER 1484

I wait. All I can do is wait. I send out letters by Ned Parton and Jasper replies to me, courteously, as to a powerless woman, far away, who understands nothing. I see that the failed rebellion that cost them their army and their fleet also spoiled their faith in me as a co-conspirator, as a woman of power in the country they hoped to take. In the hot summer days as the crops ripen in the fields and the haymakers go out with their scythes and cut the hay, I see I am become as marginal as the hares that run from the blades straight into the snares because they understand nothing.

I write, I send messages, I scold Elizabeth Woodville, the sometime queen, about the behaviour of her daughters, which is reported to me in more and more detail: their beautiful clothes, their importance at the court, their beauty, their light-hearted joy, their easy Rivers charm as they flow from one amusement to another. There were many who said that their grandmother, Jacquetta, was a witch, a descendant of Melusina the water goddess, and now there are many who say that these girls weave their magic too. Finest of them all is the girl that is promised to Henry but behaves as if she has forgotten all about him. I write to Elizabeth Woodville to call her to account, I write to the vain girl, Elizabeth of York, to reprimand her, I write to Henry to remind him of his duty – and nobody, nobody, bothers to reply to me.

I am alone in my house; and for all that I have longed all my life for a solitary routine of prayer, I am most terribly alone, and most terribly lonely. I begin to think that nothing will ever change, that I will live out my life here, visited occasionally by a jeering husband who will drink wine from my cellar and eat game from my fields with the special relish of a poacher. I will hear news from court, which indicates that nobody remembers me, or my one-time great importance. I will hear from my son, far away, and he will politely send his good wishes, and on the day of his birth, his acknowledgement of my sacrifice for him; but he will never send me his love nor tell me when I may look for him.

In my loneliness I consider that we were separated when he was such a little boy and since then we have never been close – not as a mother might be to her child, not as Elizabeth Woodville always has been to her children, that she raised herself, that she loved so openly. Now that I can be of no use to him, he will forget all about me. And in truth, in bitter truth: if he were not the heir to my house, and summit of all my ambitions, I would already have forgotten all about him.

My life comes down to this: a court which has forgotten me, a husband who mocks me, a son who has no use for me, and a God who has gone silent. It is no comfort to me that I despise the court, that I never loved my husband, and that my son was born only to fulfil my destiny, and if he cannot do that, I don't know what use we are to each other. I go on praying. I don't know what to do but that. I go on praying.

Pontefract, June 1484

My lady,

I write to alert you to a treaty signed by King Richard and the current ruler of Brittany, who is the treasurer and chief officer (the duke being currently out of his wits). King Richard and Brittany have made an agreement. England is to supply archers to Brittany to help them in their struggle against France, and in return they will take Henry Tudor into imprisonment and send him home for execution. I thought you would want to know this.

I remain your faithful husband

Stanley

I have no-one that I can trust to send but Ned Parton. But I have to take the risk. I send one line to Jasper.

Stanley tells me that Richard has made agreement with Brittany to arrest Henry. Be warned.

Then I go to my chapel and kneel before the chancel rail, my face turned to the crucifix of the suffering Christ. 'Keep him safe,' I whisper over and over again. 'Keep my son safe. And bring him to victory.'

Within the month I have a reply. It is from Jasper, and short and to the point as always.

France, July 1484

Thank you for your warning that was confirmed by your friend Bishop Morton, who heard it in France. I took some of our men and rode over the border to Anjou to attract as much attention as I could, while Henry took the road to Vannes with a guard of only five. He disguised himself as a servant and rode for the border, crossing it just a day ahead of the Brittany guard. It was a close-run thing and your son was calm in danger, and we laughed about it when we were safe.

We were welcomed by the French court, and they are promising to support us with an army and funds. They will open the prison gates for us to recruit an army of rascals and I have a plan to train them. I have hopes, Margaret –

JT

WINTER 1484

The court spends the Christmas season at Westminster, and the gossip of the household tells me that Richard has put on as great a show as his brother ever did. The news of the music, the playing, the clothes and the feasting go round the kingdom and grow more glorious in the telling. My household brings in the yule log and mistletoe and holly and makes very merry without me in the kitchen and the hall.

I find the marble floor of the chapel very cold under my knees. I am without comfort, I am without place, I am without much hope. Richard at Westminster, in the glory of York power, is proudly invulnerable both to my boy and to my brother-in-law, poor pensioners of the enemy of England: France. I see them sinking into exile, I see them brought low and disregarded. I fear they will hang around the court of France for the rest of Henry's life and he will be known as a second-rank pretender: worth playing as a card in a game of treaties, worth nothing on his own account.

My husband writes one of his rare letters from Westminster,

and I fall on it as a beggar might fall on a crust of bread. I am too poor in news to be proud.

The York princess is at the top of her game, her beauty commands the court, the king follows her like a lapdog. The queen dresses her in her own gowns, they dress to match. The thin old Neville woman and this glowing, rosy girl come out to dine in dresses of the same rich cut and colour, as if they want to encourage comparison.

The queen must be ordered by the king to be so complaisant, she does everything but put her niece into bed with her husband. There are some who share your view that Richard seeks to seduce his niece only to insult your son, to show him as a helpless cuckold. If so, he succeeds magnificently. Henry Tudor is a laughing stock to this hot-blooded court. But there are others who think, more simply, that the lovers are merely reckless with appearances, forgetting everything but each other, and think of nothing but their own desires.

The court is wonderful this season; how sorry I am you cannot be here. I have never seen such wealth and glamour since Edward's time, and at the heart of it all is Edward's daughter looking as if she has come into her own again. Of course she belongs here. The Yorks are indeed the sun in splendour and to see Elizabeth of York is to be dazzled.

By the way, do you have any news of your son? Richard's spies report to him in secret, I don't know what they say; but I do know that the king has ceased to fear Henry, and his poor ally, the mad Duke of Brittany. He nearly caught him in June, you know, and there are many who say Henry will find no safe haven in France. He will simply be held by the French king as a bargaining chip, until he loses all value. Perhaps it may be that your last defeat was your last chance? What do you think? And if so, do you want to give up hope for Henry, and sue for forgiveness to Richard? I could perhaps intercede for you if I promised that you are humbled to the ground.

I send you the compliments of the season and this little book as a gift. It is printed by one Thomas Caxton on a press of his own devising, brought to England by the late and much missed Anthony Rivers, the queen's brother. I thought you would find a printed book, rather than a hand-copied manuscript, of interest. Everyone is saying that Rivers was a man of great foresight to patronise such work. His own sister Elizabeth the queen edited the first text off the press; she is a scholar as well as a beauty, of course.

What would happen if everyone could read and everyone could buy these? Would they give up on teachers and kings altogether? Would they care nothing for the Houses of Lancaster and York? And study their own loyalties? Would they cry a plague on both your houses? It is amusing to speculate, is it not?

Stanley

I drop his book to the floor in sheer irritation at the thought of Elizabeth of York and her incestuous lover-uncle dancing in the Christmas feast, while that poor thing, Anne Neville, smiles on them as if she were part of a happy family at play. When Stanley taunts me with Henry's silence, I have no riposte. In truth, I don't know what he is doing, I have heard nothing since their flight to France when Jasper said he had hopes, but did not tell me what they were. I think Jasper has advised Henry not to write to me, I think they believe that Stanley's messenger Ned Parton is unsafe; they believe he reports to my husband. They are surrounded by spies, and they have to be suspicious; but I fear that now they doubt me too. This was once our battle, this was our rebellion: us Tudors against the Yorks. Now they trust no-one; not even me. I live far from everyone, everything. I know nothing but what my husband writes to me, and he writes as a man in triumph might taunt a defeated enemy.

MARCH 1485

Another day when I rise for matins, pray as always for patience to endure my imprisonment and enforced silence, pray for the success of my son and for the downfall of his enemies, find my mind wandering as I think how Richard's downfall might come about, find myself dreaming of the humiliation of the York princess and the witch her mother, and recall myself to myself with a sudden start and see that the candles are burning down on the altar and I have been on my knees for two hours and my companions are restless behind me, giving the theatrical sighs of women who imagine they are badly treated.

I rise up and go to breakfast and see the relish with which my ladies fall on their food as if they were famished by having to come an hour or so late. They really are hopelessly venal creatures. If I could have lived in a nunnery in this time of imprisonment, at least I would have lived with holy women and not this collection of fools. I go to my room to deal with the business of my lands and the gathering of the rents, but there is almost nothing to do. It all goes to my husband's steward now, and I am a tenant in the house which was once all my own.

I make myself walk in the garden for an hour in the morning for the good of my health; but I can take no pleasure in the fat buds on the apple trees, and the bobbing yellow of the Lenten lilies. The sun is starting to grow warm again for another year of my captivity, and it is hard for me to take any joy in it. This must be the start of campaign season, my son must surely be recruiting troops and hiring ships, but I know almost nothing about it. It is as if I am trapped in a winter of solitude and silence while the rest of the world is waking to life, to opportunities, to sin itself.

I almost think it is an echo of my mood when the world seems oddly shadowed, the sunlight which was so bright and warm only a moment ago starts to feel cool, starts to look almost like candlelight, candlelight throughout the orchard, and suddenly all the birds that were singing to one another in the trees fall silent, and the hens at the end of the orchard all scurry to the hen house, as it gets darker and darker all around as if night were falling though it is not yet noon.

I freeze in my stride: at last my calling has come upon me. It has happened at last. A vision, a full daytime vision, has come to me, and at last I shall see an angel or perhaps the blessed Lady Mary Herself, and She will tell me when my son will invade, and that he will triumph. I drop to my knees, ready for the visitation that I have waited for all my life. At last, I shall see what Joan the Maid saw. At last I shall hear the voices of angels in the church bells.

'Lady Margaret! Lady Margaret!' A woman comes running out of the house, a man at arms behind her. 'Come in! Come in! Something terrible is happening!'

I open my eyes with a start and look behind me at this screaming fool as she gallops across the orchard, skirts flapping and headdress awry. It cannot be a holy vision if an idiot like this can see it. I rise to my feet. There is no vision for me today, my sight is only what everyone else sees, and it is no miracle but something worldly and strange.

'Lady Margaret! Come in! It must be a storm or something worse!'

She is a fool, but she is right in this: something terrible is happening, but I cannot understand what it is. I look up at the sky and I see the strangest and most ominous sight: the sun is being devoured by a large, dark rondel, like a plate being passed before a candle. Slowly, as I shade my eyes and squint through my fingers, I can see the plate pass before the sun and then it is completely covering it, and the world has gone dark.

'Come in!' the woman whimpers. 'Lady Margaret, for the love of God, come in!'

'You go,' I say. I am quite fascinated. It is as if the darkness and despair of my own grief has blotted out the sun itself, and now it is, quite suddenly, as dark as night. Perhaps it will always be night-time now, it will always be darkness while Richard is on the throne of England and my son is blotted from the world as the sun has been blotted from the sky. My life has been dark as night since his campaign failed, and now everyone can share the darkness with me, for they failed to rise for my son. We can all be benighted in this godforsaken kingdom without a true king, for ever. It is nothing more than everyone else deserves.

The woman trembles and then runs back to the house. The man at arms stands, almost at attention, at a distance from me, torn between his duty to guard me and his own fear, and the two of us wait in the eerie half-darkness, to see what – if anything – will happen next. I wonder if this is the world ending, and if now at last there will be a great trumpet peal from the angels and God will call me to His own, who has served Him so long and so hard, and so thanklessly, in this vale of tears.

I drop to my knees again and feel for my rosary in my pocket. I am ready for the call. I am not afraid, I am a woman of courage, favoured by the Lord. I am ready for the heavens to open, and for God to summon me. I am His faithful servant, perhaps He will summon me first, showing everyone who ever doubted my vocation that He and I have a special understanding. But instead there is the unearthly light again, and I open my eyes and look around to see a world slowly restored, the light growing stronger, the disc peeling away from the sun, the sun too bright to look at, once more, and the birds starting to sing as if it were dawn.

It is over. The ungodly shadow is over. It has to be a sign; but of what? And what am I to learn from it? The man at arms, trembling with fear, looks at me, and forgets his place so much as to speak to me directly: 'For the love of God, what was that all about?'

'It is a sign,' I say, not reproving him for speaking on this one occasion. 'It is a sign from God. The reign of one king is ending and the new sun is coming. The sun of York is to be put out, and the new sun is to come in like a dragon.'

He gulps. 'You are sure, my lady?'

'You saw it yourself,' I say.

'I saw the darkness . . .'

'Did you see the dragon come out of the sun?'

'I think so . . .'

'That was the Tudor dragon, coming out of the west. As my son will come.'

He drops to his knees and lifts his hands to me in the gesture of fealty. 'You will call on me for your son,' he says. 'I am your liegeman. I saw the sun darken as you say, and the dragon come out of the west.'

I take his hands in my own, and I smile to myself. This is how ballads are born: he will say that he saw the Tudor dragon of Wales coming out of the west and darkening the sun of York.

'The sun is no longer in splendour,' I say. 'We all saw it darkened and defeated. The whole kingdom saw the sun fail. This will be the year that the sun of York goes out for ever.'

MARCH 1485

To my wife, Lady Margaret Stanley

This is to tell you that the queen is dead. She was failing ever since the Christmas feast and she died almost unattended, from weakness of the lungs, on the same day that the sun went dark over the castle.

You will be interested to know that Richard is to publicly renounce any intention to marry his niece. Rumours have reached such a scandalous level that the lords of the north made it clear to him that such an insult to the memory of the queen – one of their own – would not be accepted. Truth is that many are terrified at the thought of Elizabeth Woodville restored as My Lady the Queen's Mother since they allowed the execution of her brother and Grey son and locked up her princes. Perhaps you would have done better to resist the temptation to scold her. If only you had urged the marriage between the York girl and Richard, it could have caused Richard's overthrow! But you did not think of that in your pride for your son. I am sure rightly.

To demonstrate his indifference to the York princess, the king has decided to put her in the care of a lady of unimpeachable morality so that the world may see that she is chaste – and not, as we have all thought, madly in love with him, and bedding him while his wife was dying.

You will perhaps be surprised to learn that his choice of chaperone . . . duenna . . . and may I say, mother? – has fallen on you, as the most proper lady to guard her reputation, since she is betrothed to your son.

I lift my head from his letter, I can almost hear his mocking laughter and see his cold smile. I find I am smiling too. The turn of the wheel of fortune is impossible to predict, and now I am to be a guardian to the daughter of a woman I hate. I hate the girl too.

The princess will arrive to stay with you within the week. I am sure you will revel in each other's company. Personally, I cannot imagine a more ill-matched household; but no doubt your faith will support you, and of course she has no choice at all,

Stanley

APRIL 1485

Grimly, I tell them to prepare a bedroom for a princess, and confirm to my fluttering ladies that the Princess of York or, as I pointedly call her, Lady Elizabeth – I give her no family name, since she has none, being declared a bastard – will come within the next few days. There is a great deal of concern about the quality of the linen and in particular the ewer and the bowl for her room that I have used, but that they consider too poor for such a great young lady. At this point I say briefly that since she has spent half her life in hiding from an ordained king, and the other half using borrowed goods to which she had no right at all, it does not matter so very much whether her jug is pewter or no, and the dent makes no difference either.

I do make an effort to make sure that she has a good prie dieu in her room, a simple but large crucifix to focus her mind on her sins, and a collection of devotional texts so that she may think about her past life and hope for better in the future. I also include a copy of our family tree and pedigree so she can see for herself that my son's birthright is as good, indeed better than, hers. While I am waiting for her to arrive, I get the briefest letter from Jasper.

In haste – the King of France has given us aid – we are sailing as soon as we get a good wind. You must secure the York princess if you can, as the Yorks will only support us if we have her, and the Lancs are slow to promise for us. Pray for us. We are on our way as soon as the wind changes. J

I thrust the letter in the fire, breathless with the shock, and at that very moment, I hear the rattle of horses' hooves. It sounds like a guard of about fifty. I go to the leaded window of the great hall and peer out. I see my husband's standard and the men wearing his livery. He is riding his big horse at the head of them all and beside him, on a big working cob, his coat burnished to bright chestnut, the captain of the guard is on a pillion saddle, and behind him, sitting sideways and smiling, as if she owned half of England, is a young woman in a riding habit of scarlet velvet.

It is the colour that makes me hiss like a cat and step back so she cannot see my white, shocked face staring out of the window as she looks up and down at the house, critically, as if she were valuing it for purchase. It is the bright redness of her dress that shocks me. I cannot even see her face yet, though I catch a glimpse of blonde hair tucked away under the red velvet cap. It is that colour which shakes me with irritation before she has even allowed my husband – my husband smiling as I have never seen before – to lift her down from the saddle.

Then it comes back to me with a rush. The year I went to court for the first time was the year that Margaret of Anjou, Henry VI's queen, showed the world the new red: that very same bright scarlet. I remember Queen Margaret looking down the great hall of the court and overlooking me as if I were not worth her attention. I remember the towering height of her headdress and the scarlet of her gown. I remember feeling then, as I find I am feeling now, the seething resentment of someone who deserves the highest attention, the greatest respect, and yet is being overlooked. The Lady Elizabeth has not even stepped over my threshold, and yet she wears the colour of a woman who wants to capture the attention of everyone. Before she has even set foot in my house I feel sure that she will draw every eye from me. But I am determined that she shall learn to respect me. She shall know who is her better; I swear it. The power of the Lord is mine, I have spent my life in prayer and study. She has spent her life in frivolity and ambition and her mother is no more than a lucky witch. She shall honour me in God's name. I shall make sure of it.

My husband himself throws open the door for her and steps back to let her precede him into the great hall. I come forwards out of the shadows and she immediately recoils as if I were a ghost. 'Oh! My lady Margaret! You startled me! I did not see you there!' she cries, and she sweeps into a curtsey which is precisely judged – not as low as for a queen, low enough for the wife of a great lord of the realm, low enough for the woman who might be her mother-in-law, but a little raised, as if to remind me that I am in disgrace with this girl's uncle and I am under house arrest on his word, and she is his favourite and he is king.

I make the smallest, smallest movement of my head in return, and then I step towards my husband and we exchange our usual frosty kiss of greeting. 'Husband, you are welcome,' I lie politely.

'Wife, I give you joy,' he replies. For once his smile is bright, he is richly amused at bringing this blooming flower into the cold wasteland that is my home. 'I am glad to bring you such a companion to cheer your solitude.'

'I am happy in my own company, with my studies and my prayers,' I say at once, and then, as he raises an eyebrow at me, I have to turn to her: 'But of course I am very glad of your visit.'

'I will not intrude on you for long, I am sure,' she says, flushing a little at the rudeness of the icy welcome. 'I am sorry to do so. But the king ordered it.'

'We did not choose it; but it is a happy arrangement,' my husband says smoothly. 'Shall we go to the privy chamber? And take some wine?'

I nod to my steward of the household. He knows to fetch the best of the bottles, my husband is now acquainted with my cellar and is always served with the finest, now that he is master here. I lead the way and I hear her light footsteps coming behind me, her high heels tapping on the paving stones of the hall, the very tempo of vanity. When we reach my room I gesture that she may sit on a stool, and I take the carved chair and look down on her.

She is beautiful, that much is undeniable. She has a heart-shaped face and a creamy pale complexion, straight eyebrows of brown, and grey, wide eyes. Her hair is fair, blonde at the front and curling, to judge from the one lock which has escaped from the cap and which falls in a ringlet to her shoulder. She is tall, she has her mother's grace, but she has an endearing charm that her mother never had. Elizabeth Woodville would turn a head in every crowd, but this girl would warm a heart. I see what my husband means about her radiance, she is tremendously engaging. Even now, as she pulls off her gloves, and holds her hands to the warmth of the fire, unaware that I am looking her up and down as I would a horse that I might buy, she has a sort of vulnerable appeal. She is like a young animal that you cannot see without wanting to pet: like an orphan fawn, or a long-legged foal.

She senses my eyes on her and she looks up. 'I am sorry to disturb your studies, Lady Margaret,' she repeats. 'I have written to my mother. It may be that I will be allowed to go and stay with her.'

'Why are you sent from court at all?' I ask. I try to smile to encourage her to confide in me. 'Did you get into some silly trouble? I am quite in disgrace for my support of my son, you know.'

She shakes her head and a little shadow goes over her face. 'I think the king wanted me to be in a household where there could be no question against my reputation,' she says. 'There has been some gossip – perhaps you have heard it?'

I shake my head as if to imply that I live so quietly, so remotely, that I hear and know nothing.

'The king is very kind to me and singles me out from the ladies of court,' she says, lying fluently as only beautiful girls know how. 'There was gossip, you know how the court loves to gossip, and with Her Grace the queen dying so sadly, he wanted to make it clear that there was no cause. So he sent me to you. I am so grateful that you would take me in, thank you.'

'And what was the gossip?' I ask, and watch her shift uncomfortably on her little stool.

'Ah, Lady Margaret, you know how the world likes to whisper.'

'And what did they whisper?' I press her. 'If I am to repair your reputation, I should know at least what has been said against it.'

She looks frankly up at me as if she would have me for a friend and ally if she could. 'They say that the king would have taken me for his wife,' she says.

'And would you have liked that?' I ask steadily but I can hear my own heart pounding in my ears for rage at the insult to my son and to our house.

She blushes deep rose, as red as her cap. 'It is not for me to decide,' she says quietly. 'My mother must arrange my marriage. And besides, I am already betrothed to your son. Such things are for my mother and my guardians to decide.'

'Your maidenly obedience does you credit, I am sure,' I say. I find I cannot keep the cold scorn from my voice, and she hears it and flinches back and looks at me again. She sees the anger in my face and her colour drains away and she is white, as if she would faint.

At that precise moment, my husband walks into the room followed by the steward with the wine and three glasses, takes in the situation in one second and says urbanely: 'Getting to know each other? Excellent.'

He sends her off to her private chambers after she has drunk her glass of wine with us and tells her to rest after the rigours of the journey. Then he pours himself another measure, seats himself in a chair the match of mine, stretches out his boots towards the fire and says: 'You had better not bully her. If Richard defeats your son he will marry her. The north won't rebel against him once he has won a strong victory, and then she will be queen and you will never get out of this rat hole.'

'It is hardly a rat hole, and I don't bully,' I say. 'I merely asked her why she had been sent to me and she chose to tell me something of the truth and something of a lie, as any girl would, who does not know the one from another.'

'She may be a liar and indeed, in your terms, she may be a whore, but she will be the next Queen of England,' he says. 'If your son comes in like a dragon from Wales – did you know there is a new ballad doing the rounds about the dragon from Wales? – then he will have to marry her to secure the York affinity, whatever her past has been. If Richard defeats your son, as seems most likely, then Richard will marry her for love. Either way she will be Queen of England and you would be wise not to make an enemy of her.'

'I shall treat her with perfect courtesy,' I say.

'Do that,' he recommends. 'But listen to me, and do something more . . .'

I wait.

'Don't take this opportunity to ride roughshod over her, in case, when the times change, she rides her horses over you. You have to appear to be on her side, Margaret. Don't be a Beaufort filled with wounded pride – be a Stanley: get on the winning side.'

MAY 1485

I disregard my husband's advice and I watch Lady Elizabeth and she watches me. We live together in a state of armed silence, like two armies drawn up, pausing before battle.

'Like two cats on a stable roof,' my husband says, much amused.

Sometimes she asks me for news of my son – as if I would trust her with the humiliation he has had to suffer at the French court to raise funds and support for his attack on England! Sometimes I ask her if she has heard from her sisters, still at court, and she tells me that the court is to move to Nottingham, the dark castle at the heart of England, where Richard has chosen to wait for the attack that he knows is coming. The younger York girls are to be sent to Sherrif Hutton for safe-keeping, and I know Elizabeth longs to be with them. She obeys the rules of my household without demur, and she is as silent in prayer and as still as I am myself. I have kept her for hours in my chapel without her breakfast and she has never breathed one word of complaint. She just grows paler, more and more weary in the devotional silence of my private rooms, and I imagine that she finds the days very long. The rose that she was when she rode in through my gate in her red riding dress has now faded to a white rose indeed. She is still beautiful; but now she is again the silent girl that her mother raised in the shadowy sanctuary. She had only a little time of glory, poor little thing: a very brief moment when she was the unofficial queen of a merry court. Now she is in shadow and silence again.

'But your mother must live as I do,' I remark one day to her. 'She too lives alone in the country, and she has no lands to command and no people to supervise. She is robbed of her lands and alone as I am. She must be penitent and sad and quiet.'

To my surprise she laughs aloud, and then puts her hand over her mouth and apologises. But her eyes are still dancing with the joke. 'Oh no, my mother is a very merry woman,' she says. 'She has music and dancing every evening, and the mummers come, and the players, and the tenants have their festivals, and she celebrates the saints' days. She rides out with a hunt most mornings and they often picnic in the woods. There is always something happening at her house, and she has many guests.'

'It sounds like a little court,' I say. I can hear the jealousy in my own voice and I try to smile to conceal it.

'It is a little court,' she says. 'Many people who loved her still remember the old days and are glad to visit her and see her in a lovely house and in safety again.'

'But it's not her house,' I insist. 'And she once commanded palaces.'

Elizabeth shrugs. 'She doesn't mind that,' she says. 'Her greatest loss was my father and my brothers.' She looks away as she mentions them and swallows down her grief. 'As for the rest of it all – the palaces and the clothes and the jewels matter less to her.'

'Your mother was the most venal woman I have ever known,' I say rudely. 'Whatever she pretends, this is her downfall, this is her poverty, this is her defeat. She is in exile from the royal court and she is a nobody.'

She smiles but says nothing in disagreement. There is something so utterly defiant in her smiling silence that I have to grip my hands on the arms of my chair. I should so like to slap her pretty face.

'You don't think so?' I say irritably. 'Speak up, girl.'

'My mother could have come to court at any time she wished, as the most honoured guest of her brother-in-law King Richard of England,' she says quietly. 'He invited her and promised she would be the second lady in the kingdom after the queen. But she didn't want to. I think she has put worldly vanity behind her.'

'No, it is I who have put worldly vanity behind me,' I correct her. 'And this is a struggle of mastery over one's greed and desire for fame, a goal only won by years of study and prayer. Your mother has never done such a thing. She isn't capable of it. She has not surrendered worldly vanity; she just didn't want to see Anne Neville in her place.'

The girl laughs again, this time smiling at me. 'You are quite right!' she exclaims. 'And almost exactly the very thing she said! She said she couldn't stand to see her lovely gowns cut down to fit Anne Neville! I truly believe she wouldn't want to go back to court anyway, but you are quite right about the gowns. Poor Queen Anne.'

'God rest her soul,' I say piously, and the girl has the face to say: 'Amen.'

JUNE 1485

My son must come soon. Richard, from the castle at Nottingham, sends a commission to all the shires of England to remind them of their duty to him, and proclaiming the threat of Henry Tudor. He orders them to put aside all local disputes and be ready to muster in his cause.

He orders Elizabeth to leave me and to go to Sherrif Hutton with her sisters, to join the orphaned children of George, Duke of Clarence, in a safe place. He is putting all the York children in the safest place he can find, his castle in the north, while he fights for their inheritance, against my son. I try to keep her with me – the men of York will only support my son if they think he is betrothed to her – but she packs in a moment, she is in the red riding dress in a second, she is ready to leave me within the hour, and when the escort comes for her she all but dances out into the yard.

'I daresay we will meet again when all this is over,' I remark, as she comes to make her farewell curtsey to me. I let her come to me in the great hall and I stay seated in my chair and make her stand before me, like a servant being dismissed.

She says nothing, she just looks at me with her beautiful grey eyes as if she is waiting for me to finish my sermon and release her.

'If my son comes in like a dragon from Wales and defeats King Richard, then he will be King of England, he will take you as his wife, and you will be queen. It will be in his gift,' I say. 'You have no name now, he will give you one if he chooses to do so. You have no title, he can make you Queen of England. He will be your saviour, he will rescue you from shame and from being a nothing.'

She nods, as if shame is not a curse for a woman.

'But if Richard defeats my son Henry, then Richard will take you, his whore, and wash your reputation clean with a late marriage. You will be queen but wed to the man who killed your uncle and your brothers, who betrayed your father's will, your enemy. A shameful fate. It would be better if you had died with your brothers.'

For a moment I think she has not heard me, for her eyes are on the floor and she does not flinch at this prospect. She is quite unmoved by the threat of being married to a young man who must hate her, or a man who is blamed for the murder of her family. Then slowly, she looks up at me, and I see that she is smiling, beautifully smiling, as if she were happy.

'Either way you will be disgraced,' I say harshly. 'You should be aware of it. Shamed in public for all to see.'

But the bright happiness in her face does not falter. 'Yes, but either way, shamed or not, I shall be Queen of England, and this is the last time you will sit in my presence,' she says shockingly. Her confidence is extraordinary, her impertinence unforgiveable, her words terribly true.

Then she sweeps me a curtsey, turns her back on me with absolute disdain, and walks out of my great hall and into the yard where the soldiers are waiting in the sunshine to take her to safety far away.

I have to say, she leaves me stunned into silence.

My husband comes home, his face grim. 'I can't stay,' he says. 'I have come to muster my army. I am calling out my tenants, I am taking them out to war.'

I can hardly breathe. 'Whose side?' is all I can ask.

He glances at me. 'D'you know, that is the very question that King Richard asked of me,' he says. 'He doubts me so much that he has taken my son as a hostage. He let me go out to recruit only if George is in my place as a pledge. I had to agree. I have to get my affinity out into the field. This will be a battle which will decide the next King of England, the Stanley banner has to be there.'

'But on which side?' I ask.

He smiles at me, as if to reassure me after such a long time of waiting. 'Ah, Margaret,' he says. 'What man could resist having his stepson as King of England? Why do you think I married you, all that long time ago, if not to be here today? Arming my thousands of men to put your son on the throne.'

I can feel my colour rising in the warmth of my cheeks. 'You will bring out your army for Henry?' I ask. The Stanley army will be many thousands of men, enough to determine the course of a battle. If Stanley will fight for Henry then Henry is certain to win.

'Of course,' he says. 'Could you ever have doubted me?'

'I thought you would only take the winning side?' I ask.

For the first time in our marriage he opens his arms to me and I step willingly towards him. He holds me warmly for a moment and then smiles down into my face. 'If I am fighting for him, then Henry will be the winning side,' he says. 'Is that not your wish, my lady?'

'My wish, and God's will,' I say.

'Then God's will be done,' he confirms.

JULY 1485

The network of spies and reporters that I had around me during the rebellion slowly emerges again, and my husband sends me word that I can meet with whoever I want, at my own risk. Dr Lewis returns from Wales with a promise that the Welsh will be loyal to the name of Tudor, Pembroke Castle will throw open its doors to its old ruler, Jasper Tudor. Rhys ap Thomas, the greatest chieftain in Wales, has given his word to Richard, but he will play him false; Rhys ap Thomas will rise up for Henry. My man Reginald Bray goes quietly around the great houses of England promising that Henry Tudor will bring an unbeatable army, and that he will take the throne and bring justice at last to the House of Lancaster and reconciliation with York.

I receive a letter from Jasper:

To Lady Margaret Stanley

It is to be at the end of this month or early next. We will have fifteen ships and about two thousand men. This will be our last chance, I think. This time we have to win, Margaret.

For the sake of your son, you must make your husband take the field. We cannot do this without him. Henry and I are counting on you to bring out the Stanleys. Please God I shall see you at our boy's coronation or else I shall never see you again. God bless you either way. This has been a long good cause, and I have been proud to serve your son and you.

Jasper

AUGUST 1485

The fifteen ships set sail from Harfleur, financed by the French for the destruction of England, loaded with the worst men in Europe, drilled by Swiss instructors into some semblance of an army, commanded by Jasper, and led by Henry, more frightened than he has ever been before in his life.

He has reached the English shore before, and sheered off, too afraid to face this enemy, certain he would be defeated. Now he has his chance once more and he knows this will be his last chance. The Bretons supported him before but he did not even land. The French support him now but they will not do so again. If this fails there will be no-one else to join him. If he fails now he will spend the rest of his life in exile, a pitiful pretender to the throne, begging for his living.

They sail through summer seas, the winds are warm, the sea calm, the night is short and the dawn clear. The southern counties are held down by Richard, they do not dare land in the south. So they land as far west as they can, at Dale, in West Wales, hoping that Richard's spies will not see them, hoping to enlist a flood of recruits eager to march against the tyrant, before he even knows that they are in his country.

It doesn't happen. They are greeted mostly with indifference. The men who marched out with the Duke of Buckingham and were defeated by rain don't want to march out again. Many of them are loyal to Richard, some of them may even send a warning to him. Henry, a stranger in the country he is claiming as his own, cannot understand the Welsh language in this harsh western accent. He even speaks English with a Breton accent, he has been abroad too long. He is a stranger; and they don't like strangers.

They march north cautiously. Jasper's former towns open their gates from old love and loyalty, others they skirt. Henry calls on Welshmen to support a Welsh prince. But the Welsh are not stirred by this call from a young man who has spent most of his life in Brittany, who marches with a French army of convicts.

They cross the Severn at Shrewsbury. Henry has to confess he had a fear that the river would be up – as once it destroyed another rebel against Richard – but the crossing is low, and the evening mild, and at last they are in England, a raggle-taggle army of French convicts, German mercenaries and a few Welsh adventurers. And they cannot even decide which way they should march.

They start to march on London. It will be a long march across the breadth of the west country and then along the valley of the Thames, but both Jasper and Henry believe that if they can take London, then they have the heart of England, and they know that Richard is north of them, mustering his armies at Nottingham.

To Jasper Tudor and my son Henry Tudor

I greet you well.

My husband and his brother Sir William Stanley have assembled two separate mighty armies, and are ready to meet you near Tamworth in the third week of August. I am in touch with the Earl of Northumberland who, I think, will prove true to us also.

Send me news. Reply to this –

Lady Margaret

In Nottingham, Richard the king commands Lord Stanley to return to court at once, and bring his army. He waits for the reply, but when it comes he lets the letter sit on the table before him, and looks at the folded paper and the red seal stamped with the Stanley crest. He opens it as if he knows what he will read.

Stanley writes that he sends his king his love and loyalty. He writes of his duty to his king and his urgent desire to serve him at once. He writes that he is sick, dreadfully sick but as soon as he is well enough to ride, he will come to Nottingham ready to do his duty.

Richard raises his eyes from the letter and meets the stony gaze of his friend Sir William Catesby. 'Fetch Stanley's son,' is all he says.

They bring George, Lord Strange, to the king though he trails his feet like a prisoner. When he sees Richard's face and the letter with his father's seal on the table, they see him start to tremble. 'Upon my honour—' he starts.

'Not your honour, your father's,' Richard interrupts. 'Your father's honour is what concerns us. You in particular, for you might die for his failure. He writes that he is sick. Is he meeting Henry Tudor? Has he agreed with his wife Lady Margaret that they will repay my kindness with treason?'

'No! Never! No!' the young man says. 'My father is true to you, Your Grace. He always has been, from the first, from the first days. You know that. He has always spoken to me of you with the most devoted—'

'And your uncle, Sir William?'

The young man chokes on his assurances. 'My uncle, I don't know,' he says. 'He might . . . but I don't know. We are all faithful . . . our motto is *Sans Changer* . . .'

'The old Stanley game?' Richard asks gently. 'One on one side, one on another. I remember them telling of Margaret of Anjou waiting for your father to come up and fight for her. I remember her losing the battle while she waited.'

'My father will come in time for you, Your Grace!' the miserable young man promises. 'If I could write to him and bid him to come in your name!'

'You can write to him and tell him that you will be killed without sentence or ceremony if he is not here by the day after tomorrow,' Richard says swiftly. 'And get a priest, and get yourself shriven. You are a dead man if your father is not here the day after tomorrow.'

They take him to his room and they lock him in, they bring him paper and a pen and he shakes so badly that he can hardly write. Then he waits for his father to come for him. Surely, his father will come for him. Surely, a man such as his father would not fail to come for his son and heir?

Henry Tudor and his army marches east to London. The hay is in and the hayfields greening up with the new growth. The fields of wheat, barley and rye are golden. The French in particular have to be marched in strict columns, they see the rich villages and think of pillage and theft. They have been on the march for three weeks, they are tired, but the captains keep them together, and there are few desertions. Jasper reflects that the advantage of foreign mercenary troops is that they have no homes to run to, their only way home is with their commanders. But it is a bitter thought. He had counted on his people flocking to the Tudor standard, he had thought that men whose fathers had died for Lancaster would come out for their revenge; but it seems that it isn't so. It seems he has been gone too long and they are accustomed to the peace of Richard III. Nobody wants another war, only Jasper and Henry and their army of strangers. Sitting heavily in the saddle Jasper thinks that this is an England he doesn't know. It has been many years since he was commander of an English army. Perhaps the world has changed. Perhaps – he makes himself wonder – perhaps they serve Richard as a rightful king and see his boy, the Lancaster boy, the Tudor boy, as nothing but a pretender.

The promise of a meeting with the Stanleys, the first great recruits to their cause, makes them halt their eastward march on London and turn for the north. Sir William Stanley comes out with just a small bodyguard to meet them as they get to the town of Stafford.

'Your Grace,' he says to Henry, and puts his fist to his chest in a soldier's salute. Henry shoots a quick glance at Jasper. This is the first English nobleman on English soil to greet him with the title of a king. Henry is well schooled, he does not grin, but he returns the salute with warmth.

'Where is your army, Sir William?' he asks.

'Just one day away, awaiting your orders, sire.'

'Bring them to join us, we are marching on London.'

'It will be my honour,' Stanley says.

'And your brother, Lord Thomas Stanley?' Jasper asks.

'He is raising his men and will join us later,' Sir William replies. 'He is at Lichfield, a little south of here. He was going to bring them to Tamworth. We thought you would march on Nottingham and give battle to Richard at once.'

'Not London?' Jasper queries.

'London is all for Richard,' Sir William warns. 'They will close the gates and you will face a hard siege, they are well armed and Richard has prepared them. If you sit down before London, Richard will come marching up behind you.'

Henry's young face is still, he shows no fear though his hands tighten on the reins.

'Let's talk,' Jasper says and motions Henry to dismount. The three men turn off the lane into a field of wheat, the men of the army fall out from their ranks on the road and sit on the grassy verge, drinking small ale from their flasks, spitting and swearing at the heat.

'Will you march with us on London? Will Lord Stanley?'

'Oh, neither of us would advise it,' says Sir William. Henry notices that this does not answer the question.

'Where would you join us?' he asks.

'I have to go to Tamworth, I am promised to meet my brother there. I can't come with you immediately.'

Jasper nods.

'We would come after,' Sir William assures him. 'We would be your vanguard for your march on London, if you are determined on London. But Richard's army will come along behind us . . .'

'We'll take counsel with Lord Stanley and yourself at Tamworth,' Jasper rules. 'And decide then what to do. But we will march all together or not at all.'

Sir William nods. 'And your men?' he asks tactfully, gesturing to the motley bunch of two thousand, scattered down the road.

'They call it the English adventure,' Jasper says with a harsh smile. 'They are not here for love but for money. But they are well drilled and they have nothing to lose. You will see that they will stand against a charge, and advance when ordered. They are certainly as strong as a bunch of tenants called from their fields. They will be free and wealthy if we win. They will fight for that.'

Sir William nods as if he doesn't think much of a convict army, and then bows to Henry. 'Outside Tamworth then,' he says.

Henry nods and holds out his hand. Sir Willliam bows to kiss the gauntlet, without a moment's hesitation. They go back to the lane and Sir William nods to his guard to bring up his great charger. His page kneels in the mud and he steps regally on the lad's back to reach the stirrup and swing into the saddle. Once there, he turns to Henry and looks down on the young man.

'My nephew, Lord Strange, our family's heir, is held hostage by Richard,' he says. 'We can't risk being seen with you before the battle. Richard would kill him. I will send a servant to guide you to us at night.'

'What?' Jasper demands. 'Secret doings?"

'He will show you my ring,' Sir William says, shows them the ring on his glove and then turns his horse and trots away, his guard falling in behind him.

'For God's sake!' Jasper exclaims.

He and Henry look blankly at each other. 'We have no choice,' Henry says grimly. 'We have to have the Stanleys. We will fail without them, we just don't have the numbers.'

'They won't declare for us.' Jasper keeps his voice low, glancing around at the men at arms. Any one of them could be a spy rather than a volunteer. 'They are finding ways to delay.'

'As long as they are there when battle is joined . . .'

Jasper shakes his head. 'That's only the half of it. If everyone knows the Stanleys are for you, then everyone knows that we are the winning side,' he says. 'If they meet you in darkness, or here, half-hidden in a bloody wheatfield, then they are not declared for you. They could still turn out for Richard, and everyone knows that. Damnation. Damnation. I hoped your mother had secured her husband for us, but if his son is held by Richard, he could spend the whole battle sitting on the side, doing nothing for us, and join Richard for a final charge. Damnation.'

Henry takes his uncle's arm and marches him away from the listening men. 'What shall we do? We have to go on.'

'Yes, we can't retreat now without even having met Richard, but we are in a worse state than I had hoped, my boy.'

'Should we march on London?'

'No, they will be right about London being all for Richard, and now we will have them hot on our heels, not knowing if they are friends or enemies, and Richard close behind them. For all we know, they are not our vanguard but his fore-runners. And now we have told them that we are headed for London. Damnation.'

'So what?' Henry presses. His face is pale, his young face grooved with lines of worry.

'We turn north and go to meet them, we do our best to persuade them that we can win. We do our best to get their promise. And then we will go onwards, north, and choose the best battleground, for Richard in Nottingham will know where we are by tomorrow, know our numbers and our disposition. I don't doubt that Stanley will deliver all that information to Richard by midnight tonight.'

'We agree to meet the Stanleys in secrecy? What if it's a trap? What if they will serve Richard by handing me over to him?'

'We have to try. We do whatever will bring them to our side,' Jasper says. 'I don't think we can beat Richard without them. I am sorry for this, my boy.'

'Your Grace,' Henry reminds him with the ghost of a smile.

Jasper puts his arm around the young man's shoulders. 'Your Grace, Your Grace, and England never had a braver king.'

From Lady Margaret Stanley

Husband, I greet you well.

Ned Parton tells me he can find you, and that he knows where you are. In that case, he knows more than your wife or your pledged ally, my son.

Husband, with all my heart, I beg you to remember that you could be the stepfather of the King of England within the week. Richard may have made you Constable of England but that will be nothing to the future we might have. We will be the royal family and our grandson will be king. Nothing can be greater than this, it must be worth every risk.

I hear that Lord Strange, your son, is with Richard, and held by him, as warranty for your loyalty. Husband, for all our sakes, order him to escape, so that you can be free to support the true king, and we can find our way to our destiny as the rulers of England.

And know this, that the Earl of Northumberland has not called out the north for Richard, he will serve my son. The nobles of England are coming out for my son, will you not be the foremost?

I beg you to serve your own best interests.

Your wife,

Lady Margaret Stanley

Henry's march brings him to Lichfield, where Lord Stanley's army have occupied the town. He hopes that his stepfather will open the gates to him and bring out his own army to join the march, but this doesn't happen. As soon as Stanley's scouts bring him news that Henry Tudor's army is on the road to the town, he simply withdraws and advises the townspeople to open their gates to avoid bloodshed. Richard in Nottingham, like Henry at the town gates, cannot be certain whether this is a gesture of rebellion or loyalty. Lord Stanley's army marches away and is now quartered at Atherstone, his brother a little to the north. They look like armies choosing a battleground. Lord Stanley sends daily messages to Richard, telling him where the Tudor army is headed, their numbers, their discipline. He does not come himself, as he should do, but he appears loyal.

Richard orders his army out of Nottingham Castle and onto the road south. He orders square battle – as his brother Edward would have ordered, with men in square ranks and the cavalry riding up and down the line, on guard. The king himself and his household guards ride at the front, everyone can see the royal standard ahead of them, everyone knows that Richard is determined to crush this threat to his peace once and for all. This will be the last rebellion of his reign, the end of the long wars of the cousins.

Before they leave Nottingham, Catesby delays the king with a question. 'The Stanley boy?'

'He can come with us. Under guard.'

'Should we not kill him now?'

Richard shakes his head. 'I can't make an enemy of Stanley on the very eve of battle. If we kill his son we guarantee he goes to Tudor for his revenge. Bring Lord Strange with us, in my retinue, and if Stanley moves against us, we will behead him on the spot.'

The royal army and the Tudor army are not the only forces marching to meet. The two Stanley armies are positioned and waiting, the Earl of Northumberland is bringing a force of cavalry behind Richard, promised faithfully both to his service and to Margaret Stanley. The greatest single army to take the field is undoubtedly the king's. But the Stanleys' and Northumberland's forces would tip the balance.

19 AUGUST 1485

Jasper, his big warhorse jogging in a trot beside his nephew's charger, leans over and clasps his gauntleted hand on the reins. 'Courage, my boy.'

Henry flashes him a tight, small smile.

'Let them get ahead.' Jasper nods to their own slowly advancing army. 'Let them get out of sight and then double back. I'll get them settled for the night and then come out for you. Do what you can with the Stanleys. I won't show myself unless you get into trouble.'

'You don't think they'd kill me?' Henry asks, as if it is a question of tactics.

Jasper sighs. 'I don't think so. I think they are more likely to tell you their terms. They must think you have a good chance, they wouldn't even be meeting us if they were not intending to back you. I don't like you meeting them alone, but with his son as hostage, Stanley has to be careful. You have your knife in your boot?'

'Of course.'

'And I won't be far behind you. Godspeed, Your Grace. I'll

be just behind you. I'll have you in earshot for most of the time.'

'God help us all,' Henry says bleakly. He checks the road ahead to see that the stragglers of his army have turned a corner and he is out of sight, and turns his own horse and rides away to meet the Stanley servant, waiting, cloaked, on his own horse, in the shadow of the hedgerow.

They ride in silence, Henry scanning the darkening landscape to be sure of finding his way back to his army. The servant gestures to a little roadside inn, the skeletal holly bush strapped over the door as a sign that it is open for poor business, and Henry dismounts. The servant takes his horse to the back of the building, and Henry ducks his head, takes a deep breath, and pushes open the door.

He blinks. The room is filled with smoke from the dirty rush lights and the greenwood fire; but he can make out Sir William, and three other men. He can see no-one else, there is no way of knowing whether to expect an ambush or a welcome. With a Breton shrug, Henry Tudor steps into the darkened room.

'Well met, Your Grace, my son.' A tall stranger stands up and drops to his knee before Henry.

Henry puts out a hand that shakes only slightly. The man kisses the glove, and the other two men, and Sir William, drop to their knees as well, pulling off their caps.

Henry finds he is grinning in relief. 'Lord Stanley?'

'Yes, Your Grace, and my brother Sir William, who you know, and these are men of my household for our safety.'

Henry gives Sir William his hand and nods at the other men. He has a sensation of having fallen from a very great height and somehow, luckily, landed on his feet.

'You are alone?'

'I am,' Henry lies.

Stanley nods. 'I bring you greetings from your Lady Mother, who has pleaded your cause with me with such passion and determination from the very first day she did me the honour to marry me.'

Henry smiles. 'I don't doubt it. She has known of my destiny from my birth.'

The Stanleys get to their feet and the unnamed servant pours wine for Henry and then his master. Henry takes the glass furthest from the one he is offered and sits on a bench at the fireside.

'How many men do you have under your command?' he asks Stanley bluntly.

The older man takes a glass of wine. 'About three thousand under my command, my brother has a further thousand.'

Henry keeps his face composed at the news of an army twice the size of his own. 'And when will you join me?'

'When will you meet with the king?'

'Is he marching south?' Henry answers a question with a question of his own.

'He left Nottingham today. He has summoned me to join him. My son writes to me that he will answer with his life if I don't go.'

Henry nods. 'Then he will be upon us within – what? – the week?'

The Stanleys do not remark on Henry's lack of knowledge of his own country. 'Perhaps within two days,' Sir William says.

'Then you had better bring your troops up to mine so that we can pick out the battle ground.'

'Certainly, we would do so,' Lord Stanley says. 'But for the safety of my son.'

Henry waits.

'He is held by Richard as hostage for our support,' Stanley

says. 'Of course, I have commanded him to escape, and as soon as he is in safety, we will bring our army over to yours.'

'But if he escapes without getting word to you? The delay could be serious . . .'

'He won't do that. He understands. He will get word to me.'

'And if he can't escape?'

'Then we will have to join with you, and I will have to mourn my son as a man of courage, and the first of our family to die in your service,' Stanley says, his face grave.

'I will see him honoured, I will see you rewarded,' Henry says hastily.

Stanley bows. 'He is my son and heir,' he says softly.

There is silence in the little room. A log shifts on the fire and in the flare of the flame Henry looks into the face of his step-father. 'Your army doubles the size of mine,' he says earnestly. 'With your support there is no doubt that I can win. Our combined forces will outnumber Richard. You hold the key to England for me.'

'I know that,' Stanley says gently.

'You would command my gratitude.'

Stanley nods.

'I have to have your word that when I am on the battlefield, facing Richard, that I can count on your forces.'

'Of course,' Stanley says smoothly. 'I have given my word to your mother, and now I give it to you. When you are on the battlefield you may be sure that my army is yours to command.'

'And you will march to the battlefield with me?'

Regretfully, Stanley shakes his head. 'As soon as my son is free,' he says. 'You have my word on it. And if battle is joined before George can escape, then I will join with you and make the greatest sacrifice a man can make for his rightful king.'

And with this, Henry has to be content.

'Any good?' Jasper asks him, as Henry comes out of the inn and leads his horse from the poor shelter to mount him on the road.

Henry grimaces. 'He says he will be there at the battle for me, but he cannot join us while his son is held by Richard. He says that the moment Lord Strange is free, he will come to us.'

Jasper nods, as if he expected this, and the two ride on in silence. The sky starts to lighten, it is the early summer dawn.

'I'll go ahead,' Jasper decides. 'See if we can get you into camp without anyone noticing.'

Henry turns his horse to the side and waits while Jasper trots into camp. At once, there is a flurry of activity, obviously, they have already missed Henry, and are in a panic that he has run away. Henry sees Jasper get down from his horse, gesticulate as if explaining that he has been riding around. The Earl of Oxford comes out of his tent to join the conference. Henry spurs his horse onwards and rides towards his camp.

Jasper turns. 'Thank God you are here, Your Grace! We were all anxious. Your page says your bed has not been slept in. I have been out looking for you. But I was just telling my Lord de Vere that for sure you were meeting some supporters who are coming over to our cause.'

A sharp look from Jasper's blue eyes prompts Henry to take up the story. 'Indeed I was,' Henry says. 'I cannot give their names for now, but be assured that more and more are coming to our cause. And this new recruit will bring in many men.'

'Hundreds?' asks the Earl of Oxford, glancing around at their small army with a worried scowl.

'Thousands, praise God,' says young Henry Tudor, smiling confidently.

20 AUGUST 1485

Later that day, with the army on the move again, shuffling through the dust of the dry roads and complaining of the heat, Jasper brings his warhorse alongside Henry. 'Your Grace, give me leave,' he says.

'What?' Henry starts out of a reverie. He is pale, his hands tight on the reins. Jasper can see the strain on his young face, and wonders, not for the first time, if this boy is strong enough to enact the destiny his mother has seen for him.

'I want to ride back the way we have come, and secure safe houses on the way, set some horses ready for us in their stables. I may even go as far as the coast, hire a boat to wait for us . . .'

Henry turns to his mentor. 'You are not leaving me?'

'Son, I could as easily leave my own soul. But I want an escape route for you.'

'For when we lose.'

'If we lose.'

It is a bitter moment for the young man. 'You don't trust Stanley?'

'Not as far as I can throw a rock.'

'And if he does not come to our side then we will lose?'

'It's just the numbers,' Jasper says quietly. 'King Richard has perhaps twice our army, and we have about two thousand now. If Stanley joins with us, then we have an army of five thousand. Then we are likely to win. But if Stanley joins the king, and his brother with him then we have an army of two thousand and the king has an army of seven thousand. You could be the bravest knight in all of chivalry and the truest king ever born, but if you go out in battle with two thousand men and face an army of seven thousand then you are likely to lose.'

Henry nods. 'I know it. I am certain that Stanley will prove true to me. My mother swears that he will, and she has never been wrong.'

'I agree. But I would feel better if I knew we could get away if it does go wrong.'

Henry nods. 'You'll come back as soon as you can?'

'Wouldn't miss it for the world,' Jasper says with his half-smile. 'Godspeed, Your Grace.'

Henry nods, and tries not to feel a sense of terrible loss as the man who has hardly left his side in the twenty-eight years of his young life turns his horse and canters slowly away, west to Wales.

When Henry's army sets out the next day, Henry rides at the head of them, smiling to right and left, saying that Jasper has gone to meet new recruits, an army of new recruits and bring them to Atherstone. The Welshmen and the English who have volunteered are cheered by this, believing the young lord that they have sworn to follow. The Swiss officers are indifferent, they have taught their drills to these soldiers, it is too late to train more, extra numbers will help, but they are paid to fight anyway and extra men will divide the spoils into smaller portions. The French convicts, fighting only to earn their freedom and for the chance of spoil, don't care either way. Henry looks at his troops with his brave smile and feels their terrible indifference.

20 AUGUST 1485: LEICESTER

The Earl of Northumberland, Henry Percy, marches into Richard's camp at Leicester with his army of three thousand fighting men. He is brought to Richard while the king is eating his dinner under the cloth of state, in his great chair.

'You may sit, dine with me,' Richard says quietly, gesturing to a seat down the table from his own.

Henry Percy beams at the compliment, takes his seat.

'You are ready to ride out tomorrow?'

The earl looks startled. 'Tomorrow?'

'Why not?'

'On a Sunday?'

'My brother marched out on an Easter Sunday and God smiled on his battle. Yes, tomorrow.'

The earl holds out his hands for the server to pour water over his fingers and pat them dry with a towel. Then he breaks some manchet bread, and pulls the white soft crumb inside the crunchy crust. 'I am sorry, my lord, it has taken me too long to bring my men. They will not be ready to march tomorrow. I had to bring them fast, down hard roads, they are exhausted, they are in no state to fight for you.'

Richard gives him a long, slow look from under his dark eyebrows. 'You have come all this way to stand to one side and watch?'

'No, my lord. I am sworn to join you when you march out. But if it is to be so soon, tomorrow, I will have to volunteer my men for the rear guard. They cannot lead. They are exhausted.'

Richard smiles as if he knows for a fact that Henry Percy has already promised Henry Tudor that he will sit behind the king and do nothing.

'You shall take up the rear then,' Richard says. 'And I shall know myself safe with you there. So.' The king speaks generally to the room and the heads come up. 'Tomorrow morning then, my lords,' Richard says, his voice and his hands quite steady. 'Tomorrow morning we will march out and crush this boy.'

SUNDAY 21 AUGUST 1485

Henry waits as long as he dares, waits for Jasper to come back to him. While he waits, he orders the pikemen to practise their drill. It is a new procedure, introduced by the Swiss against the formidable Burgundian cavalry only nine years earlier, and taught by the Swiss officers to the unruly French conscripts, but by steady practice, they have perfected it.

Henry and a handful of his horsemen play the part of the charging enemy cavalry. 'Take care,' Henry says to the Earl of Oxford, on his big horse, on his right. 'Over-ride them and they will spit you.'

De Vere laughs. 'Then they have learned their task well.'

The half-dozen mounted men wheel and wait, and then, at the command 'Charge' they start forwards, first at the trot but then at the canter and then the full terrifying cavalry gallop.

What happens next has never been seen in England before. Previously a man on the ground, facing a cavalry charge, always slammed down the shaft of his pike into the ground, and pointed it upwards hoping to spear a horse in the belly, or he swung wildly at the rider, or he made a desperate upward stab and a downward dive, arms wrapped around his head, in one terrified movement. Usually, the greatest number of men simply dropped their weapons and fled. A well-marshalled cavalry charge always broke a line of soldiers, few men could face such a terror, they could not bear to stand against it.

This time, the pikemen spread out, as usual, see the charge start to gather speed towards them, and obeying a loud yell from their officers, run back and form into a square, ten men by ten men on the outside, ten men by ten men inside them, another forty crammed inside them, barely room to move, let alone fight. The front rank drop to their knees, grounding the shaft of their pikes before them, pointing upwards and outwards. The middle rank hold them firm, leaning over their shoulders, their pikes pointing outwards, and the third rank stand, wedged together, with their pikes braced at shoulder height. The square is like a four-sided weapon, a block studded with spears, the men crammed against each other, holding onto each other, impenetrable.

They race into formation and are in place before the cavalry can get to them, and Henry wrenches the charge aside from the bristling deadly wall in a hail of mud and lumps of turf from the horses' hooves, pulls up his horse, and then trots back.

'Well done,' he says to the Swiss officers. 'Well done. And they will hold if the horses come straight at them? They will hold when it is for real?'

The Swiss commander grimly smiles. 'That's the beauty of it,' he says quietly, so the men cannot hear. 'They cannot get away. The one rank holds the other, and even if they all die, their weapons are still held in place. We have made them into a weapon itself, they are no longer pikemen who can choose whether to fight or run.'

'So shall we march now?' Oxford asks, patting his horse's neck. 'Richard is on the move, we want to be out on Watling Street before him.'

Henry notes the sick feeling in his belly at the thought of giving the order without Jasper at his side. 'Yes!' he says strongly. 'Give the order to fall in, we march out.'

They bring the news to Richard that Henry Tudor's little army is marching down Watling Street, perhaps looking for a battle-ground, perhaps hoping to make good speed down the road and get to London. The two armies of Sir William Stanley and Lord Thomas Stanley are trailing the Tudor – ready to harry him? ready to join him? Richard cannot know.

He gives the order for his troops to form up to march out of Leicester. Women swing open the upper windows of houses so they can see the royal army going by as if it were a midsummer-day parade. First go the cavalry, each knight with his page going before him, carrying his standard, fluttering gaily, like a joust, and his men following behind him. The clatter of the horses' hooves on the cobbles is deafening. The girls call out and throw down flowers. Next come the men at arms, marching in step with their weapons shouldered. The archers follow them with their longbows over their shoulders and their quivers of arrows strapped across their chests. The girls blow kisses, archers have a reputation of being generous lovers. Then there is a bellow of shouts and cheering for there is the king himself, in full beautifully engraved armour, burnished white as silver, on a white horse, with the battle crown of gold fixed to his helmet. His standard of the white boar is carried proudly both before and behind him, with the red cross of St George along-side, for this is an anointed King of England marching out to war to defend his own country. The drummers keep a steady beat, the trumpeters blast out a tune, it is like Christmas, it is better than Christmas, Leicester has never seen anything like it before.

With the king rides his trusted friend the Duke of Norfolk, and the doubtful Earl of Northumberland, one on the right hand, one on the left as if they could both be relied on for defence. The people of Leicester, not knowing the king's doubts, cheer for both noblemen and for the army that follows: men from all over England, obedient to their lords, following the king as he marches out to defend his realm. Behind them comes a great unruly train of wagons with weapons, armour, tents, cooking stoves, spare horses, like a town on the move, and behind them, straggling as if to demonstrate either weariness or unwillingness, the Earl of Northumberland's footsore army.

They march all day, stopping for a meal at noon, spies and scurriers going ahead of them to learn the whereabouts of Tudor and the two Stanley armies, then in the evening Richard commands his army to halt, just outside the village of Atherstone. Richard is an experienced and confident commander. The odds on this battle could go either way. It depends on whether the two Stanley armies are for him, or against him; it depends whether Northumberland is going to advance when he is called for. But every battle Richard has ever experienced has always been on a knife-edge of uncertain loyalties. He is a commander forged in the fire of civil warfare, in no battle has he ever known for sure who is a friend and who an enemy. He has seen his brother George turn his coat. He has seen his brother King Edward win by witchcraft. He places his army carefully, spread out on high ground so that he can watch the old Roman road to London, Watling Street, and also command the plain. If Henry Tudor hopes to rush past at dawn and on to London, Richard will thunder down the hill and fall on him. If Tudor turns aside to give battle, Richard is well placed. He is here first and he has chosen the ground.

He doesn't have long to wait. As it gets dark they can see the Tudor army turn from the road and start to make camp. They see the camp fires start to twinkle. There is no attempt to hide; Henry Tudor can see the royal army on the rising ground to the right of him, and they can see him down below. Richard finds himself oddly nostalgic for the days when he was under the command of his brother and they once marched up under the shelter of night, and burned camp fires half a mile behind their own silent troops and so confused the enemy that in the morning they were upon them in moments. Or another time when they marched in under cover of fog and mist, and nobody knew where anybody was. But those were battles under Edward, who had the help of a wife who could call up bad weather. These are more prosaic days, and Tudor marches his army off the road, through the standing wheat, in full sight, and bids them make their little camp fires and be ready for the morning.

Richard sends to Lord Stanley and commands him to bring up his army to array with the royal army, but the messenger comes back with only a promise that they will arrive later, well before dawn. Lord George Strange glances nervously at the Duke of Norfolk, who would behead him at a word, and says that he is certain his father will come up at first light. Richard nods.

They dine well. Richard orders that the men be fed and the horses supplied with hay and water. He does not fear a surprise attack from the young Tudor, but he puts out watchmen anyway. He goes to his tent to sleep. He doesn't dream, he pulls the blanket over his head and he sleeps well, as he always does before a battle. To allow himself to do anything else would be folly. Richard is no fool and he has been in worse places, on worse battlefields, facing a more redoubtable enemy than this novice with his mongrel army.

On the other side of the Redmore Plain, Henry Tudor paces around his camp, restless as a young lion, until it grows too dark to see his way. He is waiting for Jasper; he knows without a doubt that Jasper will be riding through the darkness to come to him, splashing through inky streams, cutting across darkened moors, making all the speed he can. He never doubts the loyalty and love of his uncle. But he cannot face the thought of a battle in the morning and Jasper not at his side.

He is waiting for word from Lord Stanley. The earl had said that he would arrive with his massive force, as soon as the battle lines were drawn up, but now comes a messenger to say that Stanley is not going to come till dawn, he has made his own camp, his men are settled for the night, it would be foolish to disturb them in the darkness. In the morning he will come, at first light, when battle is joined he will be there, Henry can be assured of it.

Henry cannot be assured of it, but there is nothing he can do. Reluctantly, he looks west once more in case there is the bobbing torch of Jasper against the darkness, and then he goes to his own tent. He is a young man, this is his first battle on his own account. He hardly sleeps at all.

He is plagued with terrible dreams. He dreams that his mother comes to him and tells him that she has made a mistake, that Richard is the true king, and that the invasion, the battle lines, the camp, everything, is a sin against the order of the kingdom and the rule of God. Her pale face is stern and she curses him for being a pretender and attempting to unseat a true king, a rebel against the natural order of things, a heretic against the divine laws of God. Richard is an ordained king, he has taken the holy oil on his breast, how can Tudor raise a sword against him? He turns, and wakes, and then dozes and dreams that Jasper is sailing back to France without him, weeping for his death on the battlefield. Then he dreams that Elizabeth, Princess of York, the young woman promised to marry him, that he has never seen, comes to him, and says that she loves another man, that she will never willingly be his wife, that he will look a fool before everyone. She looks at him with her beautiful grey eyes filled with cold regret and tells him that everyone will know that she took another man as her lover and still longs only for him. She says that her lover is a strong man, and handsome, and that she despises Henry as a runaway boy. He dreams that the battle has started and he has overslept and he leaps from his bed in a terror, bangs his head on the tent pole, and finds himself, naked and shivering, shaken awake by his own fear – and it is still hours from dawn.

He kicks his page awake anyway, and sends him for hot water and a priest to say Mass. But it is too early, the camp fires are not yet lit, there is no hot water, there is no bread baked yet, there is no meat to be had. They can't find the priest and when they do, he is still asleep and has to prepare himself, he cannot come at once and pray with Henry Tudor. He does not have the Host ready, and the crucifix is to be set up at dawn, not now, in the darkness. The vestments are in the baggage train, they have been on the march for so long he will have to find them. Henry has to huddle into his clothes, smelling his own nervous cold sweat, and wait for dawn and for the rest of the world to get to their feet leisurely, as if today were not the day when everything is to be decided, as if today were not the day that might be the day of his death.

In Richard's camp the king is undertaking a ceremony to declare the seriousness of the battle, and to renew the oaths of loyalty from his coronation. This event only happens at moments of gravest crisis, and when a king needs to renew his oaths with his people. No-one here has ever done it before and their faces are bright with the solemnity of the occasion. First comes the priests and a choir of singers, making a measured progress before the men, then come the lords and the great men of the realm, dressed for battle with their standards before them, then comes the king, dressed in his heavy engraved battle armour, bare-headed in the warm dawn light. He looks, at this moment of his claiming his throne again, far younger than his thirty-two years. He looks hopeful, as if victory this day will bring peace to his kingdom, the chance to marry again, to conceive an heir, to establish the Yorks on the throne of England for ever. This is a new beginning, for Richard and for England.

He kneels before the priest, who lifts the sacred crown of Edward the Confessor and rests it gently on the king's dark head. He feels the weight of it as heavy as guilt, and then feels the weight lifted, he is redeemed of all sin. He rises to his feet and faces his men. 'God save the king!' comes the shout from a thousand voices. 'God save the king!'

Richard smiles at the shout that he has heard for his brother, that he has heard for himself. This is more than a renewing of his coronation oath to serve his countrymen and his kingdom, this is a re-dedication of himself. Whatever has been done to get them to this point has been forgiven. What comes next, will be the basis for his judgement. And now he knows that he is in the right, an ordained and crowned king, riding out against an upstart, a pretender, whose cause was lost in the last reign, whose affinity have stayed at home, whose support depends on foreign convicts and mercenaries, and who has attracted only the most disloyal and time-serving lords to his side – and possibly not even them.

Richard raises his hand to his army, and smiles at their roar of applause. He turns to one side and gently puts off the sacred crown and shows them his battle helmet with the helmet crown fixed lightly to the poll. He will go into battle crowned, he will fight under his royal standard. If Henry Tudor has the courage to challenge him in person, he will not have to hunt for him. Richard will be as visible on the field of battle as when the three suns of York were the emblem of the three York brothers. He will ride out in person and kill the Tudor boy in single combat. This is a king militant, this is the champion of England's peace.

The trumpeters sound the call to arms and now all the troops are arming, taking one last swig of small ale, checking their axes, their swords, their spears, twanging lightly on their bowstrings. It is time. The king is forgiven all his sins. He has re-dedicated himself to sacred kingship. He is crowned and armed. It is time.

In the Tudor camp they hear the trumpets and they are already saddling their horses, and tightening their breastplates. Henry Tudor is everywhere: among the officers, demanding that they are ready, confirming that they have their battle plan. He does not look for Jasper, he will not allow himself a moment of anxiety or doubt. He has to think now of nothing but the coming battle. He sends one message only to Lord Stanley. *Are you coming now?* He gets no reply.

He receives one letter from his mother, put into his hand by her messenger as he stands, arms outspread, as they strap on his breastplate.

My son. God is with you, you cannot fail. I think of nothing and no-one but you in my prayers. Our Lady will hear me when I pray for my boy.

I know the will of God, and it is for you.

Your mother,

Margaret Stanley

He reads the familiar handwriting and he folds it and puts it in his breastplate, over his heart, as if it could block the thrust of a sword. His mother's vision of his future has dominated his life, his mother's belief in her rights has brought him to this place. Since his boyhood, when he saw his York guardian that she hated, dragged off the battlefield to a shameful death, he has never doubted her vision. He has never doubted her House of Lancaster. Now, her faith in him and her belief that he will win is his only certainty. He calls for his horse and they bring him saddled and ready.

The two armies form lines and march slowly towards collision. Richard's guns set on the higher ground are trained on Henry's right wing and Henry's officers order the men to shift slightly to the left, so that they can come around Richard, and avoid the line of fire. The morning sun beats on their backs, the wind is behind them too, as if to blow them forwards. To Richard's army they come, with a dazzle on their raised pikes that makes them look more than they are. Henry's men break into a stumbling run and Tudor checks his horse to see the field. He looks back. There is no sign of Jasper. He looks to his left. The Stanley army, twice the size of his own, is drawn up in battle array, precisely halfway between king and challenger. Stanley could sweep down between them and if he turned to left he would attack Richard and be at the head of Henry's men. If he turned to the right he would destroy Henry's army. Henry speaks to his page. 'Go to Lord Stanley and tell him if he comes not now, I shall know what to think,' he says tersely.

Then he looks back at his own troops. Obedient to the yells of their officers they have started a run, they are rushing forwards to the royal army and there is a terrific crash as the two sides meet. At once there is the chaos of the battle, the terrible noise of slaughter, and the absolute confusion of fighting. A royal cavalryman rides down the line, sweeping his battle axe like a man scything nettles, leaving a train of men staggering and dying behind him. Then a pikeman from the Tudor army steps out and with one lucky thrust gets his sharp pike upwards and into the rider's armpit, flings him from his horse and down to the soliders, who fall on him like snarling dogs and tear him apart.

The royal guns tear into the Tudor mercenaries and they fall back, regroup, and swing to the left again; their officers cannot make them march against the fire. Cannon balls whistle towards them and plunge into the ranks like rocks into a stream, only instead of a splash there is the scream of men and the wild neighing of horses. Richard, crown glowing on his helmet like a halo, is in the middle of the fighting on his white horse, his standard before him, his knights around him. He glances back at the little hill behind him and there are Northumberland's men, as still as the Stanleys over to his left. He gives a bitter shout of laughter at the thought that there are more men standing watching than there are fighting, and lays about him with his great mace, knocking the heads off armed men, and breaking shoulders, necks, backs, as if they were dolls standing around him.

The break in the battle comes naturally, when men are too exhausted to do more. They stagger back and rest on their weapons, they gasp for breath. They look, uneasily, at the still ranks of Stanley and Northumberland, and some of them whoop for air or retch blood from their throats.

Richard scans the field beyond the immediate line of battle, holds in his horse, and pats its sweaty neck. He looks across at the Tudor forces and sees that behind the Tudor line, slightly adrift from his troops, is the red dragon standard, and the Beaufort portcullis badge. Henry has become separated from his army, he is standing back with his household guards around him, his army has pushed ahead, away from him. Inexperienced on the battlefield, he has let himself be separated from his troops.

For a moment Richard cannot believe the opportunity that he sees before him, then he gives a harsh laugh. He sees his chance, battlefield luck, given to him by Henry's momentary pause that has separated him from his army and left him terribly vulnerable. Richard stands up in his stirrups and draws his sword. 'York!' he bellows, as if he would summon his brother and his father from their graves. 'York! To me!'

His household cavalry leap forwards at the call. They ride in close formation, thundering over the ground, sometimes jumping corpses, sometimes ploughing on through them. An outrider gets pulled down but the main battle, tightly grouped, shoots like an arrow, around the back of the Tudor army, who see the danger, and stagger and try to turn, but can do nothing but watch the galloping charge towards their leader. The York horses are flying at Henry Tudor, unstoppable, swords out, lances down, faceless in their sharply pointed helmets, terrifying in their thunderous speed. The Tudor pikemen, seeing the charge, break from their ranks and run backwards and Richard, seeing them on the run, thinks they are fleeing and bellows again, 'York! And England!'

Tudor is down from his horse in a moment – why would he do that, Richard thinks, his breath coming fast, leaning over his horse's mane, why dismount? – Tudor is running forwards to his pikemen, who dash back to meet him. His sword is drawn, his standard bearer beside him. Henry is beyond thought, beyond even fear, in this, his first adult battle. He can feel the ground shake as the horses come towards him, they come like a high wave and he is like a child facing a storm on a beach. He can see Richard bending low in the saddle, his lance out before him, the gleam of the gold circlet on the silver helmet. Henry's breath comes fast with fear and excitement and he shouts to the French pikemen, 'Now! *À moi! À moi!*'

They dash back towards Henry and then they turn and drop to their knees and point their pikes upwards. The second rank lean their pikes on their comrades shoulders, the third rank, boxed inside, like a human shield for Henry Tudor, point their pikes straight forwards like a wall of daggers at the oncoming horses.

Richard's cavalry have never seen such a thing done before. No-one has ever seen such a thing before in England. They cannot pull up the charge, they cannot turn it. One or two in the centre wrench their horses aside but they just foul the oncoming dash of their neighbours and go down in a chaos of tumbling and screaming and broken bones under the hooves of their own horses. The others plough on, too fast to stop, and fling themselves onto the merciless blades, and the pikemen stagger under the impact, but wedged so tightly: they stay steady.

Richard's own horse stumbles on a dead man and goes down to its knees. Richard is thrown over its head, staggers to his feet, pulling out his sword. The other knights fling themselves to the ground to attack the pikemen, and the clash of sword on wooden haft, of thrusted blade and broken pike is like hammering at a forge. Richard's trusted men gather round him in battle order, aiming at the very heart of the battle square, and gradually they start to gain ground. The pikemen in the first rank cannot struggle to their feet with the weight of the others bearing down on them, they are cut down where they kneel. The middle rank fall back against the ferocious attack, they cannot help but give ground and Henry Tudor, in the centre, becomes more and more exposed.

Richard, his sword red with blood, comes nearer and nearer, knowing the battle will be over with Tudor's death. The two standards are only yards apart and Richard is gaining ground, fighting his way through a wall of men to Tudor himself. In the corner of his eye he sees the red of the dragon and, furious, he slashes at it and the standard bearer, William Brandon, in one huge thrust. The standard looks about to fall and one of Henry's body guard dives forwards, grabs the broken haft and holds it aloft. Sir John Cheney, a giant of a man, throws himself between Henry and Richard and Richard slashes out at him too, a vicious wound to the throat, and the Tudor knight goes down, knowing that they are defeated, calling, 'Fly, sire! Get yourself to safety!' to Henry, as his last words are choked on his own blood.

Henry hears the warning and knows he must turn and run. It is all over for him. And then they hear it. Both Richard and Henry's heads go up, at the deep, loud rumble of an army at full gallop as the Stanleys' armies come charging towards them, lances down, pikes out, swords ready, fresh horses tearing towards them as if themselves eager for blood, and as they hit, Richard's standard bearer has his legs sliced off from underneath him by a swing from a battle axe and Richard wheels around, his sword arm failing him, suddenly fatally weak, in that one moment as he sees four thousand men coming against him, and then he goes down under a flurry of anonymous blows. 'Treason!' he shouts. 'Treason!'

'A horse!' somebody screams desperately for him. 'A horse! A horse! Get the king a horse!'

But the king is already gone.

Sir William Stanley pulls the helmet from Richard's lolling head, notes that the king's dark hair is still damp with warm sweat, and leaves the rest of the looting of his fine armour to others. With a pike-head he prises off the golden circlet of kinghood and strides towards Henry Tudor, kneels in the mud, and offers him the crown of England.

Henry Tudor, staggering from the shock, takes it from him with bloodied hands, and puts it on his own head.

'God save the king!' bellows Stanley to his army, coming up fresh and untouched, some of them laughing at the battle that they have won in such decisive glory without dirtying their swords. He is the first Englishman to say this to the crowned Henry Tudor, and he will make sure the king remembers it. Lord Thomas Stanley dismounts from his panting horse at the head of his army, which swung the battle, at the last, the very last moment, and smiles at his stepson. 'I said I would come.'

'You will be rewarded,' Henry says. He is grey with shock, his face shiny with cold sweat and with someone else's blood. He looks, but hardly sees, as they strip King Richard's fine armour and then even his linen and throw his naked body over the back of his limping horse, which hangs its head as if ashamed. 'You will all be richly rewarded, who fought with me today.'

They bring the news to me where I am praying, on my knees, in my chapel. I hear the bang of the door and the footsteps on the stone floor, but I don't turn my head. I open my eyes and keep them fixed on the statue of the crucified Christ and I wonder if I am about to enter my own agony. 'What is the news?' I ask.

Christ looks down at me, I look up at Him. 'Give me good news,' I say as much to Him as to the lady who stands behind me.

'Your son has won a great battle,' my lady in waiting says tremulously. 'He is King of England, acclaimed on the battlefield.'

I gasp for breath. 'And Richard the usurper?'

'Dead.'

I meet the eyes of Christ the Lord and I all but wink at Him. 'Thanks be to God,' I say, as if to nod at a fellow plotter. He has done His part. Now I will do mine. I rise to my feet and she holds out a letter to me, a scrap of paper, from Jasper.

Our boy has won his throne, we can enter our kingdom. We will come to you at once.

I read it again. I have the strange sensation that I have won my heart's desire and that from this date everything will be different. Everything will be commanded by me.

'We must prepare rooms for my son; he will come to visit me at once,' I say coolly.

The lady in waiting is all flushed, she was hoping that we would fall into each other's arms and dance about in victory. 'You have won!' she exclaims. She is hoping I will weep with her.

'I have come into my own,' I correct her. 'I have fulfilled my destiny. It is the will of God.'

'It is a glorious day for your house!'

'Nothing but our deserts.'

She bobs a shallow curtsey. 'Yes, my lady.'

'Yes, Your Grace,' I correct her. 'I am My Lady, the King's Mother now, and you shall curtsey to me, as low as to a queen of royal blood. This was my destiny: to put my son on the throne of England, and those who laughed at my visions and doubted my vocation will call me My Lady, the King's Mother, and I shall sign myself Margaret Regina, *Margaret R.*'

AUTHOR'S NOTE

This has been a deeply interesting book to write, about a woman who triumphed in the material world and tried at the same time to serve God. She is remembered by feminist historians as a 'learned lady', one of the very few who had to struggle for the privilege of study; by Tudor historians as the matriarch who founded their house; and by less reverent memorialists as 't' old bitch' who became a mother-in-law from hell. Trying to create for the reader, a character who could grow from a child with a sense of holy destiny, into a woman who dared to claim the throne of England for her son, has been a challenge and a deep pleasure. Some parts of this novel are history, some are speculation, and some are fiction. In particular we do not know who killed the princes in the Tower, nor even that they died in the Tower. Obviously, the claimants for their throne: Richard III, the Duke of Buckingham, Margaret Beaufort and her son, were the people with most to gain from their deaths.

I am indebted to the historians who have researched Margaret Beaufort and her times and especially to Linda Simon for her biography, and Michael K Jones, and Malcolm G Underwood whose biography was the starting point for my own work. I owe Michael Jones many thanks for being kind enough to read my manuscript.

More research material and further notes are on my website at PhilippaGregory.com and readers may like to attend the occasional online seminar there.

These are the most helpful books I have read:

Baldwin, David, *Elizabeth Woodville: Mother of the Princes in the Tower*, Sutton Publishing, 2002

Baldwin, David, *The Lost Prince: The Survival of Richard of York*, Sutton Publishing, 2007

Bramley, Peter, *The Wars of the Roses: A Field Guide and Companion*, The History Press Ltd, 2007

Castor, Helen, *Blood & Roses: The Paston family and the Wars of the Roses*, Faber & Faber, 2004

Cheetham, Anthony, *The Life and Times of Richard III*, Weidenfeld & Nicholson, 1972

Chrimes, S. B., *Henry VII*, Eyre Methuen, 1972

Chrimes, S. B., *Lancastrians, Yorkists, and Henry VII*, Macmillan, 1964

Cooper, Charles Henry, *Memoir of Margaret: Countess of Richmond and Derby*, Cambridge University Press, 1874

Crosland, Margaret, *The Mysterious Mistress: The Life & Legend of Jane Shore*, Sutton Publishing, 2006

Fields, Bertram, *Royal Blood: Richard III and the Mystery of The Princes*, Regan Books, 1998

Gairdner, James, 'Did Henry VII Murder the Princes?', *English Historical Review*: VI, 1891

Goodman, Anthony, *The Wars of the Roses: Military Activity and English Society*, 1452–97, Routledge & Kegan Paul, 1981

Goodman, Anthony, *The Wars of the Roses: The Soldiers' Experience*, Tempus, 2006

Hammond, P. W., and Sutton, Anne F., *Richard III: The Road to Bosworth Field*, Constable, 1985

Harvey, Nancy Lenz, *Elizabeth of York: Tudor Queen*, Arthur Baker, 1973

Hicks, Michael, *Anne Neville: Queen to Richard III*, Tempus, 2007

Hicks, Michael, *Richard III*, Tempus, 2003

Hicks, Michael, *The Prince in the Tower: The Short Life & Mysterious Disappearance of Edward V*, Tempus, 2007

Hughes, Jonathan, *Arthurian Myths and Alchemy: The Kingship of Edward IV*, Sutton Publishing, 2002

Jones, Michael K., and Underwood, Malcolm G., *The King's Mother; Lady Margaret Beaufort: Countess of Richmond and Derby*, Cambridge University Press, 1992

Kendall, Paul Murray, *Richard the Third*, Norton and Company, 1975

MacGibbon, David, *Elizabeth Woodville 1437–1492: Her Life and Times*, Arthur Baker, 1938

Mancini, D., Cato, A., Armstrong, C.A.J., *The Usurpation of Richard the Third: Dominicus Mancinus Ad Angelum Catonem De Occupatione Regni Anglie per Ricardum Tercium Libellus*, Clarendon, 1969

Markham, Clements R., 'Richard III: A Doubtful Verdict Reviewed', *English Historical Review: VI*, 1891

Neillands, Robin, *The Wars of the Roses*, Cassell, 1992

Plowden, Alison, *The House of Tudor*, Weidenfeld & Nicholson, 1976

Pollard, A. J., *Richard III and the Princes in the Tower*, Sutton Publishing, 2002

Prestwich, Michael, *Plantagenet England 1225–1360*, Clarendon, 2005

Reed, Conyers, *The Tudor: Personalities & Practical Politics in 16th century England*, Oxford University Press, 1936
Ross, Charles D., *Edward IV*, Eyre Methuen, 1974
Ross, Charles D., *Richard III*, Eyre Methuen, 1981
Royle, Trevor, The *Road to Bosworth Field: A New History of the Wars of the Roses*, Little Brown, 2009
Seward, Desmond, *A Brief History of The Hundred Years War*, Constable and Company, 1973
Seward, Desmond, *Richard III: England's Black Legend*, Country Life Books, 1983
Sharpe, Kevin, *Selling the Tudor Monarchy: Authority and Image in 16th Century England*, Yale University Press, 2009
Simon, Linda, *Of Virtue Rare: Margaret Beaufort: Matriarch of the House of Tudor*, Houghton Mifflin Company, 1982
St Aubyn, Giles, *The Year of Three Kings 1483*, Collins, 1983
Vergil, Polydore and Ellis, Henry, *Three Books of Polydore Vergil's English History Comprising the Reigns of Henry VI, Edward IV and Richard III*, Kessinger Publishing Legacy Reprint
Weir, Alison, *Lancaster & York: The Wars of the Roses*, Jonathan Cape, 1995
Weir, Alison, *The Princes in the Tower*, Bodley Head, 1992
Willamson, Audrey, *The Mystery of the Princes*, Sutton Publishing, 1978
Williams, Neville, *The Life and Times of Henry VII*, Weidenfeld & Nicolson, 1973
Wilson-Smith, Timothy, *Joan of Arc: Maid, Myth and History*, Sutton Publishing, 2006
Wroe, Ann, *Perkin: A Story of Deception*, Jonathan Cape, 2003

A GUIDE FOR READING GROUPS

INTRODUCTION

Heiress to the red rose of Lancaster, Margaret Beaufort never surrenders her belief that her house is the ruler of England and she has a great destiny before her. Married to a man twice her age, quickly widowed, and a mother at fourteen, Margaret is determined to turn her lonely life into a triumph. She sets her heart on putting her son on the throne of England regardless of the cost. As the political tides constantly shift, Margaret charts her way through two more loveless marriages, treacherous alliances, and secret plots. She masterminds one of the greatest rebellions of all time, knowing that her son has grown to manhood, recruited an army, and now waits for his opportunity to win the greatest prize.

DISCUSSION QUESTIONS

1. In the beginning of *The Red Queen*, young Margaret Beaufort is an extremely pious young girl, happy to have

'saints' knees' when she kneels too long at her prayers. Discuss the role of religion throughout Margaret's life. What does she see as God's role for her?

2. As a pious young girl, Margaret wants to live a life of greatness like her heroine, Joan of Arc. However, her fate lies elsewhere, as her mother tells her: 'the time has come to put aside silly stories and silly dreams and do your duty' (page 26). What is Margaret's duty and how does she respond to her mother's words?

3. At the tender age of twelve, Margaret is married to Edmund Tudor and fourteen months later she bears him the son who will be the heir to the royal Lancaster family line. During the excruciating hours of labour, Margaret learns a painful truth about her mother and the way she views Margaret. Discuss the implications of what Margaret learns from her mother, and what is 'the price of being a woman' (page 63).

4. How does Jasper Tudor aid Margaret in her plans for herself and her son, Henry? What does he sacrifice in order to keep Henry Tudor safe? In what ways are Jasper and Margaret alike?

5. After the death of Edmund Tudor, Margaret marries the wealthy Sir Henry Stafford. How is Stafford different from Edmund? Margaret laments that she is 'starting to fear that my husband is worse than a coward' (page 105). What are her reasons for this? Do you see any sense in Stafford's careful diplomacy?

6. On Easter of 1461, violence breaks out between the armies of Lancaster and York. This time, Sir Henry Stafford goes

out to fight for Lancaster, only to witness a terrible battle. What does he understand about war and politics and why are these truths so difficult for Margaret to grasp?

7. Ever since she was a young girl, Margaret believed she was destined for greatness. How does her pride in her destiny manifest itself throughout the story? Identify key moments where Margaret's pride overwhelms her judgment.

8. In the spring of 1471, Stafford sides with York and supports Edward in his quest to take the throne of England once and for all. Do you understand Stafford's reasons for doing this? Is Margaret's rage at her husband's decision understandable?

9. Sir Henry Stafford suffers a mortal wound in battle. After his death, Margaret decides she must be strategic in her next marriage and so she approaches Thomas, Lord Stanley, who Jasper describes as 'a specialist of the final charge' (page 217). What does Jasper mean by this? How is Stanley different from Stafford? What does it mean for Margaret when she decides to unite her fortunes with this man?

10. In April 1483, Margaret tries to enlist Stanley in helping to get her son, Henry, and Jasper back on English shores. An argument ensues between the two of them, and the ever-shrewd Stanley confronts Margaret with his view of her true nature, much to her horror (page 236). Do you think Stanley's assessment of her is correct? Why is this so significant?

11. Discuss Margaret's feelings towards the White Queen, Elizabeth Woodville. Why does she cause her so much

anger? How does Margaret's view of Elizabeth change as she becomes her lady-in-waiting, and then as she actively plots with her – and against her – for the throne of England?

12. Once King Richard has installed himself on the throne, Margaret and Lord Stanley scheme to replace him with her son, Henry Tudor. Margaret must make the difficult decision about whether to sacrifice the two princes in the Tower for her own ambitions (page 271). Is there any way to justify Margaret's actions? Do you sympathize with her plight?

13. In the winter of 1483–84, Margaret despairs when her plans fail miserably. Under house arrest by the king, she looks back on her schemes and declares, 'the sin of ambition and greed darkened our enterprise' (page 305). Discuss Margaret's conclusion about her behavior. Do you think she takes responsibility for her actions? What blame does she place on Elizabeth Woodville?

14. As the fortunes of England shift once again, Margaret finds herself playing host to the young Lady Elizabeth, the beautiful daughter of Elizabeth Woodville. Discuss the interaction between these two headstrong women. How does Lady Elizabeth treat Margaret and what does she say on page 344 that leaves Margaret stunned into silence?

15. Discuss the final battle scenes in *The Red Queen*. How does Henry Tudor, young and inexperienced, eventually gain the upper hand, and how does King Richard lose his throne, and his life?

16. By the end of the book, Margaret, now Margaret Regina, the King's mother, has achieved all she wanted. Do you respect her and her ideals? Do you think her achievement justifies her actions?

Learn more about the War of the Roses, Richard III and the fall of the house of York at the homepage of the Richard III Society: http://www.r3.org/

Visit Philippa Gregory's website, www.philippagregory.com, to learn more about the author, view the Plantagenet family tree, and read background information on *The Red Queen*.

Read on to discover what inspired Philippa Gregory, in *The Red Queen*, to write about Margaret Beaufort, a character of enormous complexity and passion whose tale is so powerfully woven through the moving and exhilarating backdrop of the Cousins' War.

A CONVERSATION WITH PHILIPPA GREGORY

Margaret Beaufort is a very different character than Elizabeth Woodville, star of *The White Queen.* Was it difficult for you to shift perspective and write in the voice of a woman, in this case The Red Queen, who is the enemy of the main character of your previous book?

One of the most difficult things I have ever done in writing was to shift my own perspective so that after three years of thinking entirely from the point of view of Elizabeth Woodville and from the point of view of the house of York, I had to convert to the view of Margaret Beaufort and the house of Lancaster. I thought at the time that the only way to do it would be to find some sort of key to the girl that Margaret was, in order to understand her as a woman. There are three extant biographies of her and I read them all and then thought that the secret to Margaret is her genuine and deep faith. That led me to the picture of this very precocious and serious little girl and once I could imagine and love her – I could imagine the woman that her hard life and disappointments created.

Margaret's mother tells her 'since you were a girl you could only be the bridge to the next generation' (page 59). Do you feel sympathy for Margaret and her thwarted ambition? What would her life have been like had she been born a man?

Of course I feel intense sympathy for Margaret who is used by her family – as so many women of this period were – as a pawn in a game of dynasties. However, to be cheerful about it – if she had been a man she would almost certainly have been killed in a battle or in an attack – all the other heirs on the Lancaster side were killed and she sent her son away to keep him safe. Perhaps the greatest disappointment for Margaret was that she was not allowed a religious life. There is no doubt in my mind that she would have made a wonderful abbess, both as a landlord and community leader and as a scholar.

Taken together, *The White Queen* and *The Red Queen* present very different portraits of marriage in the fifteenth century. Was either woman's experience more indicative of the time?

Margaret has the more typical life of a woman of her class. Many of the noblewomen of this time were placed in arranged marriages for the advantage of their families; she was exceptionally young, but most noblewomen could expect to be married at sixteen. What is unusual about Margaret is that it seems likely that her third marriage was indeed arranged by herself, to position herself at the York court, and to give her son a stepfather of immense wealth and influence. In this she was very powerfully taking control of her own destiny, and this was unusual, even for widows. Elizabeth Woodville's first marriage is also very typical of the time. Her marriage was arranged when she was about sixteen to the wealthy heir of a great estate in a neighbouring county. The Grey family gained the Woodville's connections at court and the royal and noble connections of Elizabeth's mother, and the Woodvilles got their daughter into a wealthy house. Elizabeth's second marriage was, of course, unique. She was the first English commoner to marry a king of England, and the first queen married for love. They married in secret without the knowledge of the king's advisor and mentor. It was an extraordinary marriage.

Sir Henry Stafford is an interesting contrast to so many of the striving, power-hungry men and women in this novel. How much of his thoughts did you base on real life and how much was your own interpretation of his character?

Sir Henry, like so many men and women of his time, has left little or no record of his thoughts, and only scant records of his actions. I had to look at what we knew about him: his age, his decision not to ride out to fight in any of the many battles of the wars – except when he went out for Lancaster in 1461, and for York a decade later. Therefore I had to consider why a man would have fought in the sixth and the fifteenth battle, but no others; and why a man tied to the house of Lancaster by family and habit would change his mind so completely as to fight for York. That was all I had to go on, as well as my general reading about the feelings of so many men who were forced to take difficult decisions about their private and family hopes and fears at a time of constant challenge.

There are three pivotal women in this novel: Elizabeth Woodville, her daughter Lady Elizabeth and Margaret Beaufort. Do you think they are able to rise above what was considered acceptable for women's roles in their time?

I think what these women demonstrate in this novel is the range of responses that were possible for women; and that this range is probably wider than we, as readers of the period, might generally think. Because the history of the period has been mostly written by men (for two reasons: that until the 20th Century almost all historians were men, since only men attended universities; and that histories of war seem to attract mostly male historians) we have very scant records of what women were feeling, thinking and even doing. And those reports we do have are often biased against women who seek power. Thus we simply don't know the extent of the involvement of Elizabeth Woodville and Margaret Beaufort in the Buckingham rebellion or the Tudor invasion, we can only deduce that they were deeply involved. But we do have very negative views of Elizabeth Woodville as a mother failing to protect her children, as a panic-struck woman fleeing into sanctuary, and as a hard-hearted manipulator sending her daughters out to the uncle who may have killed her sons. That these views of her are exaggerated and indeed contradictory does not seem to trouble some historians whose view of her is determinedly negative. In contrast, the positive views taken of Margaret Beaufort emphasize her suffering and endurance and not her political skill and manipulation. In this book I suggest that Princess Elizabeth fell in love with King Richard her uncle. This is based on a letter which was seen by an historian but is now missing, and it would suggest that she also had the courage and passion to try to choose her own life. These are women of exceptional courage and determination, but I think they show that, even in a society where women are powerfully repressed both legally and culturally, there are still women who will find ways to express themselves.

How does history remember Margaret Beaufort? Do you feel that she is dealt with fairly by historians and writers?

There are two main opinions on Margaret Beaufort that have emerged for me from my reading. One, very positive, is based on the Tudor hagiography which sees her as the matriarch of the house and a woman who spent her life in the service of her son. It follows the sermon preached by Archbishop Fisher who stressed her suffering as a young woman, and her very early sense of destiny when she believed that she was advised by the saints to marry Edmund Tudor and thus have a Tudor heir to the Lancaster throne. This view sees her as a divinely inspired matriarch to a family called by God, and was incorporated into the Tudor history of their own line. The other more modern view is less admiring of her as a spiritual woman but emphasizes her political ambitions and her powers of manipulation. In this view she is sometimes regarded critically as a woman of excessive ambition and greed, and it suggests that she dominated the household of her son and influenced the upbringing of her grandsons.

Turn the page and be one of the first to read an exclusive extract from Philippa Gregory's next book, *The Lady of the Rivers*.

INTRODUCTION

The Lady of the Rivers tells the story of Jacquetta, daughter of the Count of Luxembourg, and kinswoman to half the royalty of Europe, who was married to the great Englishman John, Duke of Bedford, uncle to Henry VI. Widowed at the age of nineteen she took the extraordinary risk of marrying a gentleman of her household for love, and then carved out a life for herself as Queen Margaret of Anjou's close friend and a Lancaster supporter – until the day that her daughter Elizabeth Woodville fell in love and married the rival king Edward IV.

The story of Elizabeth, her secret marriage to Edward IV, her survival of the coup that drove her husband from England as she hid in the sanctuary of Westminster Abbey, her return to power and then her struggle with the usurper Richard III, is the subject of another book in this series, *The White Queen.*

It was during the research for this book that I discovered the amazing story of Elizabeth's mother, Jacquetta, which prompted me to add the story of her life to this series.

Of all the little-known but important women of the period, her dramatic story is the most neglected. With her links to Melusina, and to the founder of the house of Luxembourg together with her reputation for making magic, she is a most haunting heroine. The story opens as her uncle, Louis of Luxembourg, captures Joan of Arc and Jacquetta sees, for the first time, the dangers facing a girl who dares to be extraordinary.

Work in Progress

SUMMER 1430: CASTLE OF BEAUREVOIR, NEAR ARRAS, FRANCE

She sits, this odd trophy of war, as neat as an obedient child, on a small stool in the corner of her cell. At her boots are the remains of her dinner on a pewter platter, laid on the straw. I notice that my uncle has sent good slices of meat, and even the white bread from his own table, and she has eaten little. I find I am staring at her: from her boy's riding boots, to her man's bonnet crammed on her brown cropped hair, as if she were some exotic animal, trapped for our amusement. As if someone had sent a lion cub to entertain the great family of Luxembourg, for us to keep in our collection. A lady in waiting behind me crosses herself and whispers: 'Is this a witch?'

I don't know. How does one ever know?

'This is ridiculous,' my great-aunt says boldly. 'Who has ordered the poor girl to be chained? Open the door at once.'

There is a confused muttering of men trying to shift the responsibility, and then someone turns the big key in the cell door and my great-aunt stalks in. The girl – she must be about seventeen or eighteen – looks up from under her jagged fringe of hair as my great-aunt stands before her, and then slowly, rises to her feet, doffs her cap, and gives an awkward little bow.

'I am Jehanne, the Demoiselle of Luxembourg,' my great-aunt says. She gestures to my aunt: 'This is the lady of the castle, Jehanne of Bethune, and this is my nephew's daughter Jacquetta.'

The girl looks steadily at each of us and gives a little nod of her head to each. As she looks at me I feel a little tap-tap for my attention, a whisper of magic as palpable as the brush of a fingertip on the nape of my neck. I wonder if standing behind her there are indeed two accompanying angels, and that it is their presence that I sense.

'Can you speak, Maid?' my great-aunt asks, when the girl says nothing.

'Oh yes, my lady,' the girl says. She has the hard accent of the Champagne region. She is no more than a peasant girl.

'Will you give me your word not to try to escape if I have these chains taken off your legs?'

She hesitates, as if she is in any position to choose. 'No, I can't,' she says.

My great-aunt smiles. 'Do you understand the offer of parole? I can release you to live with us here in the castle; but you have to promise not to run away?'

The girl frowns. It is almost as if she is listening for advice, then she shakes her head. 'I know this parole. It is when one knight makes a promise to another. They have rules as if they were jousting. I'm not like that. My words are real, not like a troubadour's poem. This is not a game for me.'

'Maid: parole is not a game!' my aunt interrupts.

The girl looks at her. 'Oh, but it is, my lady. The noblemen are not serious about these matters. Not serious like me. They play at war and make up rules. It is a game to them. Besides, I cannot make promises. I am promised already.'

'To the one who wrongly calls himself the King of France?'

'To the King of Heaven.'

My great-aunt pauses for a moment's thought. 'I will tell them to take the chains off you and guard you so that you do not escape; but you can come and sit with us in my rooms. I think what you have done for your country and for your prince has been very great, Joan, though mistaken. And I will not see you here, under my roof, a captive in chains.'

'Will you tell your nephew to set me free?'

My great-aunt hesitates. 'I cannot order him; but I will do everything I can to see you free. At any event, I won't let him release you to the English.'

At the very word the girl shudders and crosses herself, thumping her head and her chest in the most ridiculous way: as a peasant might cross himself at the name of Old Hob. I have to choke back a laugh. This draws the girl's dark gaze to us.

'They are only mortal men,' I explain to her. 'The English have no powers beyond that of mortal men. You need not fear them like that. You need not cross yourself at their name.'

'I don't fear them,' she ignores my patronising tone. 'I am not such a fool as to fear that they have powers. It is that they know that *I* have powers. That's what makes them such a danger. They are mad with fear of me. They fear me so much that they will destroy me the moment that I fall into their hands. I am their terror. I am their fear that walks by night.'

'While I live, they will not have you,' my great-aunt assures her; and at once, unmistakeably, Joan looks straight at me, a hard dark gaze as if to see that I too have heard, in this sincere assertion, the ring of an utterly empty promise.

My great-aunt believes that if she can bring Joan into our company, talk with her, moderate her religious fervour, perhaps educate her, that she will be led, in time, to wear to the dress of a young woman; that the fighting youth who was dragged off the white horse at Compiègne will transform, as strong wine into water, and she will become a young woman who can be seated among young waiting women, who will answer to a command and not to the ringing church bells, and who can perhaps, be overlooked by the English, who are demanding that we surrender the hermaphrodite murderous witch to them. If we have nothing to offer them but a remorseful obedient girl, perhaps they will be satisfied and go on their violent way.

Joan herself is exhausted by recent defeats and by her uneasy sense that the king she has crowned is not worthy of the holy oil, that the enemy she had on the run has recoiled on her, and that the mission given to her by God Himself is falling away from her. Everything that made her The Maid before her adoring troop of soldiers has become uncertain. Under my great-aunt's steady kindness she is becoming once more, an awkward country girl: nothing special.

Of course, all the maids in waiting to my great-aunt want to know about the adventure that is ending in this slow creep of defeat, and as Joan spends her days with us, learning to be a girl and not The Maid, they pluck up the courage to ask her.

'How were you so brave?' one demands. 'How did you learn to be so brave? In battle, I mean.'

Joan smiles at the question. The four of us are seated on a grass bank beside the moat of the castle, as idle as children. The July sun is beating down and the pasture lands around the castle are shimmering in the haze of heat, even the bees are lazy: buzzing and then falling silent. We have chosen to sit in the shadow of the highest tower, behind us, in the glassy water of the moat, we can hear the bubble of a carp coming to the surface. Joan is sprawled like a boy, one hand dabbling in the water, her cap over her eyes. In the basket beside me are half-sewn shirts that we are supposed to hem for the poor children of Cambrai. But the maids always avoid work of any sort, Joan has no skill, and I have my great-aunt's precious pack of cards in my hands and I am shuffling and cutting them and idly looking at the pictures.

'I knew I was called by God,' Joan said simply. 'And that He would protect me, so I had no fear. Not even in the worst of the battles. He warned me that I would be injured but that I would feel no pain, so I knew I could go on fighting. I even warned my men that I would be injured that day. I knew before we went into battle. I just knew.'

'Do you really hear voices?' I ask.

'Do you?'

The question is so shocking that the girls whip round to look at me and under their joint gaze I find I am blushing as if for something shameful. 'No! No!'

'Then what?'

'What do you mean?'

'What do you hear?' she asks as reasonably as if everyone hears something.

'Well, not voices, exactly,' I say.

'What do you hear?'

I glance behind me as if the very fish might rise to listen. 'When someone in my family is going to die, then I hear a noise,' I say. 'A special noise.'

'What sort of noise?' the girl, Elizabeth asks. 'I didn't know this. Could I hear it?'

'You are not of my house,' I say irritably. 'Of course you wouldn't hear it. You would have to be a descendant of … and anyway, you must never speak of this. You shouldn't really be listening. I shouldn't be telling you.'

'What sort of noise?' Joan repeats.

'Like singing,' I say, and see her nod, as if she too has heard singing.

'They say it is the voice of Melusina, the first lady of the House of Luxembourg,' I whisper. 'They say she was a water goddess who came out of the river to marry the first Duke but she couldn't be a mortal woman. She comes back to cry for the loss of her children.'

'And when have you heard her?'

'The night that my baby sister died. I heard something. And I knew at once that it was Melusina.'

'How did you know it was her?' the other maid whispers, afraid of being excluded from the conversation.

I shrug, and Joan smiles in recognition of truths that cannot be explained. 'I just knew,' I say. 'It was as if I recognized her voice. As if I had always known it.'

'That's true. You just know,' she nods. 'But how do you know that it comes from God and not from the Devil?'

I hesitate. Any spiritual questions should be taken to my confessor, or at the very least to my mother or my great-aunt. But the song of Melusina, and the shiver on my spine, and my occasional sight of the unseen – something half-lost, sometimes vanishing around a corner, lighter grey in a grey twilight, a dream which is too clear to be forgotten, a glimpse of foresight but never anything that I can describe – these things are too thin for speech. How can I ask about them when I cannot even put them into words? How can I bear to have someone clumsily name them, or even worse: try to explain them? I might as well try to hold the greenish water of the moat in my cupped hands.

'I've never asked,' I say. 'Because it is hardly anything. Like when you go into a room and it is quiet – but you know, you can just tell that someone is there. You can't hear them or see them, but you just know. It's little more than that. I never think of it as a gift coming from God or the Devil. It is just nothing.'

'My voices come from God,' Joan says certainly. 'I know it. If it were not true, I should be utterly lost.'

'So can you tell fortunes?' Elizabeth asks me childishly.

My fingers close over my cards. 'No,' I say. 'And these don't tell fortunes, they are just for playing. I don't tell fortunes. My great-aunt would not allow me to do it, even if I could.'

'Oh, do mine!'

'These are just playing cards,' I say. 'I'm no soothsayer.'

'Oh, draw a card for me and tell me,' Elizabeth says. 'And for Joan. What's going to become of her? Surely you want to know what's going to happen to Joan?'

'It means nothing,' I say to Joan. 'And I only brought them so we could play.'

'They are beautiful,' she says. 'They taught me to play at court with cards like these. How bright they are.'

I hand them to her. 'Take care with them, they're very precious,' I say jealously as she spreads them in her calloused hands. 'The Demoiselle showed them to me when I was a little girl and told me the names of the pictures. She lets me borrow them because I love to play. But I promised her I would take care of them.'

Joan passes the pack back to me and though she is careful, and my hands are ready for them, one of the thick cards tumbles from us and falls face down, on the grass.

'Oh! Sorry,' Joan exclaims, and quickly picks it up.

I can feel a whisper, like a cool breath down my spine. The meadow before me and the cows flicking their tails in the shade of the tree seem far away, as if we two are enclosed in a glass, butterflies in a bowl, in another world. 'You had better look at it now,' I hear myself say to her.

Joan looks at the brightly-painted picture, her eyes widen slightly, and then she shows it to me. 'What does this mean?'

We both see the peaceful smile of a man dressed in bright livery of blue, hanging from one extended foot, the other leg crooked easily, his toe pointed and placed against his other leg as if he were dancing, inverted in the air, his hands are clasped behind his back as if he is bowing, the happy fall of his blue hair as he hangs, upside down, smiling.

'Le Pendu,' Elizabeth reads. 'How horrid. What does it mean? Oh, surely it doesn't mean…' she breaks off.

'It doesn't mean you will be hanged,' I say quickly to Joan. 'So don't think that. It's a playing card, it can't mean anything like that.

'But what does it mean?' the other girl demands though Joan is silent, as if it is not her card, not her fortune that I am refusing to tell.

'His gallows is two growing trees,' I say. I am playing for time under Joan's serious brown gaze. 'This means spring and renewal and life – not death. And there are two trees: the man is balanced between them. He is the very centre of resurrection.'

She nods.

'And look: he is not hanged by his neck to kill him, but tied by his foot,' I say. 'If he wanted, he could stretch up and untie himself. He could set himself free, if he wanted.'

'But he doesn't set himself free,' the girl observes. 'It is as if he is dancing there, held by a foot. He is like a tumbler, an acrobat. What does that mean?'

'It means that he is willingly there, willingly waiting, allowing himself to be held by his foot, hanging in the air.'

'To be a living sacrifice?' Joan says slowly, in the words of the Mass.

'He is not crucified,' I say quickly. It is as if every word I say leads us to another form of death. 'This doesn't mean anything.'

'No,' she says. 'These are just playing cards, and we are just playing a game with them. It is a pretty card, the hanged man. He looks happy. He looks happy to be upside down in springtime. Shall I teach you a game with counters that we play in Champagne?'

'Yes,' I say. I hold out my hand for her card and she looks at it for a moment before she hands it back to me.

'Honestly, it means nothing,' I say again to her.

She smiles at me, her clear honest smile. 'I know what it means,' she says.

'Shall we play?' I start to shuffle the cards and one turns over in my hand.

'Now that's a good card,' Joan remarks. '*La roue de fortune*.'

I hold it out to show it to her. 'It means the wheel of fortune that can throw you up very high, or bring you down very low. Its message is to be indifferent to victory or defeat, as they both come on the turn of the wheel.'

'In my country the farmers make a sign for fortune's wheel,' Joan remarks. 'They draw a circle in the air with their forefinger when something very good or something very bad happens. Someone inherits money, or someone loses a prize cow, they do this:' she points her finger in the air and draws a circle. 'And they say something.'

'A spell?'

'Not really a spell,' she smiles mischievously.

'What then?'

She giggles. 'They say "*merde*".'

I am so shocked that I rock back with laughter.

'What? What?' the younger maid demands.

'Nothing, nothing,' I say. Joan is still giggling. 'Joan's countrymen say rightly that everything comes to dust, and all that a man can do about it is to learn indifference.'

Philippa Gregory

The White Queen

1464. Cousin is at war with cousin, as the houses of York and Lancaster tear themselves apart . . .

. . . And Elizabeth Woodville, a young Lancastrian widow, armed only with her beauty and her steely determination, seduces and marries the charismatic warrior king, Edward IV of York.

Crowned Queen of England, surrounded by conflict, betrayal and murder, Elizabeth rises to the demands of her position, fighting tenaciously for her family's survival. Most of all she must defend her two sons, who become the central figures in a mystery that has confounded historians for centuries: the missing Princes in the Tower.

Set amid the tumult and intrigue of the Wars of the Roses, this is the first of a stunning new series, in which internationally bestselling author Philippa Gregory brings this extraordinary drama to vivid life through the women – beginning with Elizabeth Woodville, the White Queen.

ISBN: 978-1-84739-464-4
PRICE £7.99